END RUN

A
JENNIFER DONAHUE
THRILLER

END RUN

A JENNIFER DONAHUE
THRILLER

PETER S.
BERMAN

AUTHOR'S NOTE

This novel is a work of fiction in its entirety. With a few location exceptions, all characters, settings, dialogue, incidents, and other story elements are wholly imaginary. That said, I have referred to some real persons by name based upon public information. The inclusion of their actions have provided a historical setting for this otherwise fictional story.

Following an old literary tradition, I have also honored some of my friends by using their names to identify fictional characters. However, there is no connection between my imaginary characters and my real-life friends.

Any resemblance between the fictional contents of this book and real people is strictly coincidental. As for governmental institutions and business locations in Los Angeles and around the world, many of them are included to give the story the feel of realism. And while this story is complete fiction, it is based in some ways upon historical events that are publicly known.

———

Justice is occasionally elusive, but most of the time, it shows up and serves us well.

This story is dedicated to my grandchildren,
Maxwell, Charlotte, Asher, and Holden.

_____

And, as always, to Renée.

_____

Also, my thanks to Matt L'Heureux
A great lawyer and my editor.

"*To seek revenge is nothing more than returning the favor, and the best time to return the favor is when they never see it coming.*"
—Anonymous

"*I am the punishment of God…If you had not committed great sins, God would not have sent a punishment like me upon you.*"
—Genghis Khan

ONE

DOCTOR RICHARD ROSEN was running hard, and he was out of breath. But as tired as he was, he refused to slow down. At this moment he knew that he would rather die than appear to be weak, which is exactly what she would think if he couldn't keep up with her.

Rosen was a third-year medical intern currently doing a surgical rotation at the Cedars-Sinai Medical Center in Los Angeles, and that was where he first met Rachael Pendergast, a stunning brunette nurse who shared his passion for running.

At this point, she was pulling ahead like she always did, slowly at first, but invariably holding something in reserve. Losing was not in her DNA, and to his dismay, she presently showed no indication of slowing down. He tried to control his breathing, hoping to save what little was left for the final three-quarters of the block. But he was kidding himself, and he knew it. Rachael was far too competitive to ever let up. She was toying with him, and while she was just beginning to show signs of getting her second wind, he was already reeling from the first indications of serious oxygen deprivation.

Not wishing to embarrass him too much, Rachael kept her pace just slightly ahead of his. She could finish this run a lot faster, but she found herself attracted to this man, and while showing him up in this footrace was kinda fun, she was smart enough to know not to rub it in. Courting was a game to be played with finesse, and it was never a smart move to reveal all of your cards too soon.

Rosen found himself smiling. He was going to finish second, but second place had its own silver lining. Rachael had a great runner's body, and as long as she stayed just ahead of him, he was free to stare unabashedly at her exquisite derrière, without the slightest risk of being caught.

It was close to three a.m., and except for the rhythmic slapping of their footfalls on the concrete roadway, the neighborhood was as quiet as a cemetery.

Months ago, Rosen had mapped out this running course through the residential neighborhood adjacent to the hospital facility. And since both of them were working on the overnight shift rotation, they used their one-hour food break to squeeze in a three-mile run.

At this time of night, long after most people were sound asleep, there was little or no traffic. Consequently, they chose to do side-by-side running down the middle of the city streets.

The neighborhood was lined with maple trees whose foliage created a nearly solid overhead canopy.

This particular night was chilly, maybe sixty-two degrees, and the quarter moon was deep into a waning phase. The sky was dark and cloudless, the city was silent, and had anyone been out and about, the two runners would have appeared as if they were ghostly apparitions whose feet barely touched the ground.

As the hospital came into view, Rachael led them through a quiet intersection for the sprint up the final block.

Two-story duplexes lined both sides of the street, and most of them were Spanish in architectural style with thick stucco walls and red tile roofs. Because of the proximity of the street in relation to the hospital, overnight parking was by permit only, and even that was limited to the western side of the street.

They were halfway down the final block when Rosen developed a runner's cramp in his right side. As he started to slow down even further, the two of them were suddenly startled by two quick flashes of light that were accompanied by simultaneously booming explosions.

They quickly stopped running.

"Did you see that?" whispered Rachael. She was pointing at a building that was no more than thirty yards ahead of them on the eastern side of the roadway.

"Up there, on the second floor," she said.

Rosen looked up. He didn't immediately acknowledge her question, because he was actually wondering if the brief flashes and sounds had been gunshots?

They were still staring at the bay window on the upper floor when another bright flash, followed by a boom, lit up that particular upstairs room.

"Those are gunshots, Rach!" said Rosen. "We need to call the police!"

Rachael was first to pull out her cell phone, but before she could punch in 911, they heard a heavy door slam shut from the building in question. That was followed by several sets of ponderous footsteps coming down the outdoor staircase.

Rosen didn't waste any time. He grabbed Rachael by the arm and half-dragged her towards a waist-high hedge that lined the sidewalk of the nearest building. They jumped over the hedge together before he forced her face-down onto the grass. The deep shadows behind the two-foot-tall Boxwood hedge was their only real chance for concealment.

Rosen used his body to press up against hers as his way to try to protect her.

A man suddenly emerged from the front of the building where the gunshots had come from. He walked briskly to the curb, then stood stock-still to take a long, slow look around the neighborhood.

Rachael peeked at him from under the base of the hedge where she could see that he was holding what appeared to be a cut-down shotgun in one of his hands.

When the neighborhood showed no signs of stirring, the man waved his free hand as a signal to a second man who suddenly appeared from the same building. In one hand he was holding a laptop computer, and in the other what looked like a handgun.

Rosen was still doing his best to shield Rachael, but she was craning her neck to see where the two men were headed.

They were muscular in appearance, both wearing dark clothing, and her initial impression was that they carried themselves like bouncers; the kind she usually saw during her occasional forays into the Hollywood nightclub scene.

As the two men came down the sidewalk towards where they were hiding, both Rachael and Rosen cowered even more than they had before. Rachael pressed her face against the dirt that was under the hedge, shut her eyes, and held her breath. They were going to pass by within a couple of feet.

Rosen also held his breath and pleaded silently with God to spare them from discovery.

The two men walked by at a quick pace, and as they did, both Rachel and Rosen noted that they spoke to each other in a foreign dialect.

Once they went by, having failed to detect them, Rosen waited more than a full half-minute before slowly rolling off of Rachael's body. She moved to try to get up, but he used a hand on her shoulder to keep her down.

She turned her head to face his.

"Where'd they go?" she whispered.

He put a finger to his lips, then pointed down the street.

Rachael raised up higher and peeked over the top of the hedge. In the glow of a distant streetlight, she watched as the two men climbed into a dark sedan that was parked a little more than half a block away.

The engine started up, and as they pulled away from the curb, Rachael got to her feet and called 911.

"Stay here," said Rosen as he moved towards the building where the shots had taken place. "I'm gonna go see if anyone's been hurt."

He ran over to the building where the men had come from, and quickly made his way up the exterior flight of stairs.

Rachael noted the address on the building and passed it on to the 911 operator.

Lights began to go on in some of the neighboring duplexes, and three people from a building across the street were bold enough to come out and look around. Several sirens could be heard getting closer, and as Rachael began to process what they'd just been through, she started to shake as the adrenaline in her system began to wane.

Rosen hurriedly came down the stairs of the adjoining building. When he reached her side, he took her in his arms.

"You okay?" he asked.

"I think so. Is anyone hurt?"

Rosen slowly nodded.

"There's a guy up there in the front room, and he's definitely gone."

TWO

ABOUT SIX MILES away from Cedars Hospital, in the upper-class neighborhood of Brentwood, Jennifer Donahue and her partner Shari Thompson were hard at work processing a homicide scene. The two women were detectives in the elite Robbery-Homicide Division of the Los Angeles Police Department, and they had been called out to handle this particular case because of its high-profile nature.

Gabriel Orsini, a popular film producer, was only forty-two years of age, but he had already achieved legendary status among his Hollywood peers. With such blockbuster hits as *Hidden Agenda, Web of Betrayal,* and *Suspicious Deaths,* the two-time Oscar winner and rumored playboy was a daily staple for TMZ, a gossip-fueled television show.

The call for assistance had come from one of his neighbors who had spotted Orsini running nude through the bushes in his own front yard. The neighbor had noticed a long knife in Orsini's hand, and that had generated a major police response.

A half-dozen black and white units from the West L.A. Division had rolled up singly and in groups. Orsini had run back into the house, and for the moment, they were in a stand-off situation.

Normally, RHD would not have been called out until the barricaded state of affairs was completely resolved, but an alert patrol officer assigned to cover the back of the house had tripped over a young female body in the bushes while attempting to take up his surveillance post. Word went out through his watch commander to RHD, and the on-duty team was sent to the scene.

The property was three acres in size, and the main house exceeded ten-thousand square feet. The young woman's body was just about fifty yards from the home, but because of the downhill slant of the property, it was below the line of sight from the house.

The victim was nude and appeared to be in her early twenties. An obvious stab wound was visible in her center chest. Her body was far enough away from the house that Donahue and Thompson felt safe enough to preliminarily work the scene, while a SWAT team prepared to enter the home.

Donahue leaned over the body with a small flashlight and looked for distinguishing marks on the victim's body that might help them make an identification.

"She's got a small tattoo on the inside of her right wrist," said Donahue. "It looks like a the number eight on its side."

Thompson, who was taking notes nearby, said, "It's called a lemniscate. It's the mathematical symbol for infinity."

Donahue looked up and stared open-mouthed for a moment at her partner.

"You never cease to surprise me, Shari," she said.

"Scrabble," said Thompson. "You should try it."

Donahue returned her glance to the body and mumbled under her breath, "Yeah, right. That'll be the day."

Thompson chuckled. "I'll tell the photo guys to get a good shot of it, but we're gonna have to wait until the scene is secured."

Donahue got to her feet and brushed the dirt from the knees of her slacks.

The callout had come in the middle of the night. It was their turn in the barrel, a term that was used to refer to whatever team was on call for the overnight watch. And since Donahue was in possession of the take-home car, it had been her responsibility to pick up Thompson and get both of them out to the scene of the crime.

Donahue was a lanky blonde with shoulder-length hair that she kept neatly trimmed. Her partner was shorter in stature, but wore her chestnut locks down to her mid-back. Donahue was the alpha with seniority, but their arrangement was more of an equal partnership. Both women were known to be independent thinkers, and that served them well in a profession that was still predominantly male. They often relied on gut instincts, and as such, their case clearance rate was among the best in the division.

"Is your mom going to get the kids off to school for you in the morning?" Donahue asked, while she studied the victim's face in the glow of her flashlight.

"Yeah. I warned her that this might be a long one."

Thompson was recently divorced and had three young boys all under the age of twelve.

Her ex was usually pretty good about the alimony, but he rarely saw the boys on his custody days. As a result, Thompson's mother had agreed to move in with her to take care of the boys when her on-call status created a crunch.

Donahue shut off her flashlight. They would have to wait until dawn to do a thorough canvass of the scene.

"Well, I don't know about you, Jen," said Thompson as she folded up her notebook, "but I could sure use a strong cup of coffee."

Donahue nodded. "Maybe we can get a blue-suit to make a Starbucks run?"

"I don't mind going," said Thompson. "There's nothing more we can do until this whole thing settles down."

Donahue tossed her the keys.

A siren approached the winding road that led up the hill to Orsini's house. It was clearly getting closer, and when it suddenly went silent, both women noted that whoever it was had likely reached the driveway down at the base of the hill.

Thompson said, "Probably the Captain or a Deputy Chief come to take a looky-look."

Donahue sighed. "Well, no one's gonna get near this girl until the sun comes up and we get a chance to get a better look at the scene."

Too often in the history of the Department, senior police personnel would traipse through and contaminate a crime scene just to satisfy their morbid curiosity. But brighter minds had eventually prevailed, and it was now the absolute right of the detective in charge of the scene to have the final say-so as to who was allowed to view the scene during the investigation.

"I'll be back in twenty," said Thompson. "You want a pumpkin spice latte, no sugar?"

"Mmm, yes please."

Thompson wandered off through the landscaped yard while Donahue turned her flashlight on to do a cursory search for any physical evidence that might be near the body.

Three minutes later, Gibson suddenly appeared, closely followed by Thompson, who had tears in her eyes from silent crying.

Ulysses Gibson was the senior detective in their division, and at times he had functioned as the acting Lieutenant. A tall, ebony-skinned, African-American male, he had mentored both Donahue and Thompson when they first began to work at RHD.

Donahue watched them approach, but in the darkness of the yard she could not see their faces.

"Gibby?" she asked when he got closer. "What are you doing here?"

He closed the gap between them, then struggled for a moment with what he had to say.

"I need you to come with me, Jen. Shari can handle this investigation."

"Oh? What's up?"

"I need you to come with me to the car, Jen. Please?"

Two other detectives and a Deputy Chief had wandered up and were standing nearby. No one spoke, and no one even moved.

As she shifted her gaze to take in their faces, her stomach became knotted with dread. It was as if the spinning world had suddenly come to a grinding halt.

"What's going on?" she asked, looking over at Thompson. "You're all acting like someone has died."

"Please, Jen," said Gibson. "Just come with me to the car."

Donahue felt the hand of fear as it tightened around her heart.

"What is it, Gibby? What's happened?"

"There's been a shooting," he said in a broken voice. "I need you to go to the car."

"A shooting? Where? What's going on?"

Gibson wanted to crawl into a shell. He was used to tough moments, but none would be as tough as this one.

He reached out and took her arm, then leaned in and lowered his voice.

"There's been a shooting over at Sean's place. I need you to come to the car."

Donahue was frozen in place, unable to process what was being said.

"Go with him, sweetie," said Thompson through her tears. "You need to go right now."

Donahue's eyes widened as she looked from face to face.

"Sean's place? You mean *my Sean?*"

Gibson nodded.

Are you saying that Sean shot someone…?"

"No, Jen," said Gibson in a trembling voice. He held her by both shoulders, leaned in again and whispered, "Sean's dead."

Donahue shifted her gaze back and forth between Thompson and Gibson while she tried to process his words.

When it finally registered, she let out a horrible scream of pain just before collapsing into his arms.

THREE

MORE THAN HALF of the fifth floor of the Police Administration Building (PAB) in downtown Los Angeles was the domain of the Robbery-Homicide Division. With more than sixty desks in one gigantic office, all separated by waist-high privacy partitions, it had always been a central hub of activity for high-profile, publicity cases.

Donahue rode up alone to her office in one of the eight public elevators, and when she stepped out into a central hallway, she was greeted by Gibson, who gave her a hug and asked how she'd been.

"I'm okay," she replied. "My folks said to tell you hi."

Days after the funeral for Sean Walker, Donahue was ordered by her Captain to take some time off. He suggested a visit with her parents in Colorado, an idea that was more in line with an order. At that time, she was struggling with the throes of depression and was in no position to tell him no, so with the help of a few of the detectives in the squad, she got on a plane that was Colorado bound.

The visit had turned out to be a good idea. The mountains and the wild beauty of central Colorado were soothing in a way that the city could never be.

While she was gone, Thompson had arranged with a specialized firm to go into Sean's duplex and remove all of the biological waste that remained from the night of the shooting. Once that was completed,

Thompson and Gibson spent the better part of an afternoon trying to clean up the ransacked mess that the killers had made of the scene.

Gibson escorted Donahue into the squad, and after exchanging greetings and hugs with colleagues and friends, she went to a meeting in the Captain's office, where the Captain was waiting for her with Deputy Chief Frank Getty.

Captain Tom Elwood was a bear of a man. A former Marine, he was gruff when he dealt with the criminal element, but fiercely protective of the people who worked for him. Boyish in appearance, with neatly trimmed light brown hair, Elwood looked to be in his early thirties. But a hint of gray at the temples and a series of small wrinkles at the corners of his eyes were the only real clues to his age of forty-six years.

He got to his feet when she entered his office and gave her a welcoming hug. Getty also stood up, but extended his hand instead. Donahue shook it, then took a seat in front of the desk while Elwood, Gibson and Getty quickly settled in.

"How are you feeling?" Elwood asked.

"I'm good," she replied.

"That's great," said Getty. "We've missed you, so welcome back."

There was a moment of awkward silence. Donahue didn't really know Getty, but she knew he was trying to build a bridge between them, so she smiled and said, "I'm glad to be back, Chief. Thanks so much for your support."

Getty gave her a nod and a smile.

"I just wanted you to know that we're doing everything we can to assist the FBI in their investigation into your fiancé's death. Tom is the on-point liaison for the Department, and if they need anything from us, he's the man who'll get it done."

Donahue was confused, but when she glanced over at Elwood, he grimaced and gently shook his head, a sign to her not to ask Getty any questions.

She gave Elwood a quick wink. Message received, and to the DC she said, "That's great news, sir. Thanks."

Getty nodded, then got to his feet.

"I've got another meeting I've got to go to," he told them as he reached for her hand. "But I just wanted to be here to welcome you back, and to express, once again, the support of the Department. If we can do anything to help you get back on your feet, just let Tom know and he'll pass it up the chain."

She shook his hand and watched him go. Once he was out of the room, she said, "Well, that was certainly awkward."

Elwood stifled a laugh. "He meant well."

"I know. So, what's all this about the FBI? I thought we were gonna handle the case?"

"The Chief decided that we had a conflict of interest, so he asked the Sheriffs to get involved."

Donahue cocked her head. "The Sheriffs? So, how do the Feds figure in?"

"They took the case away from the Sheriffs," said Gibson. "All we were told is that Sean's death is part of a larger investigation that the Bureau guys already have in play."

"What the hell does that mean?" said Donahue with a frown. "What larger investigation?"

Elwood squirmed in his chair.

"I hate to even ask this, Jen, but are you aware of anything that might connect Sean with criminal activity of any kind?"

"Of course not," she replied without hesitation. "Sean was a real estate investor. He wasn't involved in anything shady."

"Are you sure?"

She wasn't, of course. Sean had never really discussed his business activities with her. In fact, he never really said a whole lot about his life in general. She knew that he was a man with money, how much she didn't know, and if truth be told, she hadn't really cared. But if the

Feds were sniffing around, then it seemed clear to her that there must have been something that he never mentioned or that she had missed.

"I don't know, Captain. He didn't really talk to me about his business affairs, so I guess I can't really say."

Elwood leaned back in his chair and put his thinking cap on. She waited him out, and when he finally spoke, she was surprised by what he had to say.

"When I told you to go and visit your parents, it was because the FBI asked me to persuade you to get out of town."

"Huh? Why would they want me to leave? This doesn't make any sense."

"They said they were worried that you might be in danger, but they refused to tell me why. I did what they asked because they assured me that they'd keep you under a loose surveillance in Colorado to make sure that you would be okay."

What the hell is going on? Donahue shook her head in disbelief.

"Well, if they were watching me, they were awfully good, because I never picked up on the surveillance. And for that matter, why would anyone want to kill Sean or me? And why won't they say what's going on?"

"I can't answer that, Jen," said Elwood, with a shrug. "I'm completely in the dark."

"Well, someone must know something, and I'm gonna find out what that is." She looked over at Gibson. "Were you aware of any of this?"

"Only what Tommy has told you. The FBI hasn't kept us in the loop."

She looked back over at Elwood.

"Does the Chief know what's going on?" she asked.

"If so, he hasn't said so."

Donahue folded her hands across her chest. It was clear to her that she wasn't going to get any answers by trying to go through channels. She would have to make some calls and see if any of her "friends in high places" could tell her exactly what was going on.

"So, where do we go from here?" she said. "I was planning to start working tomorrow."

"That's gonna have to go on hold," said Elwood. "I was discussing this with Getty, and if you're facing some kind of personal risk, you're going to need to be protected."

"I don't need protection, Tom. I can take care of myself."

"I don't doubt that, Jen, but you can't go it alone until we know the nature of the possible threat. Let me talk to the FBI first. Now that you're back, maybe they'll be ready to tell us what the threat is all about."

"Is this for real?" Donahue got to her feet. "Are you telling me that I can't resume working until we know what's going on, but no one knows if the Feds will even tell us what this bullshit is all about?"

Elwood leaned forward and held her glance.

"I know this sucks, and I promise you I'll, get to the bottom of it right away. But until we get a handle on what's going on, think about staying away. Maybe go back and visit your folks for another few weeks?"

"Not a chance. I love my folks, but I need my space and they need theirs." She stared at him until he blinked. "I'm coming in, boss. I'll see you tomorrow."

She got to her feet, but as she turned to head for the door, he said, "Hold on, Jen. We're not finished. Please sit back down."

It was not a suggestion, and after a moment's hesitation, she slowly returned to her chair.

"The FBI will be here in a few minutes to have a talk with you," said Elwood. "They want to interview you about the night that Sean was killed."

"*What?* They think I'm a suspect?"

"Not that I'm aware of. I had them hold off right after the incident on account of the way you were feeling. And once they wanted you out of the city, we agreed that they could put off the interview until you got back."

She looked over at Gibson and shrugged. "This just gets stranger by the minute."

She closed her eyes for a moment to consider her options. She could refuse to do the interview, but that would get her nowhere. If she did do the interview, she might be able to learn something about what was going on from the nature of the questions they planned to ask her.

"I'll do the interview," she said as she opened her eyes. "But this other stuff better get settled right away."

"I'll do what I can to find out what's going on," said Elwood, "but I want you to think about your personal security. Until we know what's happening, we can't do an assessment of what you might be facing. And that means that you and those you work with might be at risk."

She hadn't considered the fact that a threat to her might pose a risk to her partners, and that was something that she couldn't allow to happen.

"Okay, I'll think about it," she told him. "Can I go now?"

As soon as he nodded, she got to her feet and left his office. She went looking for her partner, but Shari was nowhere to be found, so she went to her desk, checked her emails, and was about to leave when Thompson walked in from the hallway and made a beeline over to Donahue's desk.

"You're back!"

Thompson leaned in and gave her a long hug, and said, "I didn't think you were coming in today, so I was gonna stop by your place after work."

"Did you know about this bullshit I'm going through?"

"Huh?" Thompson frowned. "What are you talking about?"

"Did you know about the Feds taking over the case?"

"Oh, that? Well, yeah. The powers upstairs decided it was a conflict of interest for us to work it. So, why? What's happened?"

Donahue got to her feet.

"Ladies room. *Now.*"

She headed off in a huff with Thompson close on her heels. Because the partitions in their outer office were only waist high and only came with three sides, anything said at their desks could be overheard by anyone who was sitting nearby.

Hence, the sanctity of the ladies room.

Donahue checked to make sure that the stalls were all empty, then relayed to Thompson what had transpired in her meeting with the Captain.

"Do you have any idea what Sean was up to?" Thompson asked when she was through.

"Not at all. This has to be a mistake, Shari. He never said or did anything that even hinted that he was involved in something criminal or unethical. He was just a real estate investor. He builds and owns large business properties."

"I believe you, babe. But is it possible that he just didn't tell you everything?"

Donahue felt herself tearing up.

"I don't know what to think anymore. I thought I knew him, Shari. And now he's gone and I'm finding out that he might not have been the person I thought he was."

Detective Mitzi Roberts came into the restroom. She was an attractive brunette and a talented detective who specialized in knowing everything there was to know about electronics. Among the other members of the division, she was also known for her acerbic wit.

"There you are," she said. "Welcome back, Jen. There's a couple of FBI agents waiting to meet with—"

She stopped mid-sentence when she noticed Donahue's tears.

"Are you okay?" Roberts asked.

Donahue sniffed, then pulled a Kleenex from a box on the washstand counter and blotted away her tears.

"She's just happy to be back," said Thompson.

"You want me to tell the Feds to take a hike?" Roberts asked.

Donahue shook her head. "Stall 'em, Mitz. I'll be out in a minute."

"You got it," said Roberts. She walked over and gave Donahue a hug. "You need anything babe, you let me know."

Once she was gone, Donahue said, "They want to talk to me about that night."

"That's good," said Thompson. "Maybe then they'll fill you in on what's going on."

Donahue looked at herself in the mirror, checked her face, then turned around and sighed.

"Okay. I'm ready. Let's get this bullshit over with."

FOUR

WHEN THEY CAME out of the restroom, they were met by Gibson, who took both of them aside.

"The Feds are cooling their heels in the conference room, and if it's okay with you, Jen, I'd like to sit in?"

"Yeah, sure," she replied.

Gibson acknowledged her answer with a wink.

"And if they get out of line, or you want to quit, just let me know and I'll walk you out."

Donahue turned to Thompson. "Will you be here when I get done?"

"I'm not leaving. I'll catch you when it's over."

Gibson walked her out to the central hallway and into one of the interview rooms where the two waiting FBI agents quickly got to their feet.

"Detective Donahue? I'm Kasey Smitten and this is my partner, Rebecca Folsey." She extended her hand. "It's a pleasure to meet you."

Smitten was a tall brunette with brown eyes, very little makeup, and a stern look that tended to put off her coworkers. She was the Alpha of the pair, while Folsey, a redhead, was shorter but more personable. Both wore dark blue business suits with white blouses, but Folsey augmented her outfit with a colorful scarf; a feminine touch that served as her act of independence.

Donahue shook hands with both of them and Smitten suggested that they all sit down.

Gibson grabbed a chair, and without being asked, he took a seat at the table.

"Just so you know," he started, "I'm here at the insistence of the Chief to make sure that the interview goes smoothly."

Smoothly my ass, thought Smitten. He's here to make sure that we don't badger her.

"That's fine with me, Detective Gibson." She turned her attention to Donahue. "Let me begin by saying how sorry we are for your loss. Sean Walker was one of the good guys, and we know how much he cared for you."

Donahue almost keeled over.

"You knew Sean?"

"We did," said Smitten. She looked over at Gibson then back at Donahue. "We want to talk with you today about Sean, but you might want to hear what we have to say in private."

She gestured towards Gibson with a quick turn of her head.

"Gibby stays," said Donahue.

Smitten shrugged, then nodded her understanding.

"Very well. Okay. Let's begin this way. Can you please tell me what Sean may have told you about his background?"

"Obviously, not enough," said Donahue. "And why is what he told me so important anyway?"

"We need to know if Sean said something inadvertently to you that would have enabled someone to figure out his true identity."

"What do you mean...*his true identity?*"

"In due time, Detective, but this will go a lot faster if you just answer our questions." When Donahue looked skeptical, Smitten added, "I can promise you that by the time we're done most of your questions will be answered."

Donahue thought it over. She was clearly in the dark about who Sean was and what he might have been up to with the Feds. So, if

Smitten was on the level and true to her word, she just might learn what the hell was going on.

She exhaled slowly and came to the conclusion that her best course of action was to play their cat-and-mouse game.

"Okay," she began, "he told me he came from Eastern Europe, was educated in London, and his parents were both dead. I asked him about the rest of his family but he said that he had none." She racked her brain, but nothing else came to mind. "That's all I really know."

"Nothing about his businesses?"

"Just that he was a real estate investor."

"So, you really don't know much about him at all?" said a surprised Smitten. She and Folsey exchanged a look.

"Your turn," said Donahue, whose eyes quickly narrowed. "What is it that I don't really know?"

Smitten put down her pen and met Donahue's glance. "Sean's father was *Anton Borisovich Korakovsky*, a Russian oligarch. Were you aware of that?"

"No. I wasn't."

"Okay. Well, initially, he was a close friend of Vladimir Putin. Korakovsky made his fortune in gas and oil. He founded and subsequently maintained a sixty percent share of *YURO Petroleum*. After the fall of the USSR, YURO landed the exclusive petroleum rights to the Russian Federation's area of the North Sea. The money poured in, and being a shrewd businessman, Korakovsky expanded his empire to include mining in precious metals, a dozen television stations, and an electronic components firm—-just to name a few. He oversaw this conglomerate from an office in Moscow Center. But just about five years ago, he had a falling out with Putin. That happened when he announced his intention to run for the Russian presidency on a platform of anti-corruption."

Donahue was completely dumbfounded, and Smitten noticed that her eyes displayed the fifty-yard stare of one whose mind was churning at hyper speed within the confines of her own thoughts.

"Does any of this sound familiar to you?" Folsey asked.

"What?" Donahue looked from one to the other as her mind returned to the present. "I'm sorry," she said with a shake of the head. "I'm just having a little trouble processing what you're saying. All of this is new to me."

Folsey nodded. "I'm not surprised. It's a lot to take in."

Smitten continued, "Putin doesn't take kindly to anyone challenging his authority, particularly when that person has access to a television market that covers ninety percent of the Russian Federation. So, he put pressure on Korakovsky to sell off his television stations by threatening to bring him up on charges of corruption and money laundering. Korakovsky did the smart thing. He sold his TV interests to *Sasha Vitali Berasov*, a former KGB colleague of Putin's, and an oligarch in his own right.

"Korakovsky wisely withdrew from the Presidential race, but Putin wasn't finished yet. On a trip to Oxford, London, to visit his son—your fiancé—Korakovsky became seriously ill. He was hospitalized for almost two months, and during that time he was diagnosed with severe radiation poisoning. Apparently, he ingested *Polonium 210* during a meeting with an emissary of Berasov. The Brits believe it was put in Korakovsky's tea. It took him eight painful weeks to die, and when he did, he was little more than a skeleton with skin."

"Good God!" said Donahue. She glanced over at Gibson whose wide eyes betrayed his own surprise.

"After an exhaustive investigation, MI-5 and 6 have jointly concluded that his death was a state-sponsored assassination which was sanctioned by Putin himself."

At the time it occurred, Donahue had heard about Korakovsky's death on the news. It was covered by all the news networks for weeks at a time. She remembered hearing that just moving the polonium through the city of London had left a traceable trail of radiation. It was clearly an assassination meant to deliver a message.

"You with me so far?" asked Smitten.

"I think so," said an overwhelmed Donahue. "But what about Sean?"

"I'm getting to that," said Smitten.

She leaned forward in her chair.

"Mikel Korakovsky, your Sean Walker, was Anton Korakovsky's only son. He was raised and educated in Moscow, but left the Federation to go to college after his mother passed away from cancer. He was studying economics at Oxford when his father was murdered. Anyway, because he inherited all of his father's business operations, there were worries that he, too, might become the target of an assassin. So, it was jointly decided during a high-level meeting between representatives of the United States and Great Britain that Mikel should be offered asylum in the United States where he was given a new ID and was placed in the Federal Witness Protection Program."

"Uhh...so Mikel Korakovsky is Sean's true name?" asked Donahue.

Smitten nodded. "He took the name of Sean Walker when he entered the program, and he kept it when he obtained his US citizenship."

Donahue was speechless. She'd known so little about this man she still loved. He had always deftly deflected her questions about his background, and now she understood why.

She couldn't help but wonder...*if I'd known about his history, would that have made any difference in our relationship?*

She locked eyes with Smitten.

"So, Sean was not involved in any type of criminal activity?"

"That's correct," said Smitten. "He was not."

"And the only reason that he was put in PC was for his protection and nothing more?"

"I didn't say that," she replied.

Donahue frowned.

"You're not planning to tell me everything, are you?"

"I can't, Detective, at least, not for now."

Donahue suddenly realized that she had just been handed a

not-so-subtle hint as to what had really been going on, and why the Feds had taken such an interest in Sean. Perhaps if she kept pushing, she could find out even more.

"Were you his case agent?" Donahue asked.

"I was," Smitten replied. "And that's why I'm here. Sean's true identity was classified as *Top Secret*, and yet, it looks as if they found him. It's now my job to find out how that occurred."

Sean was working for the Feds.

Donahue slowly nodded as her understanding grew. *The pieces were beginning to fall into place.*

She pursed her lips, then straightened up in her chair.

"Well, if that's what you're after, you can take me off your list. I had no idea at all about any of this."

"Will you take a poly for us?" Folsey asked.

"About this? About what I knew? Absolutely!"

Smitten nodded. "We'll set one up right away."

"So, is that all?"

Donahue felt completely overwhelmed by their revelations, and all she wanted to do at the moment was to go to her condo and get into bed. She needed some quiet time to think everything through. She wanted to go over the details of her relationship with Sean, to figure out why she had never picked up the slightest hint that his life before her had been so complex? But most of all, she wanted to understand why he hadn't trusted her enough to discuss with her the truth about his background.

"Actually, there is still just a little bit more," said Smitten. She looked over at Gibson who had yet to utter a peep. "If Detective Gibson will excuse us, I need to talk to you about something personal, but I'm not at liberty to discuss this in front of anyone else."

"I trust Gibby," said Donahue.

Smitten shook her head. "I'm sorry, Detective, but those are my orders, and they come from the top. I can't go further unless we're alone. And once we have a talk, you'll understand why."

Donahue didn't like it but she'd gone too far to bail out now.

Whatever it was that Smitten had to tell her couldn't be more shocking than what she'd already learned.

"Okay," said Donahue. She turned to Gibson. "Can you give us a few moments?"

He looked over at Smitten. "Only if I'm assured that the questioning is finished."

"It is," said Smitten. "You have my word on that."

He nodded and got to his feet.

"I'll be right outside, Jen. If she starts to ask questions again, you let me know right away."

"I will, Gibby. And thanks."

Gibson left the room, and once he was gone, Smitten said, "He's quite a loyal friend."

Donahue held her glance. She had yet to make up her mind about Smitten, who hadn't yet earned her trust.

"I'm coming down with a headache, Agent Smitten, so why don't you just tell me what you wanted to say?"

Smitten turned to her partner.

"Rebecca, why don't you go grab a cup of coffee?"

Folsey stared at her, then clearly miffed, she slid her chair back and left the room.

Smitten opened her briefcase and brought out a device which she placed on the table in front of them.

"What's that?" said Donahue.

"It's a jammer." Smitten turned it on. "It will prevent anyone from listening to or recording our conversation."

"Is that really necessary?" Donahue asked.

"It is." Smitten studied her carefully. "Can I call you Jennifer?"

Donahue nodded.

"Okay, Jennifer, here's the deal. I believe you when you say you didn't know anything about Sean's background. I say this because you seem genuinely shocked by what I've told you. Also, I spoke with Sean about you just about two weeks before all of this happened, and he said at that time that he hadn't yet told you about his past. So, if he never had that talk with you, then it's highly unlikely that you made an unguarded remark that could have put Sean's death into play."

Donahue quickly decided that she really didn't like Kasey Smitten. Sure, Smitten had known Sean a lot better than she did, and that was certainly troubling. But setting aside this twinge of personal jealousy, it was the way Smitten talked to her, as if she was somehow superior to Donahue, and that made her think seriously about punching her out.

"Let's get something straight here, Smitten—"

"You can call me Kasey," said Smitten.

Donahue frowned. "All right then, Kasey. Let's get something straight. At the moment, I have very torn feelings about what's going on. Sean's been murdered, and while I've been gone for a month, apparently at the insistence of someone in your agency—"

It was Smitten's turn to be surprised, and that didn't go unnoticed by Donahue.

"—and now that I'm back, I find out that you people have no idea who did the killing."

"That's not completely true," said Smitten.

"Isn't it?" Donahue was just getting started. "I'm not buyin' it. If you knew who was involved, you wouldn't still be working on some dumb hypothesis that perhaps I said something inadvertently that ended up getting Sean killed."

"That's not the same as knowing who killed him," said a defensive Smitten. "How they learned his true identity is different from who got paid to do it."

"So, who did it, Kasey? Because if you know who killed him, you can work your way back to the source a lot easier than starting with me and trying to go forward."

"We're working on it from both ends," said Smitten.

"Okay. If that's the case, who did it?"

"I can't tell you that, but I can say that we're working on it, and we don't plan to quit until we know how it happened and who is responsible."

"Foreign or local?" Donahue said.

"What?"

"Foreign or local? The guys who did it. Foreign or local?"

Smitten relented, "We think they were foreign."

Donahue knew she was getting nowhere. Smitten was not going to tell her anything about the hunt for the killers, so she decided to take a different approach to find out whatever she could.

"Tell me something, Kasey. Why did the Bureau want me to stay with my parents in Colorado? Why would I be in any kind of personal jeopardy?"

"Putin's a very vindictive man," said Smitten.

"There you go again, resorting to generalizations instead of hard answers. Putin would have no reason to have me killed. Even if Sean had told me who he was, why would my life be at risk?"

"As I said, he's vindictive. If you hadn't been out on a call that night, you wouldn't be alive today."

Donahue accepted the fact that that was probably true, but it was a far cry from Putin sending out another hit team just to track her down.

"I'm not buying it," said Donahue. "There's more to all of this than you've told me."

Smitten shrugged. "Think of it this way, Jennifer. Whoever killed Sean might assume that you know something that you shouldn't know."

"And what do you suppose that might be?" Donahue asked.

But Smitten didn't answer. Instead, she leaned back in her chair and said, "Let's get that polygraph out of the way and maybe I can tell you more."

Donahue stared at her for a moment, then got to her feet and gave Smitten a joyless smile.

"I'll still take the stupid poly, but until you're ready to truly level with me about everything, don't bother to call me again."

FIVE

DONAHUE GOT UP the next morning firmly resolved to learn what she could about Sean's family. She had passed the polygraph with flying colors, but the nature of the questions they asked had made her all the more curious to know what was really going on.

She wandered into her kitchen and made herself a cup of coffee. The night before she had neglected to stop at the supermarket. She'd been too blown away by her meeting with the Feds to think about anything but getting home. So, sadly, there was nothing to eat for breakfast.

She took the coffee to the living room and sat down at a small desk that she used for her home office. She turned on her computer and typed in the name of Anton Korakovsky. She read the first ten articles she found, then realized that most of the articles were focused on the use of the polonium to kill Korakovsky rather than on his business or his family. There was a great deal of repetition in the stories, but what there was confirmed everything that Agent Smitten had told her.

One article from the Times of London stated that the Russian Federation had filed charges of embezzlement against Anton Korakovsky. The writer opined that the charges were being used as leverage to try and force the British government to return Korakovsky to Moscow.

There was one other article that interested her. It focused on the meeting that Korakovsky attended when he was given the poison. It happened in a tea room in the *Exeter Hotel*, and the man suspected of delivering the poison was Anatoly Lapin, a former KGB agent who was well known to western intelligence agencies. The article went on to state that an Interpol Alert had been distributed for Lapin's arrest, but that the Kremlin had reported that several months after Korakovsky's death, Lapin was killed in a one car crash on the highway leading into the city of St. Petersburg.

On a better note, she spotted a photograph in one of the stories that showed Anton with his young son Mikel. It quickly brought a smile to her face. He couldn't have been more than maybe twelve years old, but he looked happy to be with his father.

Her cell phone rang, and although she didn't recognize the number on the screen, she answered it just the same.

"Is this Jennifer Donahue?" said a soft male voice.

"It is. Who's this?" she replied.

"Ms. Donahue, my name is James McCallum. I'm an attorney with the firm of McCallum and Roth. I worked exclusively for a single client by the name of Mikel Korakovsky, better known to you as Sean Walker."

Donahue was taken aback. What in God's name could this be all about?

"Go on," she finally said.

"Well, first let me tell you how sorry we are for your loss."

When Donahue didn't respond, he added, "Mr. Sean left instructions that in the event of his death, I was to make contact with you by phone. I was to tell you that he has left a letter for you in my possession." He gave her a moment to let what he told her sink in. "I wonder if today might be a good time for me to deliver it to you?"

A letter from Sean?

She couldn't believe it. Of course she wanted to see it right away. But bearing in mind what Smitten had said, how could she be sure that this was on the up and up?

"Rather than have you come to my location, I'd rather meet you at your office," she said.

"That's perfectly acceptable. Shall I send a car for you?"

Fat chance of that, she thought. If this was a setup, getting into a strange car would be the stupidest thing she could ever do.

"No, I'll come to your office. Can you give me your address?"

He did, and he encouraged her to look his firm up on the Internet. He also suggested that she not say anything to anyone about the name of his firm or the proposed meeting.

"You'll understand why right after we speak," he said.

He sounds just like Smitten, she thought. Both had asked her to accept what they had to say on faith.

"I'll meet you at your firm in about an hour," she said.

"Thank you," said McCallum. "I'll see you then."

⸎

The boutique law firm of McCallum and Roth was located on the tenth floor of a building on Wilshire Boulevard in Beverly Hills. Donahue left her Toyota with the building's valet, then made her way up in the elevator.

Before heading over to meet him, she had checked out the firm on the internet. She also called the State Bar Association. No complaints about the firm were ever made to the Bar, and outside of a single photograph of McCallum on the partnership website, she was unable to find any negative articles about the firm.

She'd come prepared for anything. She had a .45 caliber Sig Sauer in her handbag, and flat shoes in case she needed to fight or run.

She opened the door to the office and was met by a single secretary.

"Ms. Donahue? Welcome. Mr. McCallum will be with you in a minute. Please take a seat and I'll let him know that you're here."

She disappeared down a back hallway and returned a moment later with McCallum on her heels.

"Ms. Donahue," he said. "It's a pleasure to finally meet you. I'm James McCallum."

He extended his hand and she shook it. He then led her back down the hallway to a spacious corner office. His secretary, named Margaret, offered her coffee, which she politely declined. McCallum had her take a seat on a couch before sitting down in a chair that faced her.

McCallum was short, perhaps five-five or five-six in his black leather shoes. At sixty-eight years of age, he still had all of his gray hair, which he always wore parted and short. He was the grandfather type in appearance—respectful, but also knowledgeable on a variety of subjects. He didn't suffer fools easily, but he always managed to maintain a professional decorum even when dealing with others who were less civil.

He wore a fine quality *Kiton* navy blue suit, one that was obviously tailored to fit. All in all, he had the look of a prosperous and very successful lawyer, which, of course, he was.

Between them was a glass-topped coffee table, and on it was an open laptop computer and a set of expensive earphones.

"I must say, Mr. McCallum, your firm doesn't seem very big?"

McCallum smiled. "My firm only has only one client, Ms. Donahue, but I can assure you, appearances are deceiving."

When Donahue gave him a questioning look, he added, "The thirty lawyers in this firm occupy the entire two floors below us. I run a very private, inconspicuous practice, Ms. Donahue. It was necessary for the very confidential work that we did for Mr. Sean."

"I'm not sure I understand?"

McCallum got to his feet. In his hand was a sealed manilla envelope.

"This may help to explain things." He placed it in her hand. "I have not seen the contents, but when it was presented to me by Mr. Sean, I could feel that it also contained a memory stick. I've placed a computer on the table in front of you for you to use, and there's a set of earphones for your privacy. The computer is not hooked up to the internet, so you will be the only one who will see what's on the memory stick.

"I'll just leave you now for a few minutes. Whenever you're done, just press the green button on the intercom, which is next to the computer, and I'll return to answer any questions that I can."

She watched him leave the room, and with trembling hands she opened the envelope and pulled out two blank pieces of paper. But lying in the fold of the paper was the memory stick that McCallum had so wisely deduced by feeling the outside of the envelope.

She put the stick into the computer port, and the screen immediately came to life. She put on the earphones, clicked on the folder marked *Personal,* then watched as a video of Sean suddenly came alive on the screen.

> *"Hi, babe! If you're viewing this, then I'm obviously gone, and for that I'm truly sorry. I know that my death will hurt you, and I would give anything to be there with you now.*
>
> *"I'm also sorry that I never got a chance to explain things to you. I wanted to tell you about myself on many occasions, but I was selfish and decided to wait until I knew that you were willing to marry me. I wanted to know that you loved me for who I am… or was—it's kind of tough to say that…(he sniffed several times to keep his voice from cracking)…for who I was as a person before you found out the truth.*
>
> *"Anyway, I was planning to tell you for a while now, but I had a surprise in the works, so I thought I'd wait until you saw it. If McCallum hasn't yet told you about it—believe me, you'd know if he did—then ask him and he will tell you today.*
>
> *"I wish I could go back and change things…but I can't. I just hope you can forgive me, Jen. You're the only woman I've ever loved, and to me that love was well worth the shortness of our journey."*

There was a long pause on the recording. Sean was breathing deeply and rubbing at his eyes. He had trouble looking into the camera as he tried desperately to get control of his emotions.

For her part, Donahue had been silently crying since the start of the tape. She noticed that McCallum had thoughtfully left a box of Kleenex on the table next to the computer, no doubt anticipating that they might be needed.

She clutched a handful in her hand and used them to blot at her eyes as the taped message continued.

"Sorry for that. Where was I? Oh, yeah. I can't believe that I'm not with you now. I knew my death was a possibility, but I always thought that the change of identity would protect me…protect us. In hindsight, I was pretty naive.

"I will always be grateful for the time we had together. I often think about the way you smile and how you made me laugh. You were the sexiest woman I've ever known, and I'm so glad that you were in my life. I just hope you were as happy as I truly was.

You remember that little bet we made? I'm talking about the night we stayed at the Four Seasons hotel in Las Vegas? I know you remember what the bet was all about. I sure do. Anyway, when you lost that bet, you were supposed to read my favorite novel. Remember? Well, I know you never got around to it, so I just hope you'll take the time to read it now.

"I think you'll find that it's fascinating, a real world changer. It's a really good read, babe. Please enjoy it.

"Anyway, I'm sure by now that you know about my life and my family's background. I can't be there to protect you from what the future may hold, but at least I can see to it that you never have to worry again about your financial situation.

"James McCallum is a man I completely trust. He handled

my father's businesses for years, and when the businesses passed to me, he handled everything with professionalism and discretion. He'll serve you well, darling. He'll explain everything, and I'm sure you can rely on him to be a trusted advisor when it comes to your business endeavors.

"I love you, Jen. I know you're strong enough to handle what's coming.

"Live a good life.

"Find love again.

"And know that I'll be waiting for you on the other side."

When the video ended, Donahue continued to cry for a full ten minutes before pushing the green button. When McCallum returned to the office, he took the chair across from her and sat silently while she struggled to compose herself.

"Can I keep this?" she asked, referring to the memory stick.

"Of course. Do you have any questions?"

She nodded. "Sean said something about my business interests? But I don't have any business interests. I'm a cop and my only income is my salary."

McCallum smiled. "Perhaps Mr. Sean was referring to your new business interests?"

Donahue didn't get it at first, but it suddenly clicked in.

"Sean left me a business?"

"In a manner of speaking," McCallum said with a nod. "Do you know anything at all about his family?"

"I was told that his father was murdered in London by someone connected to Putin."

McCallum leaned back in his chair.

"Mr. Sean's father was very wealthy, and when his situation in Moscow became untenable, he hired my firm to liquidate his Russian holdings and to move his assets to the West. It took two years, but we managed the sale of most of his properties and businesses before he was killed. Mr. Sean was his only child, and as such, he was heir to his father's fortune. His instructions to us were to invest his holdings in western real estate and businesses, and that we have done."

"Okay. So what does this have to do with me?" she asked.

McCallum cleared his throat.

"When you and Mr. Sean became engaged, he ordered a new will to be drafted. He left a portion of his estate to a charitable trust, and the rest he left to you."

Donahue's eyes went wide and she shook her head.

"I don't know what to say, Mr. McCallum. I'm afraid to ask what you're talking about?"

McCallum smiled.

"I'm sure this is difficult to process, Ms. Donahue, so take your time. I can wait."

Donahue was speechless. She was now convinced that her entire life was about to significantly change.

Hell! It already had!

She started to cry again, and McCallum politely waited her out.

"Are you interested in knowing the size of the estate?" he asked when the tears went dry.

She could only nod.

"Well, the actual value of Mr. Sean's holdings is variable due to market conditions. It changes on a daily basis. But at the present time, we believe that it's in the neighborhood of forty-six billion dollars. Mr. Sean has bequeathed ten billion to a charitable trust, and he has set aside the rest for you."

"Thirty-six million?" said Donahue. "That's too—"

"Billion, Ms. Donahue. Thirty-six billion with a B."

"Oh, my God!" Donahue felt light headed. This wasn't happening. It had to be a dream.

McCallum watched as the color drained from her face.

"Are you okay?" he asked.

"No, I'm not. This feels like I'm in the twilight zone, and I think I'm gonna be sick."

McCallum quickly got to his feet and grabbed a nearby wastebasket. He managed to get it over to Donahue before she began to dry heave.

"I'm sorry," she said when the unpleasantness passed. "I—"

"No apology necessary," said McCallum. "I'm going to suggest that you take the rest of the day to process what I've told you. When it begins to feel real, we'll meet again, and I'll tell you more about the nature of your assets and the role he hoped you'd play on the board of the charitable trust."

"I can't run any kind of a business, Mr. McCallum." She rolled her eyes and shrugged. "I have no business experience."

"You'll have people to do that for you, so try not to think about that now."

"But doesn't this will have to go through probate or something like that? I don't know what the hell I'm supposed to do?"

"It's already being handled," he said. "We've been getting cooperation from the Federal government, so the proceedings should be concluded in another month or two."

"Cooperation? You mean like from the IRS?"

"Not exactly," he said with a smile. "The intelligence agencies who sponsored Mr. Sean's placement in the Witness Protection Program are guiding the court proceedings in such a way as to preserve your privacy and your connection to the assets. The Russian Federation would dearly like to get their hands on the Korakovsky holdings, and we've done our best over the years to conceal Mr. Sean's ownership by setting up a string of shell corporations."

Donahue had tuned him out. It was too much information too fast, and far too complicated for her to assimilate.

McCallum noticed this and smiled.

"We can talk about all of this another time, but because of the amount involved—and the efforts that will now be made by certain parties in the Federation to try to recover Mr. Sean's assets before they're transferred to you—I would strongly caution you not to say anything to anyone about what you've learned today. In fact, don't mention my firm by name to anyone. Our secrecy is your best protection."

He offered her a tentative smile.

"For the time being, don't tell any friends or relatives or anyone at all until you have a firm grasp on the risks involved in your situation. And as for your security, we'll need to discuss that very soon."

Her brain was screaming...*I can't fucking believe this!* She wasn't even sure that she wanted the money. *Billions? He said billions! What the hell does that really mean?*

She wanted to talk about this with Thompson or Gibson. They would know what she should say or do. But given the warnings from McCallum, a man that Sean completely trusted, she was lucid enough to know that it was better to say nothing until she had the time to think things through.

"I'd like to go home now," she said, standing up.

"Will you allow me to have our driver take you there?"

"I've got my car down in the garage."

She was feeling light headed and her legs began to wobble.

McCallum noticed and quickly came around the table to take her arm.

"I can see that you're a little unsteady. Let my driver take you home. I can have your car delivered to you in under an hour."

He was making sense. She didn't actually know if she had enough focus to make it all the way home. Her concentration was gone and she couldn't seem to wrap her head around what she'd just been told.

McCallum walked over to his desk, picked up the phone, and told his secretary to have his driver meet Ms. Donahue down at the basement Valet stand.

"Tell him to drive Ms. Donahue directly home and make arrangements for her car to be driven back there within the next hour."

He walked Donahue from his office and directly to the elevator.

"It will take a couple of days for everything to sink in. I'm sure it seems incredible now but you'll soon adjust to what has happened. I once told Mr. Sean to think of himself as simply the master of ceremonies of a very large production, so I'll give you the same advice. Your job is to provide broad guidance to a number of subordinates who will do your bidding and take care of all of the daily work. Our job, if you wish to keep us onboard, will be to ensure that your wishes are carried out."

Donahue could only roll her eyes, and for once in her life, words completely failed her.

SIX

DONAHUE MADE HER way downtown to her RHD office. She had spent a lot of time thinking about her last meeting with the Captain, and she was now more concerned than ever that the FBI's assumption of the murder investigation might have been infused with political overtones.

She arrived at her desk in the PAB, engaged in meaningless small talk with some of her close colleagues, then made her way to the Captain's office where she found him sitting behind his desk.

"What are you doing here?" he asked, when she walked in. "I thought you were gonna take some more time off?"

She shut the door behind her and took a seat in front of his desk.

"I need to talk to you about the murder investigation."

"I thought we covered this, Jen. The FBI has taken it over."

"I know, but what I want to know is whether or not you've been honest with me."

Elwood sat up straighter. "What are you talking about?"

Donahue folded her arms across her chest. "You said the FBI was keeping you in the dark about the murder investigation?"

"That's right, they are."

She held his glance while her own eyes narrowed.

"And no one ever told you about Sean's family background?"

Elwood cocked his head. He leaned back in his chair and slowly exhaled. "Where's this going, Jen?"

"I wanna know if you knew about Sean's Russian background. It's a simple question, Tom. Did you know about his family situation?"

Elwood studied her for a moment, then said, "It's pretty clear to me that someone has said something to you that I know nothing about. So, if you want to tell me exactly what it is you think I know, I'll be happy to confirm or deny your suspicions."

"Okay. Did you know that Sean was in the Witness Protection Program?"

"I had no idea. Where did you hear that, Jen?"

"The Feds told me about it when I was interviewed."

"Did they tell you why he was being protected?"

"They said his father was assassinated in London and they were worried that Sean would be a possible target."

She spent the next twenty minutes going over what she knew about the history of the Korakovsky family and the use of radioactive poison to kill Sean's father. She held back on telling him that she had become Sean's heir.

When she was finished, Elwood leaned back and slowly shook his head.

"This is pretty heavy stuff, Jen. No wonder the Feds jumped in."

"That's what bothers me, Tom. I think there's more, but the Feds aren't talking."

"That may be, but it's out of our hands now. If Sean's death somehow involves national security, we'll never be included in the loop."

"I know that, so I want to look into what happened myself. Can I get a look at our file?"

"There is no file, Jen. The Feds took everything we had."

"C'mon, Boss. Since when do we give them all of our copies?"

"You need to steer clear of the case, Jen. You hear me? If you get involved, it might taint any chance that the Feds might have to put together a prosecutable criminal case."

"But there won't be a case," she said with a shake of her head. "The Feds have had it for more than a month, and the best they can tell me is that they think the hit team was composed of foreigners."

"I'm sure they know more than that."

"I don't agree. They seem to be more focused on finding out who leaked Sean's identity than finding the people who killed him."

Elwood leaned forward again. "I'll talk to some people. Maybe I can get some more information. But I'm not gonna stick out my neck for you if you don't stay clear of the investigation."

She had no intention of following his directive, but he didn't know that, and she was not about to tell him her plans.

She got to her feet. "Thanks for your time, Captain. Please give me a call if your sources pan out."

She left the office and made her way back to her desk. Gibson was seated in his cubicle, so she made her way over and tapped him on the shoulder.

"I thought you were off for a while," he said.

"I was meeting with Tom." She then lowered her voice. "Did you keep a copy of the reports of our investigation into Sean's murder?"

"The Feds took the case, Jen. We had to give them everything."

"I can't stand around here all day, Gibby. Show me your copy of the file."

Gibson smiled. She knew she had him dead to rights when he got to his feet.

"I'm going over to Starbucks for a coffee. You want me to bring you something back?"

"I'm good," she said.

"I should be gone for about half an hour." He used his foot to tap one of his desk drawers. "If I don't see you when I get back, stay in touch."

She gave him a smile then waited for him to clear the floor before opening the desk drawer and pulling out a manila folder that held a stack of reports about a quarter of an inch in thickness.

Thanks, Gibby, she said to herself. *I owe you one.*

She tucked the file under her arm and left the squad to head for her home.

⌇

The following morning, when Thompson called, Donahue feigned illness by claiming that she felt like she was coming down with the flu. Thompson wanted to come over to offer her assistance, but Donahue objected, so they settled on staying in touch by phone.

Donahue then made a quick trip to the supermarket, but she did so only after watching to see if she had a tail. If she did, they were good, because she didn't spot one, but her heightened sense of awareness was now on full alert.

She returned home and spent the better part of the day reviewing the police reports related to Sean's murder. The first time she read them through, all she could do was cry, but after a small break to gather her composure, she read them again, and this time she did it as a professional, looking for information that might help to crack the case.

The initial statements of the two eyewitnesses were fairly detailed. They both seemed highly intelligent and very observant. She wondered if a second interview might shake loose more in the way of critical details? They were not sure of the ethnicity of the two men they saw coming out of the building, but the doctor had speculated that they might be Russian or Eastern European. Neither was sure of the make of the car, but one was found two miles away in an area known as the Miracle Mile. The car was a stolen Toyota, but there were no prints or DNA. The area was canvassed for video surveillance cameras, but nothing of any value was ever discovered.

When she got to the autopsy report, she almost broke down again. Sean had been shot three times. Two of the shotgun blasts had hit him in the chest. The third had been a head shot that had obliterated his face. On the advice of her Captain, she never saw Sean's body at the time of the funeral. The casket had been sealed, so she was spared the nightmare of seeing the damage done to his face.

Her mind drifted back to the funeral and the memories came in bits and spurts. The service was non-denominational, followed by a burial at Forest Lawn. It was attended by many friends of hers, mostly police officers, but there had been so few friends of his.

She spent most of her waking hours thinking about her life now that Sean was gone. It seemed as if she'd stumbled into an out of body experience. In the space of a few months, she had gone from incredibly happy to devastated; from financially okay to enormously wealthy.

Could her life get any stranger?

She laughed, shed tears, and had moments of introspection while she contemplated a future that was so bizarre.

The supposed amount of the inheritance was completely unbelievable. Too much money to even contemplate. She had dreamed of winning the Lotto—who hadn't—but this was too shocking to even believe.

She hated the idea of such wealth. To her it felt like blood money. The idea of getting it in exchange for Sean's life was appalling and almost too much to bear. She vacillated back and forth between telling McCallum that she didn't want the inheritance to thinking she could always just give it away.

Her confusion about what to do did not abate until mid-afternoon on the second day. At that point, she believed that she had considered her situation from all angles and what she concluded was this: if Sean loved her enough to entrust her with this overwhelming responsibility, then she would step up and do her best to make him proud. She was still ambivalent about spending money on herself, but she would see how it goes before making any decisions about giving some or all of the assets away.

She made a late-afternoon call to McCallum to tell him what she had decided, but before she could present him with her thoughts, he asked her to come back over to his office and not to say anything further on the phone.

He sent a driver to pick her up, and when she arrived at his office, she was quickly ushered into the conference room.

"I've decided to accept the responsibility of overseeing Sean's business interests. I'm not sure how to go about it, but I'll be depending on you for a while to help me see things through. After that, we'll see what happens."

McCallum smiled. "It will be my pleasure to stay on in that capacity, at least until you get your feet on the ground."

His response surprised her.

"Are you thinking of quitting?" she asked.

"Not unless you ask me to. I serve at your pleasure, Ms. Donahue, and if you lose confidence in my counsel at any time, you are free to seek other representation."

Donahue smiled.

"I doubt that will be the case, Mr. McCallum, but I appreciate your telling me the ground rules."

"Excellent," he said. "The other day, when I told you that Mr. Sean's father had my firm sell off all of his Russian assets, I neglected to mention that the Moscow Prosecutor engaged a firm to file a lawsuit in London to obtain a return of the properties, both what was sold and what was retained. They claimed that Mr. Korakovsky's initial wealth was obtained by fraud and that what remained of the assets, and any new ones purchased by the sale of the original ones, remain the property of the Russian Federation."

"Does he have a leg to stand on?" Donahue asked.

"It's uncertain. Like most of the oligarchs who rose to the top right after the fall of the Soviet Union, Anton Korakovsky relied on the patronage of President Boris Yeltsin to acquire former state-owned companies. The Federation now claims that Yeltsin had no right to agree to the sale of government assets, and it's conceivable that a London magistrate might agree with that proposition. And if such an award was made, it's suspected that the proceeds would go directly to Putin to be concealed through the use of a number of shell corporations, much like what we've done to keep him from getting what you now currently possess."

"Wow! This is a real cat-and-mouse game."

"I can assure you, Ms. Donahue, it's not a game. Mr. Putin will stop at nothing to get his hands on the assets in Sean's estate, which brings me to the question of your security."

Donahue suspected that this topic would come up again, and this time she was interested in hearing McCallum's take.

"Once Mr. Sean entered the witness protection program, we were assured that his identity would remain a complete secret. Unfortunately, that secret was somehow discovered, and it's my belief that Mr. Putin had Mr. Sean killed to force an accounting of his assets in a probate court."

"Oh?" Donahue found herself nodding. "So, if they couldn't locate Sean's assets while he was alive, then by killing him they hoped to force the inheritors to identify the assets in open court?"

McCallum smiled. "To that extent, the United States government has been very helpful. They have no desire to see Putin increase his personal wealth at the expense of the Russian people, so to keep the probate scenario from playing out, they are waiving any taxes that would normally be taken out of an estate with assets over five million, and the probate is being handled in a closed courtroom setting, under a provision that declares that what is being done is of national security interest."

Donahue's eyes widened. "Once again, Mr. McCallum, you've managed to take my breath away."

McCallum allowed himself another small smile.

"As for your security, we have no idea if the Russians know who you are or not. They may have no clue that you are his heir, but I think we must assume that when they went to Mr. Sean's residence, they probably located photographs or other items that would put you on their radar."

Donahue had not considered that. There were pictures of her and Sean in his apartment, as well as paperwork and other correspondence that might go a long way towards identifying her.

"Do we know if anything was taken from the residence the night that he was killed?" she asked.

"The FBI conducted a search as soon as they took over the case. Mr. Sean's personal computer was taken by the killers. Fortunately, he never conducted business of any kind on his laptop, but I'm afraid that any correspondence between Mr. Sean and yourself is now in the hands of his killers."

She thought about the hundreds of emails they'd sent to each other. They would have more than enough information to track her down.

McCallum cleared his throat. "Since the night of the murder, Mr Sean's security team has been keeping watch over you."

"What? I was told that the FBI was surveilling me in Colorado—"

"We replaced them," he said, and when she looked skeptical, he added, "I told you, we've been working with the Bureau. We have superior assets, so we took over the responsibility once you landed in Colorado."

"Well, your people are good. I never caught on."

"They're your people now," he told her "and if it's alright with you, I'd like to introduce you to the man who oversees your team."

He walked over to his desk, said something to his secretary, and a few seconds later, a man in a dark blue suit entered the office.

"Ms. Donahue, I'd like you to meet Mr. Zachary Bernstein. He will be in charge of your personal security."

Bernstein stood at parade rest and gave her a nod.

Donahue sized him up. He was tall and physically fit, probably in his mid-fifties. His head was shaved and his weathered face was tan and clean-shaven. There was an intensity that radiated from his countenance that led her to immediately conclude that this was a serious man who could take care of business.

"Mr. Bernstein is a former member of the Israeli Mossad. He

worked for a while for Mr. Sean's father as a political advisor to the group that still oversees the family assets. In addition to being responsible for keeping up with the Russian Federation's efforts to locate the family's holdings, his team was responsible for Mr. Sean's security."

This revelation surprised her, but before she could speak, McCallum added, "His team consists of twenty-four men, all former Special Forces operatives from the UK and the United States."

"Twenty-four? Isn't that a lot?"

Bernstein spoke up and Donahue noted that his English bore an Israeli accent.

"Ms. Donahue, we rotate your personal detail every twelve hours, and having three teams enables each group to get twelve on and twenty-four off. Most of the men speak multiple languages, so our advance teams can work efficiently almost anywhere in the world."

Donahue looked from Bernstein over to McCallum. "So, what are you proposing?"

McCallum said, "We'd like your permission to continue with the present security arrangements. Most of the time, you won't even know that they're around. However, that will require you to work closely with Mr. Bernstein. He will need to be aware of your schedule in advance."

"I can't go running around with a huge posse like some kind of rock star," she said. "I'll be going back to work soon, and for the time being, I'd rather that my colleagues were kept in the dark about what's going on."

"That won't be a problem, Ms. Donahue," said Bernstein. "We'll respect your space and your privacy. However, on some occasions, particularly when you travel internationally, we'd like to provide you with a driver and a discretely modified armored car."

"Do I have a choice?" she asked.

"You do," said McCallum, "but given what happened to Mr. Sean, I would advise you to take advantage of Mr Bernstein's expertise."

"Okay," she said. "We'll see how it goes."

Bernstein excused himself, and as soon as he was gone, Donahue asked, "Do you have any idea why the FBI was so interested in Sean?"

"That's a good question, and the short answer is, I don't. My responsibility was to oversee and respond to Mr. Sean's wishes as they related to his business interests, so I was not made privy to any information beyond those parameters."

"Spoken like a typical attorney," said Donahue, tongue in cheek. She suspected he knew more than he was willing to share, and that might not change until she earned his trust. She was the outsider coming in, and it might take a little time for her to be accepted.

"Let me ask you something else, Mr. McCallum. If Mr. Bernstein's crew is so good, then why wasn't Sean protected on the night that he died?"

McCallum sighed. "Mr. Sean refused to have the team on duty when he was in town. He believed that his new identity was sufficient for his protection in Los Angeles, and he was concerned that with your background you might spot the surveillance before he was ready to explain his situation to you." McCallum studied her briefly, then added, "He confided in me that once he was married, he would accept the security as being necessary for the two of you and any children that might follow."

At the mention of children, which now would never be, Donahue's eyes grew watery.

An embarrassed McCallum quickly changed the subject.

"If you're interested, I'd like to give you a briefing on the extent of your holdings. I would also suggest that we schedule meetings with the individuals who currently watch over your investment portfolio. Once you've been briefed and are up to speed, I'll be able to show you how we've managed to conceal the assets behind a wall of shell corporations."

"Let me have a few days to get used to this first," she told him. "I still have loose ends to deal with relating to Sean's condo and my schedule with the LAPD."

"As you wish, but I'd like to address one more matter that I believe is a bit more pleasant."

Donahue managed a smile. "That would be a nice change."

McCallum smiled back.

"It concerns your current living arrangements. If I'm correct, and if the men who killed Mr. Sean have information that can lead them to you, then you're not safe in your present condominium."

"I hadn't thought of that."

"Mr. Sean has a home in Brentwood. He planned to give it to you on your wedding day. He expected to live there with you, and I think that it would be to your advantage to move in there as soon as possible. I've been told that the project is almost complete. Mr. Bernstein's team is overseeing the security installations, but you can move in there within a week or two. That is, if you think that would be in your best interest?"

Once again, the surprises had become overwhelming. The idea that Sean intended to surprise her with a home brought tears to her eyes.

"I'm sorry," she said as she tried to conceal her emotions. "I thought I was all cried out."

"It's quite all right," said McCallum. "I've shed quite a few tears myself."

"Were you and Sean close?"

McCallum nodded. "I've been with the Korakovsky family since Mr. Sean was a baby. When his father died, Mr. Sean and I became even closer. I never married, Ms. Donahue, so Mr. Sean was like the son I never had."

She walked over and gave him a hug.

"Then we'll share our loss together," she said. "And please, in the future, just call me Jen or Jennifer."

SEVEN

IN THE TWO weeks that followed, Donahue had no fewer than nine meetings with people who ran the Korakovsky empire, and she continued to think of it that way. In her mind she was still an interloper who was going through the motions of being brought up to speed. There might come a time when she would start to believe that all of the people she spoke with worked for her, but she wasn't there yet, and likely wouldn't be so for quite a while.

Sean's assets included a forty percent share in British Petroleum and controlling shares in eleven other companies. He had holdings in such diverse sectors as commercial real estate, energy, mining, shipping, tech, aviation and pharmaceuticals. On top of that, a sizable amount of money was parked in several stock portfolios, both domestic and international, which were closely monitored by the private banking operations of a number of major financial institutions.

She began to get a sense of the scope of the inheritance, and in real terms, she was absolutely terrified. It felt as if she was playing a game, a game of Monopoly on steroids, but as the briefings jumped from sector to sector, she had to keep reminding herself that it wasn't a game, and she wasn't dreaming. The responsibility for all of the corporations and the people they employed weighed heavily on her soul. Would she ever be up to the task of guiding them into the future? She had her doubts, but she certainly hoped she would.

Although she was dying to see it, she put off looking at the house. McCallum told her that workmen were still adding the finishing touches, so she decided to wait until they were completely finished. She wanted to see it for the first time as Sean had intended, so having accepted the security detail as a practical necessity for her new reality, she spent her time going for runs to stay in shape, thinking, and deciding what to do with the rest of her life.

৵

As the days slipped by, and with no word from the FBI or her Captain on any progress being made in the search for Sean's killers, Donahue decided it was time to get personally involved. She knew enough not to do it alone, so she turned to the one woman she had trusted with her life on a daily basis.

At just after ten a.m., Donahue showed up at the PAB squad room and took a look around. Most of the men and women who worked there were out of the office; either at court or in the field where they would be conducting investigations. But Thompson was at her desk, so Donahue walked over and said hello.

"Well, look what the cat dragged in. You feeling better, I hope?" Thompson asked.

"Much better," said Donahue.

Thompson got to her feet and gave Donahue a hug. "It's been boring around here without you."

Donahue smiled. "You got a few minutes?"

"Yeah, sure. What's up?"

Donahue looked around, then lowered her voice.

"Grab your stuff and let's go. I'll sign us out."

"Must be serious," said Thompson with a questioning look. She grabbed her jacket, strapped on her gun, and met Donahue out by the elevator.

When they got to the take-home car, Donahue produced the keys and got them underway.

"So where are we going?" Thompson asked as they pulled out from the underground parking lot.

"Over to Sean's condo," said Donahue. "I need to look around."

"You haven't been back there yet?"

"I've been too busy."

Thompson settled back in the passenger seat while Donahue negotiated the entry to the on-ramp for the Hollywood Freeway.

"You didn't have the flu, did you?" said Thompson.

"I just needed some time to deal with stuff, Shari, and if I tell you something secret, I need to know that you'll keep it completely to yourself."

Thompson's interest was now piqued. She sat up taller and turned to face her best friend.

"I'm all ears," she said.

"It's your mouth I'm worried about."

"Ow! Not fair, Jen! I can keep a secret."

Donahue looked over. "If this gets out, Shari, our friendship is over."

"You mean that?"

"I honestly do. This is life and death, babe, no fooling around. So, if I trust you with this, you need to take it to your grave."

Thompson's eyes widened. "Now you've got me worried, Jen. Look, if you're in some kind of trouble, you know I've got your back, right?"

"I know that, and thanks."

"Okay, then. If it's that important for me to hold my mud, I will. But after this life and death buildup, sister, it better be a mother-fuckin', mind-blowing secret. That's all I'm gonna say."

Without mentioning anything about the inheritance, Donahue told her about Sean's true identity and how his father had been killed on orders of Vladmir Putin.

"You're not making this up? Right?" Thompson asked.

"I know. It's hard to believe, but that's why you have to keep it to yourself."

Now deep in thought, Thompson stared straight ahead.

"I got a million questions," she finally said. She turned in her seat to face Donahue again. "Is that why Sean was in Witness Protection?"

Donahue nodded.

"Did Putin have Sean killed?"

"That's what the Feds think," said Donahue. "And I'm pretty sure they're right."

"But why?" asked Thompson. "What did Sean do?"

"No one knows for sure, Shari, but it probably had something to do with his father's business interests."

Thompson studied her friend who exited the freeway at Sunset Boulevard. before heading west toward West Hollywood.

"Did you know about Sean's background before he was killed?" Thompson asked.

"Not at all. He left me a video. He wanted to wait to tell me until the surprise he had planned was finished."

"What surprise?"

"Not now," said Donahue. "Maybe later."

They rode the rest of the way in silence, each lost in their own thoughts, and when they got to Sean's condo, Donahue glanced around but didn't notice any sign of her new security detail.

She and Thompson both stood outside for a few moments before Donahue said, "Okay. I can do this."

They made their way up the stairs and Donahue unlocked the door. It appeared to her as if the place had been straightened up, and she was surprised.

"Gibby and I came over here after the hazmat folks got through. We cleaned some of the mess up, but the guys who got to Sean really trashed the place, so we did the best we could."

Donahue walked over and gave her a hug.

"I really owe you guys."

She then walked into the bedroom, put her purse on the bed, and slowly began to go through what was there.

"I packed up most of your clothes and took them over to your place while you were with your folks," said Thompson. "I didn't touch the photos or other personal stuff."

"You did great, Shari. Thanks."

Donahue moved through the duplex studying everything that was there. She gathered up a few framed photographs then carried them out to the living room. Still on the coffee table was a binder that contained clippings of items she had been using to plan her wedding. Donahue scooped it up. It was something she intended to keep.

"The FBI told me that Sean's computer was missing," said Donahue. "I don't see it here, so the killers must have taken it."

"Any idea what was on it?"

Donahue suspected that the killers were looking for info on Sean's business ventures, but she didn't want to say so now.

She went back into the bedroom and started going through some of the drawers. Most were now empty, but in one she found an old address book underneath a stack of Sean's boxer shorts.

She opened it up and noticed that most of the entries were in Cyrillic. She couldn't help but wonder why she'd never seen it around before? If she had, perhaps it would have given her a clue about Sean's real background. And if they'd talked about that a little earlier, it might have changed the outcome—

Stop it! she told herself. *No matter how hard you want to, you can't change what's happened.*

She added it to the stack of photos that she wanted to take with her.

She took another long look around, then went back out to the front room where Thompson was patiently waiting.

"Okay," she said, "we can go now."

"You got everything?"

"I think so," she said.

"Are we going back to the station?" Thompson asked.

"One more stop," Donahue replied.

"Where?"

"You'll see."

Four blocks later, Donahue pulled up to the curb at the main entrance to the Cedars-Sinai Emergency Room. It was on the ground floor of a multi-building, multi-storied hospital, just east of the city of Beverly Hills.

"So, what are we doing here?" Thompson asked.

"I want to talk with a couple of the witnesses who saw the killers leaving Sean's place."

"What? You can't do that. We turned the case over to the FBI?"

"C'mon, Shari. I thought you had my back?"

"I do, Jen, but this is nuts."

"Did you see their statements when they first got interviewed by our people?"

Thompson nodded.

"Okay, well I did, too, and there's a couple of things that need clarification."

As Donahue opened her door to get out of the car, Thompson said, "You're gonna get us into so much trouble."

Donahue smiled and gave her a wink.

Prior to driving over there, Donahue had called the hospital and learned that both of the witnesses were scheduled to show up for an afternoon shift. Donahue planned to make contact with them before their shift began.

Twenty minutes later, after jumping through a couple of hoops, the two detectives met with Doctor Richard Rosen, a tall, affable man who looked younger than his given age.

They took seats in a small ER conference room, and Donahue got right to the point.

"In your earlier statement you said that the two men spoke to each other as they walked past you."

He nodded. "We were lying on the ground, hiding behind a small hedge. I thought they were going to see us, but they didn't. Anyway, one of them said something to the other and the second guy answered back."

"Do you know what language they were speaking?"

He shook his head. "It sounded a bit like Yiddish, but the accents were so heavy that I can't be sure."

"You said they looked Russian or Eastern European. What made you settle on that?"

"The way they were dressed. They looked like mobsters from the movies with their leather jackets and hulking frames. And they were older, too. Forties… or maybe even older then that." He gave her an embarrassed smile. "I may be way off, but that was my first impression."

Ten more minutes of conversation did not reveal any new information, so Donahue thanked him for sitting down with them while Thompson went out to fetch Rachael Pendergast.

After the three women were settled, Donahue asked her a series of questions to see if she could add any details to her original statement, but Rachael had done the best she could during the first interview, so she didn't have anything new to say about the appearance of the suspects or the car they drove away from the scene.

But when it came to what she overheard them say, she surprised them with details they never expected.

"They spoke Yiddish," she said. "A few of the words were of German derivation, but essentially, it was Yiddish."

"Yiddish? Are you sure of that?"

"Of course. I speak Yiddish."

"Could you hear what they were saying?"

Rachael nodded, then slowly slipped a wayward strand of her hair behind her right ear. "The first guy who came out of the building said, *"Trinken aoyf mir in di Putin Pub."*

Donahue looked over at Thompson and smiled. "I hope you got all of that down, Shari."

Thompson laughed, as did Rachael, who generously spelled out what was said.

"Can you tell us what that means?" Donahue asked.

"It means '*Drinks on me at the Putin Pub.*'"

Donahue's eyes lit up. This was not in the report.

"Rachael, did you tell all of this to the investigators who took your first statement?"

"I don't think so? Everyone was asking about what these guys were wearing and stuff like that. I guess it never came up."

Donahue realized that Rosen had described the two men as being Russian or Eastern European, and when he told the investigators that the language spoken might have been Yiddish, no one bothered to follow that up with Rachael.

It was a small oversight, but one that might turn out to be important.

Rachael went on to say how Dr. Rosen had gone up into the victim's home, but came back out saying there was nothing that could be done.

"I thought he was pretty brave," she said, and Donahue had to agree.

When the interview was over and they were back in their car, Thompson said, "When I get back to the office, I'm gonna do a search for Putin Pub."

"If there's no such place in L.A., I think we might have to consider the possibility that he may have said 'drinks on me *at* Putin's Pub,' in which case, he might be talking about going back to Russia and getting a drink at Putin's *favorite* pub."

"I hope you're wrong," said Thompson. "And while I'm thinking of it, should we tell the Feds what we learned?"

"Let's sit on it for awhile until we know if there really is a place called Putin's Pub."

EIGHT

THE NEXT MORNING Donahue picked up Thompson at her home and drove the two of them down to the PAB. Donahue was carefully watching in the rearview mirror for signs of her personal security, but she never picked up even a glimpse of a tail. They were obviously very good; either that, or they weren't actually watching her after all?

Once they were inside the building, Donahue went straight to her cubicle. She wasn't supposed to be coming in to work, but she had learned the night before from the Captain's secretary that Elwood was taking the day off. This allowed her to slip in without having to be concerned about her being sent home.

Thompson got settled, then said, "After I got the kids into bed last night, I started searching for Putin's Pub."

Donahue glanced over. "Oh? Any luck?"

"*Nyet.* No such place in L.A. In fact, when I Googled the name, all I got was a big fat goose egg."

"Did you try looking for it by using the Russian language?"

"Yeah, right, Jen." said Thompson. "I'll just put on my super-duper, Cyrillic decoder ring and…Oh, wait a minute. I forgot. I don't speak Russian."

Donahue laughed. "Touché. So how about this. It could be the name of an off-the-books, underground club. Try calling someone over at our Russian Organized Crime Unit. See if they can come up with anything local. If not, ask whoever you've connected with to call our agency's contact at the FSB. Maybe there's such a location in St. Petersburg or Moscow."

The *Federalnaya Sluzhba Bezopasnosti,* or FSB—which is the commonly used acronym for the *Federal Security Service of the Russian Federation*—was the successor of the USSR's *Committee for State Security*, once known as the KGB.

Thompson leaned back in her chair. "So, what should our people tell the FSB when they get asked why we want to locate this place?"

Donahue gave that a moments thought.

"Tell 'em we may be coming over there soon for a high-level meeting, and we heard it was a club that was worth checking out."

Thompson smiled. That just might work.

While Thompson began searching for the phone number for the Russian Organized Crime Unit, Donahue pulled a file out of her desk and removed a long list of names and phone numbers.

During her time working in Vice, she'd met a number of Russian girls who worked the streets in L.A. as prostitutes and escorts. She tried to befriend as many as she could, and in doing so, she built up a pretty good list of informants she could call to find out what was happening in the world of drugs and vice.

She went down the list, one call at a time, getting through to one out of every three that she tried. She asked for any information on a place called Putin's Pub, but none of the girls knew anything about it.

After the sixteenth call, she was just about to call it quits. If the women-of-the-night didn't know about such a place, it probably didn't exist.

She decided to try one last contact, intending to forget the rest of the list, but when the girl picked up on the third ring, Donahue was in for a big surprise.

"I know someone originally from the Ukraine, who recently

arrived here in L.A. She once mentioned a place called Putin's Bar or something close to that."

Do you know how I can reach her?" Donahue asked.

There was silence on the line for almost thirty seconds. Then "Here's the number." She rattled it off. "She's using the name of Nina."

Donahue, who was still writing, asked, "Do you know her last name?"

"No, just Nina. But please don't mention where you got her name and number."

"Don't worry. I won't."

✍

On Sunset Boulevard, at the end of the famous strip that is known as West Hollywood, there is a *Coffee Bean and Tea Leaf* store on the ground floor of a large office building. The draw for this particular location is a large, raised, outdoor patio which is filled with umbrella tables that overlook the traffic heading west towards Beverly Hills.

As a well-known location in the area, Donahue selected it as a place to meet with Nina Padrinka, a recent émigré to the United States.

Nina was model tall with dark brown hair and a narrow jaw. And like many of the girls from that part of the world, Donahue suspected that Nina was spotted as a young teenager by Russian mob scouts who probably enticed her into their clutches with the promise of success in the modeling business.

The "modeling business" was a euphemism used by the mob for a life of involuntary servitude as a western prostitute.

Donahue had previously met many young girls who'd fallen prey to the mob, girls who'd been beaten and drugged into submission. Fear was their motivating factor for acceding to the demands of their pimps. They'd been brainwashed, raped, and tormented until they lost all hope of resistance.

The sun was out, but still low in the sky, so the temperature was a comfortable mid-seventies. Donahue chose an outdoor table, one which afforded her the best view of the patrons coming and going. Assessing possible threats to her safety was by now an old habit, brought about by years of on-the-job experience. It was so ingrained into her subconscious that she did it without ever giving it a conscious thought.

Nina showed up, and after the introductions, she took a chair at the table with Donahue. Donahue noted that she was fashionably dressed, wearing a light summer dress, open-toed sandals with one-inch heels, and dark, oversized sunglasses that were *de rigueur* for anyone who paid attention to haute couture.

Donahue had expected something else. She had expected Nina to be more connected to life on the streets, someone who attracted attention with very short skirts, cropped tops, and boots that rose to above her knees. But Nina was different. She was physically very pretty and carried herself with an air of sophistication, so Donahue quickly changed her assessment. She concluded that Nina was likely working as a high-priced agency escort.

Donahue offered to buy her a coffee.

"*Nyet,*" said Nina. "I prefer black tea."

"Then tea it is," said a smiling Donahue. She picked up her purse and got to her feet. "I'll be right back."

She returned a few minutes later with a coffee for herself and a black tea for Nina. And once they were settled in, Donahue began the questioning.

"How long have you been in the States, Nina?"

"Almost a year," she replied.

Donahue gave her a polite nod. "I ask that because I haven't seen you around."

"I don't work the streets," said Nina with a stern look. "I'm an aeronautical engineer."

Donahue's eyes widened and she blushed.

"Forgive me, Nina. I was under the mistaken impression that you might be working as an escort."

"For some reason, Americans tend to assume that all young eastern European women are prostitutes," said Nina.

Donahue sighed. "I actually got your name from one of the working girls, so I guess I made an incorrect assumption based on association."

"I have friendships with some of the young Russian women at our local Orthodox church," said Nina. "I am not quite so judgmental as to what some of them might have to do in order to survive."

Donahue sighed again. "I'm embarrassed, Nina, and I'm sorry if I jumped to a thoughtless conclusion. Lesson learned. I won't be making that mistake again."

"I forgive you, Detective," said Nina. "I have no hard feelings."

Donahue exhaled slowly. Best thing to do now was to start over.

"So, tell me, Nina. Whereabouts in Russia do you come from?"

"Actually, I'm not from Russia. I'm from the Ukraine."

Oh, boy, thought Donahue. I did it again.

Nina smiled. "I was recruited in Odessa to work at SpaceX."

"SpaceX? Wow!" said Donahue. "It must be thrilling to work in such an exciting field."

"It is," Nina replied.

Both women used the moment to take sips from their drinks.

When Nina leaned back in her chair, Donahue leaned forward and lowered her voice.

"So, let me explain why I wanted to meet with you, Nina. I don't know if you can help me, but I'm trying to locate a club known as *Putin's Pub*. I was asking around and someone mentioned to me that you might be familiar with such a place?"

"Why the interest?" Nina asked.

Donahue wasn't ready to tell her the truth, so she trotted out the story that a couple of officers were going to be in Moscow, and that they'd heard that a club with that name was well worth visiting.

Nina smiled. She didn't buy the explanation, but decided to answer the question anyway just to see where this interview might be going.

"I don't think I can help you, Detective. The club I'm familiar with is in Tel Aviv, on *Yato* Street. It's not in Moscow."

"And it's called *Putin's Pub*?" Donahue asked.

"That's right, but is not a good place."

Ahh, thought Donahue. *Tel Aviv! Hitmen who spoke Yiddish! It was starting to look like a possibility.*

"That may be the club I'm looking for, Nina," she said, now thoroughly abandoning the previous fictional explanation. "What can you tell me about it?"

"You do not want to go there, Detective. I worked in Jerusalem for a couple of years and was invited to go there several times. Many gangsters and Russian expats inside, and more importantly, they water down the drinks."

"Is it a private club?" Donahue asked.

"Not private, but tourists don't go in. Too dark, too smokey, and has bad reputation."

Donahue exhaled slowly. Could she trust this woman? On balance, she decided that it might be worth a chance.

She leaned forward again and lowered her voice.

"Okay, Nina. I'm going to level with you. The real reason I'm asking about this place is because we're looking for a couple of men who committed a murder here in L.A. They might be mobbed up, and they might be familiar with the club you've described."

"As I told you, lots of gangsters go there. It might be place you're looking for."

"Can an American blend in—?"

Nina cut her off. She slowly shook her head.

"Is not a place for tourists. They would mistake you for a prostitute."

Donahue leaned back and smiled. "I guess I had that coming."

"You did," said Nina with an even broader smile.

Donahue had what she needed, so she slipped Nina one of her business cards and slowly got to her feet.

"I'm sorry we started off on the wrong foot. I don't know any folks who work on the space program, so if you ever wanna meet with me for lunch sometime, I'd love to get your thoughts about the theory of parallel universes."

Nina laughed out loud, and when Donahue shot her a questioning look, she quickly said, "What's the expression… still waters run deep?"

Donahue cocked her head in confusion.

Nina smiled. "When you called me, I must admit I had rather unflattering opinion on what you'd be like. I suppose that was based on stereotypes. It appears that I have misjudged you, too, Detective. For that, I too, am sorry."

"We're even," said a smiling Donahue. "And you, too, are forgiven."

Nina tucked the card into her purse, then looked up. "Perhaps we can have lunch at SpaceX," she said. "I would be happy to give you a tour around the facility."

"Really? That would be great!

Back at the PAB, Donahue learned from Thompson that she had spoken with an officer in the Russian Organized Crime Unit. His contact at the Russian FSB can find no listing for a club called *Putin's Pub* in either Moscow or St. Petersburg.

"In fact, he was told that no one would dare to use Putin's name for a nightclub," said Thompson.

"And there's no place like that here in L.A.?" Donahue asked.

"Nothing even close to that comes up on the internet," said Thompson.

"Well, I fared a little better. The informant I spoke with says there's a place in Tel Aviv called *Putin's Pub*. It's a hangout for gangsters and expats."

"Did your informant work out of that club?"

Donahue smiled. "She wasn't a hooker, Shari. She's an aeronautical engineer."

"Well, that's a first," said Thompson with a grin. "So, what's our next step?"

"I want to talk to the Captain. Let's see if he learned anything about the FBI investigation from his friend in the CIA."

NINE

Her meeting with Captain Tommy Elwood took place at the *Fisherman's Outlet* on Central Avenue. It was not very far from the PAB. Elwood was in the habit of taking a late lunch over there several times a week. To sweeten the deal, he offered to buy her lunch, but Donahue told him that she only wanted tea.

"My stomach's been upset for a couple of days," she said by way of explanation.

"After everything you've been through, I don't doubt it." Elwood gave her a nod. "Anxiety can wreak havoc on your bowels. In fact, I once—"

"TMI, Boss," said Donahue with a roll of her eyes. "TMI."

"What's TMI?" he asked.

"Too much information."

"Oh."

They settled in at an outdoor table, and after his lunch of char-broiled Mahi-mahi and fries arrived—and once her hot tea was delivered—he dipped his fish in butter sauce, took a big bite, then wiped his face with a paper napkin.

"Okay," he said while he chewed. "What do you need?"

"I was wondering if you heard back from your friend?"

Elwood nodded. He took another bite of his fish, so she waited for him to finish the mouthful.

"I've been told that the Feds have composite drawings of the shooters from the two eyewitnesses. They're in the process of passing them on to Interpol."

Interpol served as an international police force and information-sharing agency. Individual members of Interpol could funnel wanted suspect information to police agencies throughout the European continent.

"Can you get your hands on a copy of those composites?" she asked.

He gave her a look.

"I told you to stay far away from the investigation, Jen."

Donahue sighed. It was time to face the music.

"Will you hear me out on this?"

Elwood knew he was fighting a losing battle. She was like a dog who had a bone in her teeth and she was not going to part with it without a fight.

"Go ahead," he said with a sigh.

"I took Shari with me over to Cedars and we spoke with the two eye-wits."

"Damn it, Jen," he said with his mouth full of fries. "I told you to stay clear—"

"You said you'd hear me out."

He wasn't happy, but after a short pause, he gave her the go-ahead with a single nod.

"The nurse, Rachael Pendergast, told us that the men spoke Yiddish. She mentioned that to the Feds, but no one asked her about what they said. Well, she speaks Yiddish, and she told me that one of the men said to the other that he was buying the first round at Putin's Pub."

Elwood stopped chewing.

"And the Feds don't know about that?"

"Not yet," she said, "but we'll tell them soon." She took a deep breath. "In the meantime, I checked around with a few of my CI's and there's no Putin's Pub in L.A., Moscow, or St. Petersburg. But there is a place in Tel Aviv. It's a hangout for mobsters and Russian expats."

Elwood was reluctant to admit it, but Donahue was really on top of her game. He was genuinely impressed.

"So, I want to get a hold of those composites," she said. "I want to send them off to a friend of mine."

"Let the Feds handle it," Elwood told her. "They're better suited to get the job done."

"That's bullshit, Tom, and you know it."

She had used his first name, a sign to him that she was not going to give up so easily.

"You know how the Feds like to do things," she said with a sigh. "They'll send a couple of suits right in the front door of the Pub, and they'll show the composites around. If the shooters are actually frequent patrons of the place, they'll be in the wind and we'll never get a line on them again."

He knew she was right. The Feds were not tactful when it came to investigations. They could flood a neighborhood with lots of manpower, but in his experience, going undercover was not their usual forte.

"I'm not going to allow you to go undercover," he said. "No way, no how."

She held up her hands in surrender. "I have no intention of doing that. My informant says that if an American girl goes in there alone, they'll assume that she's a prostitute. So, I was thinking, we could send in Shari—"

"What?"

Donahue laughed. "I'm just messing with you. I've got a few contacts over there, and I'd like to talk to them about the best way to find these guys."

Elwood wasn't pleased. She was putting him into a box, and there was no easy way out. If he denied her permission to go forward, she would do it anyway, and he couldn't fault her for that. And despite her personal interest in the case, she was a damn good investigator and she wasn't just putting out smoke. In just a few hours, she had developed a better lead than the Feds ever had in the month or so since they'd had the case.

He put down his fork and slowly wiped his mouth with a napkin.

"I'll get you a copy of the composites, but I want you to tread lightly with your Israeli sources. If the Feds find out what you're up to, they'll run to our Chief, and there will be hell to pay for the three of us."

"Speaking of that, I'd like to take Shari with me, just in case a witness is needed for a Federal prosecution."

"I can't let either one of you go on company time. You'll both have to do it off the books."

"Let me speak to her about it. I'll get back to you as soon as we work out the details."

She took a small sip of her tea, then put it down and slid out of the booth.

"You still not feeling up to snuff?" he asked.

"It comes and goes." She took a deep breath. "I'm gonna be calling your friend's messenger girl. I just thought you'd like to know."

She was referring to the CIA female agent who had been used as a courier on previous occasions. She was in tight with Elwood's source, and while Donahue had every right to call her on her own, she wanted him to know that she wasn't going behind his back.

"Mind telling me what you think that will accomplish?" he asked as he took another bite of his fries.

"She's smart and well-connected. Maybe she can find out why Sean was put into PC in the first place."

"You're not buying the Feds' story that they were worried about his safety?"

"Not one bit. That might be part of it, of course, but they're holding back. Agent Smitten said as much, and I want to know why?"

"Don't mess this up, Jen. You're skating on a very thin sheet of ice."

"I know that, Tom, but as you might have noticed, I'm one hell of a damn good skater."

TEN

DONAHUE AND THOMPSON drove over to the mall in West Los Angeles. They pulled into the underground parking lot and made their way down to the lowest level which was four stories below the street. No one else was parked down there at this time of day, so they stopped their car where they could watch the escalator while they waited for Donahue's contact to appear.

"She said four p.m., right?" said Thompson, who was checking her watch.

"She'll be here," said Donahue. "She's always on time."

Sure enough, at four on the dot, a young Asian female appeared at the bottom of the escalator.

After taking a look around for a few moments, she walked over to the car where the two detectives were waiting. She gave them a smile, then climbed into the back seat.

"Thanks for meeting with me," Donahue said. She was seated in the front passenger seat, and she had turned her body and head around to look over the seat at Charlotte Tan.

Charlotte was a well-dressed, late thirty-something, who looked more like a college student than an agent with the CIA. Donahue's best guess was that her lineage was probably Chinese or Korean. Her black hair was shoulder length, her skin blemish-free, and her eyes were both cautious and watchful.

They had worked together once before when Charlotte had helped Donahue with the L.A. portion of a case involving the abduction of a medical researcher from a conference in Alexandria, Egypt. From that experience, they had formed a solid relationship, and even though Donahue didn't know her all that well, she trusted Charlotte enough to be candid.

"Your boss got on the phone and talked with my boss about what you wanted to know," said Charlotte.

That surprised Donahue. Elwood must have done that right after his lunch.

"I hope I haven't stepped over the line?" she said.

"I don't think so," replied Charlotte. "If you had, I doubt that I would have been allowed to meet with you now."

How'd you get here so quickly?" Donahue asked.

"I was already in L.A. on another matter," said Charlotte. "My boss gave me a call, filled me in, then said to get in touch with you."

Donahue sighed. At least she was past the first hurdle.

"Oh. I almost forgot. This is my partner, Shari," said Donahue, referring to Thompson.

"I know all about Detective Thompson," said Charlotte.

Thompson's eyes widened.

But when Thompson didn't speak up, Charlotte said, "You need to chill, Detective Shari. Your private life is tame compared to others I've known." She put a finger to her lips and said, "Your secrets are safe with me."

The silence in the car was deafening, and when Thompson blushed, Charlotte laughed.

"I'm just fooling with you, Detective."

Thompson realized that she'd been had, and after breathing a sigh of relief, she smiled and said, "That's a hell of a way to break the ice."

Charlotte laughed again. "Every time I meet someone who knows where I work, they get all uptight and nervous. I just like to have a little fun, if you know what I mean?"

"I do," said Thompson. "And it's a pleasure to finally meet you."

Charlotte turned back to Donahue and suddenly became all business.

"I brought along a copy of the composites that the FBI has been sending out. Your boss said you wanted to see them?"

Donahue nodded, and when Charlotte handed them over the top of the seat, Donahue stared at them with undisguised hatred.

"I didn't get to tell you before," said Charlotte, "but I'm truly sorry for your loss."

Donahue nodded. She was memorizing the two male faces and didn't reply.

Charlotte said, "My boss called a few people at the FBI to ask about your fiancé. He got a call from the Bureau's counterpart who said, 'it was an FBI operation' and that he should 'immediately drop his inquiries.' Well, I can tell you, that did not go over well with my boss, so he pushed the issue to the top and discovered a few very interesting things.

"Apparently, this all goes back to the father, Anton Korakovsky, who decided to challenge Putin for the presidency. Putin took umbrage, and put pressure on him to withdraw. He threatened him with trumped-up charges and forced him to sell off a number of his assets. This didn't sit well with Korakovsky, so he fled to London and liquidated the rest of his holdings within the Russian Federation."

"I was told about that," said Donahue.

Charlotte nodded. "Well, here's what I'm sure you weren't told. Once his assets were secure, he requested a meeting with the FBI, the subject of which we do not know, but shortly after that he was poisoned in London. Needless to say, the meeting with the Bureau never took place. But Korakovsky met with someone at MI-6 just before he died. We think they passed on something to the FBI, but we haven't been able to confirm that." Charlotte sighed. "We still don't know why they put his son in the Witness Protection Program, but he was certainly at risk after the murder of his father."

Donahue said, "I've been told that the government is assisting with the current transfer of the assets to his heir. They've even waived any tax provisions to accomplish the transfer with speed and secrecy."

"I can see the logic for keeping the assets a secret," said Charlotte. "The Russians are trying to use the courts in the U.K. to get back what they couldn't steal outright."

"But if our government is waiving the normal taxes that are associated with such a transfer, well, it smells to me like there's something else at play?"

"I'll pass your info on to my boss," said Charlotte. "Maybe he can ferret it out."

"Is the CIA involved in the hunt for Sean's killers?" Thompson asked.

Charlotte shook her head no. "We've had no request for our assistance."

Donahue rolled her eyes. Charlotte had just confirmed her fear that the Bureau was simply going through the motions. They didn't really care if the case got solved.

As their meeting broke up, Charlotte asked to speak with Donahue privately. Thompson got out of the car and went for a short walk.

"I understand that you're Sean's heir? Is that true?"

Donahue was surprised that Charlotte was privy to that, but then again, she supposed she wasn't.

"You guys really do know a lot of stuff," she said with a shrug.

Charlotte smiled briefly, then said, "The reason I bring this up is that you need to surround yourself with very qualified people that you can completely trust. Monitor your money, set up checks and balances. You can't trust anyone, Jen. It's human nature to cozy up to people with real power, and whether you know that yet or not, that's what you've got. Be careful of strangers who want to get too close because money makes people do really crazy things."

Donahue was reminded that Sean had kept her in the dark about his wealth. He had probably done so for all the right reasons. And now that she was in the very same position, she would have to keep that in mind.

"Take care," said Charlotte. She climbed out of the car and disappeared up the nearby escalator while Thompson returned to the car.

"Strange lady," said Thompson when she got behind the wheel.

"She's okay," said Donahue. "Her sense of humor is a little weird, but she's got deep pockets when it comes to information."

"Yeah, she had me going there for a while."

Donahue laughed.

"You do know, don't you, that she was only kidding when she said that she was *just kidding?*"

"What?"

"I'm sure she checked you out, lady, and when Charlotte says she knows all of your deepest secrets, you damn well better believe that she does."

ELEVEN

DONAHUE PURCHASED A roasted chicken and some vegetables from her neighborhood supermarket before going directly home to her apartment. She opened a bottle of wine and ate alone, something she was going to have to get used to.

When dinner was finished and her dishes were put into the dishwasher, she got on the phone and placed a call to Cairo, in Egypt.

She had a drop phone number for Bryan Harb, an undercover CIA operative that she first met during a visit to the White House. Bryan had taken an instant liking to her, but because of his assignment to the Middle East and her unwavering commitment to her career in the LAPD, she kept things strictly platonic.

Bryan had lost his wife and family during the attack on the World Trade Center in 2002. Right after that, he joined the CIA, and because of his Lebanese background and ability with languages, he'd gone undercover in Palestine and never looked back.

The phone rang ten times before it finally went to message. She said hello, left her name and number, and asked him to call her when he got the chance.

About an hour later, he called her back.

"Hi, Bry," she said upon answering.

"It's been a long time, Jen," he replied.

She accepted the rebuke without argument. Once she started seeing Sean, she failed to check in with Bryan by phone.

"I know and I'm sorry. Have you got a few moments to chat?"

"Of course," he said. His voice had softened. "It's the middle of the night here so I'm going nowhere."

"Are you still working out of Israel?"

He was silent for a moment, then said, "You know I can't talk about stuff like that, particularly on the phone."

"Oh, right. I'm sorry."

"It's okay. Why are you asking?"

"Well, I'm going to be in Israel in a couple of days and I thought we might get together somewhere for dinner?"

"For business or pleasure?" he asked.

"Business," she replied, "but I really would like to see you, too."

He gave it a moment's thought.

"I'll find you," he said. "Are you traveling alone?"

"I'll probably be with Shari."

"Great! It will be good to see you both again."

"Do you want me to call when we get there?" she asked.

"No need. I'll know."

Donahue didn't doubt him. Bryan was as well connected as anyone in the Middle East. If he said he'd find her when she arrived, she knew that he surely would.

"Okay, then," she said with a smile. "I'll be seeing you soon."

⚓

The following morning, after she checked into the squad, she pulled out a cell phone that McCallum had given her. He claimed it was clean and untraceable, and for security reasons, he asked her to use it whenever she needed to talk with him.

She left the PAB and made her call in the courtyard next to the permanent monument that was dedicated to the fallen officers of the LAPD.

McCallum answered on the third ring.

"Yes, ma'am," he said.

"Too formal, Mr. McCallum. Can I call you James?"

He smiled. "Certainly, ma'am."

She laughed. "I'd prefer it if you just called me Jennifer."

"I will, but only in private."

"Fair enough. I'm calling because I need someone to make reservations for me and my friend Shari Thompson. I want to go to Israel."

"How soon do you plan to go?"

"Tomorrow or the next day, whenever you can get us a reservation."

"Will you be taking the jet?"

That question confused her.

"Of course I want to take a jet. El Al if you can arrange it. I've heard they're the safest."

McCallum was silent for a brief moment before deciding how to diplomatically give her the news.

"You have your own jet, Ms. Jennifer. It's leased and paid for through the end of next year. Mr. Sean kept it on the tarmac at LAX. It's a G4, or more precisely, a Gulfstream G450. It's maximum range is 4,350 nautical miles with a top-end cruising altitude of forty-five-thousand feet. There's a crew on standby around the clock. You just need to tell them where and when you want to go, and the plane will be made ready."

Donahue swallowed hard. *My own plane! This is crazy!*

"I want to go to Tel Aviv," she replied.

"That won't be a problem. I'll make the arrangements. The plane holds sixteen including the crew, and it has a 10 hour range. You might have to make a refueling stop, but that will be up to the Captain. What time would you like to leave?"

"Can we go tomorrow? Say… maybe noon?"

"Certainly. Would you like me to have the car pick you up? If Ms. Thompson is with you, you'll need to leave your residence by ten."

Donahue's mind was reeling. This was too amazing to actually believe.

"That sounds fine," she said.

"Will you need a hotel?"

"I suppose so."

"I'll notify Mr. Bernstein. He'll send a team with you and he'll take care of the vehicles and hotel reservations. Is your passport up to date?"

"It is."

"Very good," he replied. "I'll call you back later when everything is arranged."

For the first time since she learned about the inheritance, she was getting a taste of the perks that came with her strange new situation.

I could get used to this... was her first guilty thought.

∽

Thompson arrived at the squad room in a good mood. "Hey, you," she said to Donahue who was seated at her desk. "Want a cupcake?"

"I'll split one with you," said Donahue, who got to her feet.

Thompson studied her friend, then said, "You look awfully chipper. What's up?"

"Have you ever been to Israel?"

"Ha! I've never been east of Chicago. Why do you ask?"

"Wanna go with me?"

"Are you kidding? When?"

"Tomorrow. Can you get your mom to watch the boys?"

"You're kidding right? Why are we going to Israel?"

"I want to have a talk with Bryan Harb."

"Oh, no. I know what you're up to, and there's no way the Captain is going to approve."

"For your information, he knows what I'm up to, and he says it's okay. But it has to be strictly off the books."

"Vacation time?"

"Or overtime. You've got a ton. Do you want to go?"

"How many days?" Thompson asked.

"Four days tops."

"On whose dime?"

"Taken care of," said Donahue.

"Really?" Thompson smiled. "Then sign me up."

Donahue smiled back. "Don't you need to check with your mother first?"

Thompson shook her head, then grinned like a Cheshire Cat. "Starting tonight my ex has the kids for the next seven days."

"Lucky you," said Donahue. "I'll pick you up tomorrow at nine-thirty a.m."

Thompson looked at her watch, then picked up her purse.

"See ya," she said.

"Where are you going?"

"Where do you think? Hair, nails and packing. I've got less than a day to get ready."

TWELVE

WHEN DONAHUE PICKED her up the next morning in a chauffeured limousine, Thompson was definitely impressed. But when they pulled up at the LAX Southside Cargo Terminal where private jets were parked, Thompson went absolutely gaga.

"A G4? You've got access to a fucking G4? Are you kidding me?"

Donahue put on her serious face. "You don't think it's too small, do you?"

"What? Too small? Are you out of your mind? This is—"

Thompson stopped mid-sentence when Donahue broke into laughter.

"OK," she said, shaking her head and smiling. "You got me."

Thompson climbed out of the car and looked around. A half-dozen men and two women dressed in dark business suits were milling around the plane.

"Who are all these great looking people?" she asked.

"Our security team," replied Donahue.

"*What*? We've got our own security team?"

"Go big or go home."

"*Jeez,*" said Thompson, more soberly. "I'm guessing you're paying for this out of your inheritance. It's really classy, Jen, but you don't need to spend this kind of money on me. You don't want to blow through it too quickly."

Donahue smiled to herself.

"I'll be careful, sweetie." she replied.

Thompson looked back over at the plane and the security operatives, then slowly shook her head in continued disbelief.

"This whole thing better not change you, Jen." She studied her friend's face carefully. "Money can do that, you know?"

Donahue sighed. "It won't change me, Shari. I promise."

"A fucking G4!" Thompson rolled her eyes. "And to think, before today, we always had to fly coach."

A handsome Hispanic male made his way over to Donahue and introduced himself as Jamie Otero.

"I'll be in charge of your detail for the duration of this trip," he added.

Donahue recalled the briefing she received from Bernstein about Otero. He was just over six feet tall, all muscle, and completely professional. A former Army Ranger, he'd done two deployments in Iraq and one in Afghanistan. He was thirty-eight years old, single, and a graduate of Penn State with a degree in Business Management. And what Bernstein had failed to mention was that he was certainly easy on the eyes.

"It's nice to meet you, Mr. Otero," said Donahue, extending her hand. "This is my friend Shari Thompson."

"Please, just call me Jamie," he said with a smile. He shook hands with both of them, then said, "Once we're on board, I'll introduce you to the rest of the team."

"I notice that two members of your group are women?" said Donahue.

"Yes, ma'am. They'll be with you and Ms. Thompson whenever you go into restrooms or anywhere else where men might be prohibited."

"Oh, great!" said Thompson with a roll of her eyes. "I'll never be able to pee when someone is standing right outside the stall door."

Donahue laughed. "You'll have to forgive my friend, Jamie. She was raised by wolves."

"Siberian wolves," said Thompson with a twinkle in her eyes.

Otero smiled. "They won't be intrusive, ma'am," he said to Thompson.

"I'm too young to be a 'ma'am'," said Thompson. "So please, just call me Miss, as in...*unmarried*."

Otero blushed, and this time all three of them laughed aloud.

"It takes a while," Donahue said to Otero, "but you'll get used to her sense of humor."

"Yes, ma'am...er, Ms. Donahue."

Donahue smiled. "I guess we're ready to go, Jamie. Is everything set at the other end?"

"Yes, ma'am. Everything is taken care of."

"Good! Then let's get going."

She turned to Thompson.

"After you, Miss 'as in unmarried.'"

"You liked that, huh?" said Thompson.

"Just a touch forward, don't you think?" whispered Donahue.

"Perhaps, but it doesn't hurt to advertise."

⚘

When the plane touched down in Tel Aviv the two women transferred to a limousine that was waiting on the tarmac, and as it pulled away from the plane, it was escorted by two dark SUV's to the Carlton Tel Aviv, a twelve story modern hotel with ocean views that overlooked the beach and a marina.

The charm of Tel Aviv was the coastline. A jogging and bicycle path ran parallel to the sand for several miles. It was dotted with open-air restaurants, ice cream parlors, and souvenir shops of all descriptions. The pathway was always busy, particularly on warm days around sunset. Residents who took walks after dinner were joined by tourists and visitors who studied the small boats that were docked in the harbor while sipping cold drinks from the local vendors.

The prevalent attitude among the Israelis was to live for the day, and to treat each one as if it were their last.

On the way to the hotel, Thompson spoke about how cool it was to travel in luxury, but Donahue was thinking about her pending meeting with Bryan Harb.

"When we hook up with Bryan, I want to speak to him privately. It's important to me that our initial conversation remains confidential. But after that, I want you to join us for dinner where we won't be discussing anything related to Sean."

Thompson was a little surprised that she was going to be dismissed from the initial conversation, but it didn't change her mood at all.

"That's fine with me. I can get some shopping done for the boys."

They checked into the hotel where Bernstein had booked them spacious individual suites, each with two bedrooms and a large living room. In spite of flying by private jet, neither one had slept, so they agreed to retire to their rooms for an afternoon nap.

By five-thirty p.m., both were up and dressed for dinner. Thompson took her leave to go shopping and was escorted by two members of their security detail. Donahue hung back at the hotel and waited for Bryan Harb to call.

Twenty minutes later, he did, and he asked her to meet him in the hotel's lobby bar.

Donahue entered the bar and looked around. At first, she didn't spot him, but with a slower and even more careful scan, she noticed a man standing off to the side that looked a little bit like how she remembered him.

She walked over and saw him smile.

"Bryan?"

"Hi, Jen," he replied. He gave her a perfunctory hug.

"You've changed your hair?" It was now dark brown, and his mustache and beard were flecked with gray."

"Come with me," he said. He took her arm and immediately noticed that several military types had begun to close in.

"Are they with you?" he asked, while watching the men who were spread out in the bar.

She nodded then waved to the team that she was okay.

The men pulled back and Bryan let go of her arm.

"We need to go someplace private where we can talk, but it won't work if we're leading a parade."

"Give me just a minute," she said.

She signaled to Otero, who was standing off to the side. He joined them and she explained that she and Bryan would be leaving together for about thirty minutes and that the two of them needed to be alone.

She could tell from his face that he didn't like it, but she was the boss, so Otero acquiesced and quickly withdrew.

She walked back over to Harb and let him guide her out the back of the hotel.

They got into his car and he drove them through the city proper and up into the nearby hills. They came to a small park in a residential neighborhood which overlooked the ocean below.

Bashir "Bryan" Harb was Lebanese by birth but raised and educated in the state of Connecticut. His father had moved the family there to reconnect with relatives who had emigrated to the States a generation before. His dad was a cook, and within a year of their arrival—- and with the assistance of family members—-he opened up a restaurant. Ten years later his three locations were considered to be among the best on the east coast for authentic Lebanese food.

By that time the entire family had become American citizens. They were prosperous, happy, and the epitome of a true American success story.

Bryan, an only child, was proficient in English and Lebanese, which was a dialect of Arabic. He did his undergraduate work at Georgetown University where he graduated from the Department of Arabic and Islamic Studies while minoring in the languages of Arabic,

Hebrew and Farsi. He was gradually introduced to a recruiter by a professor at Georgetown, and after initially turning the Agency down, he went to work in one of his father's restaurants, fell in love with a young woman that his family approved of, and shortly thereafter, the two were engaged.

On September 11, 2001, he was scheduled to meet his parents and his fiancé for breakfast at the Windows on the World atop the North Tower of the World Trade Center in New York City. He had worked the night before at one of the family's restaurants and had inadvertently overslept. He was caught in traffic when the first plane was flown into the North Tower, and he watched from the sidewalk several blocks away when 102 minutes later, the building and everyone he'd ever loved came crashing down to the street.

Twenty months later, he did his first tour of duty in Iraq as a US Marine. A sniper by training, he served in downtown Ramadi, often referred to by the Marines as "the most dangerous neighborhood in the most dangerous city in the world." His kill ratio was impressive. In less than six months he had twenty-seven confirmed kills and another 34 shots that probably killed insurgents. He achieved the rank of Lance Corporal, and he was intending to re-up for a second tour, when the CIA convinced him that he could do his country an even greater service by becoming an intelligence operative.

Bryan signed on and was initially posted in Afghanistan where he worked for a while with a specialized group that was charged with tracking down Ayman al-Zawahiri. While that never happened during his tour, he played a major role in the capture or killing of dozens of senior terrorist figures, including producing the intelligence that led to a drone strike in December of 2012, that killed Abu-Zaid al Kuwaiti, Al-Qaeda's second in command, who met his fate in the tribal zone of North Waziristan, Pakistan.

After the success of that operation, he was reassigned to work in the State of Israel. There was a growing concern about the connection between the senior leadership of Hamas and their sponsors in

Tehran. The smuggling of a dirty bomb into Tel Aviv was a possible scenario, and knowing that Bryan would need substantial lead time to establish his operation, the CIA brought him in to get a read on Hamas before the situation turned into a crisis. What he needed to establish was their smuggling routes, funding sources, and the names of their Iranian-based handlers.

Bryan took to the assignment like a fish in water. He secured forged passports from a number of different countries, set up safe houses throughout the various Middle Eastern states, and began to establish identities within each region of operation. In the West Bank of Palestine, he was known as the successful owner of a clothing store, a CIA front for his intelligence-gathering activities.

"What's with the security?" he asked Donahue as he parked the car.

"A lot has changed in my life."

She told him about meeting Sean, how they fell in love, and about their plans to get married. She described who Sean really was, what happened to his father, the role of the FBI in concealing his true identity, and the details known to her about the night that he was killed.

When she was finished, Bryan leaned back and said, "You weren't kidding when you said a lot has changed."

She tried to smile, but couldn't.

"I'm sorry for your loss," he told her. "We never got a chance to really get together, but I've always only wished the very best for you."

"I know," she said. "And I wouldn't be laying all of this on you, but I really do need to get your guidance."

She told him about the killers, how both spoke Yiddish, and their possible connection with a place in Tel Aviv called *Putin's Pub*.

"I've got composites drawn up from descriptions given by the witnesses, and I was wondering if you could use your connections with the Mossad to see if anyone knows who they might be?"

"Is the FBI working the case?" he asked.

"They say they are, but they don't know anything about the connection to the bar in Tel Aviv."

"Why not?"

"Because I didn't tell them. Instead of tracking down the killers, they only seem interested in how the killers managed to penetrate the witness protection program."

"Let me see the drawings," he said.

She handed them over and he took a long look.

"It says here that this one has a tattoo on the back of his neck?"

"I know. That wasn't in the initial report, but it must have been recalled by one or both of the witnesses when they described the two men for the composites."

"Let me have these and I'll show them around."

"The composites are the FBI's, and I'm not supposed to have them."

Bryan gave her a small smile. "I'll do what I can, but that's going to limit the number of people I can show them to."

"Don't get into trouble," she said.

He smiled. "Trouble is my middle name."

"I have the feeling that Sean's death is connected with his father's death and also with Putin. And the fact that the FBI decided to put him in the Witness Protection Program makes me wonder if it was related to terrorism?"

Now intrigued, Bryan said, "I'll see what I can do."

They headed back down the hill, and Donahue relaxed. She trusted Bryan completely, and she was relieved that he had agreed to help her out.

"Shari and I thought we might drop by Putin's Pub and see what it's all about?"

"Bad idea," he said. "I know that place and you need to stay completely away from it."

When she gave him a nod that she understood, he added, "And while I'm thinking about it, don't say anything in this country that you don't want overheard. Even your hotel rooms aren't safe."

"But no one knows anything about us except for the fact that we're probably just tourists."

"You think?" He looked over and caught her glance. "After you called, I did a little checking. Because of your relationship with Sean and your future role as the inheritor of a fortune, you are of interest to everyone, including the Mossad. Just try and keep that in mind."

"Your people know about my inheritance?"

"Afraid so." He shrugged his shoulders. "Selected people only," he added.

"But you let me tell you stuff that you already knew?"

"It's always better to get information directly from a principle," he told her.

She shook her head in mock disbelief.

Oh, well. So much for keeping that a secret.

"Let's pick up Shari and get something to eat," said Bryan. "If you like blintzes, I know a place that has the best ones in the Middle East."

"Lead on."

THIRTEEN

AFTER A DINNER of blintze's that Donahue and Thompson both admitted were the best they'd ever tasted, Bryan drove them back to the hotel, followed discreetly by Donahue's security detail. Once the women were safely inside, Bryan placed a quick call on his cell phone.

He drove directly to a copy store where he made several sets of the composites before driving down to the beach in Tel Aviv. He parked in a hotel lot, made his way down the pedestrian path and along the beach until he came to a public bench that afforded a view of the boat marina.

Already seated on the bench was Mordecai Ben-Gurion, a senior member of the Israeli Mossad.

When Bryan first met him, Mordecai was posing as an Israeli tour guide.

Originally of Eastern European lineage, Mordecai discovered at an early age that he had a natural ability with languages. In addition to Hebrew and English, he became fluent in Arabic by the age of ten. A word from his rabbi to a friend in the intelligence circles first brought Mordecai to the attention of the Mossad. They met with his parents, encouraged a broadening of his remarkable talent, and by the time he was of age for his compulsory military service, he spoke half a dozen Middle Eastern languages.

Mordecai grew up in Tel Aviv, and as a Mossad agent, he spent a year along the border with Egypt, and later did a stint in the Golan Heights at an outpost that overlooked the Syrian border. But his most useful contacts were made during a two-year period when he worked closely with the Jordanian Intelligence Service. His ability with various languages was an asset during tracking operations against the many nomadic Bedouin tribes who traveled freely through the Negev desert on drug-smuggling routes that were centuries old.

Mordecai was now head of the *Political Action and Liaison Department* of the Mossad, and he was responsible for coordinating actions with allied foreign intelligence services.

"So, Bryan, have you had any good Borscht lately?"

Harb smiled. It was common between the undercover intelligence operatives from cooperating agencies to one up each other by revealing the depth of their intelligence tentacles. It was apparent that Mordecai had learned that Harb had been tasked, in addition to his work on the Palestinians, to work the Russian expats in Israel as part of the U.S. effort to get more intelligence on the Russians and their Syrian operations.

But Bryan didn't confirm or deny the innuendo. Instead, he briefed Mordecai on what Donahue had told him, and about her personal involvement in the investigation into the death of her fiancé. He talked about the death of Sean's father, and he stressed the fact that the death was caused by a dose of Polonium 210.

Mordecai remembered the incident and the problems it caused for the Brits. The killers had left a trail of radioactivity all across downtown London.

"So, it's quite possible that we're dealing with people who are possibly connected to the group that used Polonium 210 in an act of nuclear terrorism," said Mordecai.

"If you want to phrase it that way?" said Bryan.

"It'll sell better to Eli that way."

"In that case, I suppose that's not too far a stretch."

Bryan pulled copies of the two composites from his inside coat pocket and handed them over to Mordecai.

"Who put these together?" Mordecai asked.

"The FBI. Donahue's out of the investigative loop, but she managed to get ahold of a set."

Mordecai looked over the drawings, then said, "What makes the Bureau think that these men might be Israelis?"

"They spoke Yiddish," said Harb. "One of them said that when they got to *Putin's Pub* the first round was on him."

"Will you be hanging around for awhile?" Mordecai asked.

Bryan nodded.

"I'll be in touch," said Mordecai.

As he started to walk off, Bryan smiled and said, "I hear you got a promotion, and that it comes with an office and a lovely view of the western coastline. Must be nice."

"Touché!" said Mordecai with a smile. He was impressed that Bryan knew the exact location of his office.

He gave Bryan a smile. "I'll get back to you tomorrow."

FOURTEEN

THE FOLLOWING MORNING, Mordecai drove to the port area of Jaffa for a quiet meeting with Eli Ben-Judah, the current head of the Mossad, and Mordecai's mentor. Ever since Mordecai participated in a highly successful incursion into Iran to rescue a medical scientist, Eli had been grooming him to one day take over the reins at Mossad.

Mordecai parked his car on the street and made his way into the bakery cafe that was temporarily closed by the owner to allow Eli to get his cup of strong black coffee and his sugar- coated breakfast pastry without being bothered by neighbors who wanted to chat.

Eli's chief security officer unlocked the front door and let Mordecai in. The other two members of Eli's security detail were standing off to the side, quietly watching the street through the large front window. Eli was at a table towards the back. He was reading a newspaper and savoring his morning treats.

Eli Ben-Judah had risen to the leadership role as head of the Mossad after thirty years in the intelligence service. He came up through the ranks, having worked in the Collections Department for more than ten years. In that assignment he was tasked with many aspects of conducting espionage overseas. He did assignments under various covers, including diplomatic as well as unofficial. He ran the *Political Action and Liaison Department* for more than five years, and was responsible for coordinating actions with allied foreign intelligence services as well as with nations that had no normal diplomatic relations with the state of Israel.

He was a natural leader; intelligent, quick of wit, and deadly serious when it came to issues of security affecting his country.

Mordecai said hello to the bakery staff who gave him a coffee and offered him a pastry. He turned down the sugary roll, then carried the coffee over to Eli's table and pulled out a chair to join him.

"So, why did you want to see me?" Eli asked as he folded up the paper and put it on the table.

"I had a meeting yesterday with Bryan Harb."

"Oh? And how is he doing?"

"He's fine. He's added Russian expatriates to his intelligence portfolio, something I think we should also pursue."

"And you think we're not already doing that?"

"Are we?" Mordecai asked.

But Eli didn't respond. Instead, he said, "What did Bryan want?"

Mordecai ran it down for him, covering the death of Anton Korakovsky, the murder of Sean, his son, Donahue's lone-wolf investigation of her fiancé's murder, and her belief that the FBI's involvement in the case was for reasons that were yet to be revealed.

"The fact they used Polonium 210 to kill Korakovsky has me very concerned," said Mordecai.

"It has everyone concerned," said Eli, who took a sip of his coffee.

Mordecai nodded.

"Are Harb and Donahue lovers?" Eli asked.

"Friends only, or so he claims."

Eli factored that into his assessment of what he'd been told so far.

"And they believe that these killers might be Israelis?"

"That's right. Donahue provided Bryan with composite drawings of the two men. I showed them last night to a confidential source of ours—a Russian expat we've been grooming—and he identified them both."

Eli smiled. "You see, we are already pursuing the cultivation of sources among our Russian friends."

"One source, Eli. Only one. But we should be doing a great deal more."

"So, we've determined the identities of the two men involved. What can you tell me about them?"

"They're both Israeli citizens. Arkady Kuznetsov arrived here six years ago, and Rusian Fedorov arrived six months later. Both are freelancers who are believed to be running an extortion racket involving Kosher butcher shops."

Eli shook his head. "Is nothing sacred anymore?"

"Apparently not," said Mordecai. "Our intelligence people suggest that they were chosen to do the killing to provide cover for the Kremlin in the case of any blowback."

"A textbook KGB tactic," said Eli.

"SVR," Mordecai said to correct him.

The SVR, or *Sluzhba vneshney razvedki Rossiyskoy Federatsii,* was tasked with intelligence and espionage activities outside the Russian Federation. It often worked in conjunction with the *Russian Main Intelligence Directorate.*

"The tactic was originally part of the KGB playbook, Morty," said Eli. "The name of the agency might have changed, but the methods remain the same."

"We don't know the true reason for the killing of Korakovsky's son, but I'm told that Donahue believes that the Bureau might have been running an operation, and that her Sean might somehow have been involved."

Eli leaned back in his chair and signaled to his team to get ready to go.

"One more thing," said Mordecai. "I think that Bryan and Donahue are both working off the books."

Eli frowned. "If we help them out, will we be stepping on anyone's toes?"

"The Bureau might not appreciate our nosing around."

Eli gave that some thought. The fact that the killing of Korakovsky was clearly sanctioned from the very top made the killing of his son as likely coming from Putin as well.

So many questions.

What is that gangster Putin up to? And why use a radioactive poison to kill Korakovsky?

If he was making Korakovsky an example, who was the message intended for?

Eli folded his arms across his chest. "Are you asking me if we should get involved in Donahue's investigation?"

"I am," said Mordecai. "I think the pluses for doing so outweigh the negatives."

Eli nodded in agreement.

"Get surveillance photos of the two men and find out where they're staying. Give the surveillance photographs directly to Donahue and tell her, in exchange for the photos, we want to know the motive for the killing of her fiancé. If her eyewitnesses can identify them as the killers, tell Harb we'll be happy to pick them up and find out where the order came from."

"Will we give them up for extradition?" Mordecai asked.

"If they want them extradited, we'll accommodate them, but only if we're read in as to what is going on."

"And if Bryan wants to stay out of this?"

"We can make a call to the FBI and say that we have a confidential informant who tipped us off to the IDs of the two men they are looking for."

Mordecai thanked Eli for the guidance, then got to his feet.

"Hold on," said Eli. "Sit down for a second."

When Mordecai did, Eli said, "I understand that Donahue arrived here in a private jet."

Mordecai was duly impressed. He had no idea that Eli knew anything about Donahue, much less about her arrival in Tel Aviv. And the fact that he knew it was a private jet was also a surprise. His sources for information never ceased to be amazing.

"Open a file on Donahue," Eli said. "Her newfound fortune will bring her influence, and one day she might be in a position to be of some usefulness to our beloved Israel."

Eli got to his feet to signify that their meeting was over.

∽

The warm sunlight was tempered by an onshore breeze that came in from the Mediterranean Sea.

Donahue and Thompson were seated with Bryan Harb at an outdoor table that overlooked the beach. On the menu were grilled halibut steaks, baked potatoes, fresh vegetables, and wine. The conversation was light, chiefly a recap of their visit to the Wailing Wall and the Basilica of the Holy Sepulchre, where Bryan had served as their unofficial tour guide.

The sun was close to setting on the horizon, and both Donahue and Thompson felt exhilarated by their presence in such an old and sacred place.

"Do you miss the States?" Thompson said to Bryan.

"Not really. I've been working here for a long time, and to be perfectly honest, the Middle East feels like my home."

"Well, I can see why you like it here," she said, looking around. "Great weather, long dinners under the stars, and a feeling that everyone is living in the moment."

"They are," he replied. "It comes from knowing that if things don't go right, it could all be over in a matter of hours. This is a country that has never known complete peace, so it's hard to think long term when the specter of a never-ending war is always hanging over your head."

Donahue was about to chime in when several vehicles came to an abrupt stop on the nearby street.

All three looked over at once as Mordecai got out of the first one followed by a half a dozen armed bodyguards in lightweight suits and dark sunglasses.

Mordecai walked over to the table and took the seat across from Donahue. He pulled out a sealed Manila envelope which he held in his hand.

"Forgive me for interrupting, but I wanted to meet with you before you leave."

"Are we leaving?" she asked him.

"You'll probably want to after this." He slid the envelope across the table, but as she reached out with her hand to retrieve it, he held it down with his to prevent her from picking it up.

"Do not open this until you're on your plane headed back to the States."

"What's in it?" Donahue asked.

"Passport photographs of the two men you're looking for."

Donahue's eyes widened. Had they really found them already?

"Both are Israeli citizens," Mordecai said softly. "They are Russian expats, tied in with the Israeli Russian mob. You can show these photographs to your witnesses, and if you get a positive identification of one or both of them, then we will work with the FBI to get their passport information, flights to and from the US, and any other physical evidence which will help your country move forward with a criminal prosecution."

"And you're sure it's them?" Donahue asked.

"My people identified them right away from the composites. Your witnesses are very good at recalling significant details."

"This is great!" said Donahue. "Thanks so much for your help."

She reached for the envelope again, but Mordecai wasn't ready to let it go.

"When an identification is made, we will be happy to pick them up for you. Both men are still believed to be in this area. However, as a quid pro quo, we would insist on interviewing them before we turn them over to the States."

"But why would you want to interview them?" Donahue asked.

"We want to know who hired them and what connection they may have with Russia."

Donahue leaned forward. "I doubt they're going to tell you who they were working for."

"Oh, they'll tell us," said Mordecai. "We don't take kindly to being set up to take the fall for something concocted by the SVR."

Donahue decided not to push the issue. It was very apparent that the less she knew about the Israeli plans the better off she'd be in the long run.

"I suppose you know that I'm doing this without the sanction of the FBI," she said. "In fact, I was specifically ordered to stay out of the investigation."

"I'm aware of that. If these two are identified by your witnesses, if you want to stay out of it, we'll bring in the FBI and tell them that a confidential informant put us on to them."

Donahue smiled. She could get Gibby to show the surveillance photos to the witnesses. That would eliminate her conflict of interest, and would remove her from the evidence-gathering loop.

"That's very sensible," she said. "I'll keep that in mind."

"One way or the other, if they are identified, I'll see to it that you get everything we have on them and their connections."

He looked over at Bryan. "How was the tour today?"

"It was fine, but, of course, you already know that, don't you?"

Mordecai smiled. "Did you pick up the surveillance?"

"I only had a hunch, but thanks for confirming my suspicions."

Mordecai laughed, then turned to Donahue.

"So, you'll be leaving this evening?"

She nodded.

"Well, it was a pleasure meeting you," he said. He got to his feet. "And you too, Detective Thompson. You'll have to come back and spend more time in our country. If you've got a week, I can recommend a great tour service that can show you all the important sites. It will be my treat."

"That would be wonderful," said Thompson with a smile. "I'll take you up on that."

Mordecai excused himself, and Bryan walked him back to his car.

"Tell me something, Morty. Why did you let them know who you are?"

"The boss wants me to establish a relationship with Donahue. You know how that goes."

Bryan did. Donahue's new fortune gave her a chip in the big game. He suspected that the Agency would soon also recognize the value of cozying up to her, and while she may not know it yet, her money gave her political clout.

"Let me know how this sorts out," Bryan said. "I'll see them off this evening, but I'll be around."

"You want me to call you through channels?"

"Please. There's nothing worse than getting a call from Mossad while I'm doing my undercover schtick."

"*Schtick?* We'll convert you to Judaism yet."

Bryan smiled. "You can leave a message for me with Dan at the embassy in Cairo. Do you need the number?"

"I've already got it," said Mordecai.

Bryan slowly shook his head. "Why am I not surprised."

He then made his way back to the table where Donahue and Thompson were just finishing up their wine.

"Take your time," he told them. He sat down in his chair. "Enjoy what's left of the sunset."

"His offer to set up a week-long tour sounded pretty great," said Thompson. "I may have to take him up on that."

"I can assure you he'll pull out all the stops. It'll be the best tour you've ever taken."

"We just might have to do it," said Donahue. "Do you think your kids would want to go along?"

"They'll have no say in the matter," said Thompson. "They might hate it now, but someday they'll appreciate a trip to the Holy Land."

Bryan leaned forward and lowered his voice. "Just so you know, I can also guarantee that the tour guide will be an Israeli Intelligence agent."

Donahue sighed.

Charlotte was right. Be wary of everyone, even your new so-called friends.

FIFTEEN

AFTER AN ALL-NIGHT flight back to L.A. and a day at home to recuperate, Donahue dragged herself down to the PAB, where she met up with Thompson, who was still buzzing about their trip. She was describing to others in the unit what she saw on their tour of Jerusalem, and in particular, the Old City.

Clearly the group was envious of their three days off.

When Donahue got her alone, she said, "I trust you didn't say anything about the plane?"

"Of course not," Thompson replied with incredulity. "I told them we flew commercial."

Donahue nodded. She didn't mind the others knowing that they'd gone to Israel on "business," but she still didn't want anyone to know anything at all about her inheritance.

"I gave everything a lot of thought last night," said Donahue, "and I think we need to let the FBI know what we learned from the Israelis."

"I agree," said Thompson.

She was secretly happy that Donahue was willing to let others take over the investigation. The conflict of interest was just too great. Others could show a lineup card to the two witnesses, because if she and Donahue were the ones to do it, the defense would be in a position to argue that they'd pressured the witnesses to identify these particular two men, and that would be a disaster for any attempted criminal prosecution.

"I'll call Kasey Smitten," said Donahue. "She was pretty straight with me when we spoke, so she's earned the right of first refusal."

✌

Donahue was at her desk an hour later when Smitten and her partner showed up. Donahue tracked down Thompson and the four of them made their way to one of the nearby interview rooms.

Donahue described how she had obtained the FBI composites from a confidential informant, and how they had reinterviewed the two witnesses. Smitten and Folsey were not happy that Donahue and Thompson were conducting their own investigation. However, their resentment was quickly tempered by how they had used the Putin's Pub reference to move the investigation on to the state of Israel.

"I don't know how we missed that?" said Smitten, referring to the witnesses ability to speak Yiddish.

"Pretty sloppy," said Folsey, and Smitten quietly agreed.

Folsey then returned her attention to Donahue and Thompson.

"I'm concerned that your interview with them will be held against us," she said.

Thompson said, "You don't need to be concerned about the defense asserting that we somehow coerced the witnesses." She pulled a USB stick out of her purse and handed it over to Smitten. "I recorded the interview and there is nothing on there that will hurt your case. If you take the time to listen to it, you'll see that we didn't influence the witnesses in any way at all."

"We were very careful," said Donahue. "Anyway, I showed the composites to a confidential contact I have with the Mossad, and within a day they were able to identify both of them. I've got copies of fairly recent passport photos, and if you want to use them in a lineup card, they're yours."

Smitten looked at the photos, then passed them on to Folsey.

"Holy cow!" said Folsey. "The composites were right on."

Donahue continued, "If the witnesses make an ID, I have the assurances of the Mossad that they will pick them up and hold them for deportation. However, they stressed that they will interview the two suspects while the extradition is pending. Apparently, the Mossad takes umbrage with the fact that the Russians hired two Israeli citizens to do the killing in order to distance themselves from possible blowback if something went wrong."

Smitten was quick to understand that she was being handed the golden ticket. By cracking the case in this way, she would end up getting all the credit once the witnesses made an identification.

"You did a good job with this, Jennifer," said Smitten, with a smile. "I'll take the photos and we'll show them to the witnesses right away."

"Both of these guys are organized crime figures," said Donahue. "If an identification is made, the Israelis will give us a detailed background history for both of them, including dates and times they made flights to and from the U.S., and cell phone records if there are any."

"This is all great!" said Smitten. "And I'm glad you were so careful. However, I must insist that from this point forward, you need to stay clear of our investigation."

Donahue raised her hands in surrender, but she didn't say anything that could be construed as an acquiescence.

⊷

On the way out of the building, Folsey said, "I still think Donahue might have compromised the case."

Smitten stopped walking. "I disagree. Those women are talented investigators who know how to work on a complicated case. With just a little effort and some common sense and care for detail, they showed us up pretty good. We can learn a lot from them, Rebecca."

She started walking again, then paused.

"I just wish to God that we had a few more like them working for the Bureau."

Two hours later, Smitten called Donahue at her office to tell her that both men were identified by the witnesses as the killers.

Donahue sighed with satisfaction. Although she was confident that they had the right suspects, it was a great relief to know that Sean's killers would now be facing American justice. She leaned back in her chair. "If you guys are ready to get an arrest warrant for them, I'll notify my contact at the Mossad and they will pick them up."

"I have to brief my supervisor first," said Smitten, "and after that, I have to take it to the US Attorney, so that may take a few days before we can get things processed."

"Understood," said Donahue. "I'll give you my contact's number, but give me time to call him first. I'll let him know that you'll be in touch, but don't call him until you have everything in place. He's well-connected and a very busy man."

"I'll keep that in mind," said Smitten.

Donahue rattled off the number and Mordecai's name.

"Say, listen, Jennifer. I can't thank you enough for what you've done. If you ever decide you might want to come to work for the Bureau, just give me a call. We'd love to have someone like you and your partner over here."

Donahue smiled. *Fat chance in hell that would ever happen.*

"That's a nice offer, Kasey. I'll keep it in mind."

When the call was ended, Donahue told Thompson about the identifications before breaking down in relief. This was quickly followed by a return to grief. Thompson comforted her for a while, then left to tell Gibson and the Captain about the progress that had been made.

When Donahue finally composed herself, she placed a call to Mordecai, and after a short delay, he came on the line.

"The witnesses identified them. The FBI is gonna move forward on it, but I've been told it'll take a few days."

"I'm glad it worked out," he said. There was noticeable satisfaction in his tone of voice. "Once we get the warrant, we'll pick them up. I'll let you know when we have them in custody."

"Will you fill me in on what you learn during the interrogations?"

Mordecai was hesitant to make a firm commitment.

"I'll let you know what I can."

She understood. There would likely be intelligence gathered that would be unrelated to the death of Sean.

"Thanks for your help," she told him, and when the call was over, she looked up to see the Captain coming her way.

"I wanted to congratulate you, Jen," he said. "You and Shari did a hell of a job."

"Thanks, Boss." She started to yawn. "But if it's okay with you, I'm emotionally exhausted and jet-lagged. I'm gonna take the rest of the day off."

"No problem. You've earned it."

Thompson overheard what he said. "Hey? Does that mean I can take the rest of the day off, too?"

"Absolutely not," he replied.

Thompson was floored. "But if Jen gets—"

She stopped when she noticed that Elwood was smiling like the Cheshire Cat.

"Go before I change my mind," he said.

"*Adios, Capitán,*" said Thompson. "You don't need to tell me twice."

⌁

Instead of going home, Donahue drove over to the Forest Lawn Cemetery with a bouquet of red roses. When she found Sean's headstone, she stood there quietly, thinking about how much she missed him, and how unfair his death seemed to be.

She laid the bouquet on the headstone, then sat down on the grass and began to talk to him before breaking into tears.

Thompson was sitting in the car, watching from a distance, before she also shed tears for her broken-hearted friend.

SIXTEEN

THE LOS ANGELES FBI Headquarters Building in Westwood, California, was a massive seventeen-story structure on twenty-eight acres of prime real estate that was surrounded by anti-vehicle barriers to prevent a suicide bombing attack.

Kasey Smitten left her cubicle on the fourteenth floor and walked directly to the office of Elliott T. Clausner, the Los Angeles Agent-in-Charge. Once she took a seat in front of his desk, she filled him in on the identification made by the witnesses in the Sean Walker killing.

She also explained how Donahue and Thompson had connected the dots, and how they made the identification of the two men involved.

"We showed six-pack photo spreads to the two witnesses from Cedars, and each one independently identified the two suspects. Both of the suspects are members of an organized crime group in Israel, and the Mossad will pick them up for us when we're ready to move forward with an extradition."

Clausner was a buttoned-down, middle-aged Caucasian who spent his childhood in Utah. He leaned back in his chair in his corner office and folded his arms across his chest. He was bothered by Donahue's and the LAPD's involvement in the case, and he didn't hold back with his criticisms.

"She's put the case in jeopardy by talking to the eyewitnesses," he told Smitten.

"The interviews that she and her partner did are recorded. We've listened to them, and they did things by the book. There's no hint of coercion, so the interviews won't be a problem."

"But the conflict of interest will be."

"She was with a partner," said Smitten, "and if it wasn't for their interview, these two men would still be unidentified. They discovered that the female witness spoke Yiddish, which we missed, and they used her translation to tie down a connection to Israel. Donahue's contact in the Mossad was able to identify the two men in a single day. I think the U.S. Attorney will decide that her involvement did not in any way taint the impartiality of the investigation."

"You better hope you're right," he said, grudgingly. "And by the way, how did they get ahold of the composites?"

"I don't know, but Donahue and her partner are very resourceful, and I'd be amazed if they didn't have a contact somewhere in our chain of command."

"Do you have a name and a number for Donahue's contact in the Mossad?" he asked.

"I do, but she cautioned me not to call him until we're ready to move forward with the extradition. Apparently, he's very high up in their administration, and she told me he's a very busy man."

"Give me the info," he said, extending his hand. "I'll see how busy he really is."

Smitten did so reluctantly.

She and her partner Rebecca Folsey were part of a special unit that worked out of the Hoover complex in Washington, D.C. She resented the fact that she had to keep Clausner in the information loop simply because he was running the L.A. operation.

Since their arrival in L.A., her interactions with him had been decidedly unpleasant. He was a real tight-ass whose reputation for being a misogynist was well known throughout the female ranks of the

L.A. office. If Donahue had been a male, Smitten had no doubt that he would be praising the way the investigation had been developed.

But she'd dealt with guys like him before, and as soon as an opportunity presented itself, she would pass on what she observed about him to people she knew had the power to weed him out of the system.

She went back to her end of the building and tracked down Folsey, who was seated in an office that had been loaned to them for the duration of their investigation in Los Angeles.

"Focus on putting together a witness list, Rebecca," Smitten said. "We're going to need it for the U.S. Attorney."

"Did Auntie-Fem sign on?"

Derived from anti-feminist, Auntie-Fem was the nickname that the FBI female agents used when speaking amongst themselves about Clausner.

"Once he stopped venting," Smitten replied.

"What will you be doing?" Folsey asked.

"I'm going to head on over to the Federal Courthouse and make contact with the AUSA. I want to pave the way for us to present the case."

※

At the office of the United States Attorney, on the twelfth floor of the Federal Courthouse in downtown Los Angeles, Smitten waited in an outer office for Susan Zajec, an Assistant United States Attorney (AUSA).

Zajac was a well-respected, nine-year veteran of the office. As a senior filing attorney, she spent the better part of her days meeting with representatives of various federal law enforcement agencies who wanted her investigative suggestions and/or charges to be filed against individuals who had broken federal laws.

Because Smitten normally worked out of the Washington headquarters building, she had never previously met with Zajec. But she had enough common sense before setting up a meeting to ask around at the Bureau's Westwood office for the name of someone who could be trusted to do the right thing; someone who would remain mum in the face of otherwise classified information.

Zajec finally invited Smitten to join her in a tiny windowless office and immediately asked Smitten for a written case summary.

"I haven't had time to put one together," said Smitten, "but I wanted to get your take on the best way to move forward with my case."

Zajec sat back and folded her hands in her lap.

"I'm all ears, Agent Smitten. What have you got?"

Smitten told her everything about the case, holding back only on the reasons for Sean Walker's initial placement in the Witness Protection Program. She talked about Donahue's relationship to Walker, and how Donahue and her LAPD partner had used a source in the Mossad to identify both killers.

"And these men are Israeli citizens?"

"That's my understanding," Smitten replied.

"Why'd they kill him?" Zajec asked.

"Our theory is to get at the assets the Russians claim the father embezzled before leaving the Russian Federation."

She went on to explain how lawyers in London had filed suit on behalf of the Federation claiming that assets removed from Russia had been shifted to legitimate businesses after being secreted behind a series of virtually untraceable shell companies.

"It's our belief that Walker was killed to force his heir to have to list inheritable assets in open court. This would enable the London attorneys to tie up those assets in litigation."

"Who is behind the killing?" Zajec asked. "Or more precisely, who hired the killers?"

"We don't know yet, but we suspect the directive came from the SVR."

"And how do you suppose they located Mr. Walker?"

"A team in D.C. is working on that," Smitten replied.

Zajec sighed. This case had gigantic international implications, possibly leading up to the highest levels of government in the Russian Federation. Just filing a case would be an international incident, and for that reason, the United States Attorney General himself would have to sign on to any prosecution.

"You want my advice on this?" Zajec asked.

"Absolutely," said Smitten.

"Okay. This is not a garden-variety murder case. It has political ramifications of an international nature stamped all over it. So, first things first. I'm going to need you to present me with a written summary of the case, including signed statements from all of the proposed witnesses. All lab work must be completed, and all possible defenses will need to be considered. You and your fellow agents will have to gather any evidence which we can then use to block those possible defenses."

"Once you have the complete package ready for me, I'm going to have to show it to my boss, and after that, it will have to go to D.C. for their consideration. Once the AG himself signs off on the case, it will come back here for presentation to a grand jury, and I would estimate that the entire process could take at least a couple of months."

"You're kidding, right? A couple of months after I get you the package?"

Zajec pursed her lips. "Just get me the package I need, and we can start the process moving forward."

Smitten shook her head in resignation.

I should have known we'd run into the usual bureaucratic buzzsaw. If a conviction wasn't guaranteed, the typical U.S. Attorney wouldn't touch it with a ten-foot pole.

"So, while I'm putting this all together, what do I tell the Israelis?" Smitten asked.

"Tell them the truth, that it's going to take some time before we'll be ready to go to a federal Grand Jury."

Smitten sighed.

God, how I hate working with spineless, promotion-hungry, government attorneys.

❧

When Smitten returned to the Bureau headquarters in Westwood, she paid a visit to Clausner's office to fill him in on what AUSA Zajec had said about their timetable.

"Take a seat," said Clausner.

She told him what Zajec demanded and the fact that it could take several months to get the case off the ground.

Clausner folded his hands across his chest and leaned back in his chair.

"Why didn't you tell me who Donahue's Mossad contact really was?" he asked.

She could tell by his tone of voice that he was about to go on a rant.

"What do you mean?" She was genuinely confused.

"You neglected to tell me that Mordecai Ben-Gurion is the Director of the Mossad's Political Action and Liaison Department."

Smitten's eyes widened.

"Oh? Okay. What's that?"

"He's number two in the Mossad. He coordinates all Israeli intelligence activities with foreign intelligence agencies."

Smitten could hardly suppress a smile. Donahue's ability to surprise her with the level of her connections was staggering.

"I had no idea. Remember, I told you she said not to call him until we were ready to extradite, so I had no reason to check him out."

"Well, you should have. I told him we'd be ready in a day or two."

He was clearly embarrassed for having jumped the gun, and he made no bones about trying to hang some of the blame on her.

He leaned forward in his chair.

"You'll need to call him back and let him know that it's going to take a lot longer than we first thought."

She was not surprised that he'd thrown this back on her. He wasn't much of a leader, and he was certainly not willing to admit that he hadn't paid attention to Donahue's admonition.

"Anything else?" she asked. She was finding it hard to sit and endure his condescending attitude.

"No, that's it. Just get the write-up over to the AUSA as soon as you can."

She left his office more intent than ever to use her connections back in D.C. to get Clausen transferred to some satellite office in a place like North Dakota. As far as she was concerned, he could spend the rest of his professional life freezing his ass off in miserable isolation.

Once she got back to her desk, Smitten immediately called her boss in D.C. and filled him in on where they were at.

"When you get the murder case written up, give me a call. In the meantime, I'll talk to the Justice Department here in D.C. and we'll see if we can get the case heard in this jurisdiction. Once we get that squared away, I'd like you and Rebecca to get back here as soon as you can. We're going to need more help to figure out who passed on Walker's identification information."

"Any progress on that front?" she asked.

"I've got several of our teams working with the U.S. Marshals. They're doing background checks on all personnel who had contact with, or access to, the confidential file on Walker. It's tedious, I know, but it needs to get done."

"I'm sure you're right, but there may be another way. I want to get the background info on the two killers. Maybe we can work backward to find out who hired them, and if we're lucky, that person might have a phone or email link with someone who knew about Walker's true identity?"

"Okay, but can you do that from back here?"

"I'd rather stay out here, boss. Donahue may be the key to getting cooperation from the Mossad, and besides, the weather here beats being back in D.C. at any time of the year."

"Okay, let me think about that. But in the meantime, drop a dime on the Mossad contact and see if they can put a watch on the two suspects until an arrest can be made."

"I will," she told him. "Now, while I'm thinking about it, the Agent-in-Charge out here is a real dickhead, and I think you guys might want to move him to Bumfuck Montana or some other appropriate dead-end assignment before the lawsuits start flooding in."

"Oh?" He leaned back in his chair. If Smitten was concerned enough to bring this up, he had better take a moment to listen.

"Is it really that bad?" he asked.

"His nickname out here is '*Auntie-Fem*.' Need I say much more."

"*Shit!*" He leaned forward and reached out for his computer keyboard, then shook his head and sighed.

"Okay. Lay it on me…"

⌁

Mordecai showed up at a small cafe in eastern Jerusalem without his security detail. Bryan Harb was inside, and he led Mordecai to a basement room where he knew they could talk without interruption or detection.

"Are you friends with the owner?" Mordecai asked.

"He owed me a favor," Bryan replied.

Mordecai nodded. "So, I heard from the FBI in Los Angeles. They're preparing a warrant for the two suspects, but it might take several weeks or even several months for the process to be completed."

"What do you plan to do in the meantime?" Bryan asked.

"We'll keep looking for them."

"Well, keep your people out of *Putin's Pub*. It's a very closed shop."

Mordecai's eyes widened. "You've been in there?"

"An informant of mine vouched for me," said Bryan, with a nod. "I've been in there the last three nights."

"Any sign of the guys we're looking for?"

Bryan nodded affirmatively.

"The smaller one came in two nights ago. I followed him to an apartment on *Carlebach Street*. I had a team of my people come out and mount a camera across the street. The feed is being monitored at my embassy in Tel Aviv. They're watching for suspect number two."

"You've been busy," said Mordecai with a smile. "But just so you know, when we pick them up, we'll be handling the interrogation. You're welcome to watch, if you want?"

"I wouldn't miss it," said Bryan.

"On a different subject, do you realize the size of the inheritance that has fallen into Donahue's lap?"

"I don't know the exact amount, but I imagine it's more than comfortable."

"It's staggering," said Mordecai.

Bryan sighed. "I feel sorry for her. She's such a sweet lady. A lot of problems come with having big money. I just hope she's got the savvy to handle it."

SEVENTEEN

Two weeks later, when the okay was received to go forward with the prosecution, the case was presented to a grand jury in the Federal Courthouse in downtown, Los Angeles. Because of the political sensitivities connected with the case, senior administrators in the Justice Department sent a prosecutor from D.C. to L.A. to handle the case. His name was David Langley, and by all accounts he was a budding legend when it came to putting on high-profile murder prosecutions.

A federal grand jury would normally meet in secret to consider whether there was sufficient evidence to justify a formal criminal charge against a suspect. The jury was composed of twenty-three members who normally met only once a week. Even so, at least sixteen members were required to be present for the grand jury to conduct any business. They would hear only the prosecution's side of the case, as a reasonable suspicion that a crime had been committed—and that the person suspected was the one who did it—was all that had to be shown.

Proof beyond a reasonable doubt was the standard for a trial, not for a grand jury criminal indictment.

The first witness called to testify in the case involving the Israelis was the first patrol officer to arrive at the scene of Sean's killing. She and her partner got the initial call, and had responded to the duplex within three minutes.

The officer explained that they were met by two witnesses, a doctor and a nurse who told them what they saw and heard. When she and her partner entered the upstairs duplex unit, she noted right away that the place had been ransacked. On the floor in the living room was the body of an obviously deceased male.

After the rest of the duplex was cleared, she left her partner at the door to guard the scene. She returned to the street, and based on the eyewitness statements, she put out a description of the suspects and the car they were believed to be driving.

Other units arrived and a canvass of the neighborhood was conducted for witnesses and video surveillance cameras.

Next to testify was Ulysses Gibson, the ranking detective at RHD, who was first to arrive at the scene. He coordinated the callout of other RHD detectives, then left the scene to locate the fiancé of the deceased, who also happened to be a detective with the RHD.

A firearms investigator was called, and after qualifying as an expert, he explained that three empty shotgun casings were picked up at the scene. After a microscopic examination of the casings, he told the grand jurors that a single shotgun was used to accomplish the killing.

The Coroner who conducted the autopsy on Sean Walker was called, and she testified that he had been shot twice in the chest and a third time in the face.

The presentation was temporarily recessed when two jurors became ill after looking at the autopsy photographs.

When the case resumed, Agent Kasey Smitten was called. She identified the victim of the murder as Mikel Korakovsky whose father was a Russian dissident who had been murdered in London by associates of the Russian SVR. Because of that killing, Korakovsky's son was put into the Federal Witness Protection Program. His name had been changed to Sean Walker.

She went on to explain that the getaway vehicle was found three miles from the scene of the killing. It was apparently stolen two hours before the incident from the lot of a new car dealership. No prints or other physical evidence was found at the scene, but composites of the suspects were drawn up by an FBI artist after consultations with the two eyewitnesses. After circulating the composite, the suspects were identified by representatives of the Israeli Intelligence Service. Photographs were obtained, and both men were positively identified by the two eyewitnesses as the men they'd seen leaving the scene of the crime.

But AUSA Langley wasn't finished with his presentation. He called Dr. Richard Rosen who described what he and Rachael Pendergast were doing at the scene. Rosen told the grand jurors about seeing the flashes of light in the window of the duplex, and the sound of the shotgun when it went off. He looked at the photographic lineup cards, and then confirmed that the two men that he identified from the lineup card were the same men who came out of the duplex carrying a shotgun and a laptop computer.

Without calling Rachael Pendergast to testify about the conversation she overheard between the two killers, Langley gave his final summation. He closed by asking the jurors to indict each of the two men on one count each of premeditated murder.

Thirty minutes later, after being instructed on the law, the jurors began their secret deliberations, and after a single vote, both men were indicted for murder.

EIGHTEEN

MORDECAI WAS ON the phone, seated in his corner office, toying with a pen while he listened intently to the voice on the other end of the line. An FBI agent named Kasey Smitten was filling him in on the details of the arrest warrants that now existed for Arkady Kuznetsov and Rusian Fedorov. Both were indicted for the murder of Sean Walker.

When the conversation was over, he buzzed for his secretary.

Jeanette Fond came into his office with a steno pad and a pen in her hand.

"Please contact Dan Taylor for me. He's CIA head of station at the American Embassy in Cairo. Use a secure line. Tell him to have Bryan Harb call me as soon as it's convenient."

Jeanette scribbled down the information as fast as he could dictate.

"Will there be anything else, sir?"

"An agent named Smitten from the FBI is sending you an email with an attachment. It's a certified copy of a criminal indictment with supporting documentation. Please see that four copies of everything are printed, and bring them to me as soon as that's done."

"Yes, sir."

Once she was out of his office, he picked up his phone and placed a call to Yoram Ha-Levy, the current head of the Israeli Police in the Jerusalem District.

"What can I do for you, Morty?" said Ha-Levy.

"I'm in the process of putting together two American arrest packages for suspects in an assassination that was perpetrated in the States. Both men are Russian expats who were given Israeli citizenship. They're also members of Russian organized crime."

"When do you want us to make the arrests?"

"Tomorrow morning."

"Do we know their whereabouts?"

"I'll send a courier over with everything you'll need, but I want to caution you. This information and the arrests are highly sensitive. Secrecy concerning the entire operation is mandatory with everything on a need-to-know only basis."

"I understand. Will there be representatives from outside agencies?" He was referring to foreign intelligence services.

"Possibly one. I'll let you know when he confirms."

When Mordecai hung up the phone, he settled back in his chair. His people would be doing the interrogations, so the two suspects would be taken to a military base where details of their arrest and detention would not leak out to the press.

≈

By four a.m., everyone was assembled at the National Headquarters of the Israel Police in Kiryat Menachem Begin, Jerusalem. Mordecai was present, as was Bryan Harb, who showed up in time to be present for the pending arrests.

The Israeli police unit involved in the operation was known as *Yasam*. They were the district's on-call tactical counter-terror unit, and because of the international implications of the pending arrests, they were designated to serve the arrest and search warrants on the two separate suspect residences.

Arkady Kuznetsov was the suspect that Bryan Harb had initially followed from Putin's Pub several weeks before. In addition to the camera mounted by the CIA, the Mossad had been watching the location through a camera which was also mounted across the street. But even with two cameras for all those many nights, the second suspect had never shown up. But two nights before the warrant came through, the investigators got lucky. The second man showed up at Putin's Pub, and he was followed by Mossad to his current residence. A hastily installed camera was set up across the street and a surveillance was begun right away.

"Once the teams go in and have both men in custody, you'll be free to go through their apartments," said Chief Ha-Levy.

Mordecai nodded. He and Bryan would go through both locations, and once everything was photographed as is, detectives and agents from the Mossad would comb through the two apartments looking for any form of actionable intelligence.

According to the surveillance reports, Kuznetsov showed up at his home at five-thirty p.m. the previous evening, and as far as they knew, he was still inside. Fedorov was observed going into his apartment at just after nine p.m., and he, too, was still inside his place. Both men lived alone, so the risk of harming others was minimal. But even so, the plan was to evacuate the neighboring apartment units on the off-chance that the arrest teams would encounter armed resistance.

Two separate caravans of police and tactical teams left the police building at just after five a.m. Upon arrival at the two locations, which happened to be several miles apart, they quietly went to work removing nearby residents to a predetermined safe location a block away from each of the suspects' apartments.

Bryan was with the team assigned to take down Kuznetsov, while Mordecai went to Fedorov's location. The raids were timed to be executed simultaneously, and at exactly five-thirty-five a.m., the front doors were hit and the teams went in.

Mordecai's cell phone rang, and when he answered it, Bryan Harb said, "Kuznetsov is dead."

Mordecai sighed. "Fedorov has suffered the same fate." He looked around, then lowered his voice.

"The Israeli police will be handling the investigation. I'll stick around here and see what we can develop. Why don't you get a unit to take you back to the station, and I'll be in touch just as soon as I've got any news."

"How do you suppose they knew we were coming, Morty?"

"By 'they,' I assume you mean whoever did the killing?"

"That's exactly what I meant," said Bryan.

"I don't know, but I intend to find out."

NINETEEN

MORDECAI MET WITH Bryan Harb at the *Mount Zion Hotel* on Hebron Road in Jerusalem. Security was uppermost in the minds of both men. There was the ever-present fear of a terrorist attempt on Mordecai's life because of his role as a leader within the Mossad, and the realistic possibility that Harb—a well-entrenched agent of the CIA—would have his cover blown if he was seen in public with a known Israeli Intelligence agent.

The historic five-star boutique hotel was on the outskirts of the Old City, and its history ran back to the days of the Crusaders. It was expensive and therefore secure enough to enable the two men to meet without fear of discovery by hostile foes.

They were on the tenth floor in a hotel room rented by a travel agency that Mordecai had once used as a cover for his recruitment of Middle Eastern assets. Mordecai's ever-present security was all but invisible, but they guaranteed that the two men could meet in secret and without interruption or fear of attack.

"We've got a lead on the killer," said Mordecai. He and Bryan were sipping coffee from a cart delivered by room service, and Bryan looked over and away from the window he'd been using to study the city below.

Mordecai continued. "The video taken from the security camera at the complex where Kuznetsov lived showed a man entering the location in the latter part of the evening, ten minutes after Kuznetsov got home. We can't put him in Kuznetsov's apartment, but he shows up later that evening on the video feed at Fedorov's apartment. Our facial recognition software has identified him as Sergei Ivanov. We picked him up again on video at the airport in Tel Aviv where he boarded a flight to London. He arrived at Heathrow several hours ago, and MI-5 tracked him out of the airport, but the vehicle that picked him up was stolen and later found abandoned in an underground parking lot of a crowded shopping center in Kensington.

"Somehow, Ivanov and the driver avoided the security cameras at the mall. It's unknown if they left on foot or by another vehicle."

"So who is he?" Bryan asked.

"He's reputed to be an SVR operative from *Service A*, a group responsible for planning and implementing active measures. At this point, he's what you Americans refer to as a person of interest."

Bryan gazed out the window again, lost in thought.

"Cause of death?" he finally asked.

"Small-caliber weapon, apparently silenced. Two to the head of each man," said Mordecai.

Bryan nodded. No question in his mind that the killer was a professional.

"The Russians wanted to sever the final link between the two killers and their government," said Bryan.

"That's what we've concluded," replied Mordecai. "They used Israelis for the hit as a way to deflect their involvement in Mikel Korakovsky's murder."

"Have you notified the U.S. authorities?" Bryan asked.

"Not yet. I wanted to let you know first, but we'll be calling the FBI in a couple of hours to fill them in on what we have."

Bryan sighed, then shifted his gaze back over to Mordecai.

"They're going to want a set of prints, photos, and autopsy reports to confirm the identities," he said.

Mordecai nodded.

"And let's hold off on telling Jen Donahue," said Bryan. "I'd rather we had something positive to tell her about the guy who took them out."

"It's your call," said Mordecai.

Bryan came around the couch that he'd been standing behind.

"I'd like access to whatever you have on this guy Ivanov. Photos, background, the works. My people will want to follow the trail, and I suspect that I'll be asked to help them with the hunt."

Mordecai handed him a packet, and while Bryan looked it over, Mordecai said, "I've got a source at MI-5 who's already looking into it for us. I'll call him just as soon as we're done to let him know that you're on the way."

꒰

Bryan caught a flight from Israel to Barcelona before transferring to a British Airways flight to Heathrow, London. Once he made it through Immigration, he walked to the baggage claim counter of Terminal One, and after a twenty minute wait to retrieve his bag, he made his way to Customs, where he turned in his form and was quickly ushered through.

Once outside, he spotted a man holding up a sign that bore the name "M. L. Rickman." Bryan identified himself as Rickman and the man escorted him to a waiting car driven by a second male.

Bryan turned up his coat collar to deal with the cold and the wind, a stark reminder that he was no longer in the warm weather of the Middle East.

Once his suitcase was in the boot and he was in the backseat, the driver took off and introductions were made. Both men were members of MI-5, Britain's domestic intelligence service.

"The man who is helping you is waiting at a safe house just east of London proper," said the driver.

"His name?" Bryan asked.

"Major Andrew Whitney, Special Air Service," said the passenger. Bryan nodded. He'd heard the name before.

The weather was cold and rainy. Low gray clouds completely filled the sky. The intermittent showers bogged them down in traffic, and Bryan, who felt drained from the long flights, had trouble keeping his eyes open.

An hour and forty-five minutes later, after crawling along on the M1 and M23 highways, they arrived at a small home on a farm in East Sussex.

The farm was a safe house operated by MI-5, the sister-service to MI-6, which was the United Kingdom's foreign intelligence service.

Bryan stepped out of the car, and while he waited, one of the men removed his bag from the boot. Bryan dragged it into the cottage, where he was met by Whitney, who welcomed him in with a cup of hot tea.

Major Andrew Whitney was the son of a British diplomat who held posts throughout eastern Europe. His mother was a teacher. She traveled with his father and taught at the embassy schools. Whitney studied abroad at his father's postings, but returned to England to get a degree in engineering at Cambridge. Once he graduated, he put in for a posting with the Royal Air Force. He served three years as a helicopter pilot before being accepted into the Special Air Service (SAS). He then spent three years in Belfast where he ran a clandestine intelligence team whose sole responsibility was to identify members and sympathizers of the IRA. For the next two years he was assigned to covert operations, and after that, he was loaned to MI-6 as a liaison officer responsible for foreign inter-agency cooperation.

Whitney was six-foot-two in height with thick brown hair and chiseled features. His bearing as a soldier was obvious; back straight, chin high, and green eyes that took everything in.

The two men took chairs in front of a warming fireplace, and for the next twenty-five minutes, Bryan described for Whitney the details surrounding the death of Anton Korakovsky and the murder of his son

Sean Walker. When he mentioned Walker's relationship to Jennifer Donahue, Whitney cocked his head.

"You say she's a Detective with the LAPD?" he asked.

Bryan nodded.

"I know Jennifer Donahue," said Whitney. He went on to explain to Bryan the details of the investigation he was involved in with LAPD against the IRA, and how he worked with Donahue, who was a good friend of Renée Marin, a prosecutor and the woman he hoped would one day become his wife.

"Small world," said Bryan, who then filled him in on a case he worked on in the Middle East, where Donahue was tangentially involved.

When talk of the mutual acquaintance was completed, Whitney confirmed how they lost Ivanov and his driver in a busy mall.

"MI-5 is doing a computer analysis on all of the CCTV tapes from around the projected time of arrival in the city," said Whitney. "All cameras on routes leading into London will be scanned. The license plate on the car that picked him up was stolen hours before his flight arrived, and they likely had a second car at the mall or close nearby."

"How long before we know something?" Bryan asked.

"Analysis could take a few days, but I'm hopeful that we'll get a lead sooner than that."

"Our mutual friend Mordecai will be sending over a dossier on Ivanov as soon as it's prepared. In the meantime, I brought along a surveillance video showing Ivanov's face. If you want it for your facial recognition file, it might help identify him if he tries to take a flight out of London."

He handed Whitney a thumb drive, and Whitney handed it to one of the MI-5 guys who was having a cup of tea in the kitchen.

"Can you drive this down to HQ and tell them to enter the guy into our facial recognition system?" he said.

"Will do, sir."

When the aide took off, Whitney walked back into the front room and resumed his seat in the fireside chair.

"We've already got people looking for him at all the airports and at the stations along the route through the Chunnel. But that tape of yours will certainly help."

"What's the plan once you locate him?" Bryan asked.

"We'll pick him up and hold him for the Israelis."

"He needs to be interviewed about his employers," Bryan said. "And once he starts talking, I can get word to our NSA and they can check for intercepts in Europe."

"You hungry?" said Whitney.

"Starving," Bryan replied.

"Then grab your coat. There's a place nearby with great food—that is, provided you're okay with fish and chips."

"As long as they've got catsup, I'm good."

✍

Three hours later, Whitney received a copy of a dossier from Mordecai on Sergei Ivanov, the suspected killer of the two Israelis. He thanked the driver who drove it out from the HQ in London. A note explained that the delay had been caused while the contents were translated from Hebrew to English.

He sat down at a table across from Bryan, and after he reviewed each of the documents, he passed them on for Bryan to read.

Sergei Ivanov was a known agent of the SVR who was assigned to London as an aide to a Consulate Trade Representative working out of the Russian Embassy.

"Fortunately, he doesn't have diplomatic immunity," said Whitney. He passed the page he'd been looking at over to Bryan.

"It says here that he's a principal in a Russian-owned security company that operates primarily in Western Europe," said Bryan looking up. "EurX Security? Have you ever heard of them?"

Whitney nodded. "EurX deals primarily with corporate information and computer security systems. But they also offer protection services to executives who travel to areas where physical security is sketchy."

"Well, if that isn't a case of putting the fox in the henhouse, then I sure as hell don't know what is."

Whitney nodded. "It poses the real risk of Russian access to the information storage at all of the companies that *EurX* deals with, as well as corporations doing business with their so-called 'protected companies.'"

"I'm thinking more along the lines of the *physical security* aspect of the corporation. Any chance it might serve as a cover for SVR assassinations?"

"How so?" Whitney asked.

"Oh, I'm just thinking out loud here, but I wonder if Anton Korakovsky was using EurX for his personal protection at the time of his assassination?"

Whitney frowned as he pondered Bryan's question.

"The killer who brought the Polonium to the hotel came in through the front door. He left a radioactive trail, and he's on the hotel's security tape showing up after Korakovsky was already seated in the dining room.

"Still," said Bryan, "the Russians must have known Korakovsky's schedule, and whoever carried in the poison must have had help getting it into Korakovsky's tea."

"You make a lot of sense," said Whitney.

"One more thought," said Bryan. "Doesn't it strike you as suspicious that a guy who is a principal in a large security company is serving as an aide to a consular level representative? It feels like a cover to me."

Whitney nodded. "I'll pass your thoughts on when I get back to HQ."

"Well, now that we know about his connection to the Russian Embassy, it should be easy to track down where he's staying."

"What we've got here is a copy, so I suspect they're already on it. But let me make a call and we'll see where we're at."

Whitney excused himself, and after going into a nearby room, he pulled out a secure satellite phone and placed a call to the Government Communications Headquarters, (GCHQ), an agency responsible for providing signals intelligence and information to the government and the armed forces of the United Kingdom.

Five minutes later he rejoined Bryan.

"We've got his residence in London under surveillance. He's living in a brownstone near the Stonebridge Gardens, in Haggerston. Once the watchers determine that he's in there, the Metropolitan Police Anti-Terror Unit will hit the location and pick him up."

"We're gonna want to get ahold of his computer and phones. That's the best chance we've got to find out who he's working with."

Whitney wholeheartedly agreed. In his role as a Major with the SAS, he had frequently gained a great deal of actionable intelligence from the cell phones of captured terrorist suspects.

"Will your people be monitoring his calls?" Whitney asked.

"Before I got on the plane, NSA told Mordecai that they would, so they'll do a computer run and pull whatever calls they've got where his name comes up. But if you can get a number for his phone, provided he's not using a one-and-dump prepaid phone, we can cut down the search and speed things up."

"Good idea," said Whitney. "In the meantime, I've got a car waiting for us outside. I think we should head back to central London just in case he's home and an arrest goes down right away."

"Sounds like a plan," said Bryan.

As the two men made their way out of the farmhouse, Whitney smiled and said, "Any other thoughts? I'd hate to have to keep calling my boss with *one-at-a-time* ideas."

Bryan smiled back.

"Nope. That's it...*for now*."

TWENTY

FOR THE PAST few days, Donahue did what she could to get back into a set routine. She was still feeling worn down from the trip to Israel and the bug that she was certain she had picked up on the trip.

Her current routine was to go in early to the office, do a workout in the basement gym, shower and change, then work on old cases that still needed to be tied down. She had lunch with colleagues, more work at her desk, then home by five. A long run through the neighborhood was followed by dinner and a few hours of going over the information that her attorney, James McCallum, would send over each day to help her become familiar with her inherited business holdings.

She was only now beginning to realize the enormity of the responsibility that came with the Korakovsky family inheritance. The benefits to her were obviously enormous…but at what cost was still an unknown.

She looked at the time on her cell phone and noted that it was close to eight p.m. She called up Thompson's contact number, and after five rings, it was answered with a typical Thompson quip.

"Shari's Bar and Grill, where kids do the eating and the Mama drinks."

Donahue laughed.

"What's up?" Thompson said.

"Nothing, really. I just wondered if you felt like coming by?"

"Lonely, huh?" She put down the phone for a moment, and Donahue could hear her talking to her mom.

"Okay," she said, "my mom will help me put the boys down. I'll come by as soon as they're tucked in."

"Thanks," said Donahue. "See you then."

An hour later, Thompson showed up at her door, and after they embraced, Donahue led her into the kitchen where she opened a bottle of wine. She poured Thompson a glass of Chablis while sticking to water for herself from a plastic bottle on the counter.

"You're not drinking?" said Thompson who accepted the glass of wine.

"I've still got a queasy stomach, so I don't want to compound it with alcohol."

"Well, cheers," said Thompson. "Thanks for taking me to Israel."

"You're welcome." Donahue took a small sip of the water.

Thompson studied her friend carefully over the top of her glass, and when she did, she found herself becoming markedly concerned. Jennifer looked gaunt. Her hair had lost its shine, her wrists and arms looked thin, and her usual, jovial, irreverent self had seemingly gone into hiding.

Moron! Of course she's not herself. Sean is dead and her life is in a tailspin.

"You look like you've lost a little weight?" said Thompson casually.

"Almost twenty pounds," said Donahue. "I haven't been hungry, and this damn flu bug keeps hanging around."

"My God, Jen! Twenty pounds? You need to check in with your doctor."

Donahue shook her head. "I'll get better once this bug has run its course."

"That twenty-pound-loss isn't all from the flu. You're suffering from depression. That's why you're not eating."

"I'm just not hungry, that's all."

"That's a classic sign of depression. Are you still running?"

"Yeah, when I can."

"Well, maybe you should give it up for a while, at least until you put some of your weight back on."

"It helps to center me," said Donahue with a sigh. "Makes dealing with Sean's death a little easier to take."

"Well, if you don't stop losing weight, I'm gonna drag you in to see a doctor myself. You need to talk about things with a therapist, Jen. There's no shame in admitting that you might need help."

"Fine. Since it appears that you're going to harp at me until I agree, I'll consider it."

"Good, and now that we've got that settled, let's drink to better days."

Thompson sipped her wine and Donahue took another tiny sip of water, which because of her nausea, stayed in her mouth until she could finally swallow it down.

She put down her plastic bottle, then said, "I've been thinking about this inheritance thing and it turns out that I never have to work again. So, I've been wondering if I should just quit the job?"

Thompson chuckled. "If I was in your situation, I sure as hell would quit, but I'm not sure that's the best thing for you just now."

"How so?"

"Well, first and foremost, there's the loss of Sean. You'd be completely on your own. No partner to share the inheritance with. And then there's the issue of your identity and self-worth, both of which currently revolve around your role as a homicide detective. Your work gives your life stability. And I'm saying this from experience, Jen. When I went through my divorce, I kept saying to myself 'at least I've got the kids, and I've still got my job.' If you pull the pin now you've got neither to back you up. You'll have money, sure, but what good is money without people around that you care about and love?"

Donahue shrugged. "I've still got you, don't I?"

Thompson rolled her eyes.

"Of course you do, always and forever, but that's not what I'm talking about. You need human contact every day, Jen, but without the job and the friends you've got in the squad, you might find yourself completely isolated for a good while, and you certainly don't need that kind of loneliness now."

Donahue seemed to weigh what Thompson was saying.

"Maybe you're right."

"Of course I am, and look at it this way. By staying on the job now, it gives you time to plan your future out. It's too important a decision to make in haste. In six months time you might have a completely different outlook on your life."

Donahue hung her head, then sighed.

"What I'd really like to do is find out who ordered Sean's killing and why? I'm not buying the argument that it's just about stealing the family fortune. I think there's more, and I'm not sure that I can answer those questions if I stay on the job?"

"Oh, please!" said Thompson with a laugh. "You've never let the job stop you from doing whatever the hell you wanted to do anyway, so don't give it another thought. We'll solve the case together. That's what friends are for."

She held up her wine as a toast again, and Donahue smiled before raising her bottle of water in a joint salute.

TWENTY-ONE

Andrew Whitney and Bryan Harb raced back to London in an MI-5 sedan, one that was equipped with police lights and a siren, but as they closed in on the area of Haggerston, their driver—a female agent with eight years of experience with the service—shut off the lights and siren when she got within two kilometers of Stonebridge Gardens.

"Do you want me to go straight to the Gardens, sir?" she asked.

"No. We're going to go to the staging area first."

He gave her an address that turned out to be within six blocks of Ivanov's residence. It was an underground parking facility that had been co-opted by the Metropolitan Police as a staging area for units that would be responding to Ivanov's residence for the service of the arrest warrant.

Whitney, who had his earpiece in, was monitoring the radio communications being made by the teams involved in the surveillance operation.

He suddenly turned his head and looked over at Bryan.

"A unit on stakeout is reporting that Ivanov has just arrived at his residence. He showed up in a cab and went into his house. Once the driver dropped him off, the cabbie was followed out of the area before being pulled over. MI-5 wants to get the location where Ivanov got into the cab. That will be followed up by a search of CCTV cameras in that area to see if they can trace his pre-cab movements back to other contacts."

When the Officer-in-Charge of the Yard's Anti-terrorist Squad verified that their target was in his residence, he gave the order for the operation to begin. The first stage involved the use of beat officers to block off the street at both ends. While this was being done, the entry squad got into vehicles and drove in convoy formation directly to the residence location. Whitney's driver followed the convoy, taking the last place behind an ambulance that was there in case of any possible emergency.

They did not use lights and sirens, but each intersection they went through was staffed by a traffic officer who saw to it that the convoy did not have to stop for red lights.

When they got within two blocks, the convoy split into two groups to enable them to arrive at the location from two different directions.

Having prepared for the worst, the team stopped short of the residence building to enable the officers involved to approach the final fifty meters on foot.

The operation went off without a hitch, and in less than thirty seconds, the entry unit crashed through the front door and captured a surprised Ivanov, who had just stepped into the bathroom shower.

A search was begun while Ivanov was given a towel and taken to the front room. There he was allowed to dry off and put on clean clothing that came from his closet in the flat's single bedroom.

Once he was dressed, a bag was put over his head, his wrists were shackled, and he was taken outside to a car where he was placed into the back seat. Four MI-5 agents squeezed into the car and then drove him to a safe house where he was going to be held until they could complete the arrangements necessary to take him to a military base for an in-depth interrogation.

Whitney and Bryan stuck around for the first hour of the search. They wanted to learn what they could about Ivanov's life. They were looking for possible weaknesses that would assist them during the interrogation process. Photographs, love notes, bank books, and food choices—anything relevant was noted and/or taken if it might prove to be of value or give them some form of leverage.

Ivanov's computer and cell phone were seized, and a careful search was conducted by intelligence agents of every piece of paper found within the unit. Anything that offered information of interest was seized, as was anything written in Russian.

When Whitney and Bryan were done looking around, they had their driver take them to the location where Ivanov was currently being held.

It was a safe house just outside of East Cumberland. The location had a basement room which was perfect for conducting interrogations. All four walls were plastered over brick, no windows, and only one door that led to a stairwell that went to the first-floor entry hall. The room was wired for video and sound, and was currently outfitted as an escape-proof jail cell.

When they arrived in East Cumberland, they discovered that the interrogation of Ivanov was already underway. They took seats in the front room on the first floor level, and watched on a TV screen while the two specialists from Five did what they could to soften Ivanov up.

They were already an hour into the questioning when an agent who had been watching the progress of the interview turned his attention to Whitney to give them a catch-up briefing.

"He speaks very good English," said Jim Freeman, a thirty-five year-old from Bournemouth, a seaside resort on the southern coast of England. "Initially, he denied knowing either man, but when he was confronted with the video of him going in and out of Kuznetsov's unit, he admitted that he paid them each a visit, but he says that they were tip-top when he left 'em."

They listened in for the next two hours, but Ivanov was firm in his denials. When one of the Fives came out to catch a break, he huddled with Whitney and Bryan.

"I don't think he's going to crack for a while sir," said Devon Schier, a grizzled, experienced interrogator who was formerly a Sergeant with the Special Air Service (SAS).

Bryan turned to Whitney and asked, "How long can you keep him here?"

"We can hold him in pre-charge detention for twenty-eight days under the terrorism act. After that, we can send him to Israel, where they can hold him indefinitely," said Whitney.

"Then we've got plenty of time. He's already shown that he'll change his story when confronted with video, so maybe we should let him cool his heels while we go through his computer and phone. That way, if we come up with something, we can hit him up with it which will likely force him to change his story."

"That makes sense, but let's shake him up a bit first," said Whitney. "I'd like to leave him thinking that we know a lot more than we do."

"I'm down for that," said Bryan. "Let's do it."

Whitney had Schier go back into the room and call his partner out. After letting Ivanov stew alone for fifteen minutes, they put on balaclavas to hide their faces, then entered the room and took seats at the table directly across from him.

"Hello, Sergei," said Whitney. "Are you comfortable?"

Ivanov looked confused.

"Not really." He raised his hands to show that they were cuffed and chained to a ring in the table top.

Whitney smiled behind the mask.

"If that makes you uncomfortable, Sergei, then you're in for a very rude awakening, mate. This is the best it gets. Once you leave this room, I can promise you it's going to get a whole lot worse."

By not identifying himself, and by planting a seed designed to heighten Ivanov's anxiety, Whitney hoped to set the mood for Bryan's simple recitation of facts.

"Look at me, Sergei," said Bryan.

Sergei shifted his glance from the hooded Whitney to Bryan who could now see the fear in Ivanov's eyes.

"You're probably thinking that all this is just temporary; that your country is going to come to your aid and get you set free. But that's not going to happen, Sergei. No one knows where you are, and if we don't change our minds, no one ever will."

Whitney leaned forward in his chair and Sergei shifted his gaze away from Bryan.

"My American friend here has given us details about the murder in Los Angeles."

"What murder?" Sergei asked. "I've never even been to America—"

"You're insulting us, Sergei," said Bryan. "You know exactly what murder we're talking about."

Bryan also leaned up on the table, where he slowly encroached on Ivanov's personal space. "The killing in L.A. has been classified as a terrorist incident, and that designation has brought my friend and I into the investigation."

"You have a very attractive wife," said Whitney. "And those two little girls of yours are just adorable."

"It's a shame you'll never see them again," said Bryan. "In fact, in a year or two, we'll pass the word on to them that you've gone to the other side and left them behind."

"You can't do that," said Ivanov. "That violates the Geneva convention on the treatment of—"

Whitney laughed out loud.

"You hear that, partner? He still doesn't get it." He reached out with his hand and turned Sergei's face towards his. "No one is ever going to know what happened to you, Sergei. You're going to become a living ghost."

Sergei's initial bravado was beginning to dissipate. He'd been trained to resist torture during his time with the former KGB, but never in his wildest dreams did he believe that he would be kidnapped by a foreign power that would never let anyone know what they'd done.

Bryan jumped in. "You executed the two hit men involved in the L.A. killing, and that means you were a co-conspirator in the L.A.

assassination. According to the laws of the United States, that will subject you to the death penalty."

"Then again," said Whitney, "You committed a double murder in the State of Israel, and that's going to get you a life term without parole in *Rimonim Prison*."

Sergei could sense that they weren't bluffing. They obviously wanted something or they wouldn't be going through this rundown of his likely future if he couldn't find a way to bargain for his freedom.

"What is it you want to know?" he asked.

Whitney nearly smiled. Sergei had flinched first. He looked over at Bryan who gave him a slight nod.

"No promises, Sergei, but we're after the people who put you into this situation. But I don't want you to give us any names today because I'm sure you're gonna hold back, and I'd rather not waste my time. I think it's important that you get a taste of our hospitality first, you know, so that you can make a well-informed decision later down the road."

Sergei was flabbergasted. They didn't want him to talk because they had something awful they wanted him to experience first.

Who does things like that? Who are these men?

Whitney and Bryan got to their feet, but before they left, Whitney said, "We're going to look at your computer records and all your calls for the last five years. I would encourage you to think carefully about whether or not to cooperate. Your spot in this game is over. The only question that remains is whether or not you live or die, and what you'll go through first if execution is in the cards."

They walked out of the room and went upstairs to watch Sergei's actions on the flatscreen. He was staring straight ahead, obviously in thought, and for a moment he let his guard down and tears appeared in the corners of his eyes. He moaned once, then lowered his head to reach his hands so he could wipe away his tears.

"I think we got him," said Whitney.

"He's definitely rattled," said Bryan. "But let's see what a few days in custody will do for his willingness to speak before we start to celebrate."

A young man from Five came into the room and handed Whitney a note. He looked it over, smiled, then glanced over at Bryan as he crunched it up.

"Mordecai sends his best. The Israelis have an interview team on the way. He suggests we let them have a crack at Ivanov."

Bryan smiled. With both murders committed by Ivanov having occurred in Israel, the Mossad would have all the leverage needed to force him to talk for a deal.

"By all means. This should be fun."

The drive from the safe house to the *Doughnut,* in Benhall, was several hours in duration. The Doughnut was in the suburb of Cheltenham, Gloucestershire, in South West England. It was the nickname given to the headquarters of the Government Communications Headquarters (GCHQ), a British cryptography and intelligence agency.

The Doughnut housed 5,500 employees, and was the largest building constructed for secret intelligence operations outside of the United States. The Doughnut was circular in shape, open in the center, and surrounded by car and bicycle parking in concentric rings, thus giving rise to its famous nickname.

Because the original building turned out to be too small for the number of staff that were needed, a second secret building was added at an undisclosed location in the Gloucestershire area. It was staffed by teams from GCHQ, and it was to this location that the two men were headed.

Whitney parked the car in a secure lot and the two of them entered the building using a security system that scanned Whitney's irises to confirm his identity. Once inside, Bryan was presented with a visitors' pass that allowed him to access certain floors in the building. They then made their way to an office where a group of individuals was pouring through the contents of Sergei Ivanov's phone and computer.

"Any hard answers yet?" Whitney asked the chief technician.

"Not yet, sir. We were able to quickly bypass the initial passcode by using *PRISM.* That's a program that gives us backdoor access to programs from nine of the world's top internet companies. His laptop contains five-hundred gigabytes of information while his iPhone contains sixty gigabytes. A quick scan of what we found on both his phone and the laptop indicates that his documents and search histories are primarily written in Standard Russian. That's the modern Russian language since the mid-twentieth century. So, we're going to have to get the information run through a language translation computer program at JTLS, and that might take a few days."

JTLS was the shorthand way to refer to the *Joint Technical Language Service*, a British translation service.

"Anything of interest in his phone directory?" Bryan asked.

"His directory contains phone numbers and contacts, and those will be run through various programs at the Center to see exactly what comes up."

Bryan nodded. He had hoped that the process would be a little faster, but these people were experts and he had no doubt that they were working as fast as they could.

Whitney sighed. Things never went smoothly in any investigation, and this one was no exception.

He turned to Bryan. "Shall we go get something to eat?"

"Maybe later for me," said Bryan. "I need to let my people know what's going on."

"Okay. I'll show you where the SCIF is. You can use it to ensure confidentiality."

A SCIF, or Sensitive Compartmented Information Facility**,** was a high-tech enclosed area within a building that enabled conversations to be held in secrecy. It was also used for the transmission of sensitive or classified information to keep it free from interception by outside interests.

"Where will you be?" Bryan asked.

"I'll be down on the second floor in the cafeteria. Meet me there when you're finished."

Bryan nodded, then followed Whitney to the SCIF. He would update his handler, Dan Murphy, in Cairo, and have him forward a progress report on to Langley.

⁓

After giving Murphy a complete rundown of the events in both Israel and London, Bryan decided to call Donahue and let her know that things were moving along.

He dialed her cell phone number, half expecting that he wouldn't get through, but she answered on the fourth ring.

"Jen? Hi. It's Bryan Harb."

Donahue checked the clock on the nightstand. It was just after 3:00 a.m.

"Hi, Bryan. Is everything okay?"

"Yeah." He took a quick look at his watch, then made the calculation. "I guess I forgot to check the time where you are. Sorry if I woke you up."

She sat up in her bed and turned on the nearby lamp.

"It's okay. It's good to hear your voice."

Bryan sighed. "I can't tell you anything about what's going on. My phone is secure, but yours isn't. I've passed along an update to my friends, and someone you know will be setting up a meet in the very near future."

Donahue understood. It was good to know that her friends were still trying to do something with the lead she'd given them.

"However, I will say this," he added. "Things are going well. We're making progress."

"Thanks, Bry. That's very reassuring." She felt a smile coming on. "How's the weather where you are?"

"Rainy and cold," he replied, then smiled to himself.

She probably thinks I'm still in Jerusalem.

"I'm in London," he said. "Long story. You'll hear all about it later."

She was surprised, but the fact that he wouldn't talk about it meant that there must be a lot of progress related to the search for Sean's killers.

"Well, I'll let you go back to it," she said. "Thanks for everything you're doing."

"My pleasure," he replied. There was a long moment of awkward silence. Then he added, "Hopefully, you can see your way back sometime for another, but longer, visit."

She smiled.

"I'd like that, Bry, thanks."

When the call from Charlotte came in, Donahue was at home in her apartment. She was seated at her breakfast table studying a photograph of Sean that she had taken only a few months ago. He was smiling at her with that twinkle in his eye that she so desperately missed. She tried to blot out the fact that he was permanently gone, preferring to think of his absence as akin to a passenger on a ship that was just below the horizon. Maybe she couldn't see him now, but he lived on somewhere in the great beyond, and one day in the future, they would be together again.

Her previous life seemed to be a distant memory, having ended in a moment of unforeseen violence. She was suddenly mindful of the old Yiddish adage…"*Man Plans, and God Laughs.*" She felt adrift, no longer sensing a purpose for her life. Her work as a detective now seemed to be irrelevant. The new responsibilities she'd inherited still seemed overwhelming and akin to an out-of-body experience. She didn't belong in the role of a CEO, and instead of bringing joy and a feeling of well being, the riches that flowed from her new but unwanted life brought her guilt and a deep sense of sorrow. To be endowed with such good fortune at the expense of her lover's life was a trade off of happiness for money tinged by blood.

How can I enjoy it when every penny I spend will be a constant reminder that it came from the death of the man I still love?

She had been working for the past two hours on putting together a photo album of pictures of herself with Sean, alternately crying and laughing. So, when her phone began to ring, she answered it with a voice that was husky from crying.

But if Charlotte noticed, she was too polite to say anything about it.

"We need to meet," said Charlotte. "Same place, one hour."

"Okay…" But before Donahue could say more the line went dead.

That girl is all business. I wonder what she's like off the clock?

She took time to change from shorts and a t-shirt to jeans, a blouse, and a jacket. She wore her handgun in a shoulder holster, and when she stepped outside, she found her driver waiting at the curb. He had taken to parking outside her apartment during the days. The only time he was gone was during the evenings when she told him that he wouldn't be needed.

She knew her security detail was close behind, so once she was in the car, she dialed the number she had for Bernstein and told him she was headed for the Westside mall.

"Once the driver drops me off, I want the team to remain on the upper level. They're to stay out of the below-ground parking structure."

Bernstein was confused.

"Are you sure you want to be alone?"

"I'll be fine," she assured him. "I'm meeting an informant related to my work, and this person will take off if any members of my team are spotted."

"Understood," he told her. "I'll phone Mr. Otero and give him the necessary instructions."

When they got to the mall, Donahue had her driver drop her off at the curb just outside the main entrance. She made her way into the structure, located the escalator, and took it down two floors. She waited there at the bottom of the escalator, watching to see if anyone came down after her. But no one did, and once she was convinced that her team members were doing what they'd been instructed to do, she ventured down to the fourth level below ground where people rarely ever parked.

She waited at the bottom of the escalator, and right on time, Charlotte showed up. She led Donahue to a dark corner of the lot where Donahue explained to her about her security detail and the fact that they were waiting for her up on level one.

"It's my new reality," said Donahue with a shrug.

Charlotte appreciated the candor and the heads up.

"It will take a while to get used to," she said, "but soon you'll forget that they're even there."

"I was told you would have a progress report for me," said Donahue. She was anxious to know what was going on.

Charlotte nodded. "The two suspects in Jerusalem were identified and tracked down. Unfortunately, both of them are dead." She gave Donahue a few seconds to digest the information. "Apparently, they were shot to death in their respective apartments, likely to sever their connection to the people who ordered your fiancé's death."

Donahue started to shake. This was a scenario she had never anticipated. Now she would never know who ordered Sean's death.

"Our agent involved in the investigation has reported that the man suspected of killing the assassins was tracked from Israel to London. He is a Russian."

Donahue's eyes lit up.

They know the identity of the man who killed Sean's killers? Thank God! There's still a trail.

"Where is he?" Donahue asked.

"In custody. The authorities picked him up without incident. He's being held by MI-5. They can hold him for twenty-eight days, and at that point, he'll be transferred to the Israelis who can hold him without trial indefinitely." Charlotte smiled. "Because of the trail that seems to lead back to Russia, the two killings are being classified as a terrorist action conducted to impede an investigation into a murder committed in Los Angeles."

"Can you tell me his name?"

Charlotte shook her head no.

Donahue was disappointed, but grudgingly understood. There could be many reasons for keeping everything close to the cuff. Sources, logistics, timing, politics…all were factors that needed to be considered when dealing with international intrigue.

"Do we know what he's saying during his interrogation?" she asked.

"He underwent a preliminary interrogation, but has not yet revealed what was behind the killing of your fiancé or who ordered it. And he still hasn't revealed who ordered the killing of the two hitmen. But eventually he'll tell us what he knows. I'm sure of that."

Charlotte knew a great deal more than Donahue did about what went on during black operations, so Donahue knew that she was just going to have to wait and take what Charlotte said at her word.

"I've been told by my boss that the NSA has been asked by MI-6 to provide them with any and all telephone intercepts from conversations between the subject and all numbers they can connect to him. There are quite a few, so it could take a while before they can review them all."

"I'm so glad that you guys are willing to see this through," said Donahue. "I was afraid that I was going to have to do everything on my own."

"I know I don't need to say this, but I will anyway. Everything I've told you is confidential and classified as top secret. The fact that you're being read in on all of this is dangerous to us and to you. So, don't repeat any of this to anyone, not even your partner. Understand?"

"I won't say a thing. Please thank your boss for keeping me up to speed."

"I'll tell him," said Charlotte with a smile.

"I don't suppose you guys have any new information on why Sean was in protective custody?"

Charlotte shook her head. "The FBI is unusually close-lipped about that. My boss says only a couple of people at the top of the Bureau have ever been read in, and they're not yet ready to speak about it to the CIA."

"How about the Marshals Service? Wouldn't they know?"

"Someone there would know. They'd have to in order to set up a plan for his security."

"So, if the leak is with the Marshals, how would they go about discovering who it was?"

Charlotte took a quick look around before she was reassured that they were still alone.

"The FBI is working on it, but it's slow. They've compiled a list of everyone involved in the planning and relocation, and warrants have been issued for phone and banking records. I would imagine that they'll soon begin interviews and mandatory polygraph examinations, so if one of them is involved, they'll get to the bottom of it."

"Okay," said Donahue. "Thanks for the briefing. Let me know if I can do anything to help."

Charlotte smiled. "How are you adjusting to your new role as a corporate CEO?"

Donahue rolled her eyes. "It's in the hands of the lawyers for now, but once the court is done with the probate, and once I have a grasp of the entire operation, then I'll figure out what I can do and exactly who I can rely on."

"Stay safe," said Charlotte. "Until we know what's behind Sean's death, we can't say for sure that you're not at risk."

"I will," said Donahue. "Thanks."

TWENTY-TWO

DONAHUE WROTE DOWN the address, then thanked McCallum before hanging up. She got to her feet, picked up her purse, then looked over the partition into Thompson's cubicle.

"You got time to take a ride with me?" Donahue asked.

"Sure," said Thompson. "What's up?"

"Surprise," said Donahue.

They signed out on the board in the squad room, writing, "*In the field*" after their unit designation. No one ever questioned such an entry, as detectives in the RHD were afforded great latitude concerning how they spent their time during their on-duty shifts. The unspoken rules of the job were clear. When there was work to be done, it took preference over everything else, even family, sleep, or vacations. It wasn't unheard of to work for days in a row on a case with only a few hours of sleep when collapse was imminent. But when the work tapered off, no one ever batted an eye when personal business was required to ensure an even keel to life outside of the department.

They walked from the PAB to their car which was parked in a nearby multi-story lot. After making their way west on the Santa Monica freeway, Donahue switched to the 405 northbound, finally getting off on Sunset Boulevard. She headed west for a mile or so, then turned north towards the foothills in Brentwood.

As she drove up a winding road into the hills, Donahue slowed each time they passed a gated driveway, seeming to be searching for a specific address.

"What are we looking for?" Thompson asked.

Donahue looked over and smiled.

"You'll see."

When she finally spotted the address she was looking for, Donahue brought the car to a stop in the street, put it into park, and simply stared at the gate and what lay beyond.

Donahue's security detail had pulled up behind her and were waiting patiently two car lengths to the rear.

The wall around the property was at least twelve feet high. The front gate was solid with decorative iron scrolls. The home, wherever it was located, was completely hidden behind the gate and the walls.

Donahue sighed, still unable to accept the fact that this property was now hers.

"So who lives here?" Thompson asked, which broke Donahue out of her trance.

Donahue sighed. "Apparently, I do."

"What?"

Donahue put the car into gear and turned from the street into the driveway, stopping right up at the still closed gate.

A camera was visible up on the wall, and when Donahue looked up, the gate began to open.

"Holy shit!" said Thompson who watched the gate slide back. "No fucking way!"

"You're telling me," said Donahue, who was now thoroughly shaken. This was her first visit to the home, and the entire experience was causing her to deal with a stream of memories and conflicting emotions.

"Did you just buy this?" Thompson asked as they drove up the winding driveway towards the house.

"Sean bought it for me as a wedding present. This is the first time I've seen it."

Thompson didn't know how to react to that, so she didn't respond. But her mouth remained open in undisguised surprise.

The grounds were lush and the driveway was wide and circular. She pulled up next to a black Mercedes sedan that was parked to the right of the front entryway.

"Let me guess," said Thompson. "Is the Mercedes yours, too?"

"It belongs to James McCallum. He's the lawyer who oversees everything connected to the estate."

For a few moments, all they could do was stare at the home. It was clearly a mega mansion, one that would rival anything in the Brentwood area.

"I'm just blown away, Jen. I can't wrap my head around all of this. Yours is the biggest place I've ever seen."

"How do you think I feel?" said Donahue. She couldn't stop staring at the home.

"I can't imagine, babe. It's like we've just gone down the rabbit hole and ended up in Jennifer's Wonderland."

The front door opened and McCallum walked out onto the front porch. Next to him was a matronly woman of Hispanic descent who was dressed in the uniform of a housekeeper.

"Who's that?" said Thompson.

"That's McCallum, the lawyer. But the lady with him? I have no idea."

They climbed out of the car, and Donahue introduced Thompson to McCallum who introduced them both to Marcelina Revolorio.

"Marcelina is your *grand dam*. She will oversee the house and the other staff members who will work here to keep your house in order."

Thompson looked over at Donahue and silently mouthed, *No shit?*

"Would you like to come in?" McCallum asked.

Donahue nodded, and as he led them inside, he said, "Your home is Mediterranean, fifteen-thousand square feet, on five acres of hilltop land. There are eight bedrooms and fifteen bathrooms, a theater, a solarium, a professional kitchen, a gym, several pools and hot tubs in the backyard, a tennis court, and a ten car garage."

"Several pools?" said Thompson. "You mean more than one?"

"Two," said McCallum. "One is a small pool with current which allows you to swim in place. The other is a full-size pool for entertaining."

Thompson could only close her eyes and slowly shake her head. Words failed her.

The tour of the downstairs was interrupted when Donahue left them to open a rear door that led out into the back yard. Thompson and McCallum followed her out, while Marcelina remained inside.

The border on the back of the property was below the horizon. On the upper level were the two pools and a pool house, and from the upper yard, the view of the city was panoramic. It extended from downtown Los Angeles to the Pacific Ocean, and in the distance, on a clear day, one could see the Island of Catalina. It was as spectacular a view as money could buy.

The lower two acres contained a lighted tennis court and a large section of the property was devoted to a garden that was full of fruit trees and a large glass hot house.

According to McCallum, the previous owner, a CEO of a business tech firm, was an avid grower of orchids.

Beyond the property line, farther down the hill, were multi-million dollar mega homes on sizable residential lots.

"This is a lot to take in," said Donahue.

"It's pretty freakin' amazing!" said Thompson. She noted that Donahue was displaying conflicted feelings, so she walked over and gave her a hug.

"Sean really loved you, honey, and by living here, you'll be making him smile."

They slowly wandered back up to the house, admiring the pools and the hot tub. When they got inside, McCallum explained that he had to leave for a previously-scheduled meeting that he was reluctant to cancel.

Donahue told him to go, and he explained that he would return just as soon as he could. He wanted to explain to her the ins and outs of the home's security features.

"So, if you'll excuse me, Ms. Donahue, I'll have Marcelina give you a tour of the inside of your home."

He left the location, and Marcelina escorted the two women through the rest of the house. When Thompson saw the theater with the twelve individual reclining seats, she flopped into one and smiled.

"I know who's gonna be throwing the next Super Bowl party."

Donahue winked. She was over the shock of the size and beauty of the home, and she had to admit to herself that it was a place that had everything one could only possibly imagine.

When Marcelina finished giving them the tour, she excused herself to go to her office which was just off the kitchen. She explained that the new staff had been given the day off in anticipation of Donahue's wanting to tour without distraction.

"They'll be back in the morning, Ms. Jennifer."

Donahue and Thompson settled on a couch in the living room. They talked about the furnishings, which Thompson felt were "just perfect," particularly the four framed, blown-up photographs of Sean and Jennifer together which lined one of the living room's inner walls.

"They're beautiful," said Thompson, referring to the photos. "Who took them?"

"A photographer friend of Sean's," said Donahue. "We had them done right after we got engaged."

The way she said it, Thompson could tell that Donahue had very mixed emotions about the photos.

"You can always take them down if they make you sad, then hang them up later when you feel the time is right."

"I suppose," said Donahue. Thompson was making good sense.

"Don't say anything to anyone about the house, Shari. You're the only one I trust to know about this stuff."

"I've got your back, Jen. I'll never say a word unless you tell me to. So, when are you planning to move in?"

"Later this week. Mr. Bernstein says there's still work to be done to harden this place, so it's going to take a few more days to get everything wired up properly."

"With a place this big, you're probably going to need to have security guards here as well."

Donahue sighed. "Apparently, the security system is going to be state-of-the-art, and there will be a full team on duty around the clock. They're going to be using a cottage near the front gate for their base of operations."

"Makes sense," said Thompson. "What are you going to do about Sean's duplex?"

"McCallum has advised the leasing company that we'll be moving everything out sometime this week. I'm going to go over there later today and sort things out. I'll keep some of the stuff, but the rest will go to charity."

"Do you want some help?" Thompson asked.

"Thanks for the offer, but I need to do it by myself. It will give me a bit of closure."

"Well, if you change your mind, let me know."

Donahue got to her feet and checked her watch. "We should probably go back to the office for a while."

Thompson nodded. "I want you to invite me back when you get moved in. I want to see your view of the city at night."

Donahue smiled. "I'll have the cook whip something up, and if the weather's good, we can eat outside under the stars."

"You have a cook?" Thompson asked.

"According to Marcelina, I do."

Thompson shook her head in disbelief.

"Jeez, Jen! This just gets better and better. And I was telling myself

I wasn't going to be jealous, that you're a good person, and that you deserve all of this. But you've got a cook? *Oh, my God, Jen!*"

Her eyes met Donahue's. "Any chance you'd consider adopting me?"

TWENTY-THREE

KASEY SMITTEN LEFT her desk and made her way down the hallway to Clausner's outer office. She spoke to his secretary who asked her to take a seat while she buzzed him on her phone.

When she hung up, she said, "He'll see you now, Kasey. By the way, nice shoes."

Kasey smiled. She got to her feet, knocked on his door, then entered and closed it behind her.

"Grab a seat," said Clausner. He folded his arms across his chest and leaned back in his chair.

Smitten did as instructed, then waited for him to tell her to proceed.

"So, where are we at?" he finally said.

"With the homicide investigation or the search for a possible leak?"

"Both," he said. "Let's start with the homicide."

For the next ten minutes, she covered old ground, telling him everything they knew about the murder and the two men involved, but when she got to the killings in Israel, he sat up straighter and listened with new intensity.

"The Mossad has tracked the killer to London, and it's my understanding that he's been taken into custody. MI-5 and the Mossad are presently putting him through an intense interrogation, and once they're finished, he'll be extradited to Israel to face the music there."

Clausner smiled. "So, that means we can close out the Sean Walker case. You've done a good job, Smitten."

She frowned. Clausner appeared to be interested only in his clearance statistics, and while she hated to burst his bubble, she also took pleasure in knowing that her protection came from higher up in D.C., and for the moment, he was nothing more than a mild irritation.

"Actually, sir, the investigation isn't over. We still have to determine how Sean Walker was identified, and we want to know who ordered his killing and why?"

"That's for your people in D.C. to worry about." Clausner cocked his head. "As far as I'm concerned, your work here is concluded now that Walker's killers have been identified and neutralized."

She stared at him wide-eyed. Was he telling her that it was time to go back to D.C.?

"Look, sir. I don't know what I've done, if anything, to warrant your apparent irritation with my partner and I being here, but I would remind you that I answer to a different supervisory chain in D.C. and not directly to you." She got to her feet. "I'll be speaking to my boss about the situation here, and I suspect he'll be calling you to clarify my operating instructions."

Clausner may have been a life-long misogynist, but he wasn't a complete fool. After all, he was Agent-in-Charge in one of the Bureau's most prestigious field offices. His problem was simple. He had long resented the influx of young women into what was once an old-boys bastion of God-fearing, conservative, mostly Mormon, Caucasian males. And in the past, when the leadership had passed him over for plum assignments, he couldn't help but feel anger towards those who had climbed the promotional ladder with far less experience and time on the job.

He was within a few years of being eligible for retirement, and common sense dictated that he should avoid an all-out row with this fair-haired, D.C., fast-rising woman, so as not to affect his current assignment with the finish line so near at hand.

"Hold on," he told her. "Perhaps I was a little hasty by suggesting that we close the case out. I'm not sure how we got off to such a rocky start, but you're welcome to work out of this office and to have whatever resources you need to get your case done."

Smitten gave him a tight smile. "Would you like a briefing on the other part of the investigation?"

"Of course," he said, as if a tension-filled moment had not just passed between them.

"Everyone in the Marshal's Office and the courtroom proceedings involving Sean Walker's new identity have been identified. They've started giving them polygraphs, and so far more than half the names on the list have been cleared. While the polys are going on, they're expanding the investigation into Walker's personal dealings since coming to Los Angeles on the off chance that someone connected to his business operations may have had a connection with the SVR."

"Don't exclude his fiancé," said Clausner. "She has certainly ben-efitted from his death more than anyone else."

Smitten rolled her eyes. "There's no way she's involved. Her background is clean, her reputation is good, and she was completely unaware of Walker's background. I personally saw the shock on her face when she learned about who he was. She wasn't faking it. I'm certain of that."

"I'm not so sure. When there's a great deal of money involved, and there certainly is in this case, then anyone in line for such a windfall needs to be thoroughly vetted."

Smitten sighed. She hated to admit it, but he was probably right. The old adage of "follow the money" certainly applied here, and up to this point, the working theory was that the Russians wanted the family assets back.

But then again, they shouldn't ignore the obvious.

"Do you want her phones tapped as well?"

"Of course," he replied. "We need to determine who she knows, where she goes, and who she talks to. If you need some people to run a surveillance, let me know. I would also suggest that we get ahold of her bank records. Any large payouts might be money going to whoever arranged the killing. Talk to her lawyer. You know, the one who oversees Walker's assets. What's his name? McCallum? Yes, that's it. Ask him about her accounts, and impress upon him the secrecy we will need to maintain. Tell him the secrecy is for her sake if she's not involved, and for the integrity of our investigation if it turns out that she is."

Smitten got to her feet. She would look into Donahue's background, but she had no intention of speaking any further with McCallum. To tip him off would be a mistake. She had no doubt where his loyalties lay, and unless they had some tangible evidence that Donahue was somehow involved, there was no reason to stir up that hornet's nest.

But to keep Clausner at bay, she would request a FISA warrant to set up a tap on Donahue's phones. She was pretty sure the court would issue one, and if she wasn't involved, no one would be any the wiser.

My God how I hate having anything to do with Clausner. The man is a dinosaur.

TWENTY-FOUR

WHITNEY AND BRYAN were sitting in the upstairs living room in the safe house. They were once again watching the interview of Sergei Ivanov who was in the basement. The interrogation was being projected onto a wall-mounted TV screen, and the pair of agents asking the questions were a male and female from the Israeli Mossad. Also in the room was a British MI-6 specialist who was playing the role of the good guy.

Bryan leaned forward in his chair. Up to now Ivanov had told them a lot of nothing, but he looked tired and agitated, no doubt from a lack of sleep and the incessant ear worm music that had played non-stop for the past five hours. The song was the theme song from a kids TV show called Mr. Rodgers' Neighborhood, and there was no doubt in the minds of the interrogators that a few more hours of that annoying little tune was likely to turn Ivanov into a babbling idiot.

"He's tougher than I thought he would be," said Bryan. "If I had to listen to that song, I would have cracked in twenty minutes."

"But you have to admit, the Israelis are doing a good job of keeping him off balance."

Indeed, the Israelis were enjoying the role of being the bad guys, and they were brutally hammering Ivanov with questions followed by threats.

They watched the process for another ten minutes, but Ivanov still didn't break. The Israelis signaled that they were about to take a break, so Whitney turned to Bryan and asked, "You want to take a crack at him?"

"Sure," he said, "but it's going to take time. Can you give me a commitment without interruption?"

"Let me ask," said Whitney. He got to his feet and left the room.

✑

Whitney returned several minutes later with a specialist in tow from GCHQ. He introduced the man to Bryan, then the three of them sat down to discuss the situation.

"His cell phone log contained hundreds of calls to Moscow," said the specialist. "The numbers were checked against known numbers for SVR personnel and other governmental agencies. It appears that close to twenty-eight percent of his calls were to known agents of the SVR."

"I'm not surprised," said Whitney. "He's clearly an active operative."

The specialist continued, "The larger percentage of the calls were to employees of EurX, his security group, and with the assistance of the Mossad, we've discovered several calls made to the two suspects in the Los Angeles murder."

"Can I get a list of the calls made to the SVR agents?" said Bryan. "I want to pass the info on to the NSA so they can do a computer search for the calls they intercepted as part of their routine surveillance."

The specialist passed over a list of the numbers and Bryan took a quick look before putting it down.

"How about Ivanov's computer?" Whitney asked.

"His computer log listed more than twenty-five-hundred emails and more than a thousand deleted ones that were recovered. Many of them were encoded, but we used a program that identifies the coding sequence and the encrypted messages were decoded rather quickly."

"Have they been translated yet?" Bryan asked.

"It's happening as we speak."

Bryan turned to Whitney. "Ivanov was sloppy. A good agent would have changed out his computer and cell phones on a regular basis."

"Once in a while we get lucky," said Whitney.

"One more thing," said the GCHQ specialist. "My people are matching the cell phone recipients' calls with the emails on Ivanov's computer, and they will be putting them together into a timeline. If there was a hit ordered using the phone or emails, and if the NSA can provide us with the content of the intercepted calls, then you'll be able to see the progression of the planning both before and after the killings."

Both Bryan and Whitney were impressed. The amount of time being saved by having the GCHQ computers do the matching would certainly be considerable.

"Can I get a copy of the raw data for my people?" Bryan asked. "I'd like to process everything through our computers to see if we can come up with any additional contacts on our side of the pond."

"I don't see any problem with that," said Whitney. "If you link any third parties to the people we provide you with, we'd like a list of them as well. The wider we can spread this web of contacts, the better chance we have of getting a look at the SVR's bigger picture."

The specialist nodded to Bryan. "I can provide you with digital copies within the hour."

Bryan turned to Whitney. "I'll pass it on to Langley through a secure server at my Embassy."

When the specialist left the room, Whitney asked, "What happens if it turns out that the order to kill came from the very top?"

"I don't know," said Bryan, "but an assassination on U.S. soil of an American citizen will not be taken lightly, and I would suspect that it would mean a lot of headaches for Putin and the Russian Federation."

TWENTY-FIVE

KASEY SMITTEN AND Rebecca Folsey sat in front of the camera inside the SCIF, located within the FBI headquarters in West Los Angeles. At the other end of the call was their boss in D.C., Deputy Director Michael C. Hemet, the current head of the Anti-Terrorism Unit.

"How's the weather out there?" Hemet asked. He was glancing out the window of his office. "It's raining like there's no tomorrow back here."

"Sunny and seventy," said Smitten with a smile. "Not to be confused with 'sunny and seventy' yesterday and with 'sunny and seventy' tomorrow."

"Don't rub it in," said Hemet with a laugh. "I can always order you back here for a meeting."

"Or, you could come out here for the progress report," said Smitten.

"That's what I like about you, Kasey. Always working the angles." He then focused his attention on Folsey. "How's it going, Rebecca?"

"Just fine, Boss."

"Good. So, bring me up to speed?"

"We've pulled together a preliminary report on Donahue. Nothing stands out as suspicious. She lives within her means, has an unblemished record with the LAPD—has a medal of valor by the way—and our interviews of people around her indicate that no one feels that she could have been involved in Sean Walker's death. Clausner is weighing the idea of offering her a polygraph, but a decision has yet to be made."

"What do you think about giving her a poly?" Hemet asked.

"The truth? It's a waste of time. She's clean, Boss. And she's been helpful to us in identifying the two shooters. No way she's involved."

"I would agree," he said. "You tell Clausner to hold off on a poly. We need to be able to work with her in the future, so I don't want her pissed off for no good reason."

"I'll tell him, but he's not gonna handle it well. He's out of his element on this one, Boss. He's everything you warned me about."

"Well, keep this under wraps," said Hemet, "but I spoke to the Director and he's gonna do something about it."

"That's great," said Smitten.

"What about the other half of the investigation?" Hemet asked.

Rebecca Folsey cleared her throat. "Between the D.C. operation and our work out here we've made significant progress tackling the background info on all of those in L.A. with knowledge of Sean Walker's true identity. Overall, the investigation both here and in D.C. has narrowed down our possible suspects to four people. Three of them are with the US Marshals Office, and one is the FBI Agent-in-Charge in our Baltimore field office."

Hemet frowned. "You think one of our own might be involved?"

"It's not likely. We gave polygraphs to him and the three Marshals, and of the four, only one failed his preliminary polygraph exam. He's a senior member of the US Marshals Office here in Los Angeles. His name is Charles Beeson. When we confronted him about it, he chalked his failure up to nerves, but the examiner believes that the showing of deception is correct.

"So, our focus is now on Beeson. He set up Walker's new ID and handled Walker's west coast resettlement. He's been offered another test and has agreed to take it. In the meantime, we've gone over his bank and phone records, and so far, we've come up with nothing. The calls he made on his cell phone do not show any links to the FSB, the SVR, or any of their known fronts or agents."

"So, nothing to connect him to anything except for the fact that he was deceptive on his polygraph?"

"That's right," said Folsey, "but there was one call of note. It was to a number at the White House for the President's National Security Advisor, Retired General Lindsey Rush. The reason behind that call is unknown. Beeson's finances are still being checked, but the man appears to be living within his financial means."

"I think we should consider running a bank check on Beeson's wife," said Hemet.

"I agree," said Smitten.

"Get a search warrant, Rebecca, but keep it sealed. We don't want the press to get ahold of it. And as for Beeson, have him come in for an interrogation. Let's see if he lawyers up."

"Will do," said Smitten. "Also, we're waiting to hear what's going on with the suspect the Brits picked up. Any word on when we can get a look at any intelligence they might have uncovered?"

"Nothing yet," he said, "but I'll look into it. Anything else?"

"No sir," said Folsey.

"Okay, then. That does it for me, ladies. Enjoy your sunny weather."

"Try to stay dry," said Smitten.

She heard him chuckle before hanging up.

⋙

Donahue was still feeling under the weather, but when her nausea subsided, she notified her security detail that she was going to go over to Sean's old duplex to meet with the movers who were going to pack things up.

A limousine picked her up, and the drive over took less than fifteen minutes. The movers were already there and waiting, so she spoke to them for a couple of minutes, explained what she wanted them to do, then went inside by herself to take a last look around.

She began by going room to room, picking up small items, sorting clothes that would go to charity, and collecting photographs and little souvenirs that had meant so much to her in the past.

In a dresser drawer she came across Sean's favorite sweater. She picked it up and smelled it. Detecting his scent brought tears to her eyes. She went into the kitchen and located a large plastic bag which she used to seal up the sweater. She was hoping to preserve the smell which she knew she would want to experience one more time when she was back at home, alone, and free to cry out loud.

A bookshelf in the living room had been knocked down during the attack on Sean. Books were still lying in a heap on the floor, so she slowly began to pick them up. She was sorting them into two piles, those she wanted to keep and those that would be given away.

One of the books was *Crime and Punishment, by Fyodor Dostoevsky.* A Russian classic, it was one of Sean's favorites. She remembered the bet they'd made, the one she'd lost, and the fact that she'd never gotten around to paying it off by reading the book. That had been important to Sean, so important, in fact, that he even mentioned her promise to read it in his final taped message to her.

She clutched it to her breast, then settled into an easy chair for a few moments to read the first page and see if it was something she might actually be interested in reading.

The title page said that it was written in 1865. She read the first page, found it interesting, but before she could go to the second, she heard a knock at the door.

It was the moving men who wanted to get started. She let them in, pointed out the stack of clothes that were to be packed separately for charity, then asked them to box up everything else for delivery to her home in Brentwood.

As she turned to go, one of the movers said, "Do you want me to take that for you?" He was referring to the book in her hand.

"I guess so." She handed it over. "Put it with the other books and deliver all of them to my home."

She walked to the door, took a final look around, then left the duplex for the very last time.

⁓

Bryan entered the interview room without a balaclava covering his face. He figured that Ivanov was never going to rejoin the outside world again, so it might be worth the more human touch as a technique for getting him to see the futility of his situation.

Ivanov had just endured another two hours of the earworm song and was literally on the psychological edge. When Bryan walked in without his balaclava, Ivanov's face reflected concern and trepidation as he slowly concluded that a change was in the air.

The tough guy approach used by the Israelis had been the perfect foil for the softer approach that Bryan now intended to use.

He took a seat at the table across from Ivanov, who was still securely tethered to a ring that was welded to the metal tabletop.

"Can we stop the music?" Bryan said, looking around.

The music shut off a few seconds later.

"That's better," said Bryan. He locked eyes with Ivanov. "I hate that song, don't you?"

Ivanov didn't know whether to laugh or cry. He recognized the man's voice from the first interview, and he was still confused by the fact that the man was showing his face. He was also surprised by how young the man was. His previous mental picture, based on voice and eyes only, was of a quite experienced male of much older age.

"It's not so bad," said Ivanov. "*The Macarena*" is the one that really drives me crazy."

"I wouldn't say that too loudly," said Bryan. "The boss is listening, and he's going to remember that."

For a moment Ivanov's eyes widened with fear, then noticed that Bryan was smiling and that confused him even more.

"Don't worry, Sergei. We all hate that song, so it's been banned from your playlist."

Ivanov couldn't tell if he was telling the truth, but he hoped so. Tired or not, from this point on, he would have to be very careful about what came out of his mouth.

Bryan began, "When we last sat down with you, I told you that we would give you a little time to consider your situation. Since that time, we've done a great deal of work, going through your emails, resurrecting the ones you tried to delete, and tracing your phone calls back to Mother Russia. We've put together a timeline, noted your calls to the victims in Israel—both before and after the murder in Los Angeles—and whether you know it or not, and I suspect you do, the National Security Administration has transcribed all of your calls both to and from Russia, and it has given us a pretty clear picture of your involvement in the killings that occurred."

He paused for a moment to gauge Ivanov's reaction and noticed that a twitch had begun to manifest itself just below the man's left eye. It convinced him that Ivanov's stress level was slowly reaching its peak.

"I read over our dossier on you, Sergei. Is it correct that you began your tenure with the KGB when you were only nineteen?"

The change in direction confused Sergei, but he was grateful for the detour. It would give him more time to think about what this man was saying about their investigation.

Ivanov nodded. "I needed a job and it paid well. And you? When did you begin working for your government? I presume you are an American?"

"That's right," said Bryan. "I started shortly after I got out of college, right after 9-11."

"Ah, yes. That was a terrible time. On that we can both agree."

"Your wife and children, Sergei? When did you last visit with them?"

Ivanov looked away, clearly mulling it over.

"Six months, maybe more; it's been too long."

"Your wife, Natasha? She's a beautiful woman, Sergei. And your two daughters, *Lina* and *Anna*? What are they now? Six and four?"

He's demonstrating to me that he's done his homework. If nothing, this man is well-prepared.

"You are correct, six and four."

"A delightful age," said Bryan. "Which brings me to my next point. You do realize that your masters are doing everything they can to eliminate any evidence that directly connects them to the murder of Mikel Korakovsky in Los Angeles?"

"It would appear that way," Ivanov agreed.

Good, thought Bryan. *He's accepting the concept that he's at risk with his own people.*

"I'm glad you're willing to acknowledge that," said Bryan, "because we've intercepted some communications that would seem to indicate that they plan to eliminate you, too."

"They wouldn't do that," said Ivanov with a shaky voice. "I have too many friends in how you say…*high places?*"

Bryan slowly shook his head.

"You overestimate your importance to them, Sergei. They will kill everyone in the chain to protect the people at the top, and they've decided that you are expendable." He paused momentarily to let that sink in. "As I'm sure you know, or maybe you don't, the agent they sent to kill Anton Korakovsky, Mikel's father? He is now dead."

Ivanov laughed. "That's what they want you to believe. That he died in an automobile crash."

Bryan smiled. "That was their story, I agree. But we tracked him to Ozersk, in Siberia, where he received a bullet to the brain for his trouble."

Ivanov's eyes widened.

"Ah!" said Bryan. "I guess you didn't know."

Ivanov said nothing. He was trying to make sense of what this man was telling him, and to be honest, it made sense. Putin would not want to leave any proof lying around that could connect him to the use of Polonium 210 as a weapon of assassination.

"See, here's what has me worried," said Bryan. "When they discover that you've disappeared, they're going to pay a visit to your lovely wife and daughters. They'll suspect that you've gone over to the other side and they'll want to have some leverage." He shook his head in feigned sympathy. "You know how Putin likes to play the game. He'll hold them for a while, and when he doesn't hear from you, he'll assume the worst. And as we've learned with the Korakovsky killings, he's not averse to going after family members to serve as an example to others."

Bryan shrugged his shoulders and watched as Sergei hung his head.

Got him! Give him a few moments, then try to close the deal.

He watched his quarry as Ivanov slowly ran through all the permutations of his present situation and came to the conclusion that he was totally fucked. They had him right where they wanted him, he knew that for a certainty, and frankly, the possibility that he would be caught had always been a risk that he'd been willing to accept. But this man spoke the truth. His family was at risk, and that was a possibility that he had never seriously considered.

He had killed the two gangsters in Jerusalem. Apparently, they had all the proof they needed, so life in prison or death—either one—would be the end of his life as he knew it. But it was his family that was the only thing that mattered now, and if something could be done to protect them, then he was willing to sing like a bird.

"I can tell that you're beginning to realize the precariousness of your current situation, Sergei. And I'm sure that your concerns for your wife and daughters is genuine. So, since the Russians still don't know that we've picked you up, there's still time to do something to protect your wife and daughters. If you cooperate with us and give us everything we want to know, we can act right away and safely get them out. That's all I can promise you, Sergei, but here's the stick that comes with the carrot. If you don't choose to cooperate with us, the news of your arrest will be made public, and if that happens, then there is nothing we can do for your wife and your girls."

Ivanov knew that his leverage was gone. It was family or nothing. His fate was already sealed, but his Natasha and the girls still had a chance, and if that was all he could do, it might be enough just knowing that they were going to be safe.

"Putin will track them down," said Ivanov. "How will you protect them?"

"We can give them new identities, an income, and relocation to a town where your girls will grow up as naturalized citizens."

Ivanov shook his head.

"Not good enough. That didn't protect Mikel Korakovsky. So, if you want my cooperation, you'll have to do better than that."

Interesting, thought Bryan. *He might know something about how the protection program was breached?*

"I'll tell you what, Sergei. If we have your full cooperation, we can get your wife and the girls out tonight, bring them to London, and arrange for them to be protected here until we can guarantee their safety in the free world. How's that sound?"

It could work, thought Ivanov, *and perhaps I can negotiate a chance to see them again?*

"Okay," he finally replied. "I have some information that I will disclose, but I want them brought here first. I want to see them, to explain what's happened. Once I know that they're safe and that Putin can't reach them, I'll tell you things that I know you will want to hear."

Bryan would prefer to start the debriefing before agreeing to remove Ivanov's family from Moscow, but time really was of the essence, and irrespective of whether or not Ivanov accepted his proposal, Bryan had no wish for the man's wife and daughters to suffer for the sins of their husband and father.

After all, Ivanov was a professional, a soldier in the service of his country, just as Bryan had chosen to be one for the U.S.A. If he was in Ivanov's position, he could only hope that the ones he loved would be protected from the reach of those who hated him.

"You drive a hard bargain," he said to Ivanov. "But it is one, which if kept, is fair. We are both professionals, so I'm sure I don't need to tell you that if you don't carry out your end of the bargain, and if you don't have the kind of information that will be of significance to us, your wife and children will be sent back to Moscow on the first available plane. And we both know what will happen to them after that."

"I am a professional," said Ivanov, "and I am a man of my word. You protect my family and I will not disappoint you."

Bryan got to his feet and nodded.

"I'll pass this on to my companions. For this to work, you will have to make a videotape that we can show to your wife. Just sit tight and I'll return just as soon as I can. But in the meantime, I'll see that you get something to eat and a little peace and quiet."

He smiled, as did Ivanov.

Both men were thinking that if they never heard that God-awful song again, they could both die as very happy men.

TWENTY-SIX

DONAHUE WAS IN the office in her new home when the front doorbell rang. She quickly got up to answer it.

"I'll get it," she said to Marcelina, who quickly nodded and slowed down long enough to let Donahue go by.

She opened the front door to find Shari Thompson, her mother, Virginia—she preferred to be called Nana—and Shari's three little hellions; Asher (age nine), Holden (age six), and Maxwell (age five). The boys were in swimming trunks, T-shirts, and flip-flops, and all three were sporting ear-to-ear smiles.

The boys said hi as they brushed past her, eager to get a look around.

"This is quite beautiful," said Nana, who quickly moved past her to keep up with the boys.

"Thanks," said Donahue to her back.

She accepted a hug from Shari, who was carrying towels and a beach bag full of extra clothes for the boys.

Marcelina had already begun to herd the boys and Nana through the large French doors that opened out onto the upper patio.

"Thanks for letting the boys use the pool," said Thompson. She was wearing a bikini bathing suit which was barely concealed under a brightly-colored cotton sarong.

"Love the wrap," said Donahue.

"Thanks. Are your security guys around?"

"Only a couple." Donahue smiled. "They tend to hang out in the control room where they can watch everything on closed circuit TV."

"*Everything?*" said Thompson.

"Let me amend that. Everything outside. There are no cameras inside. Only motion detectors that get activated when the staff is off and when I happen to leave the property."

Thompson nodded. "Are you sure you're ready for all of us to spend the night?"

"We need to christen the house with some chaos," said Donahue.

"Okay, but if the boys get on your nerves and you change your mind, we won't take offense if you tell us to go."

"It'll never go down that way, Shari. If it gets really bad, I'll just banish the boys to the other end of the house. The security guys can deal with them a lot better than we can."

"Oh? Does that mean if I'm naughty, I'll also be eligible for the security guy treatment?"

Donahue rolled her eyes and laughed.

"You and your one-track mind."

"Guilty as charged."

Donahue laughed again. "The swimming instructor is out by the pool house. You might want to meet her. She coaches the girl's team at UCLA."

"You're kidding, right?" said Thompson.

"Not at all. Only the best for the boys."

"You are really sweet to do this, Jen."

Donahue grabbed her hand and led her through the house and out to the upper patio. They could see the boys and Nana down by the pool, and speaking to the boys was an attractive, thirty-something brunette, with a perfectly tanned body.

"That's Tina," said Donahue.

"Of course it is," said Thompson, who couldn't help but notice how attractive Tina was. "I thought female swimmers all had big shoulders and thick muscles?"

Donahue laughed. Shari was always checking out the competition.

"Lean muscle is apparently the new standard for competitive female swimmers," said Donahue. "But you've got nothing to worry about. I have it on good authority that some of the guys on the detail have noticed you and are starting to ask questions."

Thompson smiled broadly, then frowned. "Well, that won't last long, once they've seen me with the terrible trio."

"Don't be silly. The way you look, most guys would put up with just about anything to get a shot at you."

Thompson grinned. "You're too kind, Jen, but thanks."

They wandered down to the pool where Donahue introduced Nana and Shari to a smiling Tina who then wandered off with Thompson and Nina to ask questions about each boy's level of swimming experience.

Donahue had the three boys take spaced-apart seats on the side of the pool to await the start of the lesson. Once they were settled, she walked back up to the upper patio where Marcelina had just delivered a tray of small pastries and a pitcher of iced tea.

When Thompson joined her, Donahue said, "Isn't Nana going to join us?"

"She wants to stay down there and watch the boys." Thompson settled into a chair and started to tear up. "I don't know what I'd do without her, Jen. She keeps pushing me to go out and have fun. She's always ready to watch the boys."

"She does it because she loves you and the boys," said Donahue. "If she didn't love being with them, she wouldn't be volunteering."

"I know, but I don't know how to repay her for what she does."

"Just let her know how much you love her, Shari. It's all she really needs to hear."

Thompson relaxed, accepted an iced tea, and reached over for one of the pastries.

"Is this really true?" she asked, looking around.

"Is what true?"

"All this," said Thompson, gesturing to the property with her arm.

"Afraid so," said Donahue.

Thompson took a bite of the pastry. "I could get used to this," she said with a mouthful.

"It's not as easy as you might think." And then, off Thompson's surprised look, she added, "There are always people around. Privacy is hard to come by."

"Yeah, but you said the security guys stay outside, right?"

"Yeah, but there are four in the household staff, at least two gardeners, and a pool boy twice a week. Oh, and let's not forget Mr. McCallum, who drops by two or three times a week to tell me about some business situation I have no answers for."

She locked eyes with Shari, then allowed a small smile to cross her face. "I know, don't say it. 'Poor little me.'"

"Poor little you," said Thompson with a smile.

Donahue slid back with her chair and got to her feet.

"Grab your tea and the coffee cake and come with me. I want to show you something."

Thompson did as asked, and when Marcelina approached, Donahue asked her to take the tea and pastries down to Nana before leading Thompson back into the house.

They went into the living room and Donahue showed her a painting that now hung prominently on one of the walls.

"Is that an original Raphael?" Thompson asked.

Donahue nodded.

It was a painting by *Raffaello Sanzio da Urbino* called *La velata* done in 1515.

"Mr. McCallum brought over a portfolio listing of paintings that Sean had collected. They're kept in a temperature-controlled warehouse somewhere nearby, but I wanted to hang a couple of them up in the house, so I chose this one for this spot right here. What do you think of it?"

Thompson studied the painting. "What I think is that 'the tequila-swilling, let-your-hair-down' girlfriend I used to hang out with has gone the way of the dinosaur."

"What's that supposed to mean?" said Donahue, who hadn't expected such a blunt assessment.

"It means that like it or not, you've got a new role to play, one that will require you to be the well-behaved socialite whose every misstep will end up in the tabloids. And don't get me wrong, Jen. I don't mean that as a knock. It's just that everything for you is going to be so different, and I'm afraid you're gonna end up with all new friends and stuff like that, and I'll be relegated to a spot on your Christmas card list, where—"

"Oh, babe, there's no frickin' way that will ever happen. We've been through too much together to let what we have get away. I'm not gonna change, Shari, and if you ever see me starting to, just say so and—"

"You see," said Thompson, who was starting to tear up. "I was right. You already have…"

"Have what? What are you talking about?"

"Frickin'! You just said frickin'! The Jennifer I knew would have said *fucking*, not frickin'. You're already becoming gentrified…"

Donahue laughed, which also brought a smile to Thompson's face, as the two of them embraced.

"*Gentrified?*" said Donahue. "Really? Was that another one of your Scrabble words?"

"Oh, please! I did go to college, remember?"

Donahue held her tighter and continued the hug. "I think there's a bottle of tequila around here someplace. Wanna do a shot?"

"I thought you weren't feeling up to drinking?"

"I'm not, but that wouldn't have stopped the old Donahue."

"Don't be stupid, Jen. Just have a juice or something."

Donahue rolled her eyes. "You sure?"

Thompson nodded. "We don't need you to start puking up tequila because of your queasy stomach."

"Okay, then," said Donahue. "I'll get a cup of tea if you promise to do a shot for me, too."

"Now you're talking, lady! Lead the way!"

TWENTY-SEVEN

AFTER DINNER, WHEN Thompson's boys were already ensconced in one of the larger guest bedrooms, and while Nana was reading them a bedtime story, Donahue and Thompson settled in the library for an after-dinner drink.

"Mr. McCallum is insisting again that I use the security detail every time I go out."

Thompson laughed. "I can just see it now. We're racing to a homicide scene in our old blue Plymouth, followed by a limousine and two black GMC Denalis."

Donahue smiled at the thought of that.

"He says it's more than just the potential threat from being the heir to Sean's fortune. He says that because of my wealth, I'm a possible target for kidnappers."

Thompson took a sip of her drink, then put the glass down on the coffee table.

"It sounds like pretty good advice, Jen. Maybe you better give it some serious thought."

"It's so cumbersome," she replied. "Every time I want to go out, I have to notify Bernstein, and he has to call out the team."

"Aren't they already here, waiting by the cars?"

"Not really. I guess they're paid for a full shift, but if I don't give them advanced notice, I have to wait for them to respond to a call-out."

"Well, that's just bad management," said Thompson. "If they're getting paid, they damn well should be right here at your beck and call."

"But the guard house isn't big enough to hold them all. What would they do? Walk around the yard with big machine guns like badass-cartel-movie guards?"

Thompson laughed. "Having all of those good-looking guys walking around with 'big guns' wouldn't be all that bad."

"You're incorrigible," said Donahue with a smile. Thompson often referred to men with big arms as having 'big guns.'"

"You know, you could build them a bigger control room. Outfit it with a couple of pool tables, a big screen TV, and a small kitchen where they could get a quick meal. As long as the guys watching the cameras are kept separate from the rest of the shift, you'd always have people on the alert, and if something were to go down, you'd have a small army ready to respond."

Donahue gave it some thought and had to admit it made sense.

"That's a good idea. I'll mention it to McCallum."

"So, what about the twenty-four-hour coverage?"

"That's still a problem. It would never work if I want to keep working at RHD. Maybe I can cut a deal with McCallum for coverage only when I'm not on the job."

Thompson smiled. "Think like the boss, Jen. They work for you, not the other way around."

Thompson got to her feet and glanced around the room. There was a sizable collection of books all housed on one large wall.

"Where did all the books come from?" she asked. "Were they all Sean's?"

Donahue got up and walked over to the bookshelves.

"All told, there are almost five-hundred. All first editions, and for the most part, signed copies. Sean was a collector, and most of these were in storage until he bought the house. McCallum had them delivered yesterday to fill out the shelves."

She pointed out a signed Harry Potter book, and a few others by authors of note. She spotted the volume of *Crime and Punishment*, the one that had been in Sean's duplex.

She took it down from the shelf, cradled it in her arms, and told Thompson that it had been Sean's favorite book.

"In fact, he insisted I read it," she said as she opened the cover. "I lost a bet, and I had to pay off by reading the book—"

She stopped talking when she noted a cut on the inside back cover, along the spine of the book.

"Oh, no!" she said. "The movers must have damaged it."

Thompson moved over to get a look "It's torn," said Donahue, who showed her what she was talking about.

"That looks like it was cut," said Thompson.

When Donahue examined it more closely, she could see a bit of paper sticking out of the cut. She used her fingernails to pull out a small piece of paper.

There was writing on it, and when she put down the book and got the note open, she was shocked by what she read.

Nice job, babe! I knew I could trust you to find this. Call Alexi Egorov. He's in my address book. He was a close friend of my father, and he's holding a key for me. He doesn't know what it's for.

But I can tell you. The key is for a safe deposit box in my name. You'll find it in the Barclays Bank (Suisse) SA, in Zurich, Switzerland. Box 3224.

The contents are documents of significant political consequence. Keep them there or in an equally safe place. They were collected by my father and some of them are from contacts that I have cultivated. Lives are at stake. I was in negotiations with the United States government (FBI leadership) to make the documents available to them. However, I recently learned from a contact in Russia that there is a highly placed mole in the United States government, so I have withheld the documents until the mole is uncovered.

You can contact CIA Deputy Director Jamison Freely. I've come to know him personally and I trust him implicitly. Let him know that you are overseeing the documents and that you will decide when it is safe to turn them over to the FBI.

Sorry to leave you with this mess, babe, but you're the only one I trust to see it through.

But keep all of this to yourself. The documents are dangerous, and there are people looking for them who would kill you without hesitation to prevent them from being released.

I will love you always, Jen. You were my everything.

Sean

"What's it say?" asked Thompson.

Donahue had no intention of bringing Thompson into this. Sean's warning carried great weight, and the last thing she would ever want to do would be to put Shari's life at risk.

"Oh, it's just a private little love note from Sean," she said as she folded it up. The tears that followed were real.

Thompson moved over and gave her a hug.

There was nothing more for either one to say.

TWENTY-EIGHT

KASEY SMITTEN AND Rebecca Folsey took the first available red-eye flight from LAX to D.C. They were asked to return to FBI Headquarters to oversee the final phase of the investigation into the leak of information that led the killers directly to Sean Walker.

They were picked up at the airport in Baltimore by an FBI agent who drove them straightaway to the Hoover Building in D.C. for a meeting with their boss. Both women would have preferred a chance to go to their respective homes for a shower and something to eat, but when the boss says now, you don't say no.

Deputy Director Michael C. Hemet, the current head of the Anti-Terrorism Unit, was waiting for them in a conference room. With him were six other agents, all trusted individuals who had been working on the leak since the day they first learned about Sean Walker's death.

"Grab a coffee," Hemet told them. "I know you've had a long flight, but we're close to cracking this case and we need to do things now."

They both grabbed coffees, then took the last two seats at the table. Hemet kicked things off by telling the group that both Charles Beeson and his wife were present in the building where they were being held in separate rooms.

He first called on Folsey, and she told the group that she ran a financial check on Beeson's wife and found an account with fifty-thousand dollars in it. It was a lump sum deposit, and the account was opened one week before Sean Walker's murder.

"His wife is Jane Beeson," she told the group, "and they have no kids."

"Is there an alternative explanation for the money?" Hemet asked. "Like an inheritance, an insurance payout, or something like that?"

"We don't know yet," said Folsey, "but I'd like to ask her about it as long as she's here."

Hemet nodded. "The plan is to have you two do the interviews," he said, referring to Smitten and Folsey. "But before you confront her, I want you to trace back the deposit. Find out if it was in cash or a check?"

"Will do," said Folsey.

He turned his attention to Smitten.

"Anything new on the fiancé?"

"The taps are in place," said Smitten. "We're doing sporadic surveillance, but she has her own security team and they're pretty good. We don't want to get too close, so the teams are keeping it very loose."

"What about a GPS on her car? Is that a possibility?" he asked.

"Her security guys are on the car twenty-four seven, so unless something changes, we'll have to keep things visual."

"How about an air unit?" asked one of the other agents.

"If we get wind of a long trip, we'll call one in," said Smitten. "But her people are good. All ex-military, special forces. If the chopper gets upwind, they'll hear it. We need to be very careful."

"When she's not working at the LAPD headquarters," said Folsey, "she's pretty much staying in her new home. She has frequent meetings with an attorney named McCallum, the same gentleman who oversaw Walker's business operations. He's acting as her financial advisor while she learns about the extensive holdings she now controls. Her only friend who comes to visit her is her LAPD partner, a divorcee named Shari Thompson, the mother of three young boys, and Thompson's mother, a woman named Virginia Sloan. But Thompson and the boys call her Nana. They recently spent the night at Donahue's home, but other than that, Donahue doesn't go out."

"Are you running a full background on Thompson?"

"We started one," said Smitten, "but we had to stop to get back here."

"Get someone else to handle that," said Hemet. "I want you to focus for the moment on Beeson and his wife."

⁓

Ivanov was being kept in a cell at Chetwynd Barracks at Chilwell, an army facility in Nottingham, U.K., but the conditions of his confinement had changed significantly once he told them he'd cooperate. The food was much better, there was more of it, and there was no more earworm music. Just blessed silence. They even arranged for a few books for him to read, one of them being the Holy Bible, which at first he thought was a joke, but it turned out to be the one that he couldn't put down.

The first thing they did when the deal was cut was to have him make a video of himself talking directly to his wife. The American who spoke to him—he never did get his name—told him that the video would be forwarded to the Embassy in Moscow and agents would show it to his wife. If she and the girls were willing to leave, they would be driven out of Moscow to Saint Petersburg, and from there they'd be put on a cruise ship that would bring them back to London.

"You can do that?" he asked. "You can get them on a cruise ship?"

"Sure," said Bryan.

"But they don't have passports?"

Bryan smiled. "It's not a problem, Sergei, so just relax."

⁓

Kasey Smitten entered the interview room where Charles Beeson was patiently waiting. He and his wife had been instructed to come in for an interview, but once they arrived, they were quickly separated, and Charles Beeson hadn't spoken with anyone for the last several hours.

"Mr. Beeson? My name is Agent Smitten. I'm sorry we've kept you waiting, but I just flew in from L.A. and the plane was a little late."

"Where's my wife?" Beeson asked.

"She's here, in another room. My partner is talking with her now."

Beeson nodded. He still had no idea why he was there, but he suspected it had to do with the murder of Sean Walker, the guy he had personally handled during the transition into the Witness Protection Program."

"I'll tell you what, Agent Smitten. I already told the other Bureau guys everything I could about the Walker case, so I'm a little confused about why you wanted to see me and my wife?"

Smitten exhaled slowly.

"Well, as you know, Mr. Walker was murdered in Los Angeles, and we believe the people responsible were the ones we were trying to protect him from. That means that someone got very lucky and just happened to spot him out in public, or the more likely scenario is that someone on the inside sold him out. You with me on this?"

"Of course I am. I know I'm not the guy you're looking for, so I want to help, really I do, but I've told you guys everything I know."

Smitten held his glance for a while, then said, "The polygraph you took? You came back deceptive."

"What? That's impossible! I didn't lie about anything."

"That's why I'm here, Mr. Beeson. Can I call you Charles?"

"I guess so. Yeah, sure."

"We need to see if we can figure out why you didn't pass?"

Beeson sighed. "Can you tell me what questions I failed?"

"No, but I can tell you it had to do with your financial situation." And off his surprised look, she said, "We're concerned about the money your wife deposited into her own account. Where did it come from, Charles?"

It caught him up short, and he knew it showed.

"Ah, the money was a loan from my wife's parents. We're gonna use it as a deposit on a new home."

"And her parents will confirm that?"

"Of course," he told her, but it didn't sound convincing.

"Did you tell anyone about Sean Walker's true identity?"

"No. Of course not."

She smiled broadly, a smile designed to unsettle him, and with a nod she got to her feet. "We're gonna give you another poly right now," she said softly. "We'll speak again when it's over."

⁓

In a small room, on a separate floor of the J. Edgar Hoover building on Pennsylvania Avenue, Rebecca Folsey sat with Jane, the wife of Charles Beeson. Jane, who had demonstrated a quiet hostility towards the idea of being made to wait to be interviewed, was irritated to the point of being snippy. On the drive in to the Hoover Building, her husband had explained to her that their interviews were part of a process in the search for a leak in the Marshals Office relating to the death of a Russian man who was in the Witness Protection Program.

But Jane was no dummy. She was an executive secretary to one of the partners of the Burch, Collins, and Singleton law firm. Their lobbying expertise in D.C. made them players to be reckoned with. She was on good terms with her boss, Ben Collins, so if things were about to get messy, she was sure that Ben would step in and save the day.

She thought about giving Collins a call when they made their way into the building, but Charley said no, that Collins would charge them an arm and a leg just to take the call. He urged her to wait, to let things play out. Neither one of them had done anything to be worried about, so "just go in there and tell them the truth."

Folsey had been making progress with Jane by tossing her softball questions about her career, her outside interests, her family background, and her love for the Washington Capitols, a team that Jane had followed since her early teens. But the small talk could only get her so far, and Folsey was now ready to get to the meat of the interview.

"Jane, I want to ask you about a checking account you recently opened up at a Wells Fargo Branch in Bethesda. The initial deposit was fifty-thousand dollars. I'm sure there's a reasonable explanation, but can you tell me where the money came from?"

The question caught Jane by complete surprise. Charley had told her the investigation was focused on a possible leak within the Marshals office, so what the hell was this agent doing by trying to open a second and entirely separate can of worms?

"How did you find out about my checking account?" Jane asked.

"Routine background information," said Folsey. She had noted Jane's burgeoning hostility and was now alert to the need to tread softly so as to keep the information flowing.

"Well, I resent the fact that you people are digging around into our personal business."

She folded her arms across her chest, waiting for Folsey to make the next move.

"We're not trying to embarrass you, Jane. We don't just randomly poke around in someone's personal business. We ran across this deposit, which I'm sure you'll agree was rather significant, and while there is probably a very logical explanation for how the money was acquired, we need to find out what that is so that we can move on with our investigation."

"Well, you're just going to have to ask my husband about that because I'm not going to answer."

She studied Folsey's face, but saw no indication that the woman was going to let her off the hook, so she decided to play her trump card.

"I want to speak with my attorney," she said. "Ben Collins. You know who he is?"

"Yes, ma'am, I do. We'll stop the tape now for a few moments and I'll be right back."

"Am I free to go?" Jane asked, now feeling that she was in the alpha position.

Folsey gave her a tight smile.

"I'm afraid not. Sit tight, Mrs. Beeson. I'll be back in a few minutes."

When the door shut behind Folsey, Jane Beeson got to her feet and tried the handle. It was locked.

Uh, oh, she said to herself. *What have I gotten myself into?*

TWENTY-NINE

SERGEI IVANOV SAT on his bunk with his back up against the wall. The room contained a single cot with a metal frame that was bolted to the floor. A two-inch-thick mattress lay on top of the solid metal platform. A sheet covered the mattress, and a thin blanket lay on top. There was no pillow.

Sergei had given his life a lot of thought since his arrest. Yes, he was a soldier. And yes, he'd done what he'd been ordered to do. But he also gave consideration to who he'd been working for—the man at the top who'd been giving the orders—and he couldn't help but think that he'd been used. The people in power were in it for themselves. They didn't give a damn about the homeland, and as a good soldier he had followed orders, but at what cost to himself and his country? What was good for Putin and the Duma—the nest of cronies in lockstep with Putin—was not always in the best interest of the motherland, and it certainly hadn't been good for him.

There was something to this book he'd been reading. A philosophy about life that he had never been exposed to. Would it cause a change in his immediate behavior? He didn't think so, but it gave him a whole lot to think about. And as he pondered his present situation, he slowly came to the realization that he owed his masters nothing.

He'd given them everything for the good of his country, and they'd used his loyalty as a means to further their own ambitions.

He shook his head. He was disgusted with himself.

How could I have been such a fool?

Bryan entered the cell alone, carrying a thermos and a small plastic bowl. He put the bowl down on the small eating table, then poured the contents of the thermos into the bowl.

"I understand you like *borscht*," he said, looking over at Ivanov.

Sergei smiled, put down the Bible, and walked over to the table where he took a seat. *Borscht,* or cabbage soup, was his very favorite meal. It brought back pleasant memories of his life back home.

"You are very kind, sir," he said.

Bryan handed him a plastic spoon.

"Enjoy it, Sergei. It came from a restaurant here in town. I'm told it's the best around."

Sergei tried the soup. "It's delicious, sir," he said, looking up.

"Call me Patrick, Sergei."

Sergei nodded, but he was wise to the game. A good agent would never reveal his true identity, so he could only believe that the name he'd been given was nothing more than a *nom de guerre.*

"I have something else for you," said Bryan. He held up an iPhone that contained a message from Sergei's wife.

He turned on the video and held up the phone for Sergei to see.

My dear husband. I don't know what you've done, but your children and I are following your orders. We have gone with these men and they have taken us to Petersburg where we were given identification and put on a large passenger boat. I have been told that we are on our way to London and the girls and I are looking forward to seeing you again. We are now safely at sea. The men with us are very nice and they are watching after our girls. I am worried about you, but I will trust that you know what is best for us. I love you. We love and miss you.

Sergei put down his spoon and started to cry. All that mattered to him now was the safety of his family. He looked up at Bryan and nodded his thanks.

"I am ready to tell you what I know," he said.

Bryan nodded. "Finish your soup, Sergei, before it gets cold. We'll have plenty of time to talk when you're done."

❧

In a room upstairs, Whitney sat with the two Mossad agents, and all three were glued to the TV screen. Sergei had resumed eating the soup and Bryan ventured a quick glance up at the camera and gave a very fast wink.

"The American is really good at this," said one of the Israelis. "Notice how deferential the subject has become?" He turned to Whitney. "Can we get a copy of the feed? I'd like to take it back for training purposes."

Whitney smiled. "I don't see why not, but we'll have to blur out the American's appearance. He's still involved in undercover work."

He got to his feet, pulled out his cell phone, and made a quick call to his boss.

"The Russian is ready to talk," he said.

"Good," said the voice on the other end. "Keep me up to speed when you can."

❧

The interview with Sergei went off without a hitch. He was moved to a more spacious interview room where a table for eight occupied the center of the room. In addition to Bryan who was going to lead the interrogation, Whitney, the two Israelis, and two members of MI-6 were there to listen to what he had to say. And of course, each one was focused on their own special interests.

Bryan began the questioning in the classic manner. He sought general information first. It was a well-known and practiced technique: build rapport, get him comfortable with talking, study his responses, and look for physical tics that might demonstrate that he was withholding the truth.

Two hours into the interview, and after a short bathroom break, Bryan and Whitney concluded that Sergei was telling them the absolute truth. Whatever switch had been flipped, Sergei was going to live up to his commitment to tell them everything they wanted to know.

The team reassembled back in the interview room, and Bryan resumed the questioning.

He covered the killing in Los Angeles, but Sergei steadfastly swore on the life of his children that he wasn't involved in the L.A. operation. They came at him from a dozen directions, but no matter how hard they tried, they couldn't catch him in a contradiction.

Maybe he wasn't involved in the L.A. incident, thought Bryan, so he switched his approach and asked about the killings in Israel.

Sergei cleared his throat and began an extensive narration.

"I was at my apartment when I got a call from a voice I recognized. It was Oleg Kozlov. He is my country's Ambassador to the United States, currently assigned to Washington, D.C. In conversation, he told me that someone would be contacting me to do a job. The work was sanctioned, and it needed to be done as soon as humanly possible."

"What does sanctioned mean?" said Whitney.

"Approved by the state. I knew at once it meant killing someone, but I didn't expect him to say anything else on the phone." His gaze shifted from face to face at the table, and that was followed by a smile. "The American NSA would be recording all his calls, and I suspect that the Israeli Mossad was doing the same."

"Had he done that before?" asked Bryan. "You know, asked you to do something that was sanctioned?"

Sergei nodded.

"On two other occasions I was given orders to liquidate men who presented a threat to our political hierarchy. Both were oligarchs, and both were taken out in my country." He went on to describe in detail the methods he used to complete his tasks.

"What happened to the assets of these men that you killed?" asked one of the Israelis.

"They were forfeited to the state," he replied before breaking out in a nervous laugh. "The state is Putin, and Putin is the state." He raised his arms up and shrugged his shoulders. "What else can I say."

He was suggesting rather forcefully that he believed that Putin got the lion's share of the assets.

"What happened after you got the call from Kozlov?" Bryan asked.

"A man named Vladislav Zhukov came by to see me one day later. He gave me a file on the two men they wanted me to kill. It had their addresses and pictures of each man. He wanted them hit late at night in their own homes. He wanted it done the same night so that the second one would not get wind of what had happened to the first one."

"Okay, did you choose when to do the killings?"

"I was given forty-eight hours."

"And this man who gave you the order? What was his connection to the Russian Federation?"

"He's a Colonel in the SVR. I never met him before, but I knew of him. He came to Israel solely for the purpose of speaking to me in person. I believe he was headed back to Moscow, but I'm not really sure about that."

Ivanov went on to describe the killings he'd committed, the details of which the Israeli's had already pieced together.

"What did you get for killing them?" Whitney asked.

"Ten-thousand U.S. dollars for each."

"So twenty-thousand dollars in total?" Bryan asked.

Ivanov nodded. "It was deposited into my checking account the very next day. It came in by wire transfer, and I sent most of it to my wife back in Moscow."

"Tell me about Ambassador Kozlov?" said Bryan.

"What do you want to know? He was former KGB, now SVR. He came up through the ranks with Putin. He's considered by the Americans to be a spymaster. He recruits by the classic techniques:

honey traps, financial need, and intimidation. Those are his chosen methods."

Bryan leaned back in his chair.

"So, why did Kozlov choose you for this job?"

Ivanov sighed. "Because I'm stupid," he said flatly. "I believed I was doing it for the good of my country, but now that I've thought about things, I realize that I was being used to help the political elite to enrich themselves at the hands of my country's oligarchs."

To say that Bryan and Whitney were surprised by the answer would be putting it mildly. It seemed likely that Ivanov's conversion away from the dark side was now a *fait accompli*.

"Let's step outside?" said Whitney to Bryan.

Once they were alone, Whitney said, "What if we cut him loose and sent him back into the game?"

"I don't know," said Bryan. "It might mean having to send his wife and kids back, and I'm not sure he'd go for that."

"If we could get him to work for us it could be a window into the Russian game plan. Remember, this guy has got a high-end security company that does computer security for companies throughout western Europe. So, in addition to knowing what his security group is up to, we might end up getting a little advance warning when hits are scheduled to take place."

"I see your point," said Bryan. "His position in the Embassy hierarchy is what intrigues me. Maybe we could make it work."

"You want to bring it up?" Whitney asked.

"I can mention it, maybe plant the seed. It would have to be cleared by our people, but let's see what he has to say?"

They went back into the room and once they were seated, Bryan said, "We appreciate the fact that you've been so candid with us, Sergei. We're gonna want to talk to you a few more times. We need to go over stuff that's on your computer and the calls you made on your phone."

"Any chance I can see my wife and kids?" he asked.

"We're thinking about that, but in the meantime, I've got a little something I'd like to talk to you about. When I listen to you talking, I get the feeling that you've come to realize that your country considers you to be expendable."

"I think you're right," he said.

"Well, what if you came to work for us?"

It was out there now, and Bryan held his breath. Would Sergei even consider it? Would his life be at risk if he did?

"I'm not a fool, Mr. Patrick," he finally said. "If I don't work for you, I'll be in prison for the rest of my life. But if I do go to work for you, does that mean I'll be free to rejoin my family?"

"Nothing is guaranteed yet," said Bryan. "I'm just throwing it out there. But if you went to work for us, we'd want you to go back to what you've been doing. We would want information that you learn from the Embassy. We want information from your work in the private sector. We want to know whatever we can about everything we can get on Putin, the SVR, and anything else of intelligence value."

"You're asking for a lot," said Ivanov. "What's in it for me?"

"Besides your freedom?" Bryan asked.

Ivanov smiled. "I need to make a living."

Bryan nodded. "If that's all that's holding you back, we may be able to work something out."

Ivanov, who'd been holding his breath, slowly let it out.

"Can I speak to you in private?" he said to Bryan. "No tapes, no video?"

Bryan looked over at Whitney who nodded, then got to his feet as did the others.

When everyone left the room, Bryan said, "What did you want to tell me, Sergei?"

"You need to be very careful," said Ivanov. "I've heard rumors that Kozlov has a high ranking person in America who's been feeding him Grade A information. I don't have any idea who it is, but the gossip I've heard is that it comes from the White House, or possibly the FBI.

The indication is that it's someone who is in a position to influence policy or who is being read-in at the highest level."

"And this information is coming from where?" Bryan asked.

"From things I've overheard over the last several years. Nothing specific, but little things that have enabled me to come to that conclusion." Sergei sighed, then added, "If your people learn that I'm working for you, there's a good chance I'll be found out before I've begun."

Bryan had to agree. A mole at the highest levels of the U.S. Intelligence apparatus was an instant game changer. He was going to have to discuss this with people he could trust, but until then, he would let the debriefing continue as planned.

"Anything in particular you'd like for dinner?" Bryan asked with a smile.

"Fish and chips," said Ivanov without hesitation. "And a cold beer, that is, if that's not pushing things too far?"

Bryan smiled. "I'll see what I can do."

◆

Outside the interview room, Bryan cornered Whitney in private. "Did you overhear what he told me?"

"Nope. I figured we didn't need to. If it was something important, I knew you'd tell me."

Bryan was glad that he could trust Whitney. It made what he had in mind that much easier to propose.

"Sergei says there's a high placed mole somewhere in D.C. who's in a position to influence policy. He suggests it could be in the White House or someone senior in the FBI, but he's not sure. Whoever it is, Kozlov is running him."

"This is serious," said Whitney.

Bryan nodded. "I can take care of things at my end. I'll notify my boss and we'll get the proper people looking into it. But I think it would be a mistake to let anyone at my end know about Sergei. I think the better course for us right now would be for your people to take him on as a source. You can keep it in-house, and that way our mole won't know anything at all about him."

"What about the Israelis?" asked Whitney. "They want him for a double murder?"

"Let me talk to Mordecai about that," said Bryan. "As long as you share what you learn from Sergei with the Israelis, I'm sure he'll be on board."

"What about Kozlov?" Whitney asked.

"One thing at a time," Bryan cautioned. "Let me speak to my people about the possible mole. Once that is done, we can figure out what to do about Kozlov."

"His family will be here the day after tomorrow," said Whitney.

"Yeah, that could be a problem. It would be a lot better if we could get them back without anyone in Moscow being any the wiser."

"I'll work on that," said Whitney. "You make your calls. I'll get the guys in Six to start interviewing Sergei about his phone log. Let's touch bases in a couple of hours."

THIRTY

BRYAN HARB LEFT the Chetwynd Barracks and was driven by an MI-5 agent to the U.S. Embassy in the London Borough of Wandsworth. It was the largest American embassy in Western Europe, and the building—which resembles a crystalline cube swathed in shimmering sails of plastic, set on a plinth (a heavy base)—is surrounded by a moat-like pond on the edge of the River Thames. Using his CIA identification, he entered the facility where he used a SKIF and placed a call to Dan Taylor, the CIA station chief in Cairo. Taylor was his mentor and immediate supervisor.

Taylor, a former Marine, was a tall man, almost six-foot-four, with dark hair, a kindly face, and a broad, warm smile. He'd been an undergrad at Princeton who majored in political science. It was there where he was first approached by the CIA to consider working as an analyst. He took the job right after graduation, but found working ten hours a day behind a desk to be something he had no interest in. He applied for a transfer to field work, and once he was accepted, he began to excel. He had a knack for recruiting agents, and before long he was assigned to work in the Middle East. After five years in the field, he was promoted to Head of Station in Egypt, a role that kept him out of the daily grind while allowing him to oversee the most important operations.

Bryan spent fifteen minutes bringing Taylor up to speed on the murder in Los Angeles, the murders in Jerusalem, and the identification and apprehension of Ivanov. He detailed the interrogation results, the link to Oleg Kozlov in D.C., and Ivanov's willingness to become an enthusiastic double agent.

Taylor listened patiently, and when Bryan was finished, he said, "It sounds like you did a good job."

"Thanks, but there's more. We've got a serious problem in D.C."

He told Taylor what Ivanov said about a possible mole in the White House or a senior person in the FBI.

"He's passing on innuendo, but he's so convinced that it's true that he told me not to pass his name up the chain of command because he believes it will make its way to Putin."

"I know Kozlov," said Taylor. "I met him once at a function in D.C. If I'm not mistaken, he's former KGB."

"Ivanov says he's a true spymaster. His speciality is recruitment."

"Okay. So, how do you plan to work Ivanov?" Taylor asked.

"I'm recommending that we let Six run him. That way, no one in our chain will have any idea that he's turned."

"Then what's your recommendation for how we deal with Kozlov?" Taylor asked.

Taylor sighed. The CIA was prevented by law from working a case domestically. They could furnish leads and information to other agencies, but the FBI has exclusive jurisdiction over federal crimes committed in the United States, and until they knew for sure that the Bureau wasn't the source of the leak, he was reluctant to let them take the investigation.

"I'm going to leave that conundrum in your hands," said Bryan. "That's why they pay you the big bucks, right?"

"Let me work on that," said Taylor with a chuckle. "You get the situation with Ivanov worked out while I see what we can do about Kozlov."

Dan Taylor made a quick call to Deputy Director Jamison Freely of the CIA on a secure Embassy line, and after he finished telling him about the possible mole, Freely stated that he would pass on the concerns to a person that he trusted completely at the FBI.

"What about Kozlov?" Taylor asked.

"There have been rumors swirling around him for a number of years," said Freely. "It's going to be up to the FBI to deal with it, but maybe we can help with a concurrent investigation by reviewing his electronic communications."

"What do you want me to tell Bryan Harb?"

"His instinct is right. Let the Brits handle Ivanov. Tell him to gather what he can from the debriefings, but he's to pass all actionable intelligence on to you, and I want you to report it directly to me. The fewer people who know where it's coming from, the better it is for the informant."

⤚

Deputy Director Freely walked up the steps to the Lincoln Memorial which was located on the western end of the National Mall in Washington, D.C. The statue of a sitting Lincoln was placed at the top of the stairs, and the interior walls of Indiana limestone were engraved with two of Lincoln's most famous speeches; the Gettysburg Address, and his Second Inaugural Address.

Jack Cullen, the current Assistant Director of the Federal Bureau of Investigation, was waiting for him at the top of the stairs.

At sixty-three years of age, Freely's career with the CIA began when he was twenty-seven. He was recruited into the Agency while at Harvard Law School, and after passing the bar he did his first five years in Berlin where he was focused on recruiting and counterintelligence operations. Berlin was followed by a posting as the Resident Agent-in-Charge in Moscow. Fluent in Russian, he ran recruitment and intelligence-gathering operations, and he cemented his reputation at the Agency when he was able to recruit a high-ranking member of the Politburo. He was elevated to the role of Director of the National Clandestine Service (D/NCS), where he oversaw the Directorate of Operations. He ran this from a desk at Langley, in McLean, Virginia. Four years later, he was elevated to Deputy Director of the Central Intelligence Agency. He was so well thought of by everyone in the Agency that he retained that position during the new Administration.

Cullen's background was very different. He was at one-time a police officer in the city of Beverly Hills. But for him, it wasn't enough to be a small-city cop, so he enrolled in law school at night. After four years of study, he graduated from Southwestern University School of Law at the top of his class, and then went to work directly for the FBI. He worked bank robberies in Detroit for three years, then was transferred to New York when the Bureau decided to upgrade their resources and capabilities in the field of Counter-Terrorism.

His rise to stardom within the Bureau came out of the blue when after recruiting a Somali immigrant, he learned about a plot by *Abu Sayyaf* to set off propane explosions in the Grand Central Station. Timely arrests of all of the principals involved averted a major catastrophe, and after that, his rise through the ranks was nothing short of stellar. Within three years he rose to the rank of number two within the FBI.

The two men shook hands, and Cullen said, "Tell me something, Jim. You ever take the time to read Lincoln's Second Inaugural Speech?"

"It's been a while," said Freely, who looked up at the words engraved in the limestone on the North chamber wall.

Cullen pointed out the speech. His favorite part was the ending of Lincoln's Second Inaugural Address which he began to read aloud:

"...With malice toward none; with charity for all; with firmness in the right, as God gives us to see the right, let us strive on to finish the work we are in; to bind up the nation's wounds; to care for him who shall have borne the battle, and for his widow, and his orphan…to do all which may achieve and cherish a just, and a lasting peace, among ourselves, and with all nations."

Cullen slowly turned back to face Freely.

"It's so beautifully worded; so unifying. I get inspired every time I get a chance to read it."

Freely concurred.

"You don't realize how important it is to have a President who is also a great orator until you have one in power whose entire vocabulary consists of *greatest, biggest, wealthiest, and me, me, me…* "

Cullen suppressed a smile. "The demise of many of the great societies in history can be traced to the leadership of greedy, self-serving, insecure men with certifiable delusions of grandeur."

"You think he's putting our nation's democracy at risk?" Freely asked.

Cullen held his stare and winked. "I know he has, and as far as I'm concerned, he can't be gone soon enough."

Freely sighed. Cullen wasn't usually this outspoken about his dislike for the man in the White House. He must be having a very bad day.

The monument itself generally had a lot of people coming and going, and tonight was no exception.

Freely looked around. "Let's take a walk."

The two men walked down the stairs, then followed the tree-lined pathway that was parallel to the Lincoln Memorial Reflecting Pool. As they strolled along, they were carefully watched over by a shield of FBI agents who were discreetly scattered around the area.

They were old friends, both career government officials, and they had worked together on many serious investigations and top-secret operations. Both men felt that the current President was a man that had to be worked around, and both suspected that if they kept their heads down, they would still be in their jobs long after their nemesis was out of office and just an embarrassing historical footnote.

Freely told Cullen everything he knew about the murder of Sean Walker, the death of the two Israelis, and the detention of Ivanov by Britain's MI-5.

Cullen barely flinched.

"I'm up to speed on that investigation," said Cullen. "A team of agents that directly reports to me has been working that investigation from out in L.A."

"I was aware of that," said Freely with a nod, "but what I told you is preliminary to your understanding of what the interview with Ivanov has disclosed. He's interested in working for us. And as a sign of good faith, he says that Ambassador Kozlov in D.C. is running a recruitment program. Kozlov was the person who notified Ivanov that he had a job for him, and that someone would soon meet with him to give him the details for the assignment. That person was an SVR colonel named Zhukov who presented Ivanov with the order to kill the two Israelis."

"There have been rumors about Kozlov for the last two years," said Cullen.

"I'm not finished," said Freely. "Ivanov said he doesn't want his assistance being known by anyone but the two men who are handling him in London. He says that the scuttlebutt about Kozlov is that he has a high-ranking source in either the White House or the FBI. He doesn't know which, but apparently the source is in a policy-making position."

Cullen stopped walking. This was deeply troubling news.

"If the mole is in my shop, it could explain how they got the information they needed to track down Sean Walker," said Cullen.

Freely sighed. "I don't know what's worse, a mole in your organization, or one in the White House."

"Either way," said Cullen, "we've got a big problem."

"So, how do you want to handle this?"

Cullen started walking again and Freely now matched him stride for stride.

"We've been focused on a U.S. Marshal as a possible source for the leak of Walker's identity and whereabouts," said Cullen. "But if what this Russian is saying is true, this might be the link we need to get to the person who actually corrupted him."

"You think this US Marshal might have given the info directly to Ambassador Kozlov?"

"I don't know, but we'll have to work backward through his phone calls and emails. I'll put a full team on him right away."

"That might be a mistake," said Freely. "I'm just thinking out loud here, Jack, but this U.S. Marshal is probably not the mole. If you put a D.C. team on him, and if it turns out the mole is in your operation, then the whole thing might be blown before it even gets off the ground."

Cullen gave that a moment's thought.

"You make a good point. I'll bring a group in from L.A. Their work will be independent of the D.C. office. Only you and I will know anything about them; who they are, and what they're doing."

Freely nodded. "What about Kozlov? Are you going to put a team on him?"

"We can do that, but it probably won't yield much. With a guy like Kozlov we need to dig up all we can on his electronics, and once again, until I can determine who the mole is, I'll have to bring in people from outside the D.C. office."

"I can loan you a few teams, but you'll need to swear them in as FBI agents."

Cullen smiled. "I'll keep that in mind, but I'm pretty sure I've got enough people I can trust to do what needs to be done."

"Will you be coordinating with the NSA?" asked Freely.

Cullen nodded. "We'll get every call Kozlov has made in the last five years."

"What about the people within your D.C. office? Do you plan to give polygraphs to all of them?"

"We'll begin the process with the cover of a routine, annual exam. That way suspicions won't be aroused."

"I've got a half dozen good poly examiners. You want me to loan them to you?"

"That would be a great help," said Cullen. "They can work with my people and it should help us get through it in half the time."

They walked a little further, then started back towards the Lincoln Memorial.

"Can we keep this just between us," asked Freely. "I'd rather we didn't let any of this go up the ladder."

"I don't trust him either," said Cullen, "so until we determine if, in fact, there really is a mole, and until we know who it is, then as far as I'm concerned this stops with us."

"Thanks, Jack," said Freely, who shook his hand. "I knew I could count on you."

THIRTY-ONE

Two HOURS LATER, Kasey Smitten received a call advising her to meet with Assistant Director Cullen in his office.

"When does he want me to come by?" she asked the secretary who gave her the message.

"As soon as you can be here."

Smitten sighed. "Okay. I'm on my way."

When she got upstairs to his office, Cullen directed her to a seat in front of his desk.

"Fill me in on where we are on the investigation into the U.S. Marshal."

"Yes, sir. Beeson's wife Jane has insisted on getting an attorney and our polygrapher has just reported to me that Beeson has proven deceptive in his second polygraph."

Get a warrant for Beeson's home and office and make sure that it covers everything." Cullen leaned forward. "Seize their passports with the warrant and keep them both here while the search is underway."

"Yes, sir."

"We'll need evidence from the search or we're going to have to release them. And if that is the outcome, then I want them followed. Make sure a tracker is on their vehicles."

"We already looked at his phone records," she reminded him. "And there was only a single interesting call to a person of any importance."

"Oh? And who was that?"

"Retired General Lindsey Rush, the President's National Security Advisor. And if I can get your okay, I'd like to get a FISA warrant to seize Rush's phone calls."

Cullen shook his head no.

"That's mildly interesting, Kasey, but without a pattern of calls between them, and without hard evidence that either man is involved in criminal activity, you've got no PC for a warrant, especially when your target is a senior government official."

"But the call was made five days before Sean was killed? Honestly, Boss, it's the only lead we've got."

"It's not enough." But he thought about it for a moment more. Cullen didn't rise to the top of the organization based upon his good looks. He had been a damn good operative in the field, always pushing the envelope when it came to investigations, much like Smitten was trying to do right now.

He cleared his throat. "You're saying the call went from Beeson to Rush?"

"That's right," she told him.

"Get a warrant that's narrowed down to a search of Rush's phone records, but only for Beeson's phone number. Inform the court that once the records are made available and sealed by the phone company, we want a special master to be appointed to go through the records and look for calls from Rush's number to Beeson's. Stress that we don't want to know about any of Rush's other calls."

"What's our PC?" Kasey asked.

Cullen leaned back and studied her for a moment. He'd been mentoring Kasey for the past three years, and had complete trust in her basic integrity.

"I'm going to tell you something, Kasey, but you will not repeat this to anyone. Put it in the application for the warrant, but make sure that the court keeps the affidavit sealed indefinitely. Are we clear about that?"

Kasey's eyes widened.

"Of course, sir."

Cullen proceeded to tell her that a confidential Russian source had indicated that there was a mole in the United States government, possibly in the White House or the FBI. He told her to use Beeson's having failed the poly on two occasions—and that his call to a member of the National Security Team in the White House would seem to indicate a possible connection between the two men and the informant's warning.

"Can I make a suggestion, sir?"

Cullen nodded.

"I've got Beeson sitting downstairs. I'd like to ask him about the call he made to Rush's number before I try to get the warrant. If there is an innocent explanation, then we don't want to jump the gun with Rush in case he turns out to be the mole. But if his explanation for the call doesn't hold water, then it will improve our PC while getting Beeson's lie down on tape."

"I like that," he said. "Get it done, and get back to me right away."

CHARLES BEESON WIPED the sweat from his brow with the back of his hand. It was warm in the interview room and he'd been sitting there for so long that it felt as if the walls were closing in.

He got to his feet and moved around. It was small, eight by ten. There were four solid walls, one with a solid door, and a CCTV camera in an upper wall corner that no doubt was filming his every movement.

He was in trouble and he knew it. It was a big mistake putting the money into his wife's bank account. He should have kept it in cash, or deposited it in a number of different accounts in much smaller denominations. He should have been smarter than he was, but it was too late now, the die was already cast.

He took the second polygraph as requested, and while the polygrapher didn't tell him how he did, he could tell by the man's face that he had not done well. And while the investigation seemed to be focused on the killing of Sean Walker, it won't be long before they discover the truth about the money, and when they do… *I'm gonna be toast.*

The door suddenly opened and in walked Agents Smitten and Folsey. Smitten told him to take his seat, which he did, and the two women sat at the table across from him.

Smitten held his glance for a while and she could tell that he was nervous.

You're hiding something, Beeson, and I'm gonna find out what it is.

"We've got another problem, Charles," she began. "Your wife didn't back up your story about where the money in the account came from."

The silence was deafening, and it told her legions about Charles Beeson.

"We've got her upstairs now and we're sending agents out to interview her parents."

Smitten waited. Perspiration had appeared at the hairline of Beeson's brow, and as a drip made its way down to his left eye, he wiped at it with the back of his hand.

"Where did the money come from, Charles?" Folsey said.

Beeson took a deep breath and decided to talk.

"The fifty-thousand is money I've been saving at the house to help out my parents. They live in New Jersey, and both have been ill. There's a pile of medical bills that we've put off for far too long, so a lot of the money was going to be used to pay down the hospital expenses."

"That's not what I asked you," said Folsey. "Where did the money come from?"

Beeson sighed. "I made it selling coke."

Folsey looked over at Smitten whose eyes were as big as saucers. *Did he just admit that he's selling cocaine?*

But Beeson didn't notice the surprised looks on their faces. He was too busy getting up the courage to tell them what they wanted to know.

"Early in my career with the Marshal's Office, I met a coke distributor and I asked him about securing a route. The guy had one that covered night deliveries, so I took it. I knew it was wrong, but the money was good, so I did it. My folks weren't doing well, so I thought I could help them out."

"So, you were a distributor and not a street dealer?"

"I delivered to stores in the greater D.C. area; places like supermarkets and wholesale buying clubs."

"Wait a minute?" said Smitten. "What are you talking about?"

Beeson looked over at her through narrow eyes.

"I'm a Coca-Cola distributor. I work a second job at nights."

"I thought we were talking about cocaine," said Folsey.

"Cocaine? Oh, God, no!" He started to smile. "I'm not a drug dealer. I sell Coca-Cola as a wholesaler."

"Then why the secrecy?" said Smitten. "Why didn't you just come out and say that the first time?"

"Look, having a second job is forbidden by the U.S. Marshals Office. We put the distributorship in my wife's name, and that's where the money came from."

"Is there anyone who can verify what you're telling us?"

"My general manager," he said with a nod. He gave them a telephone number and a name.

"Stay put," said Smitten. "We'll be right back."

She and Folsey made their way out of the room.

"If he's telling the truth, then we've been wasting our time," said Folsey.

"Oh, shit!" said Smitten. She turned to Folsey. "I forgot to ask him about the call to Rush's office. Can you check out this distributorship info for us? I need to go back in there and pin him down about the phone call."

Folsey nodded and kept on walking towards the elevator while

Smitten returned to the interview room. Beeson was still sitting at the table and he looked up rapidly while she resumed sitting.

"Am I going to lose my job?" he asked when she was seated.

"I don't know, yet. We need to verify that you've told us the truth about the money, and if you have, I'll check with my boss and see if we can keep your second job to ourselves."

Beeson nodded, now clearly showing a more relaxed attitude.

"But even if we decide to let it go, you should give some serious thought to telling the Marshals Office about your dealership, because sooner or later they're gonna find out, and when that happens, you won't be able to negotiate a favorable solution."

"You're right. I'll let them know and maybe they will cut me some slack."

"While we're waiting for my partner to return, I have another question for you, Charles. We went through your phone records and discovered a call you made to the White House, specifically, to the office of Retired General Lindsey Rush. Can you tell me what that call was all about?"

"Sure. One of his assistants called me. The man said he was calling on behalf of the General and that the White House wanted to know where Sean Walker was living and how he was doing?"

As he spoke, he suddenly realized the import of what he was saying. They were investigating the murder of Sean Walker, and he'd given the address information to someone in the White House.

"Oh, my God!" he said. "It never occurred to me to tell you guys about that call. The request came from the White House."

"You know that for sure?" Smitten asked.

He nodded. "When he made the request, I told him I'd call him back when I had what he needed. It took me a couple of hours, but when I got it, I dialed the callback number, and it went through the White House switchboard. I know that for a fact."

"Anything else about that call?" she asked.

"He said his boss needed the info for a report to the President, so I gave him what I knew."

"What was the name of the man you spoke with?" Smitten asked. She was trying to keep the excitement out of her voice.

"I don't remember offhand," said Beeson, "but the name is in my call-in log book. It's at the office, in my desk."

Smitten got to her feet. "Sit tight, Charles. I'll be back in a few."

⚬ᔭ

Smitten got on the elevator and took it up to the floor where her unit was housed. She located the agent who was writing the warrant for Beeson's home and office and told him to put it aside.

"I don't think we're going to need it," she said, "but if we do, just save what you've already got."

She then tracked down Folsey, who had just gotten off the phone with Beeson's supervisor at the distributorship.

"They've paid him almost sixty-thousand since he started working for them," Folsey told her. "He's telling the truth. He's a legitimate distributor."

"Go get the car started," said Smitten. "I'll get Beeson. We're gonna take a ride."

THIRTY-TWO

DONAHUE REACHED MCCALLUM on the second ring. She was still splitting time between her apartment and the big house, and this morning she was in the apartment. She was hesitant to move into the big house because of the guilt she felt over having so much money at the expense of having lost the love of her life. On top of that, the thought of packing up and moving from her apartment seemed overwhelming, especially when she still felt physically ill and emotionally depressed.

Her appetite still hadn't returned, and the very thought of eating would sometimes trigger a wave of nausea.

There was so much to do, so much responsibility. Sometimes she just wished she could get back into bed, pull the covers up over her head, and completely shut out the rest of the world.

But today was not the day for that. There were things she needed to accomplish, and if she could get even half of the must-do's done today, she knew she would feel better about herself and perhaps become inspired to do a little more the next time.

She picked up the phone and called McCallum who answered on the very first ring.

"That was fast," she said. "Were you anticipating my call?"

"Actually, I was just starting to read the morning papers and the phone was laying on the table next to me."

"Well, I hate to disturb you, James, but I need to make some travel arrangements."

McCallum listened to her describe where she wanted to go, and once she was finished, he told her, "Once again, I'm going to put Jamie Otero in charge of your security for this trip. As you know, he's a former Army Ranger and a decorated combat veteran. He's handled trips to London and Zurich before, so when would you like to leave?"

"Tomorrow morning, if I can?"

"That's plenty of time for him to get everything in place. We'll take care of the hotel arrangements in each city. Open ended, so you can adjust your schedule in whatever way suits your purpose. Once you leave the States, any requests you have should be handled by Jamie directly. Will you be traveling with Ms. Thompson again?"

"I haven't asked her yet," said Donahue.

"Well, if she's going to go with you, we will need to know as soon as possible so we can adjust our planning accordingly."

"I'll call her right away," said Donahue. "Oh! And one more thing. I've decided to accept your recommendation about making full use of my security. I'm going to move up to the big house as soon as I get back from Europe, and other than when I'm working for LAPD, I'll accept the security detail whenever I go out."

"That's a very comforting concession on your part, Ms. Donahue. I'm sure it will work out just fine."

"Also, I'd like you to arrange a meeting for me with the architect who did the renovations on the big house for Sean. I want to add a much larger facility on the property for the security team."

"Oh? Has something happened?" McCallum asked.

"Actually, I think the threat risk is going to go up, so I want to be able to have a full team around the clock, and to do that, we need to give them a few advantages for having to hang around all the time when I'm not going out. I'm thinking about adding a bunk room, a kitchen, a dining area, and a relaxation room with flat screens, a pool table, and a gym with a dressing room."

If McCallum was surprised by what she was thinking of doing, he never let on. It was what she liked best about him. If her ideas were good, he didn't waste time with needless chatter, but if they didn't pass muster, he would tell her so in such a way that she would end up following his sage advice.

"How soon would you like the meeting with the architect?"

"This afternoon, if possible."

"I'll make it happen."

❧

She made a quick call to Thompson, who was still at home. She was getting the boys ready for school. But when she told her about the quick trip, Thompson begged off, stating that she needed time to hang with her kids.

"Besides, I've almost used up all of my overtime, and I need to hang on to my vacation days for the school holidays around Christmas. But thanks for the offer. Any other time I'd jump at the chance to go."

"There will be more trips in your future," said Donahue. "I'll likely be gone a week, so I'll check in with you when I get back."

"Have you told the Captain yet?"

"Not yet, but I'll fill him in later this morning."

❧

Donahue's next call was a bit more sensitive. Per the instructions in Sean's note, Donahue then went to Sean's address book, located the number for Jamison Freely, and gave it a call. Donahue wasn't sure how much to say on the phone, but if she couldn't get through this first hurdle, Sean's plan would go no further.

"Deputy Director Freely's Office," said a secretarial voice.

"Hello. My name is Jennifer Donahue and I'd like to speak with Mr. Freely."

"May I inquire what this is all about?" the secretary asked.

"I'm afraid that's private, but Mr. Freely will know."

"Can I have a callback number?"

"I'll hold," said Donahue.

The line went to canned music, and almost a minute later, a male voice said, "This is Jamison Freely."

"Mr. Freely, my name is Jennifer Donahue. I'm a homicide investigator with LAPD. Sean Walker was my fiancé and he left me instructions to give you a call."

"I know who you are, Ms. Donahue. How are you?"

"I'm okay. Sean left me a note that said you could be trusted—"

"Not on the phone, Ms. Donahue. Your line is not secured."

"Okay. I'd like to meet with you, Mr. Freely, if that would be possible?"

"I think that's a good idea. Would you like me to come to you?"

"The number I have for you looks like a Washington D.C. area code. Is that where you are now?"

"That's correct," he said.

"Well, I can be in D.C. in the next twenty-four hours or so. Can I call you when I arrive and we can set up a time and place to meet?"

Freely paused for a moment, then said, "When you arrive here, get a hotel room. I'll give you a number to call once you're settled in and we can work something out."

He gave her the number, then said, "If you'd like, I can have someone you've met before meet you at the airport?"

"That won't be necessary," said Donahue. "I'll be traveling with a security detail."

"Very well, but when we meet, it will have to be just you. I hope you understand."

"Yes, of course," she replied.

"I'll wait for your call," said Freely.

"One more thing," said Donahue. "You said you know who I am. Have we met before?"

"We share a mutual friend, Ms. Donahue."

It suddenly clicked for Donahue. *Freely must be the confidential source that her Captain knows; the one who uses Charlotte as a go-between.*

It certainly was a small world.

THIRTY-THREE

SMITTEN AND FOLSEY drove Beeson to his office in downtown D.C. Once they entered and cleared security, Beeson led them to the duty room where a U.S. Marshal was stationed around the clock to answer any calls from people in the Witness Protection Program who needed help of any kind or felt threatened in any manner.

"Hey, Coolio," said Beeson to the Marshal who was minding the phone. "I need to take a look at the call-in log."

"Who are these folks with you?" asked Coolio. His real name was Calvin, but someone had tagged him with Cool in high school, which morphed into Coolio when he started as a Marshal.

"Need to know, only…my son," said Beeson. "If I told you, we'd have to kill you."

Smitten stepped up. "FBI, Mr. Coolio."

Beeson laughed. "Coolio is his nickname. His real name is Calvin."

Smitten gave Beeson a hard look, then she and Folsey produced their ID's for Calvin's inspection.

"We just need to verify a call that should be in the log book," she told him.

Coolio smiled. He then handed over the log book directly to Beeson, who carried it over to a nearby empty desk and began to thumb back through the pages to the approximate date in question.

"All calls in and out are logged in by hand," Beeson told the two agents. "By not entering them into the computer, there's no way the info can be hacked."

"What about the security of the book?" Smitten asked.

"It stays in this room," said Beeson, "and we're the only ones who get a chance to see it."

He found the page he was looking for, then pointed the entries out to her.

"Here's the initial call. I logged the name of *Phillip Greenwood* as the caller, the time of the call, and the callback number." He moved his finger down the page. "And here's the callback I made to the White House. I spoke with Greenwood and gave him the information he requested."

Smitten asked for a copy of the page, one which would have the other calls and info redacted, and Beeson said he could arrange it, but she'd need to get a warrant to enable him to release it.

Smitten nodded. She had assumed that would be the case.

Beeson returned the book to the Marshal on duty and the three of them quickly made their way from the building.

"I'll take you back to our office," said Smitten. "You're free to go, but our interest in Greenwood must remain completely confidential. Do not mention any of this to your wife or anyone else. If you do, we'll arrest you for obstructing an FBI investigation and for lying to an FBI agent. Both are felonies, Mr. Beeson, and if we have to do that, your future will be fucked."

"I understand," he said.

"Incidentally," said Folsey from the driver's seat. "Your wife lied to us, too. We'll let her go as well, but you might want to mention to her that we're giving her a pass as well on the lie, but we'll keep the tape of the interview on file in case she mentions our investigation to anyone, including her lawyer."

"Her lawyer? My wife got a lawyer?"

"She requested one," said Folsey, "but we didn't let her call him yet."

"I'll take care of it," he said. "On that you can rely."

THIRTY-FOUR

DONAHUE'S PRIVATE FLIGHT arrived at the Baltimore International Airport on a cool and blustery day. The sky was full of darkness and moisture-saturated clouds. The humidity was high and a downpour seemed inevitable.

Otero and five other men and one female were with her on the plane, and they were met on the tarmac by three more men in two black SUV Denalis. Donahue was loaded into one of the cars with Otero, two men and the female, while the other six took the chase car.

As she sat in the rear seat during the ride into D.C., Donahue could only wonder how much this security entourage was costing, and if it was really necessary?

She knew that when it came to money, she would always have a middle-class state of mind. It was going to take a lot more time to come to grips with the reality of her new situation— that no matter what she did, she would likely never run out of money.

She was driven to the Omni Shoreham Hotel on Calvert Street NW, in Washington, D.C. It was a hotel that had hosted presidents and other world leaders. The Omni was located in a premier residential neighborhood; an elegant urban retreat of over eight-hundred rooms which was situated on eleven lush garden acres.

Donahue was escorted to a suite on the tenth floor, and once she was settled in, she called the number given to her by Freely, who advised her there was going to be a change of plans. Instead of sending someone for her, he himself would be coming to her hotel within the hour.

∽

When Jamison Freely arrived at the hotel, he called her room to tell her that he was on his way up. When he arrived at her door, he was met by Otero and one other man who patted him down and checked his identification.

Once he was permitted inside and they were seated on chairs in the living room area, Donahue showed him the note that Sean had written to her. He read it carefully with real interest, then passed it back.

Freely pulled out a small piece of electronic equipment from his pocket and placed it on the coffee table directly in front of them. He turned it on, then looked over at Donahue.

"It's a signal disruptor," he said with a smile. "It's one of our shiny new toys. It will garble any attempts to electronically intercept our conversation."

"It's very James Bond," she said with a smile.

He then pulled out a piece of paper from his jacket pocket and passed it over to Donahue with a pen.

"It's a confidentiality agreement," he said. "You need to sign and date it before we speak. And while you're looking it over, keep in mind that if you reveal anything I tell you to anyone, it will constitute a national security breach, and if that occurs, you will guarantee yourself a very long stretch in prison."

Donahue read the document over and quickly signed it, all the while chiding herself for not giving any thought to the depth of the security that would be needed now that she was a potential target of a hostile nation-state.

Freely lowered his voice and said, "Sean's father, Anton, was providing us with intelligence after he left Russia and settled in the U.K.

He claimed that Putin was looting the country, industry by industry, and he was beginning to supply us with information about Putin's financial dealings, hoping that we could use it to undermine Putin's next election campaign. Anton believed that once the Russian people discovered what was going on, they would elect someone who would clean up the corruption in Russia."

Donahue rolled her eyes. "So, he was working with you personally?"

"I met with Anton several times, but he was given a case officer and worked directly with agents assigned to our Russian desk."

"So what happened? You said Anton gave you some information?"

"He started to. A task force was set up to investigate his claims and to authenticate the first few documents he turned over to us." Freely leaned back in his seat and crossed his legs. "Just so you know, we were willing to accept the kind of information that Anton was providing, but before we even considered doing anything with it, we had to thoroughly vet it. It's rare but not unheard of for us to receive disinformation; the kind that is intended to mislead or embarrass us, so the vetting process itself can take a very long time. Anyway, as far as Anton was concerned, the investigation into his proofs was taking too long. He wanted the documents released in time for the last Russian presidential election, so he went behind our backs and made contact directly with the FBI. He believed that they would act much faster, but before a deal for the documents was finalized with them, he was poisoned in London. After he died, our task force was eventually disbanded."

"But what about the documents you were given? Wasn't there enough there to at least cause Putin some public embarrassment?"

"There was, but we were told to sit on what we had by the current administration, ostensibly because our President wanted to try and improve our relationship with the Russian Federation."

Donahue sighed. The current administration was already under investigation by a special counsel for possible conspiracy with the Russians during the last American presidential election. If the Russians had dirt on Trump—as was suspected by a majority of Americans—then it wasn't a stretch of the imagination to believe that Trump would want to keep the contents of Anton's documents a secret. It would give him leverage with Putin, a tit-for-tat card to play in case the Russians attempted to squeeze him too hard.

"And Sean?" she asked, already suspecting that she knew the answer. "How did he figure into all of this?"

"It would appear from his note to you that he inherited an additional stack of documents from his father."

Donahue's mind was racing.

"Did you know about these new documents?" she finally asked.

"I did not," he replied, "and I suspect that no one in my agency did either."

"What about the FBI? If they were working with Anton, wouldn't they have known that he had more documents in his possession?"

"Quite possibly," said Freely, "but if they did, they never passed that information on to me."

Donahue sighed. There was so much she still didn't know. How was she supposed to make an intelligent and safe decision about what to do?

"So, what do you think? Should I turn Sean's documents over to the FBI?"

"Not now," said Freely. "I'm hesitant to tell you this, but it's possible that there's a mole within the Bureau or the White House. It's being looked into, but until we know for sure, I would suggest that you hang on to the documents and lay low."

"A mole?" Donahue's eyes went wide. "Are you serious?" The pieces were rapidly falling together. "Oh, my God! Is that how the Russians found their way to Sean?"

Freely shrugged. "That's being looked into, Ms. Donahue. That's all I'm at liberty to say."

When he said no more, it was abundantly clear to Donahue that at this point the Bureau could not be trusted.

She sighed. This was so much more complicated than she ever imagined.

"I'm heading to Zurich as soon as we're done," she told him. "I need to get a sense of how many documents we're talking about."

"Look them over, if you have to, but leave them there and make sure that you're not followed to where they're being stored."

"My team is pretty good. I'm not worried about my security."

"You should be," he warned her. "Your enemy isn't a person, Ms. Donahue, it's a state, and if they want you dead, they'll find a way. You need to keep that in mind."

"Thanks for scaring me to death," she said with a frown.

Freely smiled tightly. "It's better to know what you're facing than to go off exposed and half-cocked."

"Do you have any information on how the investigation into Sean's death is going?"

"As I'm sure you've been told, the two men who killed him have themselves been killed, and the man who killed them has been captured. I'm told he's talking, but that has to remain confidential." He gave her a melancholy look. "And that might be as far as we can go with the investigation."

"Why?" she asked.

"We think the man who gave him the order may have diplomatic immunity, and if that turns out to be true, then there's little we can do except to expel him from our country."

"So, he's here in the States?"

Freely nodded.

"Are you going to tell me who he is?"

"Not until we know for sure. But at some point, maybe those documents will bring about some measure of justice to the people behind Sean's killing."

He slowly got to his feet. "Please keep me apprised of your location. If we learn of any threats, I'll let you know right away."

"I will," she said as she got to her feet. "Thank you for meeting with me."

"My pleasure," he said, sighing heavily. "We'll find the mole, Ms. Donahue. I promise you that. In the meantime, just keep yourself safe. When the time comes, we'll talk about the best way to deal with Mr. Putin and those documents."

THIRTY-FIVE

KASEY SMITTEN WAS waiting for Cullen when he came back from a luncheon meeting.

"You got something for me?" he asked as he took off his coat and put it on a coat rack that stood behind his government-issued desk.

"Yes sir. The man who made the call from Rush's office is named Phillip Greenwood. He is thirty-eight years old, married, in debt, but no criminal record."

"You want to bring him in?"

"Not yet, sir. I'd like to have someone talk to General Rush first. I'd like to know if he asked for the information, and if so, if Greenwood ever gave it to him?"

"And if he knows nothing about it?"

"Then we'll pick up Greenwood and see where it goes from there."

&

Agent Rodger Mason sat patiently in the waiting room just outside the office of Retired General Lindsey Rush. It was Rush's West Wing office, and on the door, the nameplate said *Assistant to the President for National Security Affairs,* commonly referred to as the NSC advisor.

Mason was a seasoned agent who was rapidly working his way up in the Bureau's ranks. He was tall, mid-forties, and in good shape. His career had already included a number of assignments in various cities throughout the United States, but now that he was assigned to D.C., he was planning to keep his nose to the grindstone so that his family could remain in one city for at least five years.

When Rush's secretary advised him that the General "will see you now," Mason got to his feet, straightened his tie, then followed the secretary into the General's office.

It was a surprisingly small room. There was an enormous desk and several easy chairs in a small seating area for both important and informal conversations. The furnishings were well made and expensive, as befitted an office in the West Wing.

"Agent Mason, is it?" Rush asked. He was seated at his desk and he peered at Mason from over the tops of his reading glasses.

"Yes, sir, General."

"Well, take a seat, son. What can I do for you?"

Rush directed him to a chair in front of the desk, an indication to him that the meeting would be formal.

"We're conducting a routine audit of the Marshal's Office, specifically the Witness Protection Program, and we noticed in the call logs that a call was made from your office by a gentleman named Phillip Greenwood."

"Phillip is an assistant of mine," said the General.

"Yes, sir. Well, he requested certain information of a confidential nature which was provided to him. We wanted to confirm that you requested that information, and whether or not you ever received it."

"And what was the information we supposedly requested?"

Mason was surprised. He was anticipating that Rush would immediately know exactly who they were talking about.

Was it possible that the General had requested information on other occasions from the Program? If that wasn't the case, and if this was the only time, did he not know what his assistant had been up to?

It was Mason's first inkling that something wasn't right.

Mason cleared his throat. "It was the location of one of the program's protected witnesses."

Rush held his glance, then said, "I never made such a request, Agent Mason, and I never received any information relating to a protected witness. If you'd like, I can call Phillip in and we can ask him about it right now?"

"Actually, sir, we'd prefer that you didn't say anything to Mr. Greenwood. We'll conduct a full investigation, and we'll advise you before we take any action."

"As you wish," said the General.

"In the meantime, sir, I would suggest that you limit his access to confidential or secret information, and do so without letting him know that he's being cut out of the loop."

Rush nodded. "A good suggestion, Agent Mason. Please let me know if I can be of any further assistance."

"I will, sir." Mason got to his feet. "And thank you, sir, for your time."

◆

When Mason got back to the office, he told Smitten that Rush denied requesting the information, and that he said he never received it. He also added that Rush was cooperative, but betrayed no emotion upon being told that his assistant had illegally obtained top-secret information.

"He was a General," said Smitten. "You know, a highly disciplined guy. So, he is probably very good at concealing his emotions."

"Yeah, there's that," said Mason, "but he was way too cool."

"Meaning what?" she asked.

"Just my observation. He didn't even ask who the subject was, and he wasn't curious enough to ask if the protected witness's security had been compromised in any way."

"Strange," said Smitten

"My thought, exactly."

◆

Three hours later, an FBI undercover surveillance team watched as Greenwood, his wife, and his infant child came out of their house in Bethesda, Maryland. They drove to a nearby mall where they had dinner at a *Panda Express.*

While the family was eating, an FBI tech team, under the authority of a FISA warrant, entered their home, downloaded the contents of Greenwood's computer, added a keystroke program to monitor his future writings, then inserted miniaturized microphones into several light fixtures that would pick up conversations in most of the rooms in the house. The verbal conversations would then be broadcast several blocks away by a transmitter concealed in Greenwood's backyard, under a Mulberry bush.

THIRTY-SIX

Ambassador Oleg Kozlov's black Mercedes pulled out of the Russian Embassy on Wisconsin Avenue NW, in D.C., and headed for the historic *Hay-Adams Hotel* on 16th Street NW. The car was being driven by an SVR intelligence officer who acted as Kozlov's driver and bodyguard. Right behind it was a second Mercedes with three more SVR security agents.

Kozlov was a very recognizable public figure in the Washington political scene. He frequently made the rounds at Embassy parties, willingly did television interviews on the Sunday morning network shows, and even managed to secure an occasional invitation to White House functions, courtesy of an administration that inexplicably tended to overlook his reputation as a recruiter of spies.

A block behind the black Mercedes was a silver Toyota containing two FBI Counter Intelligence agents, both members of the Los Angeles FBI team. They were flown in during the day by Jack Cullen to handle the secret surveillance of Oleg Kozlov.

Kozlov was dropped off in front of the Hay-Adams. He waited for his security team to get settled before getting out of the car. A second FBI counter surveillance team, one which had been running a parallel route, stopped on the block behind the hotel to let three agents out of their vehicle. One by one, they entered the hotel by means of a seldom-used back entrance.

The FBI team located Kozlov and his escorts in the main lobby. Kozlov was shaking hands with two men dressed in blue business suits, and the three of them chatted quietly before making their way into the hotel's *Lafayette* room, a destination considered to be one of the best fine-dining restaurants in the Washington, D.C., area.

The two female members of the surveillance team were dressed like businesswomen. They followed their target's progression into the restaurant and were seated at a table about thirty feet away from the one that was given to Kozlov and the two businessmen.

They posed as female friends out for drinks and dinner after a long day at the office. Both ordered dry martinis and their conversation was animated and full of good cheer.

Both women had cameras secreted in their small purses which lay on the table between them. Once their drinks arrived, one adjusted her purse so that the lens on the micro camera contained within was pointed across the room at the Kozlov party. The lens filled a small opening in the cloth side of the designer purse, which enabled the rest of the camera to remain concealed. Using her cell phone, she operated the video camera using the bluetooth feature which allowed the feed to be directly transmitted to the building that the task force was now using as their base of operations.

The building was a hastily-rented warehouse in the horse country in Virginia. In need of a name for radio purposes, they referred to the warehouse as "the barn."

The feed was run through facial recognition software and the two men with Kozlov were quickly identified as bankers from the D.C. branch of *HSBC* bank.

Meanwhile, the two agents who initially followed Kozlov from the embassy to the restaurant were replaced by a second shift that set up across the street from the hotel. The first team then returned to the barn where they worked on their field log before heading to a nearby motel where they could catch a few hours of sleep before rotating back on the surveillance.

The counter surveillance team was made up of true professionals, and along with the support group of computer operators and makeup specialists from L.A., they were intent upon building a minute-by-minute summary of Kozlov's activities and contacts.

⌣

As the key investigators in the Walker murder case, Smitten and Folsey were attached to the Greenwood surveillance operation. Cullen had insisted that both of them undergo polygraphs relating to their work as handlers of Sean Walker, and both had passed with flying colors. Convinced that neither one could be the mole, Cullen authorized them to work with the Bureau surveillance teams that he had imported from Los Angeles. They were given access to the barn, and they were quickly assimilated into the ongoing operation.

Now hanging out in the barn, Folsey had just filled her coffee cup from a percolator when Smitten called her over from across the room. Folsey joined her and a computer technician who was standing by Smitten's desk.

"You need to hear this," said Smitten.

"Oh, what's up?"

The computer tech, an agent named Hawthorne, cleared his throat.

"I was reviewing the contents of Greenwood's computer and I got a good look at his calendar. He had an entry for a meeting with someone named 'Mr. Jones' five days after the Sean Walker killing."

"So? Who is this Mr. Jones?"

"That's just it," said Hawthorne. "On most of his other meetings with people, he lists the location and time of the meets. But there's no location listed for Jones, which means that if they had a meeting, it was at a location already known to both of them."

"And the time of the meeting? Was that listed?"

"Eleven p.m.," he replied.

"Okay," said Smitten. "Where are we going with this?"

"He has another entry for a meeting with 'Mr. Jones' on his calendar for tomorrow. No location, but the time of the meet is six-thirty p.m."

"An early evening meeting? Now that is interesting." Smitten looked over at an agent who was monitoring the surveillance radios.

"Is Greenwood still at dinner with his family?" she asked.

The agent nodded.

Smitten smiled. "Well done, Hawthorne. We'll take it from here."

She turned to Folsey. "Tell the team leader on Greenwood that we need to get that meeting covered tomorrow. We'll need photos of Jones, sound from the meeting if possible, and if the meeting actually does take place, we're gonna want this Jones person followed until we can make a positive ID."

"Five bucks says Jones is a female and he's having an affair," said Folsey.

"You're probably right," said Smitten. "But if he is, it might give us some leverage when we brace him up about the call that he made to Beeson."

THIRTY-SEVEN

DONAHUE AND HER entourage of security personnel arrived at London's Heathrow Airport, and after connecting with the vehicles that Otero had arranged for, they drove down the M4 and A4 highways into downtown London proper.

Reservations had been made at the Claridge's Hotel, a luxury landmark in the Mayfair district of London, and once she was settled into her suite, she pulled out Sean's address book and placed a call to a number that was listed for Alexi Egorov.

When Egorov answered she explained who she was.

"I know who you are, Ms. Donahue," he said in a thick Russian accent. "Mikel told me all about you."

Egorov was a fifty-three year old, Uzbek-born, Russian ex-pat oligarch, who was listed in the Bloomberg Billionaire index. He made his wealth through precious metals, mining, and pharmaceuticals. He also owned a hotel chain, with properties in the Czech Republic, Scotland, and most recently in northern England.

"I'm here in London," she said, "and I was wondering if we could meet?"

"Of course. Where are you staying?"

When she said the name of her hotel, he told her he could be there in an hour.

"I'll call you when I arrive," he added. "Perhaps you'll let me buy you a drink in the bar?"

Donahue was reminded of the fate that befell Sean's father, who had met with a Russian in a hotel restaurant for a cup of tea. She had no intention of meeting him for a drink, but rather than tell him that, she preferred to keep him off balance. So, once he arrived at her hotel, she would bring him up to her room where she could control her environment.

"That sounds fine," she said. "Mikel told me that you were holding something for him. I would appreciate it if you would bring it along."

"Of course." He paused for a moment, then said, "I'm looking forward to meeting you."

When he showed up fifty minutes later, she advised him to come up to her suite. When he arrived, he was carefully searched by Otero before being allowed to make entry into the room.

He was dressed in an expensive gray business suit with a starched white shirt and a pale maroon tie. He extended his hand and gave her a warm smile, and Donahue responded in kind.

"You have quite a security presence," he said, once they had shaken hands.

She offered him a seat on the couch, which he readily took. Room service had already delivered tea and pastries which she had thoughtfully placed on the coffee table.

"I'm afraid that certain events have necessitated that I take precautions when I travel," she said while she poured him a cup of tea.

"I understand," he replied, and after taking the cup, he leaned back on the couch and sighed.

"Let me begin by telling you how sorry I am that Mikel has been killed. He was like a son to me, and when he told me about how much he loved you, I could tell that you were very special. I'm sure his death has been awful for you, and if there's anything I can do to help you in any way, please, just let me know."

"I appreciate your condolences, and I'm sure that Mikel's death has also been painful for you, too."

"It has."

His voice caught for a moment, and in the silence that followed, Egorov placed what was left of his tea on the table.

"I don't know what Mikel told you about me, but I was very close to Anton, his father."

"I knew nothing about you," she told him. "In fact, I knew nothing about Mikel's family or his background until after his death." She briefly shut her eyes as she recalled in a flash the moment that she was told that Sean had been killed. "I only learned about you from a letter that Sean left for me."

Egorov was surprised. He had always assumed that once Mikel was engaged that he had informed her about his background.

"I was unaware of that," he told her. "But Mikel was a very careful man, so it doesn't surprise me that he would not want to expose you to the horrors of his family's dealings with Putin and his thugs."

Donahue sensed that Egorov might well be in a position to tell her more about what happened to Anton than what little she'd been able to glean from news reports. She studied him intensely, and for a moment she debated with herself whether or not it would be prudent to ask him about Anton, and what significant events may have led to his death.

With Sean now dead, she decided she might never meet anyone else who was in a position to paint for her a first-hand portrait of the Korakovsky family history, and why things ended up so tragically.

"May I call you Alexi?" she asked.

"Of course, Ms. Donahue."

"Thank, you, Alexi. And please, call me Jennifer."

Egorov nodded. He was beginning to like this young woman. No wonder Mikel was so attracted to her. She was beautiful, that went without saying, but she also possessed a dignity that masked the aggressiveness that was likely a hallmark of her chosen career as a police officer. He suspected that she was very intelligent, and that was good, because she had been thrust into a situation where intelligence and courage would be necessary for her to remain safe.

He wondered if she understood the rules of the game, and if she had the fortitude to face what might be coming? Would she cut and run, or did she have the strength and tenacity to see Anton's and Mikel's quest through to its conclusion?

He locked his eyes on hers and was about to speak when she beat him to the punch.

"I've read about Anton's murder, but there's very little that's publicly available. So, Alexi, I wonder if you would be willing to tell me what you know about what happened, and the perceived reasons for Anton's killing?"

Egorov smiled and nodded. His assessment of this woman was right on point. She was going to be a fighter, and because of that, he would give up what he knew in the hope that it would level out the playing field and help her to survive.

But before he dragged her into this mess, he would need to know that her commitment was real and not just a figment of an old man's wishful thinking.

"You have unwittingly been dragged into a very difficult and dangerous world, Jennifer, one that could lead to your death. I will tell you what I know because I know how much Mikel believed in you and trusted you, but once I tell you what is going on, I want you to think very carefully about taking the next step. You have no real sense of how diabolical these people are and the lengths they will go to in order to keep the status quo." His eyes slowly narrowed. "Are you sure you want to know what is really going on?"

Donahue nodded. "I loved Sean, Alexi, and he loved me. That meant that we had each other's backs. Whatever he was involved in, I know that he believed that what he was doing was worth the risk, and since he's not here to see it through, it falls to me to do what I can to continue his actions. But I'm not a fool. I know that I'm floundering around in the dark. And to be honest, I have a feeling that the people I've been dealing with in my own government are just as ignorant as I am as to what is going on. So, if I'm going to see this through, I need to know what the hell I'm getting myself into, and to that extent, if you know anything that will help me get a better picture of what I'll be facing, then please fill me in and let me worry about the rest."

Egorov slowly nodded. Mikel had told him once that she was a remarkable person, and it was pretty clear to Egorov that Mikel was right.

"As you wish, Jennifer. Let me begin with Mikel's father. Anton was a shrewd businessman. When the USSR collapsed in '91, Russia was very much like the wild west. Those with connections to Yeltsin were able to purchase the main assets of the Federation, and Anton was able to borrow a large sum of money to purchase the rights to communications, oil, and mining operations. And while Anton built up his fortune, Putin focused on politics.

"In '90, after years in the KGB, Putin was appointed as an advisor to the Mayor of Saint Petersburg. He was responsible for promoting international relations and foreign investments. In '96, when Putin's mentor lost the Mayoral election, Putin was called to Moscow and became a Deputy Chief of the Presidential Property Management Department. In this position, he was responsible for the foreign property of the state. His role was to organize the transfer of the former assets of the Soviet Union to the Russian Federation. In '97, Boris Yeltsin appointed Putin to be Deputy Chief of Presidential Staff, and during this time, he held other positions as well, all of them involving various aspects of the transition and the control of power."

He held her glance for a moment, and was pleased to note that he still had her undivided attention.

"I'm sure you can see that these positions gave him a leg up on the competition when it came to knowing their weaknesses and where the skeletons were buried. Anyway, in '98, Yeltsin appointed Putin as head of the FSB, and also as a permanent member of the Security

Council of the Russian Federation. He now had all the knowledge and the backing of the Intelligence Services to position himself to take advantage of an ailing Yeltsin's decline. In '99, he was appointed a First Deputy Prime Minister, and later that same day, Yeltsin appointed him as acting Prime Minister. When Yeltsin unexpectedly resigned in '99, Putin became the Acting President of the Federation, and since that time, he has firmly held on to the reins of power."

Egorov suddenly coughed. It was phlegmy and sounded quite bad.

Donahue offered him a glass of water from a nearby carafe which he eagerly sipped.

When he put his glass down, he said, "After Putin's third inauguration, Anton began using his television network to crusade against corruption. Putin had formed a cabal of oligarchs, men he trusted from his earlier days in the KGB and FSB, and Anton was slowly beginning to align himself with other oligarchs who opposed Putin's personal grab of assets and secret holdings that were being hidden by members of his cabal. This assault on corruption incurred the wrath of Putin. Anton was ordered to divest himself of his television network holdings or he would face an indictment on charges of financial corruption.

"Anton knew that he'd met his match, so he liquidated his holdings and shifted his investments into western businesses. He moved to London with his son, Mikel, and when Putin realized what Anton had done—that he'd taken all of his large fortune out of Russia— he had the Prosecutor General prepare false charges against him.

"But Anton was a fighter, and rather than succumb to Putin's threats, he announced from London that he would run against Putin for the presidency. Putin tried to have him extradited from the U.K., but the British refused to give Anton up. So, quite naturally, because Putin couldn't take the risk of going up against Anton in an election, he gave orders to the FSB to make sure he didn't run."

Egorov sighed and shrugged. "To keep him from running, they poisoned Anton with radioactive Polonium 210."

"But why do it that way?" Donahue shook her head in disbelief. "Why put so many people at risk? Why anger the western world and incur governmental sanctions when a bullet would have been less controversial?"

"Putin wanted to send a message to the others in the oligarch class. *'Go against me and you will suffer while you pay the ultimate price.'* And as for the western nations, the use of Polonium 210 was his way of announcing to leaders of the West that he is a person to be reckoned with."

Egorov leaned forward and shrugged. "But it didn't end there. What you don't know is that there has been a trail of retribution killings, all stemming from Anton's death. And by the way, the victims are not all Russian oligarchs."

"In '07, an American named Paul Joyal, a friend of Anton's, appeared on NBC's *Dateline* TV show to discuss the death of Anton. He was a longtime Putin critic, and he accused Putin of ordering Anton's murder. Four days later, he was arriving home after meeting with Oleg Kalugin, the former chief of KGB Counter Intelligence. Kalugin was a defector and also a critic of Putin. When Joyal arrived home, he stepped out of his car and was attacked by two men. One of the men shot him, and both men fled when the gun jammed before it could give off a second shot.

"Eight days before this, another person on the same program ended up dead. Daniel McGrory, a senior London Times reporter, died of a heart attack. His death initially seemed unsuspicious, but after the poisoning of Anton, the British authorities decided to take a second look at his death, and the death of all the others.

"A few years later, Boris Berezovsky, a former Russian billionaire and a harsh critic of Putin, was found hanged in his bathroom at his home in London. He, too, was a close friend of Anton's."

Egorov shrugged his shoulders and gently sighed.

"There are more, Jennifer. The list is long. I tell you about these things to make sure you understand that Putin is a vengeful man. He has enormous wealth and the power of the Russian Federation behind him. Mikel thought that the American government could protect him, but Putin has once again demonstrated to the world at large that when he decides he wants someone dead, then even the Americans' famous Witness Protection Program is no guarantee of safety."

Donahue slowly closed her eyes for a moment. This was one hell of a vicious opponent that she was about to face, and to be honest, it was causing her to have second thoughts.

"I had no idea," she told Egorov. "I will definitely reassess my involvement, but tell me, Alexi, why did Putin decide to come after Sean? I know there are documents of some kind, but where did they come from?"

Egorov leaned forward. "Well before he died, and before he left the Federation, Anton began collecting information from others who'd been victimized by Putin. You see, Putin takes a large share of every asset that he has forced his enemy oligarchs to sell. It has become a large part of his enormous wealth. His share then disappears behind a number of shell corporations, and is often listed publicly as an asset controlled by one of his oligarch cronies. And, just so you know, it's no secret that Putin is now believed to be one of the richest men in the entire world."

Egorov coughed again, then produced a cloth handkerchief which he used to catch what he needed to expel from his mouth.

"Please forgive me," he said as he tucked the handkerchief back into his pocket. "I apologize for my cough. I'm afraid it is the result of too many cigarettes for too many years."

He took another sip of the water, then resumed his story.

"These days Putin prefers to put his money into western businesses and properties, and that is why he's been pushing so hard to have your President remove the sanctions that have tied up many of his investments."

"What about the people who were involved in Anton's killing? Do the authorities know how they got to him?"

Egorov leaned forward.

"Andrey Lugovoy, a millionaire and former officer in the *Federal Protective Service of Russia,* met with Anton on the day he fell ill. He visited London at least three times in the month before Anton's poisoning. It was the fourth time when it actually happened. Traces of polonium-210 were discovered in all three hotels where he stayed, so the plot was clearly underway well before Anton was actually given the poison. Lugovoy was himself treated for poisoning back in Russia, although the Russians would not confirm that it was due to polonium-210. The British Crown Prosecution Service has charged him with murder, but the Russians have refused to honor their extradition request.

"A second man was also involved. He was Dmitry Kovtun, a Russian businessman and an ex-KGB agent. He was also with Lugovoy when Anton was poisoned. He arrived in London on a flight that passed through Hamburg, and he left a trail of polonium-210 in his car and at his ex-wife's home where he spent the night before his flight to London. He was later hospitalized with polonium-210 poisoning, and the case against him is still under investigation.

Egorov shifted his weight in his chair and sighed heavily.

"The Brits believe that these two men were idiots. Their carelessness in handling it made both of them ill, so even though they made several separate attempts to poison Anton, they may not have known that the poison was radioactive. But when the third attempt failed, the Russians added one more killer to the mix, and he's a man we know very little about. The Brits refer to him as Vladislav, but he is also known in western intelligence circles as *Igor the Assassin.*

"From what I've been told, on the day that Anton was poisoned, Kovtun and Lugovoy ostensibly went to the Millennium's hotel bar where they met with Anton to discuss a business deal. When the three men later went to Anton's room at the Millennium, they were joined by a man who called himself Vladislav. This Vladislav was vouched for by Lugovoy. Anton later told the British that Vladislav was offering to help him win a lucrative contract with a Moscow-based private security firm. My source in British Intelligence tells me that they believe Lugovoy distracted Anton while Vladislav poisoned the tea. He was later photographed leaving the country on an EU passport. He's believed to be in Russia, but his true identity is still unknown."

For the moment, Donahue's head was spinning, and she decided that she'd heard enough. This was so much more complicated than she had ever imagined, and while her sources in Washington had given her only a small part of the picture, she couldn't help but wonder if they actually had a handle on the scope of Putin's deadly vendetta.

She was going to need time to process what she'd learned, and as a first step, she needed to know a little bit more about the documents that Sean had secreted. And to do that, she had to visit the place where Sean had placed them in storage.

She leaned up and said, "Did you bring the item I asked you for?"

Egorov nodded. He pulled a sealed, letter-sized envelope out of his suit pocket and held it out for her to take.

"Here is the key to a safe deposit box," he told her.

Donahue's eyes narrowed. "Sean's letter to me said that you didn't know what he was asking you to hold on to?"

Egorov gave her a genuine smile.

"My dear, Jennifer. If you squeeze the envelope, you can easily tell that it contains a key. And what else could a key like this be for if not for a safe deposit box?"

Donahue slowly smiled. Egorov was right. It didn't take a genius to identify a key in a sealed envelope. She took the envelope from his hand and placed it on the table in front of her.

"Alexi, I would appreciate your discretion when it comes to keeping what we've talked about a secret," she told him.

"Of course, Jennifer. Anton and Mikel were like family to me, and you have taken their place in my heart."

"I appreciate that, Alexi. If you learn anything more about the people involved, I hope you'll give me a call."

"I will, Jennifer. And if there's anything more that I can do for you, just ask."

He got to his feet, gave her an awkward hug, then cautioned her to be careful before leaving her suite.

Donahue found that her hands were shaking and her knees were ready to buckle. She sat back down in her chair and tried to process what she'd been told.

Her first sane thought was to get back on her plane and get the hell out of London. But then the left hemisphere of her cerebral cortex took over, and she realized that she was already in too deep to even think about backing out now. It was entirely possible that Sean's killers knew about her from the time they spent when they were in Sean's duplex. If that was the case, then it was more likely than not that Putin would quickly discern that she was probably going to be the beneficiary of Sean's will.

I'm already fucked, so running away now would be futile. I guess I'll just have to see things through.

THIRTY-EIGHT

DONAHUE'S PLANE TOUCHED down at *Flughafen*, the international airport in Zurich, Switzerland. And just as he had done on the earlier stops on this trip, Otero had arranged for everything. She was quickly hustled through customs and immigration, then driven for eighteen minutes from the airport by limousine to the nearby foothills and the castle-like Dolder Grand Hotel, where she was quickly ensconced in a massive suite that overlooked the city of Zurich.

The sky was gloomy. A moist, cold fog had swooped in and enveloped the city, but Donahue was prepared for the inclement weather with a heavy wool overcoat, a pair of leather gloves, and a pair of long underwear beneath her jeans. The outfit was the result of a purchase she made at Harrod's in London before taking off from Heathrow.

She was slowly beginning to realize that there were certain advantages to having one's own plane and an unlimited budget. And a good psychiatrist would say that it was a sign that her undeserved guilt over the inheritance from Sean was slowly beginning to fade.

Once she was settled in, she asked Otero to escort her without the usual security entourage to the *Credit Suisse AG, Private Bank, at Bleicherweg 33,* in Zurich.

"It's important that my visit to this location goes unnoticed. I want to slip in and out without attracting any undue attention."

Otero asked for an hour to set things up, and once he left her suite, she went to the bedroom and laid down on the bed. Her nausea had returned, and she decided that as soon as she got back to L.A., she was going to get a full checkup from her doctor.

Otero returned forty-five minutes later carrying a small bag.

She heard him enter the suite, so she got to her feet, willed the queasy stomach away, and came out of the room.

"I purchased a few items that will help with the deception," he said. "The bank is going to have cameras."

He emptied the bag out on the dining room table. The contents included a shoulder length brown wig, a pair of dark sunglasses, and a black rain umbrella.

"I've sent a few members of your team to the bank to scout it out, and I've decided that we'll catch a cab to and from the bank. One of my teams will follow the cab discreetly."

Donahue tied back her hair and slipped on the dark wig.

"It makes me look like Jackie Kennedy," she said, as she preened in front of the dining room mirror.

"That's good, I guess, as long as you don't look like you."

Donahue smiled. "Is it still cold outside?" she asked.

Otero nodded. "Light rain, low forties."

"Let me get my coat. I want to get this over with."

She was growing more anxious by the moment. This trip to the bank was the first active step to possible exposure, but she understood that she was on a path that offered her no easy offramp. She wished that Shari had come along on this trip with her. It would have been nice to have her independent counsel.

"Are you still feeling under the weather?" Otero asked.

"A little, but it comes and goes."

"I can arrange for a doctor—"

She shook her head. "I'll be okay for now, but I plan to see one as soon as we're back in L.A. Hopefully, I haven't been poisoned."

Otero blanched. "If there's any chance that's happened, Ms. Donahue, then I insist that we get you checked out right now."

Really stupid, Jen, she told herself. He doesn't get my warped sense of humor yet.

"I was just kidding, Jamie. It was a bad joke. I'm sorry."

"Yes, ma'am," he said, and she could see the relief on his face.

She grabbed her coat, put on the sunglasses, then picked up the umbrella.

"Okay," she said. "Let's go."

They walked out of the hotel, had the doorman summon a cab, and were driven to an office building directly across the street from the bank branch. Once the cab was out of sight Otero escorted her to the nearest corner where they crossed the street and made their way into the bank.

Otero left her sitting in a waiting area while he spoke to an assistant manager who quickly accompanied him back to Donahue. When she advised him that she wanted to get into her safety deposit box, he escorted them over to a private room where he was given the box number and shown the numbered key that Sean had left with Alexi Egorov.

She was escorted down a flight of stairs to a secured basement vault, and once they were past the security door, the assistant manager used his key and hers to open the double-locked box. It was two feet long and twelve inches wide. Otero lifted it out for her and placed it on a nearby counter before he and the assistant manager then left her alone.

Once they were gone, Donahue lifted the metal cover and examined the contents of the box.

The stack of documents was almost three inches in height. They were not bound in any way, so she pulled out the top quarter inch and began to look them over.

They were mostly written documents, almost all of which were in a language that was not English, and if she had to guess, she suspected that most of them were in the standard Russian language.

In the stack, she came across a number of photographs, eight by ten in size, and Vladmir Putin was in at least five of them. They appeared to have been taken surreptitiously, and she suspected that the people he was with were what made the photographs important to Sean's father.

There was little she could do with the documents. She had no desire to remove them from the bank, but at some point, she was going to have to have them translated so that she'd know exactly what she had.

But the photographs were different. She could show them to Freely, and with a little effort, perhaps he could make a quick assessment of their potential importance.

She pulled out her iPhone, and using the camera feature, she took pictures of the photographs containing Putin. There were other photos of people she didn't recognize, but they looked like undercover surveillance photographs of people in a clandestine meeting. She snapped pictures of those as well as a few of the documents, and when she felt that she had a large enough representative sample, she put everything back in the box, closed the metal lid, then pressed a button on the counter that signaled that she was ready to go.

Otero and the assistant manager came back into the room and the box was returned to its slot in the wall. Once it was locked back up with the two keys, Donahue was given hers back.

Outside the bank, Donahue and Otero caught a cab back to the hotel, and on the way, Donahue told Otero that she was ready to go back to L.A.

"The pilots and crew are required by law to get a certain amount of rest," he told her. "I can hire another crew if you'd like, but the team we came with has already been vetted, and they'll be ready to go again first thing tomorrow morning."

She hadn't realized that there would be a rest requirement involved, but it sure made sense. Her nausea had subsided, probably because she was no longer anxious about what was in the box.

"We can wait until tomorrow," she told him. "And I'm feeling a little better, so maybe I can do a little sightseeing and shopping."

"With or without the wig?" he said with a smile.

She laughed. "It feels a little itchy, so I think I can do without it."

THIRTY-NINE

GREENWOOD FINISHED UP the last page of his notes which summarized the document he'd just been reading. He then printed out his report, added it to the original document, and after knocking on the door of Rush's office, he walked in and dropped the file into the inbox that was on the left side of Rush's desk.

Rush was standing in a corner of the office, staring out the window. He turned when Greenwood entered and watched him place the documents into the inbox.

"What's that?" he said.

Greenwood was momentarily startled. He hadn't realized that the General was still in the room.

"Oh, hi! I didn't know you were still here, sir. It's an agricultural report for the southern region of the U.S. It's pretty dry, so I summarized it for you."

"Thanks," said Rush. "I've been meaning to ask how your family is doing?"

"Everyone is fine. Penny is hoping to get back to teaching soon. Next term she's scheduled to take the third grade."

"What about the baby?" Rush asked.

"Her mom has volunteered to take her during the day. Her parents live a few miles from our place, so it is going to work out nicely."

Greenwood was beginning to think that something was up. Rush rarely engaged any members of the staff in small talk, so his questions about Greenwood's family were disconcerting.

An awkward silence followed, which put Greenwood even more on edge.

When Rush finally spoke again, he said, "We'll have to get together one day. Maybe we can get a drink after work?"

"Aaa…yeah, sure. That would be great, sir."

After looking at his watch, Greenwood excused himself by telling Rush that he needed to catch the six-fifteen Metro.

Back in his own office, Greenwood gathered up his laptop and backpack before making his way to Dupont Circle Station where he used his pass to catch the Metro Red Line.

He was headed to the Woodley Nature Sanctuary, a forty-acre property in Chevy Chase, Maryland. It was home to the Audubon Naturalist Society, a non-profit environmental organization dedicated to conservation and education. The grounds were open to the public, and it was perfect for hiking excursions, with easy trails that traversed the woods and open meadow spaces.

Technically, the sanctuary was officially closed at dusk, but there was no way to lock people out. Once he arrived, he entered the park and took a seat on a public bench where he pulled out his laptop and began to respond to his emails.

A few minutes later, a man walking a small dog came down the path and stopped when he got to the bench. Greenwood reached out to the dog, who got up on his hind legs and allowed Greenwood to rub his head.

✎

When Greenwood entered the park, the Counter Intelligence teams were on it. Several agents in jogging clothes made a quick pass, then took up concealed positions further down the pathway. An unmarked van pulled up at the curb on a street with a line of sight to the bench.

In the back of the van, a second team was engaged in fine-tuning their technical equipment.

A program had been installed on Greenwood's laptop which made use of the computer's microphone. It picked up sounds around the computer, then transmitted them over the internet to the equipment in the truck.

The agents in the truck could clearly hear and record the conversation which took place between Greenwood and the man with the dog.

A few minutes later, the man with the dog walked off. Greenwood closed up his computer, put it back inside his backpack, then left the park to go to the nearby Metro station.

⌎

At the barn, Smitten and Folsey were standing with the Agent-in-Charge of the agents involved in the Woodley Nature Sanctuary surveillance team. They were waiting for the agents in the field to transmit their recording of the meeting.

Greenwood was being followed by agents on the Metro and also by a team in an undercover car. The man with the dog—ostensibly named Mr. Jones—was now himself under surveillance by two additional FBI teams.

When the broadcast of the tape was received, it was played through speakers so that all three, and several nearby agents, could hear exactly what had been said.

"Hey, puppy! What's his name?"

"Gringo," said the man.

"Hey, Gringo! What a good boy!"

"I need you to do something for me," the man with the dog asked. *"I need you to find out who stands in line to inherit Sean Walker's estate."*

"I can't do that," said Greenwood. *"My boss is acting strange. I can't take a chance."*

"Sure you can," said the man. *"Just make the call to the Marshals Office like you did the last time."*

"It won't work. The guy was killed, and if I even try to ask, they will be onto me like white on rice."

"I can't go further without that information," said the man. *"I know it's going to be tough, but I've got great confidence in you, Phil. You feel the same way I do. This has to get done."*

There was a prolonged moment of silence, then Greenwood said, *"Okay. I'll try."*

"Call me when you get it," said the man.

The group stood there in silence for a few moments while they digested what was said by the targets.

"Can we pick up Greenwood now?" Folsey asked.

"Not yet," said the surveillance team leader. "I need to clear it with Mr. Cullen. We might want to see if we can turn Greenwood into a double."

"He's too low on the totem to be a double agent," said Smitten, but she knew that was a decision better made at the top.

"That may be, but I still need to make the call and kick the decision upstairs."

Smitten sighed. "While you're doing that, I'll wait for the video feed. I want to run this Mr. Jones character through our facial recognition program. We need to know who he is."

FORTY

JACK CULLEN SAT across the desk from his boss, Robert Landers, the current Director of the FBI.

Landers was a former United States Attorney for the southern district of New York. Having been educated at Harvard law school, he spent ten years as a prosecutor before doing a brief stint in private practice. But he was not enamored with the constant need to accumulate billable hours, so he changed careers again when he was elected to become a Justice of the Supreme Court, in New York's trial court of general jurisdiction.

As a judge, he quickly built up a reputation for being fair and impartial. He loved the drama of the work, and believed that he had finally found his true niche in life. But his reputation as a by-the-book jurist soon made it's way to the top of the political world, and when he was asked by the President to become the director of the Bureau, he knew he couldn't refuse.

The investigation into the death of Sean Walker had reached a point where Cullen was obligated to brief Director Landers or face the possibility of being forced to resign. Cullen wasn't too sure about his boss. After all, he was a political appointee, and the President who had chosen him seemed to be more interested in personal loyalty than he was in an individual's integrity.

But this was going to be a first test for Landers, and he owed the man a chance to prove that he would put country and the good of the nation over political loyalty to his party.

He spent almost thirty minutes going over the details of the investigation, beginning with the murder of Anton Korakovsky, followed by the murder of Walker and the killings in Israel of the two men involved. He danced around the capture of the assassin in London, and withheld the news that the man had become an informant. Instead, he shifted the conversation to the fact that the CIA had passed on information that there might be a mole within the Bureau, or possibly within the White House.

"You mean there are two possible moles?" Landers asked.

"No, sir, we don't think so. And actually, we've made some progress on that front."

"I'm all ears," said Landers.

"We've focused on an administrative assistant named Phillip Greenwood. He works in the office of Retired General Lindsey Rush. Greenwood made a call to the U.S. Marshal's Office and obtained information on Walker's whereabouts. He claimed to the Marshal's Office that the call was on behalf of the General himself, and shortly after he obtained that information, Mr. Walker was assassinated."

"Have you picked him up?" Landers asked.

"Not yet. We've got surveillance in place, and we're hoping to identify his Russian handler."

"Does he still have access to sensitive information?"

"Not anymore. We've briefed General Rush, and he'll see to it that Greenwood doesn't get close to anything of intelligence quality."

Landers gave that some thought.

"I don't like it, Jack. He could still end up seeing something when the General is out of his office."

"It's a possibility, sir," said Cullen, "but I think we need to take a chance. And there's one more wrinkle I haven't yet mentioned."

"Now would be a good time," said Landers, as he folded his arms across his chest.

"Greenwood had a meeting last night with a man named Morris Zuckerman. It turns out that Zuckerman is a journalist with the Washington Post. Zuckerman asked Greenwood to call the Marshal's Office again and find out who inherited Walker's estate."

"Why is that important?" Landers asked.

"Walker was holding on to certain documents detrimental to President Vladmir Putin. That's why we put him in PC, to protect him while we negotiated for possession of what he had. But there is another aspect to this that I need to mention. The Russians filed a lawsuit in London over the ownership of Walker's assets. They wanted to flush him out. Once they got the information they needed, they sent in a hit team that killed him.

"Now here's the rub. The lawsuit is still pending, and we believe that they are now attempting to use the lawsuit to determine the identity of the person inheriting his estate. They want the family assets and the documents that implicate Putin in criminal activity. If they ever get ahold of her identity, they'll do whatever it takes to get their hands on those documents, including taking her out."

Landers got to his feet and began pacing around his desk. He always thought more clearly when he was moving around.

"As I see it," he began, "we've got several things going on at the same time. We've got the Russian efforts to get their hands on Walker's assets and documents, and we've got the second bigger issue which is a possible mole within the White House or the Bureau."

"That's correct, sir," said Cullen, "and the two issues might be related. The CIA has information that Ambassador Oleg Kozlov may be running the spy in the Bureau or in the White House. That spy might possibly be involved in passing on the information that was gleaned from Greenwood's call to the Marshals. Greenwood might be the spy, or maybe it's Zuckerman from the Washington Post. But at the moment, we don't know for sure if it's either one."

"So, what's your plan?" Landers asked.

"I don't think that Greenwood is a true believer. It's more likely that he's being blackmailed or doing it for money. So, rather than wait to see if he leads us to his handler, I want to pull him in and press him hard. If we can get him to tell us what's going on, and about his connection to Zuckerman, I think we can speed up this investigation without tipping off the Russians that we're moving up the chain."

"You may be right, Jack," said Landers. "Would this be something worth briefing the President about?"

Cullen was afraid it would reach this point, but he'd given it a lot of thought on the way to this meeting, and his opinion as to how to move forward was now very carefully considered.

"No, sir, I don't believe that now is the time to give him a briefing. We're at a very sensitive point in the investigation, and within a day or two we might have a much better picture of what's going on, and how, if at all, the White House is involved. I would urge you to wait until we have more information before we alarm the President and his staff with an allegation that we haven't completely resolved."

Landers smiled. "Have you ever considered a career in politics, Jack, because you've got the patter down to a T."

Cullen smiled. "I'm trying to keep politics out of it, sir."

"Yes, you are," said Landers in agreement. "We'll keep the White House out of the loop until we know a lot more about what's going on. But in the meantime, I'd like to talk to Jamison Freely over at the CIA. Do you have any objection to my doing that?"

"No, sir. I've spoken to Assistant Director Freely, and he's up to speed on what's going on."

"Very well. Go ahead and pick up Greenwood. Let's see what he has to say."

❦

Thirty minutes after Cullen got back to his office in the Hoover Building, the first thing he did was place a call to Jamison Freely.

"I've briefed Landers," he said when Freely picked up the phone. "He's going to give you a call."

"He already did," said Freely with a chuckle. "I told him we'll offer any overseas assistance regarding identifying others in the chain. He plans to get the NSA on board. They'll be able to act once they have the names of possible Russian contacts."

"Did he mention that I've decided to have Greenwood picked up?"

"We didn't get into details," said Freely. "But don't you want to wait and see who his handler is?"

"I think he's weak," said Cullen. "We'll make faster progress if we can break him down."

"Okay. Keep me in the loop."

"I will."

When the call was over, Freely placed a call to Donahue, who was still in Zurich and in the midst of a shopping spree.

"Can you talk?" he asked when she picked up the call.

"I'm in Zurich in a hotel and on a cell," she told him.

"Okay. We're making progress on that matter we've previously discussed. I'll have more for you later when communications are secure."

"I'll be back in D.C. tomorrow," she said. "I want to show you something."

"Call me when you arrive. What I have to tell you can keep until we get together. But in the meantime, there's something that won't wait. We have information that leads us to believe that someone is definitely trying to identify you, so you need to make sure that precautions are taken. Do you understand what I'm saying?"

"I do," she said, now worried. "Is the threat imminent?"

"We've got it contained for the moment, but we'll need to talk more about this when you get back."

❧

When she got off the phone with Freely, she promptly went into the bathroom and threw up. She knew it was only nerves, but it seemed to her that her nausea was compounded by the bug she seemed unable to shake.

What if it's the start of an ulcer?

She supposed that was possible, considering the nervous strain she'd been under since learning about Sean's murder. And it wasn't getting any easier, particularly now that she was going to become a potential target of the Russian Federation.

She came out of the bathroom and placed a call to Jamie Otero, who was in the room next door to hers. He came over right away and joined her in the sitting room.

"I just talked with a friend of mine in the government. Apparently, an unknown person or persons are attempting to determine my identity, so we're going to have to be even more circumspect with my security detail. More people at the house when we get back to L.A., but less visible security when we go out."

"I'll take care of it," he told her.

She liked that about Jamie. No BS of any kind. You give him an order and he carries it out. It was great to have someone she could rely on so completely.

"We're going to make a stop again in D.C. before we go to L.A. Can you set it up?"

"I'll notify the flight team right away. Will you need a hotel room?"

She thought about the fact that the flight crew might once again need a break.

"Go ahead and reserve some rooms, but we'll decide what we'll do after we get to D.C."

Otero got to his feet to leave. "Will you be going out tonight?" he asked.

"I'm still not feeling one-hundred percent, so I'm gonna stay in."

Otero nodded. "I'll release some of the guys to go and get dinner. You want them to bring something back for you?"

"I'm going to order soup from Room Service, but thanks for the offer."

He nodded and quickly left.

FORTY-ONE

A MEETING WAS called of the special surveillance team leaders at the building they called "the barn." Smitten, Folsey, and Jack Cullen were present, as were four team supervisors. They were seated around a large table that had been brought in during the afternoon. Now that they had three separate surveillances going on around the clock, it was determined that they needed some kind of overall coordination to avoid stepping all over each other's investigations.

"How are we doing on the FISA warrant?" Cullen asked.

"We'll have it within the hour," said Smitten. "It's an open warrant, one which will enable us to capture calls from any phone being used by any of the three men involved. However, the calls captured that involve Zuckerman, the journalist, will have to go to a special master because of potential problems with the Reporter's Privilege."

Cullen knew that the Reporter's Privilege was a protection under constitutional and statutory law. It prevented a reporter being compelled to testify about confidential information or sources. To that extent, the calls from sources other than Greenwood would have to be culled out by an independent, court-appointed special master, to guarantee that law enforcement did not make use of any information that they were not entitled to get.

"Have we lined up a Russian translator for any of the calls made in Russian by Kozlov?" someone asked.

"NSA is onboard," said Smitten. "They'll run the calls through a computerized translation program, then it will be listened to and verified by a Russian-speaking expert working for the agency."

What Cullen didn't tell the group was that six months ago, the CIA learned that the Russians had been purchasing all of their prepaid phones at a particular outlet in Virginia. Once that was discovered, a break-in team had entered the store and substituted all of the models of the phones favored by the Russians with exact duplicates whose numbers were known by the NSA. This enabled NSA and the CIA to track all calls made by all Embassy personnel who were using the prepaid phones.

Kozlov's current phone was very quickly identified, and his unsecured calls for the past six months were already being reviewed.

Procedures for creating surveillance zones were developed, and teams in the field would be told when and where other teams were operating. Whenever their surveillances were on the move, the other teams would know in real time what was going on.

Cullen let them know that more agents were being brought in from western states to augment the present surveillance teams. It was anticipated that additional agents would be needed to assist in putting together background checks on each person contacted by any of the three individuals who formed the core of the investigation. Shifts would remain at twelve-on and twelve-off until further notice. Lastly, teams were reminded to refrain from contacting friends at the D.C. Bureau. The work they were doing was confidential because of a possible leak within the D.C. operation, so no one was to know what they were up to, or that they were even in the general area.

Cullen said, "If word leaks out about these investigations, or about the possibility of a mole in the government, everyone will be going on the poly, and anyone who fails will be criminally prosecuted to the fullest extent of the law."

That little nugget came as a surprise to the team leaders, but it added to the importance of what they were doing. None of them wanted to believe that there was a traitor within the Bureau or the White House, but if there was, then finding that person was now their number one objective.

⚜

After a bumpy landing on runway 10, Donahue stepped off her plane in Baltimore. She had to turn up her coat collar to the frigid and unrelenting mist that filled the air on what was a cold and cloudy day. Rain and possible snow flurries were on the horizon, so she hurried to the vehicles that were waiting for her on the side of the tarmac.

Otero and his team escorted her in a convoy to the Sofitel Hotel at Lafayette Square in Washington, D.C. Once there, she headed for her reserved suite, then put out a call to Freely. He told her that he would come by a little later in the day. She then called the front desk to find out if they had a doctor on call? She was told that they didn't, but the manager said he could recommend one. She advised him that she wanted a female general practitioner, preferably one who would make a house call. The manager gave her the name and number of a doctor who he claimed had treated many visiting dignitaries, and after she researched the doctor on the internet, she placed a call to her office, described her symptoms, and after a short delay, the nurse advised her that the doctor would stop by in a couple of hours.

Donahue called Otero's cell and told him to expect the doctor, then made her way into the bedroom where she curled up under the covers to await the doctor's arrival.

Ten minutes later, she was bored, so she used her cell phone to give Thompson a call.

"How's it going?" Donahue asked when Thompson answered her phone.

"You need to come back, Jen. It's lonely here without you."

"Aw, thanks, Shari. I miss you too."

"They've got me paired up with Rich Bengtson, and he's driving me crazy. He never stops eating, Jen. Lots of nuts and seeds, and he spills them all over the car. He's like a giant, sloppy, squirrel."

The two of them shared a laugh, and Donahue realized how much she missed their daily banter.

"I'll be headed home tomorrow. I'm in D.C. at the moment, trying to tie up some loose ends."

"I'd ask how it's going, but I'll wait to do that until we can talk in person."

Donahue smiled. She didn't have to explain anything to Shari when it came to security.

"Any calls for me or messages left on my desk?" Donahue asked.

"No notes, but Bryan Harb called. He said he'd call you back in a few days."

Donahue was sorry that she missed his call, but she had other things on her mind. If Bryan was okay waiting to call her back, then whatever he wanted to tell her could likely wait as well.

"How are the boys?" Donahue asked

"They're fine."

"Good. I've still got that damn flu bug, and I was just wondering if it might be going around?"

"You think my kids might have given it to you?"

"Of course not. But if it is the flu, it usually shows up first in schools."

"You got that right," said Thompson with a chuckle. "They're fine, and no one else has got it that I know of, so if it is the flu, Lady, then you're probably the typhoid Mary."

Donahue was now more worried than ever. If it turned out that she didn't have the flu, then maybe she had picked up a parasite of some kind.

"You really should see a doctor?" Shari said, softly.

"I've got one coming by in a few hours. I'll let you know what she has to say."

"It's probably something you picked up that only attacks rich folks," said Thompson with a laugh. "I'll bet you got it at one of your fancy, exotic, foreign destinations."

"Are you jealous?" Donahue said through a smile.

"Damn straight."

"I invited you to go along, remember?"

"I haven't forgotten, and if I wasn't such a good and responsible mom, I would have taken you up on that generous offer."

"Well, I'll make it up to you. We'll plan a girls' weekend away. You name the destination, and we'll go."

"You mean it?"

"Of course," replied Donahue.

"Wow, Jen! If you were a guy, I'd let you do me."

Donahue laughed. "That's what I love about you, Shari. Your sense of humor has no boundaries."

"No, I mean it! Just get a sex change and I'll prove it!"

Thompson began to laugh at her own joke, and Donahue said, "On that note, I'll call you tomorrow and let you know when we're heading home. And take my word for it, you and your boys need to get a flu shot as soon as possible, because if this is the flu, it fuckin' sucks."

∾

Phillip Greenwood got off at the Metro station that was nearest to his home and began walking toward his house. Because it was so cold outside, no one else was around.

Two cars suddenly pulled up nearby, and three FBI agents jumped out and ran over to grab him. They flashed their ID's, cuffed him behind his back, then marched him over to the nearest car and put him in the back seat.

The two cars headed off towards the barn, and the agents involved reported that no one had witnessed them make the arrest.

∾

When Greenwood was brought into the barn, he was taken to a small room that was hastily converted into an interview room. It was just big enough for four people, and a camera was visible in the upper corner of the room facing the spot where Greenwood was seated.

Smitten and Folsey came into the room and took seats at the small metal table. Greenwood was still handcuffed behind his back, and they could tell from his expression that he was wary and nervous.

"Why am I here?" he asked. He already had a general idea, but he was hoping he was wrong.

"You're in a lot of trouble," said Smitten. "There are others involved, so I want you to know that now is your only chance to cooperate. If you fail to take this opportunity, it will not be offered again. We'll soon be taking others into custody, so you need to decide right now if you want to help yourself. Otherwise, you're going to be booked on a charge of treason."

"*Treason?*" Greenwood was floored. "What in the hell are you talking about?"

"You furnished classified information to the Russians," said Folsey.

"*What?* No! I did no such thing. This has to be a big mistake."

"Do you want to tell us what you know?"

"I'm not a spy. What the hell is all this about?"

Smitten advised him of his constitutional rights, and Greenwood quickly waived them.

He hung his head, then said, "Does this have something to do with the death of Sean Walker?"

"That's exactly what it has to do with," said Folsey.

"Tell me about your call to the Marshal's Office," said Smitten.

Greenwood looked up and shifted his eyes from one to the other.

"General Rush asked me to call the Marshal's Office and get a current address for Mr. Walker."

"We spoke to General Rush. He claims he never asked you for that information," said Smitten.

"Then he's a liar," said Greenwood.

Folsey turned on a digital recorder, hit the playback, and studied Greenwood's face as he listened to the audio of his meeting with Morris Zuckerman, the reporter for the Washington Post.

When the audio was finished, Folsey shut if off.

Greenwood caught her glance. He sighed, then shook his head in disbelief. They had monitored his meeting, and that was what he had feared the most.

"I can explain," he said softly.

"We're listening," said Smitten.

"I got the address information from the Marshal, then gave it to the General. A few days after that, I was reading the Post online, and I saw a report that said that Mr. Walker had been killed in Los Angeles. I knew right then that it wasn't a coincidence, you know, that I gave the General the information, and the next thing you know, that poor guy was dead. I figured our government had a hand in it, so not knowing where to turn, I called Zuckerman and told him what I knew. I said I thought our government assassinated Sean Walker. Zuckerman said he was going to investigate, and when he called me to meet him today, I thought he was going to tell me what he'd found out. But he wanted me to get him more information, and I definitely wasn't going to do that."

Folsey was about to speak, but Greenwood jumped in before she could.

"I know what you're thinking. I told him I'd try to get the info, but I wasn't going to make the call."

Smitten said, "Why didn't you notify the FBI?"

"I didn't know who in the government to trust. Hell, I don't even know if I can trust you. Maybe you guys picked me up just to make sure I can't tell anyone else."

He held Smitten's glance, but she didn't look away.

"We're here to find out who ordered Mr. Walker's death. We're not here to cover up the killing."

Greenwood seemed to relax a bit.

"I don't know who did it, but what I do know is that at his request, I gave the information to General Rush, and whatever happened after that...I just don't know."

"We're gonna give you a polygraph examination," said Smitten. "Is that okay with you?"

"Hell, yes! Bring it on. I'm telling you guys the truth."

"I'll get it set up," said Folsey.

She got to her feet and left the room.

"Am I in trouble for telling the reporter what I thought had happened?" Greenwood asked.

"I don't know," said Smitten. "Let's see if you pass the poly before we get around to discussing that."

FORTY-TWO

OTERO OPENED THE door to Donahue's suite with a keycard that she'd given him. He led the doctor into the front room, then walked over to the bedroom door and gave it a knock. When Donahue called out, he told her that the doctor had arrived.

Donahue came out of the room in a bathrobe and Otero took his leave. Doctor Shelly Goetz then introduced herself before asking Donahue to take a seat on the couch.

Goetz was in her fifties, well dressed and very cordial in her presentation. She exuded a level of confidence that Donahue found reassuring.

Goetz immediately took Donahue's blood pressure, which was followed by taking her temperature. When the thermometer was out of her mouth, Goetz asked her to describe her symptoms.

"Nausea and occasional vomiting. I've lost a lot of weight in the last two months. Maybe twenty pounds. My fiancé was murdered, and I haven't had much of an appetite since it happened. There are days when I don't feel like getting out of bed, and I do a lot of crying that comes out of nowhere."

If Goetz was surprised, she didn't show it.

"I'm sorry for your loss," she said. "Depression can explain a lot of what you're experiencing, and I'm going to recommend that you see a grief counselor. Where do you call home?"

"Los Angeles," said Donahue.

"I know a couple of good psychiatrists out there. When we're finished with our examination, I'll get you a couple of referrals."

Goetz pulled a stethoscope out of her bag and listened to Donahue's breathing from both the front and from her back.

"Your lungs are clear," she said.

The examination went on for another five minutes, and when it was concluded, Goetz asked, "Have you been sexually active?"

"Not since my fiancé was killed?"

"And exactly how long ago was your last intercourse?"

"About nine or ten weeks? Something like that."

"Were you on birth control at the time?"

"Rhythm method," said Donahue, who was starting to get the gist of where this was going.

Goetz nodded, then reached into her bag. She pulled out an *Easy@ Home* urine test strip and handed it to Donahue.

"Go pee on the stick," she said.

"But I can't be pregnant," said Donahue.

"Has your cycle been normal?"

Donahue shook her head. "I'm a runner, so I sometimes don't have my period for a couple of months at a stretch."

"Humor me and go pee on the stick. If you're not, then we're going to have to go to the hospital for additional tests."

Donahue shook her head. She was beginning to realize that the possibility was real, that perhaps her bouts with nausea were really hormonal in nature.

She was suddenly petrified.

I can't be pregnant. That can't be the reason I've been so sick...

She got up and went into the bathroom, and when she didn't come out in a couple of minutes, Goetz walked over to the door and gave it a knock.

"Are you okay," she asked through the door.

She could hear Donahue crying. The door suddenly opened, and Donahue held up the stick which was blue.

"Congratulations," said Goetz. "You're officially pregnant."

She walked Donahue back into the living room and the two of them sat on the couch.

"Do you have an OBGYN back in L.A.?" Goetz asked.

Donahue nodded. "Jacklyn Crandall at UCLA."

"I want you to make an appointment with her right away. What you're experiencing is nausea caused by a change in hormones. It is usually gone by twelve weeks. Dr. Crandall will want to give you a baseline checkup, and she'll give you the spiel about not drinking alcohol or smoking. She'll tell you a lot more, but there's nothing to be concerned about. Once you get your appetite back, I'm sure you'll put on all the weight you've lost and then some." She smiled. "Cheer up, Jennifer. I have three kids of my own and I can assure you that your life is about to change for the better."

After Goetz was paid by credit card, and after she gave Donahue two references for grief counseling, Donahue sat back down on the couch and waited until Goetz was on her way down the hallway before she started to cry.

She was shocked that she was going to have a baby. Becoming a mom was something she always dreamed of being, but now that she was going to have to do it all alone, she was terrified. She thought about Sean, how happy he would have been, and she wished that he was there so she could tell him the news.

Her tears flowed uncontrollably, punctuated by frequent bouts of excited laughter.

Oh my God! I'm gonna have a baby! I'm gonna be a mom!

FORTY-THREE

BRYAN HARB MADE his way to the SCIF in the United States Embassy at 24 Grosvenor Square, Mayfair, in London. He placed a call to his handler, Dan Taylor, who was the CIA's Agent-in-Residence in Cairo, Egypt.

Taylor, who was Bryan's go-between, was the only one who could reach him when he was working undercover. That was a way to make sure that the wrong kind of calls didn't show up on Bryan's phone when he was in the midst of a deep cover intelligence operation.

Taylor was contacted by the on-duty SCIF operator in Cairo, and he quickly made his way from his office to the secure facility.

"How's it going, Bry?" said Taylor.

"Just great, Dan. Ivanov has been singing like a bird. He says that he has corresponded many times with Ambassador Kozlov, who he identified as his handler. They usually make contact by use of encrypted messaging from equipment at the Russian Embassy in London. At other times, he would call him or text him a code word and would later get a callback on a secure line. It also worked in reverse. GCHQ has identified a number of texts and subsequent messages sent back and forth between them, both before and after the killings in Israel."

"Will the Brits give us that information?" Taylor asked.

"That's the plan," said Bryan. "Unfortunately, the actual

conversations were on burner phones, but Ivanov knows the dates and approximate times of the calls, and the number that he called from his phone at that time."

"Send me that info by secure line, will you?" Taylor asked. "We'll have NSA do a search."

"You'll have it in about five minutes."

As soon as Bryan was off the line, Taylor went to the secure communications room and waited for the encoded message to arrive from London. When it did, and when it was decoded, he returned to the SCIF and made a call to Jack Cullen.

"I heard from Bryan Harb," said Taylor when Cullen picked up the secure line. He went on to explain what Bryan had told him, and that he was in possession of the phone numbers used by Ivanov and Kozlov.

"They were using burner phones, Jack. Does NSA have the ability to pair the numbers with intercepts that have been decoded?"

Cullen smiled because he knew that the Bureau had the numbers for all of the one-and-done phones being used by the Russians in D.C.

"It won't be a problem," he said. "Send me the info and I'll get it to NSA right away."

Kasey Smitten was seated at her desk in her fifth-floor office in the J. Edgar Hoover Building when Rebecca Folsey walked in.

"Greenwood passed the poly. He was telling the truth when he said that the information he received was requested by Rush. He also came up truthful when he was asked about why he passed on his suspicions to Zuckerman."

Smitten leaned back in her chair. "Okay, let me think." She closed her eyes for a few moments to gather her thoughts.

"Get a team to invite Zuckerman down here for a chat. Tell him we will answer some of the questions he might have about Greenwood's concerns. That should be enough to get him to hear us out without our creating some kind of an incident."

"Are you gonna get him to stop his investigation?"

"I don't know yet. I need to pass all of this on to the boss." She got to her feet. "Call me as soon as they get Zuckerman into an interview room."

Folsey took off down the hallway while Smitten called Cullen's secretary, who checked with Cullen before saying, "He'll see you as soon as you can get here."

Smitten got to Cullen's office and quickly took a seat in front of his desk. She filled him in on Greenwood's poly results, and when he was apprised of the facts, he agreed that they needed to get a FISA warrant for General Rush's conversations based on national security grounds.

"I'll get started on it right away," Smitten told him.

"You realize that I'm going to have to brief the President about Rush," he said.

Smitten was hesitant. "Is that really a good idea?"

"We have no choice. We have to assume that he'll keep the info to himself, but he needs to make sure that Rush doesn't have access to sensitive information."

Smitten sighed. She knew he was right, but just the same, she had her doubts when it came to anything Russian with the current administration.

"I want to congratulate you and Rebecca on the way you've pursued this investigation," said Cullen. "The threads were thin, but you saw past them, and you've given us our first good lead in the search for a possible mole."

"Thank you, sir. I'll pass that on to Rebecca."

⁓

At Cullen's request, the meeting in the Oval Office was between Cullen and the President without any aides or advisors. And Cullen explained why he insisted on that when he started to give his briefing.

"We believe there is a mole in the White House, sir, one who is being run by agents of the Russian SVR. Unfortunately, we've only identified one person who is involved, but until we conclude our investigation, I think caution would dictate that we assume there might be more."

The President sat across from Cullen in a yellow velvet armchair that faced the couch where Cullen had placed himself. He crossed his arms, then nodded once that Cullen should go ahead with his presentation.

Cullen began by telling him about the London murder of Anton Korakovsky by means of Polonium 210, and the subsequent murder of Mikel Korakovsky, who was in the Witness Protection Program under the alias of Sean Walker. When the President asked why the Korakovsky's were murdered, Cullen told him that Anton had gathered up documents showing the extent of Putin's corruption in an effort to challenge him later in a future Presidential election. Putin found out about it, and tried to get his hands on the documents as well as the assets that Korakovsky had acquired as a Kremlin oligarch.

"How does General Rush figure into all of this?" the President asked.

"He used an aide to contact the US Marshal's Office to get the confidential address of Mikel Korakovsky, who was murdered a few days later. When we asked him if he directed his aide to get that information, he completely denied doing so, but we've given the aide a polygraph, which he has passed."

The President seemed to consider this, then nodded again for Cullen to continue.

"We've learned from a confidential CIA informant that the spymaster here in D.C. is Ambassador Oleg Kozlov. Apparently, the Brits have obtained proof that Kozlov ordered the killing of the two assassins who murdered Mikel Korakovsky in Los Angeles."

"Sounds like they got what they deserved," said the President.

"Perhaps," said a cynical Cullen, "but Kozlov was doing this to eliminate the trail that leads directly back to Vladmir Putin."

"I see," said the President, who hadn't considered that on his own.

"We suspect that Kozlov is the agent who is handling Rush. We've begun a full investigation of General Rush, and it's our hope that we can conclusively determine if Kozlov is his handler."

"So what do I do about Rush?" the President asked.

"For the short term, I would simply ask that you do nothing to alert him that our investigation is focusing on him. Simultaneously, keep him at arm's distance. Make sure that he does not have access to secret or top-secret information. Hopefully, we can get our investigation concluded very quickly, but we need a little time to get this done right."

"I can do that," the President replied.

"One more thing, Mr. President. I would ask you not to mention our investigation to anyone here in the White House, or anyone else for that matter. There is a reporter who is onto Rush's involvement, and our agents will be talking to him later today to get him to back off until our investigation is completed. But if this gets out to any of your advisors or members of congress, well…we both know it will leak out to the national press within a matter of hours."

"I need to talk to my people about how to control the damage from this revelation," said the President.

"Sir, with all due respect, we can let you know as soon as we are ready to make arrests. That will give you time to prepare for whatever political impact this might have. But if you tell even one person, I can almost guarantee that it will be on cable news within a day or two. You can't unring the bell, Mr. President, so please, don't ring it before we've concluded our investigation."

"I'll keep Rush at arms length," said the President reluctantly, "and I'll give your suggestions some thought, but don't let this drag on too long, Mr. Cullen."

"I won't sir," said Cullen who started to get to his feet.

"And Kozlov?" said the President. "How do you propose to handle him?"

"He has diplomatic immunity, sir, so once we conclude our investigation, our recourse would be to kick him out of the country."

"Let's keep the two investigations separate," said the President. "We might be better off keeping Kozlov where he is, and by that, I mean that we know he can't be trusted, so if we send him back to Moscow, who knows who they'll send to take his place?"

"You mean as Ambassador?"

"No, we'll know that when they appoint a new one. I mean, who the new spymaster might be? It won't necessarily be the next Ambassador."

"I see your point, sir. The decision, of course, is yours to make."

FORTY-FOUR

THE SURVEILLANCE TEAMS originally assigned to Greenwood were now assigned to investigate Rush, and while he was busy at the White House, and because he was a widower who lived alone, they entered his unoccupied home in the suburbs. Under the authority of the FISA warrant, they planted bugs, dropped several surveillance programs onto his computer, and copied everything that was already on his hard drive. His phone was tapped by the local carrier service, and any calls in and out were being monitored in real time in a facility set up several miles away.

They followed him from the White House to his home in the suburbs of Virginia, and once he was inside, the teams set up where they could watch the house, both front and back.

The two agents stationed down the street from the front of the house drank coffee from a thermos and listened to the Los Angeles Kings versus the Washington Capitals hockey game. Both were from L.A., and the Kings was their team of choice.

"This could turn out to be a long surveillance," said the driver.

"How so?" his partner asked.

"You don't get to be a General if you're not smart. This guy, Rush? He's not likely to make a mistake."

"He already did. He used some kid to make the call, and then he lied about it."

"Yeah, there is that."

Two hours later, Rush came out of his front door, climbed into his car which was parked in the driveway, and drove a dozen blocks to a corner Bodega. He parked nearby and made his way into the store.

He walked up to the counter and ordered a pack of Marlboros, and when the night clerk handed it over, he slid a folded-up ten-dollar bill across the counter which the clerk picked up and put into the register. Rush pocketed the cigarettes and turned to walk out when he noticed a young female standing close behind him. She had a carton of milk in her hand.

He gave her a smile, she smiled back, then he left the store and drove back to his home.

⌑

"Hey, guys," said the female agent, once she was out the front door. She spoke into her sleeve microphone. "Does our guy smoke cigarettes?"

"Don't know," came the reply. "Let me check."

He was sitting in a car with his partner outside Rush's home. He was part of a team of six, and the one female agent assigned to the team was the buyer of the milk behind Rush in the store.

"Pipe smoker," the agent replied after consulting the profile report. "Why?"

"He bought a pack of Marlboro's, then slid his money across the counter. It was a ten dollar bill and it was folded up."

"So maybe he's gonna take up smoking?"

"The clerk never unfolded the bill. It went right into the register, and he didn't give Rush any change."

"So, how much does a pack of Marlboro's cost?" the driver asked his passenger.

"Eight bucks," said the passenger.

The two male agents exchanged a look.

"*Shit!*" said the passenger. "You don't suppose he passed a message?"

"Sounds like it," said the driver. "What'd the guy behind the counter look like?"

"Immigrant, northern Europe," said the female agent in front of the Bodega. "Possibly Russian, but he might be from one of the *stans.*"

She was referring to the former Soviet satellites, like Kurdistan or Uzbekistan.

"We're going back there," said the driver who started up the car. "We'll stay on the clerk and get photos of everyone who shows up while they're still open, and we'll follow the clerk when he closes up."

"Roger that," she said. "My partner and I will take your place in front of the primary's house. We'll handle him until it's the end of our watch."

FORTY-FIVE

THE STORE CLOSED at midnight, and the two agents watching the front were tired. They'd been snapping photos of everyone going in and out for three hours, and while there were fewer and fewer customers as the evening went on, there had been more than fifty during the last three hours.

When the clerk finally closed the doors and locked up, they moved the car to be able to cover the back entrance. A second unit from Rush's residence joined them and covered the front.

When the clerk came out the back door, they followed him from a distance as he made his way to the Metro line.

When he caught the Metro, they were with him, and when he got off four stations later, they followed him into a city park. The clerk then made his way to a bench, sat down, looked around, then apparently concluding that he was alone, he put his hand under the bench and either left something there or picked something up.

"Did you see that?" asked an agent who was watching him on a computer screen in the back of a surveillance van.

The cameraman, who was shooting footage through a brand new thermal imaging camera, replied, "I sure did."

The camera allowed them to pick out the form of a body by its heat, and the figure appeared as a light-colored ghostly human shape with red and yellow heat blotches that were framed against the darkness of the night.

The clerk left the park and made his way back to the Metro station where he caught the first train back to downtown D.C. Two agents from another team got on the same train and followed him to an apartment in the Marlow Heights section, which was just southeast of the central city.

Once the clerk was out of the park, the first two agents examined the bench. A note was affixed to the underside by a sticky, gum like substance. They removed the note, read it, photographed it, then put it back and quickly left the immediate area. The photo was immediately sent as an attachment to a computer at the barn.

They returned to their vehicle and made sure that the van kept the bench under surveillance before they called in a technical team to install miniature video cameras in trees near the bench. Once that was done, they pulled back from the area and waited to see who would show up to get the note.

Cullen was notified by phone, and he advised the team leader he was coming to the barn. He requested two additional units to rendezvous near the park to be able to take part in the surveillance of anyone who stopped at the bench to pick up the note.

※

At nine a.m. the following morning, a young woman wearing jogging gear entered the park. She ran past the bench, then around the area in a wide circle. That action was immediately suspicious to the watchers who made sure that they did not expose themselves.

She ran back to the area of the bench, stopped, then used it to support herself while she stretched her calves. And while she was doing that, she repeatedly looked around.

"She's gonna do it," said one of the techs, who was watching from the van on a Bluetooth feed from one of the cameras in the park.

"Can we zoom in to watch her hands?" asked an agent, who was watching from over his shoulder.

He adjusted the lens remotely, and the camera zoomed in just as she sat down on the bench.

"These new cameras are awesome," said the agent.

"New stuff from the battlefield in Iraq," replied the tech.

They watched her slip her hand under the bench and come out with the note in her hand. She slid it into a runner's pouch she wore around her waist, then stood up and started to jog again, this time out of the park.

A block away, she climbed into a Toyota and drove it towards the central city.

A team followed her by car while other units went ahead to make periodic trade-offs to avoid detection of the surveillance. Apparently, she never noticed that she was being followed.

Ten minutes later, she made her way directly into the gated compound of the Russian embassy.

∽

Back at the barn, Cullen watched as a full-face photo of the woman jogger was run through the facial identification program. She was soon identified as an assistant to the cultural attache.

"I want a file started on her," said Cullen to a nearby agent. "She's clearly working with the SVR, and she may lead us to others involved in espionage."

He then turned to Smitten. "Get the team leaders in here. We need to have a meeting."

An hour later, four wide-awake team leaders and four others who had been overseeing the shifts from the night before, were gathered around the conference table at the barn. All had been brought in from Los Angeles, and most were still struggling with jet lag. Smitten, Folsey and Cullen were also there, and after Smitten brought everyone up to speed on the note and the Russian courier who picked it up, Cullen took over and addressed the group.

"According to the note sent by Rush to his handler—whose

identity has not yet been determined—Rush has requested a meeting for tonight at eight p.m. No location for the meeting was in the note, so we have to assume that they have a prearranged meet location. As it stands now, only our surveillance of Rush will lead us directly to their rendezvous."

"Any chance the female jogger was his handler?" asked one of the sleepy agents.

"Not likely," said Cullen. "We're assessing her as a go-between, but that may change if she shows up for the meeting tonight." He then scanned the group. "I want two trackers on Rush's car. Forget hard wire, use batteries, and make sure both units are operational. And to that extent, use fresh batteries. I also want teams on Kozlov." He looked over at one of the day shift leaders. "Is there any way to get a tracker on Kozlov's car?"

"Not a chance," the man responded. "The driver always stays in the car when it's not parked behind the gates at the Embassy."

"How about his cell phone?" asked a second team leader. "Do we happen to know the number of the one he's using?"

Cullen turned to Smitten. "We have Rush's cell phone number, right?"

"Yes sir," she said, "but if he pulls out the chip on the way to the meet, we're toast."

He turned back to the group at large.

"Speak to Agent Smitten for the number once we break, and make sure that we're tracking it. He might not be smart enough to pull the chip, so it's worth a shot." He turned back to the group. "I also want extra teams assigned for the surveillance. Use a variety of vehicles and a couple of motorcycles if we can get them, and make sure we have people on the ground who can pick up the surveillance if public transportation is involved."

He was preaching to the choir, and the agents at the table all knew it, but he was the boss, and it probably didn't hurt to have him give them the green light to pull out all the stops.

"For what it's worth," said Cullen. "I wouldn't be surprised if Oleg Kozlov is the man who shows up for the meeting. Rush is as high-ranking an asset as one could imagine, and Kozlov is the kind of individual who would only want to work with a highly placed source."

"You want sound and video if possible, sir?" asked one of the team leaders.

"Photo's yes, sound if possible, but only if it won't blow the surveillance." He looked around the table. "I know you guys know exactly what you're doing, so I leave it up to you to develop a game plan. Use a skeleton crew for the rest of the day. I want your people to get as much rest as they can. It might be a very long night."

He looked at his watch. "Any questions?"

There were none.

"Okay," said Cullen. Let's meet back here tonight at six. That's all for now. I'll see you tonight."

⌘

When Jamison Freely showed up at Donahue's hotel room, he noted that she was dressed in jeans and a sweater. She offered him a choice of tea or coffee from a cart that she'd ordered from room service.

She was feeling a whole lot better. Sometimes, just knowing what was going on with your body can relieve a lot of anxiety, and the idea that she was pregnant and not actually dying from some form of stomach cancer—a thought that had crossed her mind when the nausea was particularly bad—was something she could live with without complaint.

Freely chose coffee while she made herself a cup of tea, and when both of them were seated in the sitting area, she opened up a cardboard folder and pulled out several photographs and a half-dozen written pages.

"Do you speak or read Russian?" she asked him.

Freely smiled. "*Nyet.*"

He had a sense of humor. Donahue liked that.

"Well, we're gonna need a translator," she told him. "I'm pretty sure these documents are all in Russian."

"I have one waiting outside in the hallway with your security people," said Freely. "Do you care if she gets a look at your face?"

"Is he completely trustworthy?" Donahue asked.

"It's a she, and she's beyond reproach."

"Bring her in," said Donahue.

The translator, a Russian-born citizen of the United States, and a fifteen year agent with the CIA, took a seat at the dining room table. She began to read five pages of documents that Donahue had photographed at the bank in Zurich before printing them out on the plane.

While the translator went to work on the documents, Freely studied the half-dozen photographs of Putin when he was meeting with other, unidentified people.

"I'd like to take these back to my office and have them run through our facial identification program," he said.

"They're copies of the originals, but I'd like to have them back."

"I understand. I'll see that they're returned to you as soon as possible."

She nodded. Her boss at LAPD, Tom Elwood, had told her that Freely was completely trustworthy, so she was okay with him handling the photos.

The translator looked up, obviously ready to report, but she was reluctant to say anything in front of Donahue. Freely immediately sensed the problem, and advised her that Donahue was cleared to hear the contents of documents.

"Go ahead, Katrina. What do they say?"

Katrina sighed. "The first two documents show ownership of shares in Oil companies that operate in the North Sea. The significant ownership share in each corporation is a shell company, and the third document lists Vladmir Putin as one of the owners of the corporation. His share appears to be fifty percent. The fourth page is an SVR document detailing the use of Polonium-210 as an agent that would cause certain and painful death. The initials VP appear at the bottom." She looked up at Freely. "That usually signifies that he has read the document, and it's dated one month before the London assassination of Anton Korakovsky. The fifth document is a memorandum written by an SVR General—to a Captain in the Russian Army—to make sure that Sarin gas containers in the Homs Governorate in Syria are not counted in the inventory to be presented to the Organization for the Prohibition of Chemical Weapons (OPCW)." She looked over at Donahue. "Those are the people who are responsible for verifying everything listed as it is transported from Syria to Russia for destruction."

Freely's eyes went wide. The documents identified Putin assets, but more importantly, they also identified Russian cheating on the Sarin gas destruction agreement, whose use during the war amounted to war crimes.

Freely looked over at Donahue.

"These documents are explosive, Jennifer. No wonder the Russians want them back so badly." He sighed. "If the rest of what you have is of the same caliber, they would afford our country significant leverage over the current Russian political situation."

"I have no idea what the other documents say, but the stack is several inches tall."

"If you turn them over to me, I will see to it that they are properly used—"

Donahue shook her head. She got up, walked over to the translator, and gathered up the five pages.

"There's no way anyone is going to get these until I know for sure that the people who were responsible for Sean's death are identified and dealt with."

Freely dismissed the interpreter, and once she was out of the suite, he said, "I'm going to tell you where we're at with the investigation, but you must keep this information completely confidential. If you speak about this with anyone, you will be prosecuted to the full extent of the law."

Donahue thought it over. She had no intention of discussing any of this with anyone, but his warning made her carefully think over her willingness to be briefed.

"I won't discuss what you tell me with anyone," she finally said.

"Okay. We believe the mole has been identified. He is a senior official in the White House, and an advisor to the President. He's already under surveillance. I've been advised that he will soon be attending a meeting that he's asked for with a high-ranking official at the Russian embassy."

"Is this White House advisor the one who got Sean's new identity and place of residence?"

Freely nodded.

"Will he be prosecuted?"

"I don't know for sure, but Jack Cullen of the FBI and I will do everything we can to put together a prosecutable case."

"And the Russian official who's running this traitor? What happens to him or her?"

"It's a him, and I'm afraid he's got diplomatic immunity. We can expel him from the country, but Russia would have to prosecute him, and if the order to kill came from Putin, there's no way that will happen."

Donahue was crushed. The people who made the decision to kill Sean were going to walk away unscathed, while the minions at the bottom were left to take the fall.

Someone needs to do something about that...

Freely reached into his pocket and handed Donahue a cell phone.

"Use this whenever you need to discuss sensitive information with me or with your friend, Mr. Harb."

"Will your people be monitoring my calls?"

Freely smiled.

"No. To do so without a FISA warrant would be a violation of law, but the phone is encrypted, and that's to preclude any foreign governments that might be eavesdropping on calls that you or others in our government are making." He gave her a tight smile. "It pays to be careful, especially when a foreign government is so hellbent on finding out who is in possession of these documents."

FORTY-SIX

DONAHUE BOARDED THE plane with her entourage, and shortly thereafter the flight took off for Los Angeles. Once they were in the air, she discussed the arrangements for arrival in L.A. before withdrawing to the master bedroom, a quiet retreat where she could lay down on the bed to get a little sleep.

Ever since learning that she was pregnant, Donahue was itching to tell someone, and that someone was Shari Thompson.

She checked the clock, then picked up her cell phone and gave her a call.

"Hey, there," she said when Thompson answered. "What are you up to?"

Thompson was standing in her kitchen packing up the kids lunches while trying to make sure that her youngest one found his missing shoes.

"I'm getting the kids ready for school. Are you back in L.A.?"

"On the way. We just left D.C., so needless to say, I won't be into the office today."

"So, how are you feeling? Did you see the doctor?"

"Yeah," said Donahue. "I saw the doctor and she said it isn't the flu."

"Really? Does she know what it is?"

Donahue smiled. "Well, she gave me a test, and I got the results. Looks like I need to make an appointment with a specialist here in L.A."

Thompson stopped what she was doing. Her stomach was knotting up in anticipation of bad news.

"What kind of test was it?" Thompson asked.

"She had me go into the bathroom and pee on a stick—"

"*Oh my God, Jen! You're pregnant?*"

"It appears so."

There was an awkward silence, then Thompson asked timidly if Donahue was okay with it?

"At first I wasn't sure, but now I'm really over the moon!"

"And it's Sean's, right?"

"What? Of course!"

"Just checking," said Thompson with a laugh. She then did the math and said, "How far along are you?"

"Eight or ten weeks, or something like that. It's early yet, so I don't plan to tell anyone else until I'm at least four months along."

"Did you tell your mom and dad?"

"Nope, only you."

"Aw, thanks. I feel really honored." Thompson smiled. "And in that case, I'm calling dibs on being Godmother."

"That goes without saying, Shari."

"*Woo hoo!* I'm glad we got that settled."

Thompson stopped for a moment to direct her youngest to look for his shoes in the bathroom where he had taken them off the previous night before climbing into the bathtub.

When Shari got back on, Donahue said, "It's just a shame that Sean is going to miss out on all of this. He would have been so happy to know that we're having a baby."

"He'll be with you in spirit," said Thompson. "And don't worry about being a single mom. Trust me, I can teach you everything you need to know, particularly if it's a boy."

Donahue laughed.

"Oh, and pray for a girl," said Thompson. "I've been told they're a hell of a lot easier— hold on a minute, Jen —*'if they're not in the bathroom, Asher, then go upstairs and look under your bed'*— Sorry, where was I? Oh, yeah, if it is a boy, are you going to name him Sean?"

"Of course," said Donahue.

"Well, if it's a little girl, please don't name her *Sean-etta* or some other ridiculous feminized variation of Sean's name. OK?"

Donahue chuckled. "You have my solemn word on that."

"I gotta run, Jen. Call me tonight when you get in. We'll talk some more."

"I will, Shari, and thanks for having my back."

"Always, babe, you know that."

FORTY-SEVEN

LINDSEY RUSH PULLED his black BMW into a turnout on the 495 highway in North Springfield, a city in Fairfax County, Virginia. The area along the roadway was mostly forest. It was thick with birch and maple trees that had lost most of their leaves due to the cold weather. He parked his car, killed the lights, and lit up a cigarette to calm his growing anxiety.

At five minutes after eight p.m., a black Mercedes pulled into the same turnout and stopped right behind Rush's BMW. The back door of the Mercedes opened, and Oleg Kozlov stepped out. He made his way to the passenger door of the BMW and quickly climbed into the front seat.

Kozlov wasn't happy to be meeting this way. Rush's note was unusual. When he had information to pass, it was always done by courier and not by demanding a meeting. The demand seemed to Kozlov to be based on panic, and not on new information that he wanted to pass along. But Kozlov also knew that in spite of his military training, Rush was not a professional spook, so little things could make him nervous.

Kozlov had previous experience dealing with scared informants, and usually all they needed was a little reassurance to calm them down.

"So, General, what was so important that we had to have this meeting?" said Kozlov in his thick Russian accent.

"The FBI came to my office. They wanted to know if I had requested my assistant to obtain information from the Marshal's Office about the whereabouts of Sean Walker."

"What did you tell them, General?" Kozlov asked, looking around.

"I denied ever asking for that information, and I told them that my assistant must have done it on his own. They told me that they talked to my assistant, and that he claimed that the request came from me."

"So, what do you plan to do?"

"I don't know what to do."

"It's simple, General. Just continue to deny any involvement. Let your assistant take the fall."

"But they won't stop, Oleg. They'll keep coming back—"

"Relax," said Kozlov, who cut him off with a gesture. He was growing weary of the man's apparent helplessness.

"I can't," said Rush, "and until the FBI has finished checking me out, I don't think we should have any more contact."

"If you think they're on to you, then why are we meeting now?"

"They aren't, but they'll be all over me until they think they've got the truth."

"Then do as I say. Keep denying that you're involved. If they want you to take a polygraph, which I'm sure they won't because of your position, you tell them you won't, that the results are not reliable, and that you've had training during your military career in how to defeat such a test."

"But I haven't had that kind of training—"

"Stop it," said Kozlov. "Get ahold of yourself. They're not going to know that you didn't. You can tell them the training was classified. You'll think of something. But if you continue to act scared, you'll give yourself away."

Kozlov reached for the door handle, then stopped before looking back at Rush.

"Did you determine who has inherited the Korakovsky estate?"

"What?" said a distracted Rush. "No, of course not. Once the FBI came by, I had to give that up."

Kozlov nodded. "I'm sure that's a good idea for now, but my superiors want that information, General, so you'll need to develop a different source."

"I can't do that, Oleg. They'll probably be monitoring my calls. If I mention it to anyone they'll be on to me." He shook his head. "It's too risky."

Kozlov opened the door, but before he stepped out, he looked back and said, "One last thing. We've paid you well for that information, General. I would remind you that they still execute traitors in your country."

He looked over and held Rush's glance. "Get us the information we want, and get it soon."

He climbed out of the car, leaving Rush to contemplate the meaning of the threat.

In a van parked just up the highway, a team from the surveillance was recording the meeting. Rush's cell phone had been turned into a transmitter by an app they had hacked into several hours earlier.

Cullen, who was in a chase car parked about a mile further down the road, turned to the Team Leader who was driving the car they were sitting in. He had just received a report of the details of the conversation between Rush and Kozlov.

He knew what he planned to do about Rush, but he wanted to consider what the options might be for Kozlov.

"Let them both go," he said to the Team Leader. "Have the teams pull back. We can pick up Rush whenever we want to. I don't want them to know that we're on to them just yet."

FORTY-EIGHT

WHEN DONAHUE ARRIVED at the Private Suite LAX terminal at the Los Angeles International Airport, she got out of the plane and stood on the tarmac while her security team offloaded the luggage. They then put hers into the trunk of one of the two SUVs that would be used to transport her and the team up to her Brentwood home.

She was tired, in need of a shower, and ready to get something simple to eat when she pulled out her encrypted security phone and remembered that she had turned it off during the flight. She was surprised to note a missed call from Freely, whose message had asked her to call him just as soon as she could.

While the security team waited patiently by the SUV's, she walked away from Otero to be able to make the call with a bit of privacy.

Freely answered on the third ring.

"Mr. Freely? It's Jen Donahue. I'm sorry, but my phone was off when you called."

"Not a problem. I was calling to let you know that the Bureau notified me that they have identified the person in our government who furnished the information about your fiancé to a Russian contact."

"That's great! Has he been taken into custody?"

"Not yet, and that's what I wanted to talk to you about."

Donahue could feel her blood pressure rising. Whatever he was about to say was not going to be good, but she had no choice but to listen.

"Go ahead. Why hasn't he been taken into custody?"

"The Head of the Department of Homeland Security and the Justice Department want to turn him. They believe that he would be in a uniquely significant position to provide the Russians with disinformation."

"They want to make him some kind of a double agent?"

"That's correct," said Freely. "Instead of prosecuting him, he'll be giving the Russians false information which they'll be hard-pressed to question. He could turn out to be a very valuable double agent."

Donahue was having trouble believing what she was hearing.

"It's not fair," she said indignantly. "He belongs in prison, or dead."

Freely paused for a moment before responding.

"I don't disagree with you on that, but it's beyond my control. Both Cullen and I have reservations about how valuable he might be, but the decision was run by the President, and I've been told that he's already signed on."

"What about the Russian, the one who may have immunity from prosecution? What's going to happen to him?"

"He'll be the conduit for our double agent, so, of course, we won't order him expelled."

Donahue began to pace, and when Otero walked over, she waved him off.

"You're telling me that two of the people most culpable in Sean's murder are going to completely avoid any consequences for their actions? Is that what you're trying to say?"

"I'm afraid that's it, exactly," said Freely. "It's a national security decision."

"What a load of BS," said a now outraged Donahue.

On the plane ride back to L.A., she had lain awake in the bedroom suite thinking about this very possibility. She had expected that there might be a speed bump or two, but this plan that was formulated by the government went far beyond what she had ever contemplated. She was led to believe that only one of them was untouchable, but now it appeared that both of them were going to avoid prosecution, and she was damned if she was going to let that happen without her raising a stink.

"Are you still there?" Freely asked.

Donahue tried to hold her temper in check, but the grief and frustration of the last two months were about to express themselves in an uncharacteristic response.

"I'm here," she began, "but I can tell you that I'm really pissed off. This isn't right, Mr. Freely. Surely there are other conduits in place for passing disinformation to the Russians. These two men need to face the consequences for what they've done."

"I agree with you, Jennifer, but my hands are tied. Cullen and I were overruled, and as I said—"

"I know what you said, but this is outrageous, and you know it, too. The White House person involved in this is a fucking traitor. He needs to be punished, not turned. Sean gave his life because he was willing to help our country to defeat the corruption of Putin and his oligarch cabal who've stolen everything of value from the Russian people."

Her hands were shaking, so she took a deep breath and tried to regain her composure.

"On the plane ride back here, I had a lot of time to think, and I would suggest that you and the people above you better pay attention to what I'm going to say. I may not be able to do anything to the bastard who has diplomatic immunity, but I can assure you and the others that if the American who passed Sean's identity and address on to the Russians isn't prosecuted for conspiracy and murder, then those documents that you want so badly you'll never see again."

Freely was silent for a moment, then said, "I hope you're kidding?"

"I'm not. If he walks, then whatever deal you thought you had with Sean is over."

Freely swallowed hard.

"Look, Jennifer, I appreciate where you're coming from, but leaving these two in place will give us an opportunity to undermine the Kremlin—"

"As will releasing the documents. So, while I appreciate where you're coming from, I'm sure you can understand exactly how much you stand to lose if you don't find a way to bring these people to justice."

Freely sighed heavily. He didn't like it anymore than she did, but he was between a rock and a hard place.

"Assuming we could bring the American to justice, we have no leverage over the Russian Ambassador. He has full diplomatic immunity. The best we can do is expel him, and the Russians will likely give him a promotion and treat him like a hero."

The Russian Ambassador? Does Freely realize that he's just given me the identity of one of the two men?

"Who's the American?" she asked.

"I can't tell you that," he replied.

"You've just identified his contact for me," she said with an air of smugness. "Don't you think I can be trusted to know who the Ambassador was dealing with?"

"I can't, Jen. You don't have the required level of clearance for top-secret information."

"If I don't have it, then you don't have the necessary clearance to review the Russia documents."

She was leveraging her holding card to the hilt. It was all that she had to trade. But would he go for it?

"It's Retired General Lindsey Rush, the President's National Security Advisor."

"And the President plans to keep him on?" she asked, incredulously.

"That's my understanding."

"That *mother*—" She bit her lip to stifle the completion of the invective.

"Look, Jennifer, I'm sure you watch the news. There's something going on between this White House and the Russians. That's the whole purpose of the congressional investigations. And until that gets resolved, you need to understand that Russia is a blind spot when it comes to this President."

His words were followed by an uncomfortable silence between them.

"Can we discuss this some more at a later time?" Freely asked. "I can come out to L.A. if you'd like?"

"I need to think about all of this," she told him. She wanted more time to process what she'd just been told.

Freely cleared his throat. "How about if I send our mutual friend out to see you, the one in D.C.? Maybe she can help you clarify things?"

"Yeah. Okay. Why not? Send her out and I'll meet with her, but don't think for a moment that I'm going to change my mind."

Donahue hung up the phone and trembled from her fading adrenaline surge. She hadn't intended to come off that forcefully with Freely, but she was not about to let that bastard in the White House turn a blind eye towards the murder of her Sean.

❧

Donahue arrived at her gated home and discovered that Shari Thompson was waiting for her in front of the house in the large, circular, gravel driveway. They embraced with a hug and Thompson said, "Welcome back, Momma-to-be!"

"Shhh," said Donahue, looking around. "One of the security guys might overhear you."

"My bad, you're right. From now on I'll just call you MTB."

"MTB?"

"Momma-to-be," she whispered. "It's code. Get it?"

Donahue laughed. "C'mon inside. I want to tell you what's been going on and get your *sage* perspective."

"Sage? Isn't that an herb?"

"It also means a profoundly wise person. Hmm, but in your case, perhaps I should have left it at get your take on things."

"That's okay, my feelings aren't hurt. You're just going through a hormonal imbalance, MTB. You'll apologize for that slander once you're copacetic again."

"Copacetic?" said Donahue. "You worked that in nicely. I take it all back, you are sage."

They walked into the house, arm in arm, chatting about the weather in Zurich and London. Donahue led her to the living room, and after Marcelina brought them tea, which was served in delicate porcelain cups, Donahue proceeded to tell Thompson about the type of documents and photos that she discovered in the safety deposit box in Zurich. She mentioned that she'd shown a few of them to Freely, who had literally salivated to get his hands on the rest of the documents.

"He and I spoke again when I landed here in L.A.," said Donahue. "He told me that they managed to identify the guy at the White House who was responsible for getting the information on Sean, which he turned over to the Russian Ambassador."

Thompson whistled. "The Ambassador, huh? Don't those guys have diplomatic immunity?"

"He does, but the American involved doesn't."

"Are you gonna tell me who he is?"

"I had to sign a confidentiality agreement, so for the moment, I can't. But, I've got an idea, Sage One, or should I just call you S1?"

"Sage One sounds sexy. Let's go with that. So, what's your great idea?"

For the next twenty minutes, the two women discussed the details of Donahue's plan, the pros and cons, and the roadblocks she would likely face in order to get it accomplished.

"Too many variables," said Thompson, "but it is a bold move."

"You think it will work?"

"I do, but you're gonna need a lot of help, Jen. Your plan has got a lot of moving pieces, and I'm not sure where you're going to find the kind of assistance that you're going to need?"

"I was thinking of asking some of my friends for a little help."

"Well, you know I've got your back, but if you're gonna pull this off, you better make sure you're on sound footing."

"You're right. I'm sure there are more than a few illegalities involved in this scheme, but I owe it to Sean to give it a try. Hell, Shari! If I don't do something, that bastard is going to get off scot-free."

Thompson sighed. "Whatever you choose to do, count me in."

⌁

After Thompson left to pick up one of her boys from football practice, Donahue got the call she'd been waiting for on the encrypted phone.

"Hello," said Donahue, when she answered it.

"Hi. It's me. My boss has me catching a flight out to your neck of the woods. I'll be in L.A. within fifteen hours. Do you want to meet in the usual place?"

"Too complicated. When I try to go out, it's a traveling circus, and I've been warned to take serious precautions. I'd prefer to meet here at my new digs. I'll tell the security folks that I'm interviewing you to be my personal secretary. Do you have a phony ID you can present to them at the gate?"

"Does the earth revolve around the sun?"

"Of course, what was I thinking. Want to give me a name so I can tell them to expect you?"

"Lynn Yi," said Charlotte.

"Is that your real name?" Donahue asked.

"What do you think, Jennifer?" said Charlotte.

"Right." Donahue slowly sighed. "By the way, is there any chance I can get a second passport in a different name? I might need one for security reasons when I fly outside the country?"

Charlotte was quiet for a few moments, then said, "I'll ask around."

"I can have someone pick you up when your plane comes in," said Donahue.

"That would be nice," she replied.

"Give me the flight information, and there will be a good-looking guy holding a hired car sign in the name of Lynn Yi."

Charlotte gave her the flight information, then asked, "By any chance, is this good-looking guy single?"

"Jeez, you're starting to sound like my partner."

⚜

The next morning Donahue paid a visit to Jacklyn Crandall, her OBGYN. Her office was in the 100 medical building at UCLA, which was right next door to the Ronald Reagan Medical Center.

Crandall confirmed that she was indeed pregnant, and she prescribed a list of vitamin supplements that she wanted Donahue to take during the pregnancy. She gave her the warnings about drinking alcohol (including wine), smoking pot, and the need to give up her rare but occasional cigarette during nights out with the girls. She then presented her with a maternity T-shirt that bore the legend, "*I'd like to think that wine misses me too.*"

"I give one to all my first-time patients," said Crandall. "A not-so-subtle reminder to take my warnings seriously."

Donahue smiled and thanked her for the shirt. Surprisingly, the shirt made the whole pregnancy experience real.

I'm actually going to have a baby!

Crandall smiled back. "I'm going to give you a prescription for *Diclectin* for your morning sickness. I want you in here once a month for checkups throughout the duration of your pregnancy."

"Aren't you going to do an ultrasound?" Donahue asked.

"Too soon," said Crandall with a smile. "Let's wait until the next visit. In the meantime, you look like you've lost a lot of weight?"

"About twenty pounds," said Donahue. "The stress of losing Sean…"

Her voice trailed off, and Crandall said, "Are you seeing anyone about that?"

"Not yet," Donahue replied.

"Well, I'm going to refer you to Mindy Cooper. She's a psychologist who specializes in grief counseling. She's someone I know quite well. I want you to see her right away. We need to fatten you up a bit, but only with the right foods. Would you like a referral to a dietician while I'm at it?"

Donahue smiled. She had no intention of telling Crandall that she had a cook on staff. She was still uncomfortable with her new wealth, and she didn't want her present relationships to change in any way.

"No. I've got someone in mind I can talk to about it."

"Okay," said Crandall. "See Molly up front and she'll set you up with monthly appointments."

Donahue got to her feet and Crandall gave her a hug.

"I know this is bittersweet for you, Jen, but in a very real way your Sean has left you with the greatest possible gift of all."

"I know. It's a real miracle, doctor. One I won't take for granted."

⁓

On the way back to her home, Donahue placed a call to Captain Tom Elwood.

"I need to take a few weeks off for personal reasons. Turns out I'm pregnant."

Elwood's eyes widened. "Jen, that's great! Congratulations!"

Donahue couldn't stop smiling.

"Do you need anything?" he asked.

"No, just keep it under your hat for a while. I want to tell the others when I'm a little farther along. I plan to keep working as long as the doctor says I can, but after that, I just don't know."

"Look, take a few weeks off, and when you come back, we'll see how it goes. But just so you know, you can work here as long as you want. I won't be replacing you as long as you indicate an interest in coming back sometime in the future."

"Thanks, Tom. I appreciate that. It's going to take a couple of weeks to get things under control around here, then hopefully I can work right up to the delivery."

"Fat chance of that. I don't want to have to deliver your child in the back of a squad car on the way to the hospital, so let's just say we'll play it by ear and see how you're doing."

Donahue smiled. "You make a good point. I'll see you in a couple of weeks."

"Have you told Shari?"

"She knows. Already put in her dibs to be Godmother."

"Is Godfather still available?"

"Aw, Tom. That's a great offer, but Gibby would kill me if I didn't ask him."

"Is there any rule that says your kid can't have two Godfathers?"

"You know, I have no idea if that's ever been done before, but on behalf of my kid, I think it's a great idea. As far as I'm concerned, consider it a done deal."

FORTY-NINE

CHARLOTTE ARRIVED AT Donahue's mansion at just before noon. She presented a Korean passport to Otero that identified her as Lynn Yi, and once the ID passed muster, he had a team member search her purse. She then submitted to a wand detector to determine if she was carrying a concealed weapon. When Charlotte passed the inspection, she was escorted onto the grounds and up to the front door. From there, Marcelina escorted her to an office, where Donahue was seated behind a desk.

Charlotte was a tall young woman in her early thirties with film star good looks. She wore a chestnut-brown, short-hair wig, one that concealed her shoulder-length, jet-black hair.

She had joined the CIA at twenty-four. She'd been an honor student at Georgetown who graduated with a degree in Public Policy. She was a natural with languages, had an ear for dialects, and in addition to English and Korean—the latter which was spoken at home by her grandparents—she had learned to speak and read Russian, German, Mandarin, and French, as if they were her mother tongues. At the language school set up by the agency, she also picked up a conversational understanding of Japanese and Swedish.

Because of her language proficiencies and her excellent scores during her tradecraft training, she was selected to be an operative under *non-official cover* (NOC). NOC's are operatives without official ties to the government who, therefore, have no diplomatic immunity.

For her first assignment in the field, she was sent to Shanghai to work in the Morgan Stanley Wealth Management Department. Her chosen *nom de guerre* for that assignment was *Sang Hee Cho*.

Shanghai turned out to be a fertile recruiting ground, and because of Charlotte's expertise and personal charm, she successfully handled nine highly-placed Chinese military and political agents for almost two years. But her success as a field agent came to a crashing halt when a mole in the United States government—one Harold William Ronson—sold her name as a possible NOC to a representative from the Chinese *Ministry of State Security*, China's foreign intelligence service.

The sale of her name occurred when Ronson was attending a meeting in Singapore. Because Ronson had been a manager in the counterterrorism branch at CIA Headquarters, he was subsequently tried, convicted, and sentenced to life at the ADX Florence Supermax prison, located in Colorado.

Because her identity had been revealed, she was pulled from her undercover assignment to work as a special assistant to Deputy Director Jamison Freely.

Donahue was unaware of Charlotte's true name or her history with the CIA. She had no idea that Charlotte was anything other than a glorified errand-runner of some kind, who did odd jobs for her boss, a man who just happened to be the Assistant Deputy Director of the CIA.

Donahue got to her feet, came around the desk, and invited Charlotte to take a seat on a nearby couch.

"How was your flight? Donahue asked.

"Miserable. There were adorable two-year-old twins on board, six rows back, and they cried on and off throughout the flight."

"That's just bad luck.

"Tell me about it. Even the earplugs didn't help."

Donahue laughed. "Before we get started, would you like something to eat or drink?"

"If I could get a cup of coffee, that would be great."

Donahue picked up the phone, made a few requests to the cook in the kitchen, then hung up before leaning back in the chair that faced her guest.

"This is quite a home," Charlotte said, glancing around.

"I know. A little large for one person, but with all the hired help needed to run this place it sometimes seems too small."

"Are you complaining?" Charlotte asked, with a twinkle in her eye.

Donahue shrugged. "I guess I'm just having trouble getting used to such a major change in my life. Big money brings its own type of big problems, Charlotte, and for all the benefits it does provide, I can tell you that it doesn't buy happiness."

"Sounds like a sentiment for a Hallmark card," said Charlotte with a laugh. "But once you get adjusted to it, I suspect you'll discover that money is power, and it gives you a voice and a platform that will be respected. And if you find a cause that's important to you, you'll have a good shot at making a difference."

Marcelina showed up with a silver pot of coffee and a few freshly-baked pastries. She left the tray on the coffee table in front of Charlotte, then made her way out of the room.

"Aren't you having some?" Charlotte asked, after noting there was only one coffee cup.

"I'm on a schedule to put on weight. I just finished a power shake before you got here, so I've got another two hours to go before I have another."

"You are looking a little thin," said Charlotte. "I was gonna ask you about that."

"Loss of appetite," said Donahue. "But I've got a nutritionist now, and she's in charge of what-and-when I eat."

Charlotte chuckled. "While the entire female world worries about losing weight, you get the luxury of putting weight on without guilt."

For the present time, Donahue had no intention of letting

Charlotte know what was behind her need to put on a few pounds, so she quickly changed the subject.

"Where do I stand with your boss?" she asked.

"You've got him rattled. He's afraid your pursuit of justice is going to overshadow what may be in the best interest of our country."

"I've been a cop for a long time," said Donahue with a sigh, "and I've learned that there are times when the people at the top don't recognize the need to stop trading upward. If you've got a traitor in the highest levels of government, you don't let him keep operating in the hopes that he can be used to pass disinformation to the Russians. You need to put him in prison or give him the death penalty to put others on notice that working with a hostile power will get you no mercy."

"You're preaching to the choir," said Charlotte, "and to be honest, I suspect that Director Freely feels the same way. But he has to answer to others, and unfortunately, the current President seems to have cold feet when it comes to calling out the Russians."

"But Rush is one of ours," said Donahue. "His value as a double agent won't begin to make up for the role he played in a Russian scheme to murder a man in protective custody."

"I know you see it that way, Jen, and I can't disagree, but you're playing with fire. If they want to use Rush as a double agent, they're gonna do it. And if Ambassador Kozlov is his handler, then he's now a known quantity. They can feed false info to Rush, who'll feed it through Kozlov to Moscow. And because we will know what is going on, we can monitor things every step of the way."

"Then they'll never see the Putin papers," said Donahue. She crossed her arms over her chest.

"Don't be so sure," warned Charlotte. "They know you've got them, and they can hit you up with a subpoena for those records on the grounds of national security."

"Is that what Freely has in mind?"

"It's what he's afraid will happen. Look, Jen, the Director is in your corner, but the problem starts at the very top. I'd love to tell you that

Rush is gonna go down and that Kozlov is gonna be shipped back to Russia, but it's probably not going to happen."

"Then why are we meeting like this?" Donahue asked.

Charlotte kept her voice unemotional.

"The Director is worried that you're going to withhold the documents. He wants you to reconsider turning them over. If you do, he says to let you know, that he'll forever be in your debt."

"What does that even mean?"

"It means that you'll be holding a marker, one that may help you out should you ever need help in a pinch."

Donahue shook her head.

"I appreciate his offer, but my answer is no. I've given this a lot of thought, and maybe I'll just have to do something on my own."

"You want to tell me what you have in mind?"

"Are you serious?"

Charlotte shrugged. "I suppose not."

"Then there's nothing more to say," said Donahue. She got to her feet.

"Hold on," said Charlotte. She waited for Donahue to sit back down. "Can we go off the record?"

Donahue nodded.

"Okay, I want you to know that I agree with you about everything. Rush needs to go down, and Kozlov can't be allowed to operate with impunity. I know you're not going to tell me what you have in mind, but if I can be of any assistance to you, I will. Off the books, of course, but I'm willing to have your back."

Donahue gave it some thought. Charlotte had contacts that Donahue couldn't even dream of having. Perhaps she could be of some help. But was it fair to enlist Charlotte's assistance? If anyone ever discovered what Donahue had in mind, everyone involved might end up in prison.

"Why would you want to help me?" she asked.

"My career was disrupted by a traitor, so I guess I know firsthand what you're feeling."

Donahue was surprised. "Care to elaborate?"

"Maybe someday, but not now."

Well, that's interesting, thought Donahue. *If she really does identify with how I feel, then maybe I actually can trust her.*

"I wouldn't want to put you at risk?" said Donahue. "I'm thinking about your career and your personal safety."

"I'm not worried, Jen. If what you're asking me to do is too risky, I'll let you know."

"Let me think about it," said Donahue. "In the meantime, where are you staying?"

"I've got a flight back later tonight," said Charlotte.

"Can you bump it over a day?"

"Sure. I prefer the weather here in L.A."

"Okay. Put it over and hang out here. I'm gonna make a few calls, and after dinner, I'll let you know if you can help."

"Will you let your security people know what's up?" Charlotte asked.

"You've had a long trip just to get here, and I want to get to know you better before making a decision on whether or not to hire you," said Donahue. "Otero will buy it, no problem."

"Sounds good to me," said Charlotte. "Have you got a pool here?"

Donahue smiled and nodded. "I'll get Marcelina to get you a suit."

"Lying in the sun will be great. I might even catch a little nap," said Charlotte.

"I thought Asian women didn't like to get tan?"

"Not this girl. Brown is beautiful, and I love everything about being outdoors."

Donahue picked up the phone, punched in the intercom, and when Marcelina answered, she asked her to join them.

"Marcelina," she said when the door swung open. "Miss Yi is going to be my guest overnight. Can you set her up in one of the upstairs bedrooms, and find her a bathing suit. She's going to hang out by the pool while I take care of a little business."

"Certainly, ma'am. Will you be having dinner in tonight?"

"Do you like sushi, Miss Yi?" Donahue asked.

"Are you kidding? I was raised on sushi," said Charlotte.

Donahue turned to Marcelina. "We'll be eating out tonight."

Marcelina nodded. "Miss Yi, if you'll come with me…"

Charlotte smiled at Donahue, then made her way out of the room.

Donahue notified Otero of her plan to have Miss Yi stay over, then she put a call in to Thompson who had been summoned to her kids' school to pick up one of her boys who was running a temperature.

"Can you make it up to the house tonight? Charlotte is here and she's going to stay over, so I thought we could take her to *Sushi Sushi*."

"Ah, I hate to tell you this, but pregnant women are supposed to refrain from eating raw sushi."

"Really? Donahue frowned. "Okay. I'll check with my doctor tomorrow, but in the meantime, since she didn't mention that when I saw her, I'm gonna play dumb and do it one last time."

"You sure?"

"I'm drooling just thinking about it. I'm sure."

"Okay then. My mom's on board for watching the boys, so yeah, I can do it."

"Good. I haven't told Charlotte what I'm going to do, but she's volunteered to help. I'll explain everything later, but I think it's a good idea to have a witness present when I tell her what I'm going to need."

"What time do you want to meet up?" Thompson asked.

"How's seven-thirty sound? Just go straight to the restaurant."

"I'm down. I'll see you there."

༄

Dinner at *Sushi Sushi*, a traditional Japanese restaurant in Beverly Hills, had the potential for being a bit of a circus. Donahue was hoping for a quiet dinner where she and Thompson and Charlotte could toss around a few ideas, but the burden of having to go everywhere with her security detail weighed heavily on the prospect of achieving her goal. A significant security entourage was bound to attract attention, particularly in Beverly Hills, so Donahue held a quick meeting with Otero, and they worked out a plan which would allow her and Charlotte to get out of the car a block away from the restaurant. That would enable them to walk to the restaurant alone. The security team would shadow them from nearby, and once they arrived at the restaurant, only Otero would go inside.

She had called ahead, so when they arrived, they were escorted to a table in the corner of the room. Otero took a seat at the counter, about fifteen feet away, where he could keep tabs on who came in and out. Thompson was already there, enjoying a cup of tea at the table, and once the three women were all seated, a charming young waitress greeted Donahue by name and brought them hot towels and green tea. Donahue told her they would order *Omakase* style, which was the Japanese word for saying that the dishes to be served would be selected by the chef.

"You're gonna love this food," Thompson said to Charlotte. "The owner is a fanatic when it comes to freshness."

"Do you come here often?" Charlotte asked Thompson.

"About once a month. I've got three kids, so I don't get out all that much. But Jen is in here every week."

Charlotte shifted her glance to Donahue.

"If that's true, you need to make sure that you vary your times and days. Can't be too careful if you think the Russians might be on to you."

Donahue sighed. "I hadn't given that enough thought, but you're right. I'm going to have to be a lot more careful."

The first round of fish arrived, and as the waitress put the plates down, she said softly, "*Shige* says '*no soy sauce.*'"

Donahue laughed and looked over at Shige, the Chef/owner, who waved one finger from side to side. She gave him a nod, then turned to Charlotte.

"He's such a love. He's very particular about making sure we eat it with maximum taste value. He'll let us know if soy or wasabi is needed."

Charlotte popped a piece of *Chutoro* into her mouth. It was the medium-grade fatty part of the tuna, and as she chewed, she slowly rolled her eyes.

"Oh my God! This is really good," she said as soon as her mouth was empty. "It literally melts in your mouth!"

"That's why I'm in here all the time," said Donahue.

They continued to eat for another thirty minutes while chatting about their lives and Charlotte's personal life. Charlotte claimed she didn't have one, and because of the job, there were few male prospects on the horizon. Donahue let it slip that she was pregnant, and the conversation then quickly shifted to Donahue's hopes and worries.

When the plates were cleared and another round of green tea was served, Donahue decided it was time to see if Charlotte was really interested in joining her quest for justice.

"Do you have any contacts at the NSA's CNO?"

Charlotte's eyes widened. "You're unusually well-informed."

"What's the CNO?" Thompson asked.

"It's the new acronym for the *Computer Network Operations* unit. It's a cyber-warfare intelligence-gathering operation," said Charlotte. She looked back over at Donahue. "I'm just surprised that you know the new name. It used to be called the *Tailored Access Operations (TAO)* until Snowden leaked the documents that named the unit and what it was for."

Donahue smiled. "So, do you have any contacts there?"

Charlotte nodded affirmatively. "What do you have in mind?"

Donahue leaned forward and lowered her voice.

"What I need is the best hacker that money can buy. It has to be off the books, a one-time operation. I'll pay a great deal to have it done right, but there has to be complete confidentiality and no paper trail back to me."

"How illegal is this going to be?" Charlotte asked.

"Just a little, but it's not something that I'll financially profit from."

"You're not going to tell me, are you?"

Donahue shook her head. "You'll just have to trust me, Charlotte."

"You want this person to call you directly?"

"I'll need to explain what I have in mind in person, so I prefer to go to him or her. I want to keep my ID secret for obvious reasons, so you'll have to vouch for me."

"Let me see what I can do. Is there anything else?"

Donahue nodded. "I need to know the name of a bank used by the CIA to make payouts. It has to be one that other intelligence services know is a CIA front operation."

Charlotte thought about that for a moment.

"I think I'm starting to get a sense of what you're up to, Jen, and I must say, if I'm right, I like where this is going."

"So, you'll get that information for me?"

Charlotte smiled and nodded.

"I may know just the gal you'll want to talk to. Let me talk to her first. She's expensive, but she's a wizard."

"And what about that secondary passport? Is that doable?"

"I need to clear it with Director Freely, but he can authorize that on security grounds."

"I don't want a passport that exists in the system. If the Russians are looking for me, I don't want some dirtbag in our government whose been compromised to be able to connect it to me."

"I'll mention that to the Director. Is there anything else?"

"The name and a number for someone who can check Ambassador Kozlov's travel records. I want to know if he's ever been to Cyprus, and if so, when?"

Charlotte leaned back in her chair, looked over at Thompson, and smiled. "This is better than playing Clue. Your partner here is dropping hints like crazy."

She returned her gaze to Donahue.

"I can find that out for you."

"Great," said Donahue with a satisfied smile. "Shall we order some desert?"

※

The following day, while Charlotte was lounging out by one of the pools, Donahue placed a call to Dan Murphy at the embassy in Cairo. She asked him to have Bryan Harb give her a call. Murphy knew who she was, and he agreed to reach out to Bryan right away.

Almost three hours later, Bryan returned her call. Donahue was taking a nap at the time. She was a little groggy when she first answered the phone, but when she realized that it was Bryan, she woke right up and thanked him for getting back to her so quickly.

"I have a favor to ask you," she said. "Are you on an encrypted line?"

"Are you?" he asked.

"I am."

"Good. Then we can talk freely. I'm in London at the moment. What's up?"

"I need someone outside our government who has access to a double agent, one who can pass some info on to the Russian government."

"First, why don't you tell me what you're trying to accomplish?"

She trusted Bryan completely, so she told him about what Freely had said about Kozlov's having diplomatic immunity. She went on to describe the gist of her plan, and why she needed a double agent.

When she was finished, Bryan whistled. "You really think you can pull this off?"

"I hope so."

"Don't take this the wrong way, Jen, but you've got some set of balls on you."

Donahue laughed. "I'm not sure that's a compliment, Bry, but thanks, I guess."

"It was meant as a compliment. I have a few contacts in the Middle East, but if it's okay with you, I'd like to run your request past Whitney.

MI-6 might have such an agent, and if so, I have a feeling it would be more believable if it came from a British source."

"Do you have a number for him?" she asked.

"He's here in this building. Let me run it by him. I'll get back to you in an hour or so. Okay?"

"Yeah, that's fine. I trust Whit to keep this top secret, even from his superiors. Once I start to put this in motion, my butt's gonna be hanging way out there."

He got back to Donahue in less than an hour to say that Whitney wanted a meet. She agreed to go to London as soon as a few other things were put into place.

FIFTY

THREE DAYS LATER, Donahue found herself back on an overnight flight to Washington. Charlotte had come through and said that she would be there to meet the plane once Donahue touched down at Baltimore International.

When Donahue got off the plane, Charlotte walked her into the terminal, then through an employees-only door to a room where they could have a little privacy.

"Here's a second passport for you," said Charlotte. She handed the blue covered document to Donahue. "As you requested, it's in the name of Mary Vanderbilt." Charlotte smiled. "An interesting choice of names."

"How about the NSA contact?" Donahue asked. "Any luck there?"

Charlotte handed her a piece of paper. On it was the name of *Lisa Wentworth* and a Maryland cell phone number.

"She's a brilliant girl, and if what you want to get done can be done, she's the one who can do it."

"Is this her real name?" Donahue asked as she slid the piece of paper into her jeans pocket.

"Of course not. She wants to keep her identity a secret, too."

"Understood. Is she expecting my call?"

Charlotte nodded affirmatively. "She doesn't know who you are, but she's willing to listen to your proposal, and if she's assured of confidentiality and a reasonable fee, she can probably do what I think you have in mind."

"How about the bank info?" Donahue asked.

"The CIA operates an international banking operation called Security Financial Trust. It's a private bank, very limited clientele. It's primarily used for moving funds to agencies, embassies and military personnel throughout the world."

Donahue nodded. That would be perfect.

"Is your hotel room being paid for by one of your shell corporations?"

"Yes, and I'm assured that it can't be traced back to me."

"And you're using the name of Mary Vanderbilt?"

Donahue nodded.

"Then give Lisa a call. Have her meet you at your hotel. That way you can talk in secrecy while both of you keep your true identities intact."

Donahue thanked her, promised to keep in touch, then left the small airport room to join up with Otero, who guided her out to a low-profile vehicle. It was a rental car, followed by two similar ones with her security team. They went to the *Mandarin Oriental Hotel* where a suite was reserved for her, as well as three nearby rooms for the members of her security team.

She called the number for Lisa, who answered on the fifth ring. Donahue was pretty sure that Lisa's was a burner phone that would be discarded as soon as their business was concluded. She arranged for Lisa to come to her hotel room at nine p.m., and gave her the Vanderbilt name under which she was registered.

With a little time on her hands, Donahue ate dinner alone in the hotel's *Muze* restaurant which overlooked the Washington Channel waterfront. When she was finished, she went up to her room, put on a black wig, lowered the lights in the sitting room, and removed a sequined black Domino mask from a compartment in her suitcase. It was one that covered only the upper half of her face, the area around her eyes and the space between them.

When the doorbell rang at nine, Donahue answered it and invited the young woman in. Otero was nowhere in sight, having been told by Donahue that her guest was vouched for and would not need to be formally identified.

"Good move," said Lisa when she entered the room, referring to Donahue's mask. "I should have worn a balaclava."

"Would you like a drink?" asked Donahue.

"No thanks. I'm good."

Donahue led her over to a pair of couches that were parked in front of the bay window. Lisa took a seat on one of them while Donahue sat down on the one that faced her.

Wentworth was an attractive twenty-seven year old South Korean-American woman who worked at the United States Cyber Command. Her unit was part of the Red Team, a group which conducted expeditionary and remote cyber attacks, cyber exploitation, and cyber defense operations for the U.S. Army, and for other Defense information networks. She was headquartered at Fort Meade, Maryland.

Her area of speciality was the Access Technologies Operations Branch, a team that included personnel who were brought in by the CIA and the FBI. They performed "off-net operations" that involved the surreptitious planting of eavesdropping devices on computers and telecommunications systems worldwide. This enabled them to remotely hack the overseas systems directly from their facility at Fort Meade.

None of this was known to Donahue, who was also unaware that Lisa was one of approximately six-hundred employees at the complex, all dedicated to utilizing their unique and sophisticated abilities to prepare the United States for an offensive cyber war.

"Our mutual friend has vouched for you, so let me tell you what I have in mind," said Donahue. "I want to have you hack your way into the records of a particular bank, to be identified later, and once you're in, I want you to establish an account in a particular name. Once you have the account established, I want you to show a half-dozen deposits made into that account that will go back several years. The deposits must be shown as having come from wire transfers from the Security Financial Trust bank, the particular branch yet to be determined."

"What will be the total amount of the deposits?" Lisa asked.

"Roughly six-hundred and fifty-thousand dollars."

"But there won't be any real money to back that up?"

"That's correct," said Donahue, "but this is not a scam to steal from the bank. I simply want it there for certain people to see. Once they have reviewed the records, I'll need you to go back into the system and wipe out all traces of your work." She leaned forward and smiled. "Do you think you can do it?"

Lisa nodded. "It shouldn't be much of a problem."

"It needs to be done in such a way that there will be no way that it can be traced back to either one of us," said Donahue.

Lisa leaned back and folded her arms across her chest.

"I'm gonna make a big jump here and say that this sounds to me like a CIA operation that's being conducted off the books."

"It's completely off the books," Donahue replied, "but not by the CIA. The purpose of doing things this way is to make sure that the agency has complete deniability if anything ever goes wrong."

That wasn't exactly true, but Donahue could sense that Lisa was on the fence and that this might help her reach a favorable decision.

"Our friend said there would be compensation?"

"Fifty-thousand dollars," said Donahue without blinking her eyes. "Twenty-five up front, and twenty-five when the job is completed."

Lisa's eyes went wide. This was no CIA operation. Whatever it was it had the smell of possible prison time.

"Our friend vouched for you," said Lisa, "but this sounds like it's pretty far off the books."

Donahue sighed. She was going to have to let this woman know what she had in mind or she would likely turn down the job. So, without disclosing anything about herself or Sean, she talked about the fact that the man involved had diplomatic immunity for a murder he helped to orchestrate, and that the account she wanted her to set up would be used to bring him down.

This seemed to satisfy Lisa, who after several minutes of thinking it over, agreed to do the job.

"I don't know how much you know about what we do," said Lisa, "but we have a program called QUANTUMSQUIRREL. It gives us the ability to generate false geographical location and personal identification credentials when accessing the internet. It will prevent any hostile power from tracking my work back to either one of us."

Donahue smiled. "That's great. I'm hoping to have the name of a bank in Cyprus which will be the target location for the phony deposit account."

Lisa laughed.

"What's so funny?" Donahue asked.

"Cyprus banks are the favorites for Russian mobsters and politicians who want to launder money. We've penetrated most of them already."

Donahue grinned. "That should make your job even easier."

"I suspect it will."

⁂

The next morning, Donahue had the Washington Post delivered to her room. She was interested in looking at the society section, and when she found it, she carefully perused it until she located what she was looking for. It was a column that talked about charitable events that were scheduled for the Washington D.C. area during the next several months.

It didn't take long for her to decide on an event. It was a benefit organized for the American Cancer Society: a Valentine's Ball at the Italian Embassy. There was a dinner for VIP's, live ballroom dancing, an opera presentation, a late-night DJ for dancing, and Italian food and refreshments for those who didn't attend the VIP dinner.

The ad said that there was a fifteen-hundred dollar per-person cover fee, one that was guaranteed to appeal to the VIPs.

She tore out the page that gave details about the event and tucked it into her purse.

Her encrypted cell phone rang, but the caller ID was blank.

"Hello?" said Donahue cautiously.

"Jen? It's Charlotte."

"Oh, hi. What's up?"

"I've got the info you wanted on Kozlov's visits to Cyprus."

"Is it extensive?"

"Only three visits in the last five years. One trip was for three days, the other two involved one-night sleepovers."

"Can you give me the dates?" Donahue asked.

"Have you got a pen?"

Donahue rummaged through her purse, and when she pulled out a pen and a notepad that she used when investigating cases, Charlotte gave her the dates that Kozlov had been there.

"Thanks, Charlotte. I'll be in touch."

"Let me know if you need anything else?"

"I will, and you let me know when you need a break from the D.C. weather. I'll be happy to take you out for sushi again."

"I'll find an excuse," she said with a laugh, before hanging up.

Now that Donahue had what she needed, she notified Otero that she was ready to return to L.A.

FIFTY-ONE

Once she was back home in Brentwood, Donahue worked on a *Wikipedia* profile for her new persona of Mary Vanderbilt. Thompson stopped by to help her, and together they created a backstory that was not only believable, but intriguing as well. It had to have enough details to make the persona come to life, but not enough to enable the kinds of holes in a backstory that would help someone to identify it as being a fake.

They finally settled on the following narrative, and included a photo of Donahue, whose face was partially concealed by the black Domino mask.

Mary Jean Vanderbilt, born April 30, 1976, is an American artist, poet, heiress, fashion designer, and reclusive socialite. Ms. Vanderbilt maintains homes in Paris, London, Barcelona, and Lake Como, Switzerland. Her primary residence is in the Hamptons, however, she maintains a penthouse in the upper westside of Manhattan. She is a member of the Vanderbilt family of New York, and has never been married.

As an adult, she has overseen the development of more than a dozen lines of clothing, perfumes, and household items. Because she shuns personal publicity, her products are always released under corporate names. She has a tight circle of friends, all of whom remain fiercely loyal to her. As a result, she is rarely if ever mentioned in the gossip pages. She has been rumored to have had affairs with several well-known actors, industrialists, and a Formula One driver, all of whom have denied the gossip, and who have threatened to sue if so named. She has been described by some as a stunning blonde who frequently disguises herself when out in public.

She is an anonymous patron of the arts, politically active, and heavily involved in charitable fundraising, although she rarely attends the events she sponsors. On those occasions when she does make an appearance, she often plays hostess to the creme of the world's VIP's, but these public appearances are few and far between.

Miss Vanderbilt was once quoted as saying, "Having great wealth always brings out the worst in one's friends."

Donahue did not publish the profile right away, instead, she held it back for a last-minute release when she knew that a certain person would want to know more about the reclusive Miss Vanderbilt's background.

"So, what's next," asked Thompson, who was enjoying a glass of wine. Her boys were asleep in one of Donahue's upstairs bedrooms, while her mother was watching TV in Donahue's comfortable home theater.

"I need to get the account set up at the FBME, the bank that's a front for the CIA. I'm going to make contact with Lisa again so I can give her the dates that Kozlov was known to be staying in Nicosia, Cyprus."

⤐

Lisa Wentworth went to work the following day from her base of operations at Fort Meade, Maryland. Because of her stature within her team, she had a private office which allowed her to access the government computers with a guarantee of total privacy.

Lisa was intrigued by Donahue's plan which she considered to be most ambitious. If she was able to pull it off, it could well become a template for future espionage operations. It also proved to be the extra incentive that she needed to make sure that her work went undiscovered.

She used the capabilities of the QUANTUMSQUIRREL program to enter the computer system for the Central Bank of Cyprus. She posed as a cash-transfer signal from the Security Financial Trust, a CIA-front bank in Roanoke, Virginia. Once inside the Central Bank's computer system, she accessed a backdoor entrance into the records maintained for the now defunct FBME bank, through a program known as COMMENDEER, which enabled her to compromise their computer systems.

FBME, better known as the Federal Bank of the Middle East, was originally based in Tanzania, but for years it did almost all of its business in Cyprus. In 2014, it was taken over by the Central Bank of Cyprus in the midst of a major Russian money-laundering investigation.

It was Donahue's suggestion that they set up the account in the records of the now-defunct bank, since the accounts from that bank were still viable. There would be fewer questions about the authenticity of the account if it appeared to have been set up by a Russian during the height of the corruption scandal.

Once inside the bank's records, Lisa focused on the customer accounts. She quickly created one in the name of Oleg Kozlov that matched a date in 2012, when Kozlov was known to have been in Cyprus. Once the account was established, she added the fictitious deposits, all seemingly made by money transfers from Security Financial Trust. There were six separate fake money transfers, and together they totaled just over six-hundred and fifty-thousand dollars. She added interest amounts paid on the balance for the sole purposes of enhancing the perceived authenticity.

All in all, it took Lisa less than two hours to accomplish the feat.

Before withdrawing completely from the FBME records, Lisa slipped a program called VALIDATOR into the mainframe. That program was a software vulnerability scanner that could be used for future forays into those records and the records of the Central Bank of Cyprus.

When her work was finished, and her trail was completely covered, she notified Donahue by a burner phone that everything relating to the bank account was now in place and ready to go.

FIFTY-TWO

DONAHUE SCHEDULED A quick trip to London, one that did not include taking Thompson along. She wanted to test out her new passport identity as Mary Vanderbilt, and for Shari's safety, she did not want Thompson's name to be associated with the Vanderbilt *nom de guerre.* She had no doubt that the Russian SVR would eventually discover that she was the heir to Sean's fortune, so the less they knew about Shari, the better. She had come to the conclusion that these people were evil and would stop at nothing to get what they wanted. Donahue wasn't worried about herself, but if they ever targeted Shari and her kids, she would have no choice but to give the Russians whatever they demanded.

She called ahead to Bryan Harb who agreed to meet her at her hotel. Once she was checked into a suite at Brown's Hotel, in Mayfair, London, she gave him a call. He noted the location and told her that he would come by with Major Andrew Whitney of MI-6.

She took a nap before they arrived, and after they cleared their entry with Otero and his team, she had room service deliver a high-tea selection of sandwiches and pastries, coffee and tea.

"You feeling any better?" Bryan asked, when they were settled in the suite's sitting room.

"You mean the flu bug? Yeah, much better." She was not ready to say anything yet about her pregnancy.

"How have you been, Whit?" she asked. "I haven't seen you in quite a while?"

Donahue and Whitney had worked a case involving an IRA splinter group in Los Angeles, and during that time the two of them had become good friends. He had also become involved with Renée Marin, a senior prosecutor in the DA's office, and their bi-continental relationship was still going strong.

"I rarely get to L.A.," he told her. "Renée and her daughter like to come over here, so it works out pretty well."

Donahue took a sip of her tea, then put the cup and saucer down before looking over at Whitney.

"Did Bryan fill you in on General Rush and his handler Oleg Kozlov?"

Whitney nodded.

"And, of course, you know about the documents that Sean's father collected, the ones that Putin wants, which are now in my possession?"

"You have them?" Whitney asked.

"They're in a safe place," she replied.

"I hope so."

"Well, I want to go over everything to make sure that you're still on board. My idea is to pass some information on to the Russians. It's false, of course, but it's the kind of information that's going to be scrutinized very carefully. I've taken care to set up the information part of it, but what I need now is for the information to get into the hands of the Russians through a contact of theirs that they trust. It has to seem as if the source came from intelligence shared by America with the Brits."

"You want to tell me what you plan to pass on?" Whitney asked.

"I want them to believe that Oleg Kozlov has been passing information to the CIA." She smiled. "I've set it up with a bank account in his name in Cyprus that contains sums that were paid to him over time. I also want them to suspect that he's been furnishing the Agency with information detailing the corruption of Putin. To back that up, I'm willing to furnish copies of several documents that Putin's been after that were originally in the possession of Sean and his father."

Whitney stared, open mouthed.

"That's some plan," said Bryan. "And you're doing this all on your own?"

"I've had some help from friends like you," she said. She shifted her gaze from one to the other. "But I'm doing it without the sanction of my government because the current President intends to leave General Rush and Kozlov in place. He and others want to use the pair of them as a conduit for passing disinformation to the Russians."

"No shit?" said Bryan. "That's outrageous! Rush is a traitor. You can't leave a guy like that in the Administration. Even if you feed him crap which he passes on to the Russians, he's going to have access to the real stuff, and that makes him very dangerous."

"That's what I said, and Director Freely agrees with me, but the decision has come from the very top, so this has to be done on the down-low or I'm gonna be in a whole lotta trouble."

"This is a dangerous game you're playing," said Whitney. "Even if they don't charge you criminally with treason or for undermining a national security interest, they could always go after your finances or something like that."

"They can have the money," said Donahue. "It's never been a consideration for me, and to be honest, it's changed my life in a lot of ways that I really hate."

"I wish I had your problem," said Whitney with a smile.

"Trust me, you don't. Anyway, I wanted to lay this all out for you just in case you want to change your minds about giving me some help."

Whitney got up and started to pace. Donahue knew that he was having second thoughts, so she decided to hold her tongue and wait for his reply.

"What's the likelihood that the Russians would be able to uncover this deception?" he asked.

"Pretty slim," she replied. "There are very few people who know the whole plan, and those that do, including yourselves, I trust implicitly. The only weakness I can see is if an informant is used to pass the info on, they might try to work backwards to get to you."

Whitney gave it more thought.

"You don't have to get involved, Whit," she finally said. "Maybe I can find some other way to get it to the Russians."

"Would you be willing to provide us with some of these documents you say that Putin wants to get his hands on?" Whitney asked.

"It depends on what they'd be used for. If they're going to be buried, then the answer would be no."

Whitney nodded that he understood.

"Look, Jen," he said. "As far as I can tell, there's little or no chance that anything will happen to these two men if you don't go forward with your plan. However, if you do go forward with it, you might be subject to criminal prosecution. The only way to possibly keep you out of this would be for London to take the reins and goes forward with it for you. If what Korakovsky and his son gathered has the ability to cause problems for Putin in his next "so-called" election, then I suspect Her Majesty's government would be willing to use them appropriately, if, in fact, that's what you're really after?"

"I'd love to see Putin taken down," said Donahue, "but I also want Kozlov and Rush to pay the price for what they did to Sean."

"Then let me suggest that you back away from this operation and let us take it over. If you run the risk of prosecution for undermining the decision made by the White House, then they can't touch you if we make this a British intelligence operation."

"You think your people will buy in?"

"I do."

"And you can keep me completely out of it?"

"Of course."

Donahue smiled. It seemed to be the answer to her quandary. She had no desire to end up in jail, particularly now that she was pregnant. But it was important to see this through, and Whitney might just have offered her the off ramp that she needed.

"Thank's Whit. If you can make it happen, then I can live with that."

"When do you want to put this operation into play?" he asked.

"I've got a date in mind, but I've got something else in play, and I need to see it through."

"Okay. I'll speak to my people. I have no doubt this will end up at Downing Street, but as soon as I know if we can take it over, I'll give you a call."

Donahue got up and stretched. "I don't know about you guys, but I'm starved. Care to join me for dinner?"

"What'd you have in mind?" Whitney asked.

"I was thinking fish and chips. I was told there's a place down the street that's really good. They wrap it up in newspaper, too."

"I know the place," he said. "And it's great. I'll agree to go if you agree to let me pick up the tab."

"Bry?" she asked.

He smiled. "If Whit's buying, how can I say no."

FIFTY-THREE

FOUR DAYS LATER, after hiring a nutritionist to work with her personal chef, Donahue managed to gain three pounds. She had her appetite back, and after giving approval for the design of the new security office to be constructed on her Brentwood property, she went out to the backyard patio of her home. She then placed a call to a District of Columbia number that had appeared in the ad for the Valentine's Day fundraiser at the D.C. Italian Embassy.

"I'd like to buy a table for the Valentine's Day Ball," she said to the young female who answered the phone.

"A table for six, eight, or twelve?"

"A table for eight will be fine. I also want to know who to send the donation to?"

"Oh, that's wonderful! Can I have your name, please?" said the woman.

"Mary Vanderbilt. I have my credit card, so let me know when you want the details?"

She was in possession of a corporate credit card from one of the many shell companies she now owned. It was given to her by James McCallum to help mask her personal identity. She read off the number, the expiration date, and the security code.

When the young woman completed the transaction, she asked

Mary Vanderbilt for an address where she could send the tickets. Donahue gave her the address of a dead drop that was also arranged by McCallum.

"This is a black tie event, correct?" Donahue asked.

"That's right," said the young woman.

"Wonderful! I'm so looking forward to it."

The next day, Donahue and Thompson met at Donahue's home with a graphic designer to develop fancy invitations that Donahue could mail out for the Valentine's Ball. Black, red and gold was the proposed color scheme, and the invitations were written up so that the recipients would know that they were going to be the guests of Ms. Mary Vanderbilt.

When the designer left, the two settled themselves in the home office to discuss the next step in Donahue's plan.

"Are you going to send Rush's invitation to the White House?"

"Charlotte called me yesterday and gave me his home address. She said he's single and a widower, so I'm going to send him two tickets. I doubt that he'll bring anyone along, but it will be far less suspicious than sending him just one."

"Have you decided who else to invite?"

"You mean other than you? No. I'm worried that if I do invite others, they might give away our true identities."

"I don't know, Jen. Just the three of us at a table for eight? It won't look good."

Donahue gave that some thought. "You're right. Maybe I should give Charlotte a call and see if she wants to attend?"

"I've got nothing against Charlotte, but wouldn't it be better if you gave the extra tickets to a some great looking guys? It's frickin' Valentine's day, Jen. We shouldn't let the evening go to waste."

"But I don't intend for us to stay there that long, Shari."

"I know, but if they're really hot guys, we can take them with us and hit a few clubs."

Donahue laughed. "I can see that you've already gamed this out, haven't you?"

"Waste not, want not," said Thompson.

ᴥ

The invitations went out on February 4th, and to Donahue's surprise, a representative from Rush's office quickly RSVP'd and said that the General would be attending as a single.

The RSVP number was one that was set up by McCallum for Donahue with an answering service, so there was no way to follow it back to Donahue directly.

Once she got the call that Rush would attend, she made a call to Charlotte.

"Not a good idea," said Charlotte, who had listened to Donahue's pitch. "Something could easily go wrong."

"It's your choice," said Donahue, "but to keep Shari happy, I've decided to give the unused tickets to a couple of the unmarried guys on my security team."

"Very tempting," said Charlotte, "but do you really think it's advisable for you to be meeting with him?"

"I need to do this," said Donahue, "and there's no law that says I can't invite the man to a charity party."

"But if we turn him, and if Kozlov is out of the picture, what good will it do?"

"If Rush gets turned, I'm sure the Russians will find someone else to be his overseer."

Charlotte frowned. It appeared as though there was no talking Donahue out of this, and with the papers she maintained in her possession, she still had all the leverage she needed to keep those in the know at bay.

"What about Thompson?" said Charlotte. "She can't use her own name. She'll need a cover ID."

"She wants me to call her Scarlett O'Hara, you know, from Gone with the Wind."

"She's a character, Jen, but this is really dangerous. One slip, one name accidentally spoken, and he'll have a way to trace you."

But Donahue brushed the warning off.

"We'll do the meeting, get a couple of photos, and after a few words, we'll vanish into the night."

An uncomfortable silence settled between them. Then Charlotte said, "You're hellbent on going through with this, aren't you?"

"I am, and are you sure you don't want to spend part of the evening socializing with a few guys from my security team?"

"The ones I saw were cute..." she said. "Okay. I'm in. Save me a ticket. But no pictures of me. I need to remain incognito."

"I'll send you an invite with all of the details. It's black-tie, so you'll need to get your sexy on."

"What about your security guys? Will they know what's going on?"

"A little, but they won't know the whole story. Besides, they're good-looking guys, Charlotte, and as Shari is fond of saying...'as long as they look great, they don't need to open their mouths.'"

"*Ahh!* You guys are crazy! Fun, but definitely crazy! All right. I'm in. I'll be in touch."

∼

Whitney took Donahue's plan to Sir John Stafford, the current Director of Britain's foreign intelligence service, MI-6. The meeting took place in his large window office in the Secret Intelligence Service building, on the Albert Embankment, in Vauxhall, Central London.

When Stafford learned the details of Donahue's plan, his first inclination was to say no to his government's getting involved. His main objection was that she was going behind her own government's stated intentions, and even though he believed without reservation that the current President was incapable of making an intelligent decision, he was still the President, and Stafford had no desire to create an international incident. But when Whitney told him about the documents in Donahue's possession, and the fact that she was willing to release some of them to MI-6 if they helped her with her plan, Stafford quickly realized that this was not a decision to be made without a great deal of thought.

He didn't give a damn about Kozlov. The Russian Ambassador in America was just another spy-master doing his job. On the other hand, General Rush was a threat to the U.S. and its allies. Rush had access to intelligence documents and briefings that could possibly undermine Her Majesty's government, and if their President wasn't willing to take Rush out of play, then it might be in the best interest of Six to carry out what she had in mind.

After consulting the Prime Minister, he gave the okay to Whitney, who told Stafford how he proposed to do it. Stafford listened to the details of Whitney's plan and it brought a smile to his face.

"Nice," he said, when Whitney was finished. "Go ahead and set it up."

"Should I let Bryan Harb know how we're going to pull this off?" Whitney asked.

"Do we trust him?"

"Completely. His field of operations is the Middle East. He's been asked to look into the Russian-sponsored activities in that area, so if we work with him now—once this particular situation gets resolved—he'll be a cooperative and reliable contact with invaluable Middle East experience."

"Will he want access to the documents?"

"Of course," said Whitney. "He's loyal to the CIA, but it's my opinion that even if Donahue gives them to us, she'll see to it that the CIA gets a copy of them, too."

"Okay. Fill him in, but don't identify the players by name."

"Do we want to do anything about Rush?"

"Not yet. Let's see how it plays out with Kozlov first." He gave him a smile. "Let me know when you put things into play."

"Will do."

～

Whitney left the meeting and placed a call to Donahue to tell her that Six was buying in.

"Thanks, Whit. How soon do you need my stuff?"

"The sooner the better," he replied.

"Okay. I've been putting together a package for your agent which I'll bring over for you guys in a couple of days."

"Sounds great. But before you go, any chance you could bring Renée over with you? I haven't seen her in a couple of months."

"Long distance relationships can be such a bitch!" said a smiling Donahue.

"You're telling me."

"I'll call her now and we'll see what we can do."

～

Bryan Harb and Andrew Whitney sat together in a car that was parked in a lot at the red brick, Basingstoke Railway Station, which was along the railroad line from Waterloo to Southampton. It served the small rural farming communities of Basingstoke, Worting, Newfound, Lychpit, and a half-dozen others with equally interesting names.

It was shortly after eight p.m., and the last train had just disgorged the few remaining passengers who would soon drive their cars from the lot so that they could get to their homes for a late-evening meal.

Whitney was behind the wheel, and Bryan, who was in the front passenger seat, drank coffee from an old metal thermos.

"You were going to tell me how this is gonna go down," said Bryan.

"Yeah. Okay. We've got a young kid in Six, Russian-born, emigrated here when he was fifteen. He was approached by the Russians and they tried to recruit him to spy on our operation. He came to us and said that they threatened to kill his relatives back home in the Federation if he didn't do what they asked. We talked it over, and he volunteered to work with us as a double agent in order to pass them disinformation."

"Who did the recruitment?" Bryan asked.

"The Directorate KR: External Counter-Intelligence."

"I never heard of them," said Bryan.

"When the KGB became the FSB, the old specialities were organized as Directorates. The SVR is a subgroup within the FSB, and within the SVR is Directorate KR. They're authorized to collect intelligence, implement active measures to ensure Russia's security, and to conduct espionage in Western countries. And get this, under Russian law, Putin can personally issue secret orders to the SVR without informing the Duma."

"His own private band of spies?" asked Bryan.

"Spies and assassins." Whitney looked over and met Bryans glance. "Directorate KR carries out infiltration of foreign intelligence and security services. They also exercise surveillance over Russian citizens abroad. It was an SVR team that was tasked with killing Anton Korakovsky, Sean's father."

Bryan smiled. "I guess I'm going to have to hit the books to catch up with all the new Russian organizational charts."

Whitney smiled. "Wikipedia can give you a good overview."

They entered a round-about, and Whitney kept his focus on the traffic and the route he wanted to take. Once they were out of the circle, he said, "Anyway, we'll pass Donahue's info on to this young man who will pass it on to his handler."

"Does this kid have the access necessary to successfully convince his handler that the documents are genuine?"

Whitney smiled. "His handler is an SVR-KR that we turned more than ten years ago. The kid passes it to him, and he passes it on. And because the handler is not the source of the information, he's in a position to pass back to us whatever action they take on the disinformation they've been given."

"Very clever," said Bryan. "So, he can warn the kid off if something goes wrong?"

"That's right," said Whitney.

"So, who are we meeting tonight?"

"The kid's handler, and I'm going to meet with him alone. When he pulls into the lot, I'll walk over to his car, and we'll have a little chat. You stay here and cover my back."

"No problem," said Bryan. "And thanks for the scoop on how these bastards go about recruiting. It'll help me understand what's going on when I go back into Palestine."

ᴈ

The 2014 white Toyota Yaris drove into the train station parking lot, circled it once, then parked about sixty meters away. The driver had angled it to face both the station and the vehicle that Whitney and Bryan were sitting in. The driver blinked his high beams once, then shut down his engine and turned off his lights.

Whitney got out of his car, zipped up his leather, waist-length jacket, then made his way across the lot and over to the Yaris.

"Good evening, sir," said Leonid Morozov. Whitney was in the process of settling into the front seat."

"Hey, Leo," said Whitney.

The two men shook hands.

"It must be important for you to want to meet on such short notice," said Morozov.

Leonid Morozov held the diplomatic rank of Second Secretary in the Russian Embassy, in London. He was in charge of their intelligence-collection division. He had been working in that capacity for the last five years, and was a double agent for the British since his recruitment in Brussels ten years before.

Morozov had been identified as recruitable early on in his work with the SVR when he was an agent assigned to handle recruitment of NATO personnel in Brussels. Morozov was not a true believer, and his disdain for Putin and the way the man had looted Russia of most of its treasures had been a key motivator in turning him toward the west.

Morozov's hatred for Putin and his oligarch cronies was also motivated by his belief that they had gotten rich while he had been left behind. Money was what tipped the scales for Morozov, and the payments by the Brits for his work as a double was generous, but not enough to feed his unquenchable appetite for the better, more expensive things in life.

"How's your family doing?" Whitney asked.

"They're okay," said a cautious Morozov. "Why do you ask?"

"Do you still want to send your oldest boy to Oxford?"

Morozov loosened up and relaxed. His love for his family was another one of his trigger points.

"He's working very hard in school to keep up his grades. Are you going to be able to help him out?"

"We have people working on it, Leo. As I told you before, if he keeps his grades up, he should be a shoo-in."

Whitney knew that it was already a done deal that had been arranged by Six more than a month before. But it was important to keep Morozov on a short leash, so leaving him in the dark about something as important to him as his son's education was a way to ensure his complete cooperation.

"Let me tell you why I wanted to see you," said Whitncy. "In a day or so, you're going to receive a package of information that will identify a high-ranking Russian government official as a spy for the CIA."

Morozov's eyes went wide.

"We want you to pass it on to your superiors in the *KR* without any delay."

"But why would you want to burn a western asset? That doesn't make any sense."

"Our reasons are our reasons," said Whitney. "Your job is to pass it on, and vouch for its credibility."

"What is the source of these documents?"

"The documents will be discovered by one of your recruits. He'll say that he discovered them on the desk of his supervisor who attended a briefing given by the Americans. He was able to make copies without being discovered. The documents the traitor has been furnishing to the Americans have come from oligarchs who've been helping the CIA to gather information that implicates Putin in extensive criminal activity. The handover has been going on for quite a while, and the traitor has been on the CIA's payroll for years."

Morozov was speechless. The fact that the British would want to sacrifice an anti-Putin activist ran counter to everything he believed in.

"I don't like this," said Morozov. "You know that I am doing what I do in order to eventually bring down Putin. But this—burning one of your own assets—I just don't understand that?"

"We've worked together for quite a while now," said Whitney, "and I know you trust me, right?"

Morozov nodded.

"Then this is one time when you need to trust me completely, and not ask any questions."

Morozov thought about that for a moment, then asked, "And who is this traitor to the Motherland?"

"Oleg Kozlov, the Ambassador to the United States."

"Kozlov? He's a close friend of Putin's. This is going to cause a major disruption. Does the material I'm getting have any corroboration?"

"Just pass it on," said Whitney. "When they vet it, it's gonna hold up."

Morozov shook his head. "You people play a very complicated chess game, sir. Remind me never to get you angry at me."

Whitney smiled. "Once you pass it on to them, I want to hear back from you about the fallout from these revelations. Okay?"

Morozov nodded. "And my fee?.

"Ten-thousand," said Whitney, "but don't expect us to pay this much the next time. This is an important operation, and you must make sure that it gets handled without mistakes."

"I will," said Morozov.

Whitney got out of the car and headed back across the lot. Now that Leo was securely onboard, it was time to get the package from Donahue so he could put the operation into play.

⌀

Donahue arrived in London the next day with Renée Marin in tow. Renée's daughter, Julie, had school, so Renée left her in the care of the parents of Julie's best school friend. It was an arrangement that was often mutual.

Marin and Whitney had first met during a case on which Marin was working as a senior prosecutor in Los Angeles. As an officer in the Special Air Service (SAS), Whitney had been an advisor to Marin, who was prosecuting a member of the IRA.

Once the case was over, they became romantically involved. Their bi-continental romance had continued now for several years. While both continued to work at their separate careers, Marin was beginning to consider leaving hers to relocate in the U.K.

Since the conclusion of the IRA case, Whitney had been on loan to MI-6, which helped him to develop his intelligence-gathering skills.

Whitney met Donahue and Marin at the airport, and after joining them for the drive into London, he left them at the hotel while he took the package prepared by Donahue directly to his boss.

Several documents experts were brought in to analyze what they had for the appearance of authenticity. If they didn't pass muster, the Brits were prepared to pull out of the deal with Donahue.

The first document was an official-looking, top-secret document prepared with the assistance of Charlotte—that appeared to be from a CIA accountant, allegedly responding to an inquiry made by Assistant Director Freely. It questioned the size of the amounts that the Agency had given to Kozlov over the past five years. Attached to that document were photocopies of wire transfer receipts that purported to show the total amounts that were transferred from the Security Financial Trust to a particular, unnamed bank.

Donahue and Charlotte had been wise enough to not give the Russians everything. Too much might make the Russians suspicious. With that in mind, buried in the data was the code for the bank that the money had been transferred to, as well as the number for the recipient's savings account.

There were also two documents taken from the stash in Zurich. They were the two that Donahue had already shown to Freely. They were documents, in Russian, that implicated Putin in crimes against the Russian State.

Attached to the note was a handwritten message to Freely—ostensibly from a fictitious agent—which stated, "Most recent documents turned over to us by AK."

When the package passed muster, Whitney took it to the young MI-6 agent who was pretending to be an agent for the Russians. Since the information in their possession would not be the type given by the CIA to MI-6, they had decided that the cover story would be that it had originally come from a British double agent who was working for the CIA. The Russians would be more inclined to believe that the British had stumbled upon the information which their Russian agent, in London, had accidentally uncovered in his boss's office.

Whitney had the documents repackaged, and in less than an hour, they were in the hands of the young MI-6 agent who would be turning them over to Leo a little later in the day.

After that, Whitney returned to the hotel to spend a little quality time with Renée Marin.

～

Eleven days later, Oleg Kozlov was seated in his office on the sixth floor of the Embassy of the Russian Federation, also called a Chancery, in Washington, DC. He was reviewing his schedule for the next week, and he was comfortably ensconced in his leather desk chair where he was drinking his favorite brand of black tea with milk.

His secretary buzzed to tell him that there were two men from the Presidential Security Service, (SBP), waiting in the outer office. They were insisting on seeing him right away.

Kozlov was not overly concerned. The SBP agents assigned to the Embassy were intelligence-gathering officers whose sole area of concern was the welfare of President Putin. If they wanted to see him without an appointment, it likely meant that they had uncovered something negative about one of the oligarch families who had taken up residence in the United States.

"Show them in," said Kozlov flatly.

There was a knock at the office door, followed by the entry of two men in their early forties. Both were dressed in dark suits, and both had buzz-cut hair. One was more than a foot taller than the other, so Kozlov unconsciously focused his attention to the taller one, incorrectly assuming that he was the alpha male of the team.

"Sit down, gentlemen," he said, as he gestured to the two chairs placed in front of his desk.

"Thank you, sir," said the shorter one, "but I'm afraid we don't have time for a chat."

"Oh?" Kozlov began to wonder where this was going.

"We've been directed by the office of General Valery Gerasimov to get you on an immediate flight to Moscow. There is an Aeroflot plane standing by at Baltimore International, a flight scheduled to leave in the next eighty minutes, so we must get you to the plane without further delay."

Kozlov's mind was spinning at hyper speed. A summons to the office of the Chief of the General Staff was highly unusual and very troubling. He thought about his current activities and quickly came to the conclusion that he'd done nothing that would warrant a disciplinary summoning.

"What is the reason for this summons?" he asked.

"I'm afraid I don't know, Ambassador, but the General advised us that you can confirm the order by contacting his office directly."

"I will do just that," said Kozlov. "Would you two gentlemen mind waiting in my outer office?"

"Of course, Mr. Ambassador, but I would remind you that they'll be holding the plane on the tarmac, and our instructions are not to create a diplomatic incident concerning this summons."

"Yes, yes. I understand. If you will just—"

The two men quickly left his office, which helped Kozlov to ease his anxiety. If he was somehow under arrest, he was convinced that they wouldn't have let him out of their sight.

He had his secretary place a call for him to Gerasimov's office. Gerasimov was a close associate of the President of Russia. His official title was that of Supreme Commander-in-Chief. He was also the Chief of the General Staff, the highest military position in the Federation.

When his secretary advised him that Gerasimov's office was on the line, Kozlov picked up the phone and identified himself. But instead of getting to speak to Gerasimov, the secretary transferred him to General Sergey Shoygu, the Minister of Defense.

When Kozlov identified himself for the second time, Shoygu asked, "Is this line secure?"

"Of course it is," said Kozlov. It came out a little sharper than he had intended.

"Very good, Ambassador," said Shoygu. "You are being summoned to return to Moscow to advise the President on a matter of concern relating to the security of the Federation. I'm afraid I can't take a chance and say anything more on the phone, even though the line is encrypted."

Both men knew that the NSA would be monitoring this call, and the technological gains made by the NSA meant that even encrypted calls might not be safe.

"Am I in some kind of trouble, General?" Kozlov asked.

"I'm told that you are not," he replied. "It is your expertise that is needed for the President."

Relieved, Kozlov let out a long, slow, exhale.

"I will leave right away," he said, but the line had already gone dead.

He hit the intercom button and advised his secretary to clear his calendar for at least a week.

"I'm being summoned for consultations with the President, and tell the two men waiting for me to get the car ready. I'll be coming out."

⤙

Thirty-six hours later, the Russian government issued a press release from Moscow that stated the following:

> *Ambassador to the United States, Oleg Kozlov, has been recalled by the Russian Federation to Moscow for consultations. In his absence, Ambassador Extraordinary and Plenipotentiary, Anatoly Antonov, will assume his duties.*

⤙

Five days later, Sir John Stafford was in his office for his daily intelligence briefing. A half-dozen items were discussed before the briefer stated, "We have an unconfirmed report that the former Russian Ambassador to the United States, Oleg Kozlov, has been executed."

Stafford sat up straighter.

"Really? Where is that information coming from?"

The briefer flipped a few pages.

"It says here that the information came from a well-placed Russian informant whose handler is with the BND, Germany's Federal Intelligence Service."

"What's the certainty index on that report?"

"The BND puts it at eighty-five percent, sir. The informant says the Russians are going to release a statement saying that Kozlov was charged and convicted for corruption, and has been sentenced to forty years of hard labor. But our assessment is that their statement is just a cover for his execution. Our analysts have weighed in with a ninety percent chance that the information about his death is reliable. They point out that even by Russian standards, a trial within seven days of Kozlov's recall from the United States is highly unlikely."

He looked up at Stafford, and smiled.

"Whatever Kozlov did, his fate was likely sealed even before they brought him back to Moscow."

They moved on to discuss another topic, but thirty minutes later, as soon as the briefer was dismissed, Stafford tracked down Whitney and gave him the news.

Whitney smiled. "So they went for it? I'm surprised. There were so many ways that could have backfired."

"But it didn't," said Stafford. "You might want to get in touch with Ms. Donahue and let her know what we've heard. Tell her we're awaiting additional corroboration, but the intelligence was rated very high for accuracy."

"Are the Russians giving details on the supposed corruption charges?"

"No info on that yet," said Stafford, "but it wouldn't surprise me if in the next few days or weeks the real story leaks out." He locked eyes with Whitney. "And do remind her that we'd like to get a look at the documents that she's still holding."

"I will," said Whitney.

∽

Donahue was at home when Whitney called. Thompson was with her, and they had just finished dinner with Thompson's three boys when Donahue's encrypted phone began to ring.

She excused herself from Thompson and the boys, and went directly to her office for privacy.

"Hi, Jen. It's Whitney."

"Hi," she said.

"Even though this line is secure, I want to caution you about what gets said."

Donahue's heart began to beat faster. This must be about Kozlov.

"I understand," she replied.

"Good. We showed your novel to the publisher, and they signed on. Understand?"

"I think I do," she told him. Her anxiety was mounting.

"I'm told that the main guy liked the fact that your lead character got killed off."

Oh my God! Can this be right? He's telling me that Kozlov is dead?

"I kind of thought they were gonna go with the alternate ending. You know, where the protagonist ends up in prison?"

"Apparently the head guy over there liked the ending where he gets killed off. Anyway, your agent wants to know when we can get a look at your notes for the next installment in the series?"

They want the Putin documents.

"Soon," she replied. "I'd like to wait until I get a few more reviews. I'd like confirmation that the story is really good."

"I'm sure that will be fine. I'll speak with your agent and advise him about your timetable."

"Thank you, Whit. I appreciate the call. By any chance, have you spoken recently with the publisher in Israel?"

Whit understood that she was talking about Bryan Harb.

"I haven't seen him in a few days, but I was going to call him next and pass on the good news about your story."

"Great! I'll try to get over the pond in a week or two. Will you be available to meet?"

"Sure. Just give me a little advance notice and I'll include your publisher in Israel."

"Thanks, Whit. I'll be in touch."

When the call was over, she spent a few moments thinking about the enormity of what she'd brought about. She had no qualms about Kozlov being accused of being a spy, and she had always believed that if the Russians accepted the proof, that Kozlov would end up in prison somewhere in the Federation, and that would have been just fine with her. But to find out that he'd been executed was something that she knew was possible, but didn't really believe would happen. And, to her surprise, she felt a tinge of guilt as she came to grips with the fact that she had cost the man his life.

But then she thought about Sean, how warm and kind and thoughtful he had been, and her uneasiness about Kozlov's fate soon evaporated. Kozlov had killed the man she loved, and forfeiting his life for that act was something that he justly deserved.

When her tears of relief were over, she made her way out to Thompson, who sent the kids off to bed. They were again staying over at Donahue's, and it was becoming a habit that Donahue was happy to embrace.

"I just heard from Whitney," she said to Thompson. "Kozlov was executed."

"No fuckin' way! They bought that story you put together?"

"Apparently so. I kinda thought they would put him in prison, but I guess the fact that Putin thought he'd been gathering evidence against him really pissed him off."

"Well, I'm glad it's over. You need to focus on getting ready for the patter of little feet."

"Yeah," said Donahue with a smile. "I've got so much to learn."

"I presume that the Valentine's Day party is still on?"

"You bet it is."

Thompson slowly shook her head. "I don't understand why you want to break bread with this guy? He's a fuckin' traitor, Jen, and because of his position within the White House, sooner or later, they're gonna have no choice but to take him down."

"Not so. They want to use him as a double agent," she reminded Thompson, "and as far as I'm concerned, that can't be allowed to happen."

"Hold on." Thompson gave her a suspicious look. "I thought you just wanted to talk to him?"

"Don't worry, Shari. That's all I'm going to do. But I want him to know that his secret is out, and he's going to pay the price for what he's done."

"But won't that tip him off that the Feds are on to him?"

"And if it does? said Donahue. "So what?"

"Oh, Jeez, Jen. I don't think this is such a good idea. You'll be interfering with a Federal investigation. You could end up going to prison for that."

"If that's what happens, then so be it."

"That's not smart, Jen. You need to think this through. What about your baby? Have you thought about that?"

Donahue squeezed her eyes tight, and when she opened them again, there were tears building up in the corners of her eyes.

"I can't let this go, Shari. If I'm ever going to have closure, I need to confront this guy and let him know how I feel. And if the Feds decide to let him skate, then at least I'll have had the chance to say my piece."

"And what if he tries to flee the country? What about that?"

"By now I'm sure that the Bureau has him under surveillance. If he tries to bolt, they'll bring him in, and who knows, perhaps that will put to rest any thoughts of using him as a double."

Thompson shook her head in resignation.

"I don't know, Jen. Of course, I've got your back, but this is a dangerous game you're trying to play."

"Just make sure you remember that this is my dangerous game, Shari. Not yours. If things go south, I'm the one who'll take the blame. Not you. You're just my dinner guest, and you had no idea whatsoever what I was going to say or do."

Thompson gave that a moment's thought, then sighed. Her partner was dead set on going forward with this confrontation, and there appeared no way to reel her back in.

She walked over to Donahue and gave her a hug.

"Okay, Jen. You've made your point." She gave her a smile. "Let's make this a Valentine's Day to remember."

"Have you picked out your dress yet?" asked Donahue.

"I sure have," said Thompson. "Scarlett is gonna turn heads. And can I ask, will the guys be joining us?"

"It's all set," said Donahue. "I'm sure you'll be pleased with the selection."

"Ahh, Jenny. They don't come any better than you."

FIFTY-FOUR

DONAHUE AND THOMPSON flew to Baltimore with Otero and a full security team. For obvious security reasons, they switched hotels every time she travelled.

They made their way to the historic, five-star, St. Regis Hotel in Washington, D.C., on 16th Street NW, just two blocks north of the White House. Otero had reserved a group of rooms on the top floor. She and Thompson settled into Donahue's two-bedroom suite, one that overlooked the D.C. skyline, while the security team divided up and occupied the other rooms. Thompson had arranged for a renowned celebrity hairdresser and make-up artist to get them ready for the party, and both women spent over two hours getting their looks elevated to the status of "ten plus."

For his part, Otero and his entire team wore black tuxedos, and four of the men, including Otero, were selected to sit at the table with their patron. The men were told to use an alias, and a background profile was prepared for each individual. They were to pose as executives in various fields of technology, and thanks to their military backgrounds, all four knew enough to get by. They were not expected to engage Rush in conversation, if he actually did show up, but they would be ready to play their roles should the need arise.

The rest of the security team, all armed, would be stationed outside the building as a rapid response force just in case they were needed inside.

At a little after five p.m., under a sky that threatened to rain at any time, Donahue's entourage made their way to the Italian Embassy on Whitehaven Street NW. The location was a pair of modern, five-story buildings, whose exteriors had monochromatic skins that were sliced by a diagonal cut, effectively splitting the two buildings into equal parts. Above ground, they shared a single, black, all-glass window entrance, which provided access to both sides of the two buildings.

After passing through security at the entrance, Donahue and her party were led to a vast atrium which was covered by a glass dome. The atrium was two stories in height, and was filled with tables, chairs, a stage, and an area carved out as a dance floor.

The VIP tables, reserved for those who paid for a pre-ball dinner, were sectioned off in one side of the atrium. Donahue and her entourage were met by representatives from the Embassy, who seemed to gush when they learned that the group included the reclusive Mary Vanderbilt and members of her party.

"One of your guests has already checked in," said a handsome young man serving as the official greeter. "A Miss Jae Hwa Jun?"

Donahue knew right away that it was an alias for Charlotte.

"Wonderful!" she told him. "I'm also expecting Mr. Lindsey Rush. When he checks in, will you show him where we're seated?"

"Of course," said the young man, who then asked, "By any chance, is Mr. Rush the advisor to the President?"

Donahue nodded, but put a finger to her lips as if cautioning him not to tell anyone.

"The General is traveling incognito this evening, so please don't make a fuss of any kind when he arrives."

The now-excited young man nodded sagely.

"Of course, Miss Vanderbilt. Please come this way."

They followed him to a table in the center of the grouping, and when the young man walked off, Donahue assigned seats to her security team, making sure that Thompson was seated so that she was placed in the middle of the four attractive men.

Charlotte walked up with a glass of wine in her hand and watched as they sorted things out.

"Miss Jae Hwa Jun," said Donahue to the group. She then leaned in and whispered, "You couldn't pick a more anglicized name?"

"In Korean, *Jae Hwa* means 'respect and beauty, one who is rich and prosperous.' I thought it was well suited for having dinner with a Vanderbilt."

"But you're Chinese, aren't you?" asked Donahue.

"Very perceptive," whispered Charlotte. "But dead wrong." She smiled thinly. "But don't feel bad." She glanced around the room. "To most folks here, all of us Asians look alike."

Donahue blushed. "I don't know where I got the idea that you might be Chinese, but I just hope you weren't offended?"

"Offended? No way.' Charlotte was smiling. "After all, I'm having dinner with a Vanderbilt and her sidekick is Scarlett O'Hara."

Donahue smiled at the riposte, and then said, "Between you and Scarlett over there, I have the feeling this is going to be one hell of an evening."

"I'm just glad we're all wearing name tags," said Charlotte. "It's kind of hard to know the players without a program."

She glanced around the table and noticed that Otero appeared to be studying her very carefully.

"Uh, oh!" she whispered. She turned back to Donahue. "I think the good looking one might be on to me."

Donahue followed her gaze and noted that Otero had stood up and was on his way over.

"I'll take care of it," said Donahue. She turned to intercept Otero.

"Say, isn't this the young woman you interviewed—"

"It's a long story, Jamie. Tonight she is Miss Jae Hwa Jun. Make sure the others keep that in mind."

And when he gave her a look that said *what's going on?* she quickly replied, "I'll explain everything when we're back at the hotel. Just know that everything is under control."

Otero nodded, then made eye contact with Charlotte.

"Miss Jun, it's nice to meet you."

One of the four men seated near Thompson came over and asked Donahue if she wanted a drink?

"Can you see if they have hot tea?" she asked. "If not, just some sparkling water over ice."

He nodded and walked off.

The guests for the pre-ball dinner were now arriving en masse, so Donahue took a seat to await the arrival of General Rush. She looked over at Thompson, who was holding court with two of the young men, obviously regaling them with stories, because both men were attentive and seemed to be enjoying themselves.

Otero sat down next to her, leaving the seat on her other side available for Rush.

"Miss Donahue," he began in a hushed voice, "I'm not sure what's going on here tonight. I know it's none of my business, but if you don't give me a clue, I don't know how to do my job correctly."

Donahue sighed. "Okay, Jamie, here's the deal. I set this up because I want to get a chance to talk to the man who'll be arriving soon. It's General Lindsey Rush. He's an advisor to the—"

"I know who he is," said Otero, "but why the secrecy?"

"I don't want him to know who I am. It's complicated, but you need to keep this between us. Don't share what I'm going to tell you with the members of your team."

Otero was completely confused. All he could think of was that Rush was married and that this was a romantic assignation.

"Discretion is my middle name," he told her.

"Rush is a Russian agent. He's the man who told the Russians how to find Sean."

Otero frowned. "And you're going to meet with him. Does he know who you are?"

"Not yet," she said.

"You're not planning on taking him out, are you? Because if—"

"Of course not. I would never involve you or any of the others in anything like that. I just want to say a few things to him that will likely put him on edge."

"Okay," he said with a sigh. "I don't think this is such a good idea, but you're the boss. I'm going to switch seats with Hector. I want to be on the other side of Rush in case he doesn't take too kindly to your plan."

"Fair enough. And once I have my little talk with him, we're going to leave right away. Understood?"

"Just say when and we're outta here."

⌒

Rush showed up twenty minutes after the first course had been served. He was dressed appropriately in a tux, and he looked very distinguished. He was tall and thin, with parted dark hair that was flecked with gray at the temples. No surprise, he carried himself with military bearing.

The young man who was the greeter escorted him over to Donahue's table, where he introduced himself to her, made his excuse for being tardy, then thanked her for the invitation.

She patted the seat of the chair next to her and told him to please sit down, that looking up at him while he was standing was giving her a sore neck.

"Of course." He quickly took his seat.

A waiter came over and asked the General if he wanted a drink. He ordered a Jack Daniels neat, put the napkin in his lap, then tried to play catch-up by diving into the first course, a salad that had miraculously appeared within a few seconds of his being seated.

"I've been hoping to meet you," Donahue said, without a hint of any guile. "You've had quite an interesting career."

"Well, thank you," he replied between bites. "Do you come to Washington often?"

"Lately, it seems like I'm here quite a bit."

"Where do you call home?" he asked, before taking another bite. He was trying to catch up to the rest of the guests who had already finished their salads.

"Here and there, no place in particular. I have properties all over the world. I'm kind of a rolling stone."

"I must confess, I had to look you up, Miss Vanderbilt."

"Oh? And what did you discover?"

"Not a great deal. You obviously take your privacy very seriously."

"I do," she replied. "How about you?"

"I'm afraid my life is pretty much an open book. Once you work in the White House, your privacy goes out the window."

Several waiters showed up and began to clear the salad plates. The dinner was on a schedule, so that it didn't interfere with the start of the ball. Rush took one more bite of his salad then gestured to a waiter to take the unfinished plate.

Rush introduced himself to Otero, who said his name was Oscar Hernandez. Rush noted Otero's physical build and asked him if he ever did military service?

Otero nodded. "I did tours in Iraq and Afghanistan."

"Thank you for your service," said Rush.

The dinner was served, which cut off the flow of conversation, although Thompson was still laughing and talking with the two bodyguards who flanked her on the other side of the table. But she continued to glance over at Donahue, keeping an eye on her, still not quite sure what to expect, or what Donahue planned to say to Rush.

The conversation during dinner was light. Thompson introduced herself to Rush from across the table by using the name of Scarlett, and while Rush tried to get her to talk about her background, Thompson parried by asking him about himself.

Rush related that he'd been a career military man whose wife had passed away five years before. They hadn't had any children, and he said he felt lost for a number of years, particularly after retiring, but that his position at the White House had re-energized his interest in politics.

Once the main course was over and desserts were turned down, coffee was served, and while Rush added cream and sugar to his, Donahue leaned over and asked, "I wonder if you know what the penalty for treason might be?"

Rush was completely confused. He had no idea where this question was coming from or the reason why she was asking.

"That's a rather abrupt change of topic" he said with a muted chuckle, "Why are you asking?"

Donahue locked on to his gaze and smiled.

"Scarlett and I have a wager on this. I say that lethal injection is the current method, but she's convinced that hanging is still being used."

Rush looked over at Thompson, who was studying him carefully.

"I believe it's by lethal injection," he said quietly.

Donahue shifted her glance to Thompson. "You see, I was right."

Thompson shrugged. "That's too good for traitors. I still think they ought to hang 'em by the neck."

Rush was still staring at Thompson when Donahue asked, "Have you ever been to Terre Haute, Indiana, General?"

He finally shifted his glance back to Donahue.

"I can't say that I have, Miss Vanderbilt."

"I understand that Terre Haute is the location of the Federal complex where they carry out the executions."

Rush frowned. The direction of this bizarre conversation was starting to make him uncomfortable. He decided it was time to go.

"I'm sorry, Miss Vanderbilt," he said to Donahue. He removed his napkin from his lap and began to slide his chair back from the table. "This has been a very interesting evening, but I'm afraid I'm going to have to leave. I've got a busy day ahead of me tomorrow—"

"That's not a good idea, General," said Donahue. Her tone of voice caused him to pause. "Indulge me General. I think you might be interested in what I have to say."

Rush studied her carefully. She was serious, and apparently the invitation for him to attend was for the purpose of this pending exchange.

"All right," he said, resuming his seat. "What is it you want to tell me?"

"Oleg Kozlov. Do you know who he is?"

"Of course." He was getting irritated. "He was the recent Russian Ambassador. Why? What about him?"

"He's dead, General. The Russians executed him a few days ago."

Rush's eyes went wide.

How is that possible? And how could this woman know something like that when I know nothing about it?

"Oh, my!" said Donahue. "You didn't know? Well, I have very good sources, General, and I know a great deal more than that." She leaned closer to him and lowered her voice. "I've been told that Kozlov was a Russian double agent. He was working for the Russians, but the FBI turned him several years ago. Apparently, he was a Bureau informant for the last two years, and when the Russians found out, they put a bullet in his head."

Rush's heart was now beating so loudly that he was afraid that everyone at the table could hear it.

It can't be true. Kozlov a double agent? Impossible! But if it wasn't true, then why would the Russians kill him? And if he was a double agent, was it possible he told the Bureau all about me?"

"I also heard something else interesting from one of my sources. Kozlov helped the FBI build an ironclad case against a high-ranking government official." She smiled broadly. "My sources say that an arrest will be made shortly, maybe even tonight, and that the U.S. Attorney is going to be seeking the death penalty for treason."

Rush's anxiety was quickly turning to panic. *This woman was obviously well dialed in, and if that was the case, then she must suspect that I might be...*

His mind was moving so fast that his thoughts became disjointed.

Is she setting me up? Are they just about to pounce on me here and in public?

He looked around the table and studied the men who were all now staring at him as if he was prey. They appeared to be military in bearing.

Were they all FBI?

"What's going on?" he said to Donahue. "Who are you people? And why are you telling me this?"

"Mikel Korakovsky," said Donahue. Does that name ring a bell?"

When Rush blanched, she continued.

"I'm sure you remember him. In fact, you asked your assistant, a Mr. Greenwood, to get Mikel's new name and hidden location which you then passed on to your handler."

Beads of sweat suddenly appeared on Rush's forehead.

"I don't know what you're talking about—"

She watched as he started to get to his feet.

"Mikel was my fiancé," she said. Her expression hardened. "They're coming for you General. They've built a case against you for treason. You'll become a pariah, your reputation will be destroyed, and your execution will be an example to others that when you sell out your country to the Russians, you're going to pay the ultimate price."

"You're insane," he said, a little too loudly. "I'm leaving, and you better not try to stop me."

"Stop you? I wouldn't think of it. So, go. Oh, and I plan to be there when they give you the injection."

Rush mouthed *fuck you,* turned on his heels, and hurriedly walked away from the table. His eyes scanned the room as he went, as if he were expecting to be grabbed while he tried to leave.

Donahue turned back to the group at the table. Otero and his team were already standing.

"I guess that went as well as could be expected," she said.

Thompson rolled her eyes. "Did you get it all out of your system?"

"I think so. I saw the fear in his eyes, so I guess it was worth it."

"The Bureau won't appreciate what you've done," said Charlotte. "Now that he knows they're on to him, he might try to do a runner."

"That's what I'm counting on," said Donahue. "If he does try to run, they'll have to arrest him. And if they do that, the Russians won't try to use him again. In fact, the Russians have likely concluded that since Kozlov was a double, Rush was also a plant, or, if not, already compromised." She smiled coyly. "And that means that our government will have no choice but to prosecute him for treason."

Charlotte smiled. It just might have worked.

Otero, who had been silently taking everything in, finally spoke up.

"I would like to suggest that we leave, Ms. Donahue. He has no idea about your true identity, but he still has resources. With a guy as rattled as he appears to be, you never know what he's capable of doing."

"Let's go back to the hotel," said Thompson. "Time to celebrate. The night is young and we can get some desert and coffee from room service."

"That sounds like a plan," said Donahue with a smile. She turned to Charlotte. "You care to join us?"

"Why not? I'm already hanging out on a limb, and besides, this is turning out to be a night worth remembering."

"I knew I was going to like you," said Donahue.

⸎

The next morning, Donahue and Thompson said good-bye to Charlotte, then boarded Donahue's plane for the flight back to L.A. Donahue had gone to bed shortly after they got back to the hotel, so Thompson had moved the party next door to one of the other suites.

"I'm gonna catch a little nap," said Thompson when the plane took off.

"Late night?" Donahue asked.

"Not really. Your security guys are pros. They weren't about to flirt with the best friend of the boss. But it was fun to hang with them just the same."

"Their loss," said Donahue with a smile.

"My sentiment exactly. Wake me when we're getting ready to land."

❧

Two hours later, Donahue received a call on her encrypted phone.

"Yes?" she said when she put it to her ear.

"Jen? It's Jamison Freely."

"Oh, hi," she said, cautiously. She wondered if this was the start of the fallout from what she'd done last night.

"Are you on your way back to L.A.?'

"I am." She put her hand up to cover her free ear. "It's a little noisy here, but I can hear you okay."

"I thought you might want to know that General Rush is dead. Gunshot to the head. It looks like he committed suicide."

Donahue was astonished.

"Suicide?"

"His driver found him when he went to pick him up this morning. I've been told that there was a suicide note."

"Did it say why he did it?" she asked, with more than a touch of nervousness.

"I haven't seen it, but I understand that it had something to do with his career as a public servant, and how he couldn't face the embarrassment from a single lapse of judgment. Do you have any idea what he was talking about?"

"Maybe he had a pang of conscience," she suggested.

"Rather coincidental, don't you think?"

"Whatever do you mean?"

"I don't know if you know this, but we heard from the Brits that Kozlov has been executed by the Russians."

"Actually, I did hear about that."

"Well, since Kozlov was out of the picture, Rush was no longer a potential asset, so the U.S. Attorney was going to impanel a grand jury sometime later this week."

"Maybe he already figured that out and chose the coward's way out?"

"Hmm. Yeah. I suppose that's possible. So, how was the Valentine's Ball last night?"

Donahue was shocked that he knew about the party, but did he also know that Rush had attended?

Then she smiled to herself. Of course he did. *He probably has me followed every time I come to town.*

"It was nice. A good cause, but we left right after dinner. I needed to get some sleep."

"Well, now that Kozlov and Rush are no more, I was wondering if you were inclined to turn over the documents to us?"

"About that…" She lowered her voice. "I was planning on giving some of the documents to MI-6."

"Oh? And why is that?"

"Well, let's just say that they helped me out in a pinch, so I think it's only fair that they get a share."

"Will we get a copy of what you give them?"

"I hadn't given that any thought, but I don't see why not. But I want you to know something, Jamison. I don't trust our current President. There's something going on with him and Putin, and I want to be sure that the documents get used and are not just buried to improve our relations with Russia."

"Even by releasing them, you do realize that there's no guarantee that Putin will be thrown out of office?"

"I know that, but a girl's gotta try, right?"

Freely smiled.

"Make sure you tell Six that we're getting copies, and if you choose to give us some of the originals, which I hope you will, I'll make sure that they get copies, too."

"I will," she replied. She was actually relieved that he wasn't pissed-off.

"Call me when you get ready to move the documents," he said. "I want to make sure that nothing goes wrong. And Jen, lay low for awhile. Until the documents are actually released, you're still at risk."

"I will. Oh, and I assume that Charlotte is still in your good graces?"

Freely smiled. She has finally deduced that he knew all the time exactly what she'd been up to.

"Charlotte's fine, and for your information, she hasn't said a word to me about last night, and I don't plan to ask her anything at all."

"Thank you," said Donahue. "I'm glad you're so understanding."

EPILOGUE

ALTHOUGH SERGEI IVANOV had agreed to work as a spy for MI-6 in exchange for his freedom, after six weeks of intense debriefing by Six and the Israeli Mossad, it was mutually decided that he did not have the contacts necessary to make his role as a spy worthwhile. To put it bluntly, he was at the bottom of the food chain with little ability to trade up. Consequently, the British government decided to extradite him to Israel, where he was tried and sentenced to life imprisonment for the killing of the two Israeli hitmen.

For having lied to the FBI about the money he received from his second job as a Coca-Cola distributor, Charles Beeson was fired from the U.S. Marshals Office, which included the forfeiture of his rights to a government pension. He continued to work as a soft-drink distributor, but two years later, after a protracted bout of alcoholism and an extra-marital affair with a store clerk at one of his delivery stops, his wife filed for a divorce and cleaned him out financially.

Phillip Greenwood, the assistant to General Rush, was cleared by the FBI of any wrongdoing in the delivery of information to Rush concerning the new identity and whereabouts of Sean Walker. It was decided by the U.S. Attorney that he was acting at the direction of his immediate supervisor with no knowledge of the intended use for the information. With Rush's suicide, he sought and received permission to transfer over to the office of a Congressman from West Virginia, where he currently works as an Administrative Assistant.

Initially, there had been some concern that his release of information about what had been going on to a member of the press might subject him to criminal prosecution, but the U.S. Attorney decided that he had acted in the mistaken belief that notifying the press was the only way that he could be sure that what he suspected had happened would not be covered up if he reported it to federal law-enforcement authorities.

CIA field agent Bryan Harb returned to Israel, where he continues to work undercover while ingratiating himself into the Russian expatriate community. His work with Major Andrew Whitney of the British MI-6, and Mordecai Ben-Gurion of the Israeli Mossad, has created a channel for cooperation between them that is still in place today.

True to her word, Jennifer Donahue personally delivered a complete copy of the documents from the safe deposit box in Zurich to Sir John Stafford and Andrew Whitney. She followed that up with another visit to D.C. where she presented the original documents to Jamison Freely. She kept a complete set of the documents for herself in a private bank in Gibraltar, and she told each of them that if the documents weren't released during Putin's present term in office, she would release her own copies to the world's press.

Back home, Donahue had to deal with the fact that she could no longer hide her new wealth from friends and co-workers alike, and so she held a large cocktail party at her home with everyone she could think of. And while she didn't reveal the details concerning the amount of money she had inherited, she knew that the size and location of the house would leave no doubt in the minds of her guests that she was probably set for life.

To say that her co-workers were surprised by her standard of living was putting it mildly. More than one asked her to adopt them, while others cautioned her to be careful who she surrounded herself with.

She sent long thank you letters to Mordecai Ben-Gurion, Bryan

Harb, and Andrew Whitney, telling them that she had made arrangements for them and their immediate families (and in the case of Bryan Harb, for himself and a "guest"), to spend ten days at the *Hilton Bora Bora Nui Resort and Spa*, a five-star facility famously known for its overwater villas. She was covering all the expenses, with dates to be determined by them.

All three personally called her with thanks as soon as they got the letters, and all of them invited her to join them in their respective countries whenever she would be in their general area.

With Thompson, Donahue felt a special connection. She set up a scholarship fund for all three of Thompson's boys, one that would afford them private education from grammar school through University Post Doctorate if they ever chose to go that far.

Donahue also learned from Freely that Charlotte had a birthday coming up, so she arranged for her jet to bring Charlotte from D.C. to Las Vegas for a long birthday weekend. She and Thompson joined her there, for clubbing, the pool, shows, and meals, at some of the finest restaurants in town.

A bond was formed between the three of them, the kind that would last a lifetime.

Donahue had a lot of other ideas for sharing her wealth with others, but most of them were put on the back burner while she continued to keep working as a detective, while getting ready for the birth of her child.

∽

OTHER NOVELS BY PETER S. BERMAN

**HIDDEN AGENDA * WEB OF BETRAYAL
MONEY FOR LOVE * ABDUCTED
THE STRANGLER'S KNOT * UNTOUCHABLE
SUSPICIOUS DEATHS**

This book and others by Peter S. Berman are available
at amazon.com and other retail outlets and online stores.

FOR INTERESTING INFORMATION
VISIT MY WEBSITE AT

petersberman.com

ABOUT THE AUTHOR

During his career as a Head Deputy District Attorney in Los Angeles, PETER S. BERMAN oversaw the daily operations in a series of courthouses and specialized divisions, including the Hardcore Gang Division, the Sex Crimes Division, and the Career Criminal Division. He retired in 2002.

He has lectured and trained prosecutors throughout the United States. His work has been profiled on a number of television shows, including CBS's Sixty Minutes.

He has received Citations of Recognition from the Los Angeles County Board of Supervisors, the United States Secret Service, the Association of Deputy District Attorneys, and other law enforcement agencies and groups.

From 2008 to present day, he has worked as a Specialist Volunteer with LAPD's Robbery-Homicide Division, Cold Case Specials Unit, where he actively investigates unsolved homicide cases. He was honored by the Los Angeles Police Department as the Robbery-Homicide 2008 Reserve Officer of the year.

www.ingramcontent.com/pod-product-compliance
Lightning Source LLC
Chambersburg PA
CBHW070621260626

47161CB00007B/2527